STARGATE
SG·1

ALLIANCES

There were no amenities in the stone room they were left in by Va'ton and his Jaffa subordinates. No benches. No blankets. No pillows. Typical Goa'uld hospitality. There was, however, a big messy dried bloodstain on the prison cell floor.

Daniel wasn't going to think about that.

He took off his shirt, bundled it up, and put it beneath Jack's lolling head. It wasn't much but it was better than nothing. God, he was hungry. Light-headed. More than a little shaky. The cut on his hand had long since stopped dribbling but it still hurt. He was reasonably sure it was infected. Which was nothing compared to the trouble they were in. Standard O'Neill reply: *Don't worry, Daniel. We've been in worse.*

Okay. Maybe. Once. Sitting in a corridor covered in blood, having just been shot to bits by a Jaffa staff weapon, on a mother ship rigged to the rafters with C4, knowing his wound would probably kill him first, knowing Jack and Sam and Teal'c were going to die soon, too.

He'd survived that one. So had they. But even cats only got nine lives and he wasn't a cat. How many times could he tap-dance on the brink of death before that final, fatal plunge?

Please God. Let us be rescued soon.

Jack liked to say, There is always, *always* a Plan B.

"Not this time," he told his friend. "This time, Jack, it's a miracle… or nothing."

STARGÅTE
SG·1™

ALLIANCES

KAREN MILLER

FANDEMONIUM BOOKS

An original publication of Fandemonium Ltd, produced under license from MGM Consumer Products.

Fandemonium Books
PO Box 795A
Surbiton
Surrey KT5 8YB
United Kingdom
Visit our website: www.stargatenovels.com

© 2008 Metro-Goldwyn-Mayer. All Rights Reserved.
Photography and cover art: Copyright © 1997-2008 MGM Television Entertainment Inc./ MGM Global Holdings Inc. All Rights Reserved.

STARGÅTE
SG·1

METRO-GOLDWYN-MAYER Presents
RICHARD DEAN ANDERSON
in
STARGATE SG-1™
AMANDA TAPPING CHRISTOPHER JUDGE and MICHAEL SHANKS as Daniel Jackson
Executive Producers ROBERT C. COOPER BRAD WRIGHT MICHAEL GREENBURG
RICHARD DEAN ANDERSON
Developed for Television by BRAD WRIGHT & JONATHAN GLASSNER

STARGATE SG-1 © 1997-2008 MGM Television Entertainment Inc./MGM Global Holdings Inc. STARGATE: SG-1 is a trademark of Metro-Goldwyn-Mayer Studios Inc. All Rights Reserved.

WWW.MGM.COM

No part of this publication may be reproduced, stored in or introduced into a retrieval system, or transmitted, in any form, or by any means (electronic, mechanical, photocopying, recording or otherwise) without the prior written consent of the publisher. Any person who does any unauthorised act in relation to this publication may be liable to criminal prosecution and civil claims for damages.

If you purchase this book without a cover, you should be aware that this book is stolen property. It was reported as "unsold and destroyed" to the publisher and neither the author nor the publisher has received any payment for this "stripped book".

ISBN-13: 978-1-905586-00-4   Printed in the USA

For Brad Wright,
storyteller extraordinaire.
The Other Side was an absolute inspiration
— hope I haven't let you down.

Thanks and enormous appreciation to:
Sally and Tom of Fandemonium books, for the
chance to play in the Stargate sandbox.
All the folk at Bridge Studios for creating that sand-
box in the first place.
My adored team of Beta-readers: Peter, Elaine,
Mary, Cindee, Sharon and Jenn.
The fans, who love the show as much as
I do (if not more).

Author's Note

This story takes place immediately following the events depicted in the Season Four episode *The Other Side*.

PROLOGUE

When does killing become murder? At what point does self-defence become self-interest? When does self-interest become revenge?

And does it really matter?

Dead is dead. The 'why' isn't relevant.

Jack O'Neill tossed and turned in his unquiet bed, dreaming. Remembering.

Alar's desperate. Bloody. All that plausible suaveness obliterated, the arrogance, the smooth sleek self-assurance. His world Euronda is in flames. You lit the match. Nazi wannabes. The urge to control. Destroy. Expunge what they don't approve of. Is it genetic? Coded into human DNA?

Alar doesn't understand. He's genuinely bewildered. "It could've all been yours."

You look at him, feeling sick. "I wouldn't follow us if I were you."

The team's moving out, the bunker complex collapsing around you. Of course it would be a bunker. All rats hide in a hole, eventually. Daniel dials home. He's got a brain like a rolodex, all those addresses jotted down in there somewhere. Teal'c's looking anxious. After all these missions you can read the signs, now.

You want them out of here, safe and sound. "Go."

For once, Daniel doesn't argue.

Which means it's just you and Carter, spraying bullets. Taking down the poor schmucks who think they're dying for something worthwhile. For a leader who deserves their devotion. For an ideal that's pure and noble.

God.

Alar staggers in. "Colonel. Wait. I can teach you everything I know. Just let me come with you. Please."

He's pitiful. You want to punch his lights out, put the boot in. All these fools dead and dying on the floor at his feet, for him, and all he can think of is himself.

Carter doesn't even ask you. She just goes.

You stand there, looking at Alar. You've told him once, don't follow. If you tell him again, he'll ignore you again. Doesn't he understand you yet? Doesn't he realize you're not kidding?

Do you care?

You go through the 'gate.

Carter's on the ramp, weapon up, waiting for you. She's wearing her soldier face. Hammond's waiting too, and he's not happy. You know how he feels.

You look at Carter, but you're talking to him. "Close the iris."

"Do it," says Hammond. He trusts you implicitly. You appreciate the compliment, but wonder if it's earned. This mission's screwed but good ... and you're the colonel. When your chickens come home to roost on this one there'll be bird crap everywhere.

Carter's looking back at you. She knows. It's her soldier's face, but different eyes are staring out of it. She knows. She hasn't said a word. Does that mean you're right?

Your hands slide off your weapon and you stand there, waiting. When it comes it's a tiny sound. Bug on a windshield. Death shouldn't be that small.

Hammond says, "I take it, Colonel, you were unable to procure any of the Eurondan technologies."

Sweet, sweet machines. Those remote fighters? Awesome. Provided of course your pilots don't mind ending up with brains like puréed zucchini, but Carter could've fixed that little drawback. In her sleep, probably. The fighters. The protective shield. The heavy-water power generation. The cryo-technology. All ours for the asking.

Just help Hitler, and Rabbi Rosenberg would never be your uncle.

"That's correct, sir," you tell him.

Hammond's expression changes. "I'm sorry to hear that."

You look at him. "Don't be."

O'Neill sat bolt upright as the bedside alarm clock exploded into life. Crap. It was morning. He had to get up. Run. Shower. Shave. Eat. Go to work. His heart was pounding, there was sweat in his hair. On his face. His chest. All the emotions he couldn't afford in the field pouring out of his skin.

God. He hated dreaming.

He'd learned long ago that he couldn't hide in dreams. Will-power couldn't save him. Self-control deserted him. The unconscious mind was insubordinate. Dreams came, and there was no way to stop them, or protect himself. He couldn't even change the channel.

Dreaming sucked, big time.

CHAPTER ONE

As he made the long, long elevator trip down through Cheyenne Mountain to Stargate Command Jack O'Neill pressed his fingers against his eyes, hoping to squish his gritty headache to death.

No such luck. The headache stubbornly remained, and now there were little red and black dots doing the rumba in the air before him.

Great.

The elevator bumped to a standstill and spat him out into Level 18's corridor. Airmen Leung and McCluskey slammed on the brakes and nodded at his appearance. "Morning, Colonel."

"Unfortunately," he grunted, and waved in their general direction. They took his place in the elevator, the doors banged shut, way too loudly—he'd have to tell Siler about that, Siler was a very strange man for whom too much maintenance was never enough—and he was alone in the corridor. It was early. Normal people were still eating breakfast. Maybe he should take a detour via the commissary. Eat something after all. He was a normal person, wasn't he?

His stomach rolled queasily, protesting the notion.

He headed along the corridor to see if Daniel was in his office yet. Gently tormenting Daniel was a sure-fire way to get rid of a headache.

"Morning," said Daniel, looking up from his desk. "You look like hell."

"And you look disgustingly chipper," he replied, slouching against the nearest bookcase. "Stop it. That's an order."

"Sorry," said Daniel, briefly smiling.

"So you should be." For irritation's sake he leaned over, picked up the nearest ancient stone doodad on the desk and tossed it from hand to hand. Was it his imagination, or did the little figurine's quasi-human face seem alarmed? "Seen Carter or Teal'c yet?"

Behind his glasses, Daniel's eyes were intent, their gaze fixed on the dancing doodad. "Sam's in her lab making love to the naquadah generator. I don't know where Teal'c is. Jack—"

"Daniel?" he said innocently. The most important thing was to keep a straight face. Now Daniel and the doodad's expressions were almost identical. Cool. "By the way, d'you think it's wise to discuss Carter in those terms? Last time I looked she was pretty damned handy with that P90 of hers."

"You're right, I take it back," said Daniel. He was holding a pencil, fingers clenched to snapping point. "Now can I also please take back the ancient artefact?" Dropping the pencil, he held out his hand. "Before you ruin its patina? Or break it."

"Are you calling your colonel *clumsy*, Dr. Jackson?"

Daniel's smile was edged like a sword. "I'm not calling him anything, but unless he gives me that artefact in the next three seconds Dr. Fraiser will be calling him DOA."

Bingo! With exaggerated care he placed the artefact in the centre of Daniel's palm.

"*Thank* you," said Daniel. "This happens to be an incredibly important archaeological find. Do you have any idea who this figurine represents?"

He looked at it. "Marge Simpson?"

"Close. Shri Setale Devi," said Daniel. "The smallpox goddess of Ancient India."

O'Neill nearly wiped his hands down the front of his BDUs. "What are you doing here so early anyway?" he demanded. "We're in between missions. We can afford to relax for a day or two." In theory, at least. But practice had taught him that neither Daniel nor Carter would know how to relax if their lives depended on it.

Daniel put the bug-eyed figurine aside, his irritation melting like mist in the sun. "Relax?" he echoed, with an encompassing sweep of his arm that nearly sent seven of his precious doodads flying. "When there's all this to catalogue?"

'All this' was an entire herd of figurines, human and animal, crowded on the desk. Some had faces, some didn't. They ranged in size from tiny as a thumbnail to bigger than a cat. They were made of baked clay and carved stone and dark weathered wood. What were the odds that the long-dead folk who'd made them had thrown most of them away as junk? Mass-produced kitsch? He'd lay good money the damned things were the ancient equivalent of—of garden gnomes. But to Daniel they were precious beyond measure. Boxes full of the damned things were stacked on the floor against the dangerously overcrowded bookcases. Here a doodad, there a doo-dad, everywhere a damned dusty doodad.

He'd never understand it, not in a million years.

"Fantastic, aren't they?" continued Daniel. If he turned up the voltage on his happy-meter any higher he'd burst into flames. "They came in last night from P8C-316. SG-12 found an entire ruined city with distinct parallels to what we know of ancient India. Can you believe it? 316 is *hundreds* of light-years away from Earth. It blows my mind! Doesn't it blow your mind, Jack?"

No. Basically, as far as he was concerned, it just blew. All those stolen people turned into slaves. Or worse, Jaffa. Or—the ultimate horror—Goa'uld hosts.

But he couldn't say that. Puncturing Daniel's perennial enthusi-asm for ancient doodads was like kicking a puppy. He'd do it if he had to, but if he didn't have to, well… and besides. They'd had a couple of nasty moments recently. Confrontations that peeled away the civilised tolerance they often employed with one another, to reveal the chasm of mutual incomprehension that always yawned between them. Seemed it really was possible to genuinely like and admire someone and still want to bash their head against a brick wall at regular intervals.

So. No kicking. Or bashing. At least not now.

"You're right," he agreed. "It's mind-blowing. I'm thrilled, hon-estly. Couldn't be more excited if I tried."

"Uh-huh," said Daniel. For some reason he didn't sound con-vinced. His eyes narrowed. "You know, Jack, you really do look like hell."

It was a conversation he had no intention of having. Not with Daniel, anyway. Not when the words 'I told you so' haunted that empty space between them. He was too tired for ghosts right now. He was too tired, period. "I should let Hammond know I'm here. Have fun playing with your artefacts."

Daniel smiled. Nodded. "I will," he said. Then the smile faded. Like a shadow under water, some uncomfortable emotion shifted across his face. "Actually—Jack—"

Oh no. He knew that tone. That look. 'Chipper' was a relative term. 'Chipper' could also be a mask. He should've known Daniel was incapable of leaving well enough alone. And he *so* wasn't in the mood...

"Sorry, Daniel. Gotta go. The General awaits." And, shoving his hands in his pockets, O'Neill slouched away. Going to see Hammond, yes, but taking the scenic route.

"Morning, sir," said Carter, who was indeed making love to the naquadah generator. No accounting for taste... "Could you go away, please?"

"Ah—"

She flipped a switch on the generator's casing, hurried round the bench and shoved him backwards out of her lab, pulling its door closed behind them. "Sorry. It's just I'd rather not be in there if the circuits overload."

He stared at her. This morning she was wearing her scientist face. It wasn't unlike Daniel's archaeologist face, though to her credit she tended to keep the accompanying hand-waving to a minimum. Now she was staring at the closed laboratory door, eyebrows pinched together as she waited for something—hopefully not half the base—to go 'boom'.

Time passed. There was no 'boom.' Her frown became a smile. "Excellent! I was pretty sure I had the calculations right but there's always that .0001% chance of an error." Dusting her hands together in restrained self-congratulation, she looked at him. "You wanted to see me, sir?"

"Carter..." He sighed. "If I ask what it is you're doing in there, do I have a .0001% chance of understanding the answer?"

She bit her lip. "Well..."

"Never mind. Good morning. I'm going to see Hammond. Is there anything important I should know beforehand?"

She shook her head. "No, sir, I don't think so. But if you don't mind me making an observation... you look like hell."

"See you later, Carter," he said, and kept on walking.

He'd long ago come to the conclusion that pretty much the only way to beat General George Hammond to work was to sleep on the base. And even then, nine times out of ten the damned man caught you napping. For someone on the brink of retirement *and* enjoying the shady side of sixty he had the irritating habit of never missing a beat.

"Good morning, Jack," the general greeted him from behind his immaculate desk. "Come on in. Have a seat. You look like hell."

"Really, sir?" he said, dropping into the nearest chair. "I had no idea."

Hammond's lips quirked in a smile, but only briefly and the amusement got nowhere near his eyes. "Should I be ordering you along to the infirmary?"

God, no. The infirmary meant Janet Fraiser, that pint-sized pow-erhouse of medical interferingness who took shameless advantage of a)having patched him up and saved his life more times than he cared to think about and b)technically outranking him by virtue of her medical degree. He shuddered. "No. I'm fine, sir."

"I hope so," said Hammond. "Because you and I are taking a little trip."

And just like that, the headache was back. "Don't tell me, sir. Let me guess. Washington?"

Hammond sat back in his chair and laced his fingers across his belly. His expression was grave; never a good sign. "Yes."

"I know I don't want to hear this, but....why?"

Hammond let his gaze settle on the ominous red phone; an even worse sign. When the news was good, or at least not dreadful, the general never failed to look him in the eye. "There's no easy way to say it, Jack."

That rapidly sinking sensation would be his heart, heading for his boots. "Then let me say it for you, sir. My failure to secure the Eurondan technology as promised has ruffled a few political feath-ers."

Now Hammond did look at him. In the office's harsh fluorescent lighting he looked older, and weary. "I don't like people who hog all the credit, Jack. Last time I looked the buck still stopped in this office. I could've ordered you to disregard Dr. Jackson's concerns and obtain everything Alar promised us, regardless of the ethical implications of that action. I didn't. Ultimately the responsibility lies with me."

God. It was tempting, so tempting, to let someone else shoulder the burden. The blame. But he couldn't do that. It wasn't the way he lived his life and besides, this was George Hammond. "All due respect, General, but no," he said, politely uncompromising. "I was the man on the spot. It was my call to send Daniel back here so he could cast doubt on the deal. I could easily have ordered him to stay with me on Euronda and just sent Carter with the request for the heavy water."

Hammond nodded. "And if you'd done that we'd have all that promised technology, possibly more, you and Dr. Jackson wouldn't be speaking and thousands upon thousands of innocent humans would've been slaughtered by Alar and his racial purists. Are you saying now you made the wrong call?"

"No." He pinched the bridge of his nose, willing away the vicious pounding behind his eyes. "I'm saying I wish I'd engineered a better outcome. Who is it we're meeting with in Washington?"

"A committee, who else?" said Hammond dryly. "Specially convened—and I quote—'to investigate the SGC's ongoing lack of progress in procuring military and technological assets that can be used to not only defend against the Goa'uld, but advance America's domestic agendas.'"

O'Neill felt his guts clench and his blood pressure spike. If he wasn't careful he really would need Janet Fraiser. "Oh, for crying out loud! Haven't we been through this already, with Maybourne and his NID goon squad?"

"Of course we have," said Hammond gently. "And we'll continue to go through it, Jack, again and again. This project is underwritten by taxpayer dollars, which means that as long as there are taxpayer-elected politicians with careers to protect and advance, you and I will be called upon to defend our decisions to them. It comes with the territory, you know that."

Yes. He knew that. And he hated it. Every time he watched 'A Few Good Men', part of him wanted to stand up and cheer Jack Nicholson as he made his famous speech. God, he hated politicians. Most politicians, anyway. Especially politicians like—

"Oh, crap," he said. "General, if you love me, tell me Kinsey's not behind this."

"Now you've put me in a difficult position," said Hammond, and this time his eyes did warm. "Jack ..."

"Who else?" he asked, feeling desperate. Feeling like hell and hell's little cousin purgatory. "Do you know?"

Hammond shook his head. "All I can tell you is Kinsey's chairing the investigation and it has the full support of the President."

"The *President*? I thought he *liked* us!"

"He does like us, Jack. But he's vulnerable and he's covering his ass." Another headshake, slow and resigned. "To be honest, I can't say I blame him. You know as well as I do this Eurondan business is just the last in a long line of disappointments as far as the acquisition of assets is concerned."

"*Disappointments*?" Like a fractious four-year old, he was on the brink of a tantrum. "To hell with that! We've delivered on our mission statement one hundred-fold, at least! We—"

"That's enough, Colonel!" Hammond snapped. "I'm not the person you need to convince. Save your arguments for the meeting tomorrow."

With difficulty, O'Neill got his temper under control. Hammond was right about one thing, at least: he wasn't the enemy here. "Sorry, sir," he muttered.

Hammond waved the momentary lapse aside. "I know it's hard being second-guessed by civilians, Jack. Especially civilians with agendas that don't necessarily do us any favors. I'm not saying we should get down on our knees and kiss their—" A swift, sly smile. "Boots. But, as I said, at the end of the day it comes down to funding. If we want those civilians to continue signing our pay checks, we have no choice but to play the game by their rules."

He dredged up a smile. "Maybe I should just phone Thor. Get him to beam out the contents of Fort Knox so we can become self-funded."

Hammond snorted. "Right."

"Not one of my better ideas?"

"You have better ideas?" Then Hammond frowned. "Seriously, Jack. This isn't the time for you to indulge your dubious sense of humor, or advertise your contempt for political authority." He shifted in his chair, then, looking uncomfortable. "I jumped the gun on this one. Claimed we had our hands on significant technology before it was a fact."

"Really, sir? That's not like you."

"No." Hammond pulled a face. "But there's been a lot of heat coming down from Washington in the last few months."

"I know. You said."

"I didn't say the half of it," Hammond retorted. "Didn't want you to worry. Worrying's my job, it's why they pay me the big bucks. The truth is, Jack, we had a lot riding on this Eurondan deal. I was banking on having it up my sleeve for the next round of budget negotiations. They're going to be ..." Hammond shrugged. "Vigorous."

"Oh."

"I know it's unpalatable, but it's the way things are. And every time we fail to produce a tangible asset we give Kinsey and his ilk another bullet to shoot at us."

O'Neill knew that. He knew more about the political tightrope the SGC balanced on than anyone apart from Hammond, who'd been trying to protect him, damn the man. Of course he'd kept most of that crap from Daniel and the rest of SG-1. Protected them, as best he could, because that's why they paid *him* the big—biggish—bucks. Maybe if he'd been less tender with Daniel's feelings and more attuned to the temperature in Washington...

As usual, Hammond read him like a cheap comic. "There's no point blaming yourself, Jack. What's done is done. Moreover I supported your decision at the time, and I still do. Sometimes the price you pay is just too high."

"Tell that to Kinsey."

"I'm going to. And so are you."

He stared. "Me, sir? But I don't want to go to Washington. Not if it means rubbing elbows with Kinsey."

"I don't want to go either, but we're not in charge of this train, Jack," said Hammond. "More's the pity."

"What's Kinsey involved for anyway? We haven't heard a peep out of him since his screw-up over Apophis. I thought he was old news."

"You know what they say," Hammond sighed. "Everything old is new again. I'm no happier about his involvement than you are, Jack, believe me, but I can't interfere in the civilian bureaucracy."

"I know, I know," he said, morosely. "It's just I'm not Captain Tactful at the best of times, General. Me and Kinsey ..." Just thinking about the bastard made him want to hit something. "Maybe I should sit this one out."

Hammond snorted. "Don't take this the wrong way, Jack, but I really wish you could. Unfortunately, Kinsey's insisting on your presence. There are, and again I quote, 'several points of interest in your mission report he's eager to discuss with you'."

"He's read my mission report?"

"The entire committee's read it, apparently. And the President."

That sat O'Neill up, alarmed. "Already? General, how long have you known this was coming?"

Hammond went back to avoiding his gaze. "I knew there'd be trouble the moment you said the mission had failed. Half an hour after telling the President we'd not acquired the technology as promised I got a call from Kinsey's office warning me of an official investigation."

"But that was four days ago, sir. Why didn't you say something before now?"

"To what end?" said Hammond, shrugging. "You had enough on your plate. Sufficient unto the day is the evil thereof, Jack. I don't believe in crossing a burning bridge before I have to."

"I'm sorry, General," he said, after a small silence. "I let you down on this one. I should've found a way to make the Eurondan deal happen."

"That would be water under the burning bridge, Jack," said Hammond, gently smiling. "Let's not waste time and energy on the past."

In the privacy of his own head, O'Neill could admit it. He loved this man. Loved, admired, respected. The thought of disappointing him was a sharp knife between the ribs... and he couldn't remember the last CO for whom he'd felt that. Hammond was Old School, in all the very best definitions of the term. He'd been there, he'd done that. Hell, he could open a tee-shirt shop. He fought for his people against his own side as hard as against any enemy. Harder, sometimes. Because sometimes your own side *was* the enemy, like now, and nobody can kill you deader than a friend.

"What time do we have to be in Washington?"

"Eleven a.m. I'll pick you up at your place at seven, we can go direct to Peterson from there."

Depressed, he nodded. "Yes, sir."

"Cheer up, Colonel," Hammond added, leaning back in his chair again. "It might not be so bad."

"No," he agreed, and pushed himself to his feet. "We could crash en route and miss the meeting altogether." Then he held up a hand.

"I know. I know. My humor is dubious. Sorry. Just getting it out of my system before tomorrow."

Hammond shook his head. "Close the door on your way out, Jack."

Restless, at a loose end, O'Neill headed to the control room. With any luck some massive crisis would throw them all into chaos sometime in the next five minutes, necessitating his urgent relocation off-world, for a long, long time...

The massive crisis uncharitably refused to materialise. Teal'c was there, though, working through some language-related gobble-degook with one of the technicians.

"O'Neill," he said, standing. "You—"

He raised an emphatic finger. "I swear to God, if *one more person* tells me I look like hell I will punch them on the nose!"

All around the control room, gazes were hastily averted.

Teal'c's head tilted slightly. "Indeed."

Come to think of it, that wasn't a bad idea. "Teal'c, are you busy?"

Teal'c indicated the technician. Laura Somebody. O'Neill couldn't remember her last name. They came and went all the time, he could never keep track of them. Just a bunch of lab coats babbling in too many syllables about things that made no sense... "I am assisting Ms. Hill with—"

"Great. Let's box."

"Now?"

He rolled his eyes. "No, next week. Of course now. You don't have anything better to do, and neither do I. Come on. It'll be fun." He thought about that for a moment. "Okay. So maybe not so much fun, as therapeutic. Come on. Healthy exercise, just do it."

Teal'c hesitated, then nodded. "Very well. I will join you in the gym momentarily."

"Okay," he said, rubbing his hands together. "But don't keep me waiting too long. Because the longer you have to think about this the harder you'll be shaking in your shoes."

"Indeed," said Teal'c again, after a moment.

He presented himself in the gym ten minutes' later, pulled on his sparring gear, and they got down to business.

"Since you are already endeavouring to punch me on the nose,

O'Neill," Teal'c said, easily blocking three quick jabs in succession, "I will now tell you that you do look like hell."

"I know," he said, breathing hard, the sweat pouring between his shoulder blades. "I'll get over it."

Teal'c evaded what would've been a brutal uppercut. "I know."

That was the great thing about Teal'c. He just ... got it. No navel-gazing, no anguished self-examinations, no well-meant amateur psychoanalyzing. Crap happened and you got over it. End of discussion.

An hour later, after totally failing to knock Teal'c senseless to the mat, dammit, O'Neill's dodgy knee held up a white flag and he had to stop. The headache was gone, replaced with the pain of burning lungs, burgeoning bruises and the tedious overall reminder that no, really, he wasn't as young as he used to be.

"Thanks," he said, lightly tapping gloves with Teal'c. "I needed that." His stomach rumbled. "And hey, now I need food. Is it lunch-time yet?"

Teal'c gave him a sidelong look as he pulled off his gloves. "It is a large galaxy, O'Neill. Doubtless it is lunchtime somewhere."

He smiled. "I like the way you think, big guy."

By the time they'd showered and dressed it really was lunch-time in their little corner of the Milky Way and the commissary was half-full. Sauntering in with Teal'c, seeing Carter and Daniel already in the chow line, O'Neill noticed SG-4 was back from P9D-882, sporting the very latest in nifty bandages. Nothing serious, though. Everyone still had their arms and legs. He'd catch up with Brugel later to find out what happened. Whatever it was couldn't be too bad, because they were all laughing and using their forks as catapults to hurl peas at each other.

Once his tray was loaded with chicken-fried steak, mashed potato, gravy and green beans, with a honking great piece of pecan pie for after, he joined his team at their usual table. "I didn't eat breakfast!" he protested, as they stared disapprovingly at his lunch. "*And* I just boxed the snot out of Teal'c. I *need* feeding up."

Daniel turned to Teal'c, who'd decided to live dangerously with salad. "Really? He boxed the snot out of you?"

"No," said Teal'c. "He did not."

"Didn't think so," said Daniel.

"Daniel, would you like to eat that pumpkin soup or wear it?"

"I'll eat it, Jack, but thanks for asking," said Daniel, still grinning.

Carter grinned back. "You sure about that? Orange might be your color."

And so it went, tease and bicker, bicker and tease. No pea-throwing, but then they were the flagship team. They had an example to set. An image to maintain. Besides. Peas were for pussies. *Real* soldiers used mashed potato. With extra gravy. And if he wasn't so busy eating his, he'd happily launch the first attack.

"So," he said. "I'm off to Washington in the morning. To meet with Kinsey and a bunch of other stuffed shirts. About the Eurondan mission."

As a conversation killer it was the equivalent of a direct nuclear strike. Daniel paused, a spoonful of electric green Jell-O halfway to his mouth. "Really? Um—is that wise?"

"Why wouldn't it be wise?"

"Well—because the last time you and Kinsey sat around the same table you tried to beat him to death with it?"

He raised his eyebrows. "Now, now, Daniel. Don't go trying to be subtle. You'll sprain something."

Teal'c examined a tomato as though he'd never seen one before. Saying nothing. He knew there was nothing to say.

"Just you, sir?" Carter said quietly. "Because I'm not doing anything urgent. If you want back-up... some moral support..."

Their eyes met. He let himself smile, just a little bit. "Thanks, but that won't be necessary. Hammond's going too. He's already promised to pack his whip, chair and gun. And handcuffs, in case I get antsy."

An awkward silence fell then, covered up by the background noise of a cheerful commissary. Daniel dropped his spoonful of Jell-O back in the bowl. His expression was troubled. "Look... Jack..."

"Daniel, forget it," he said briskly. "The past is another country and my passport is currently expired. I just wanted you to know where I'm going. Now, if you'll excuse me, I've got paperwork to catch up on. Adios. Arrivederci. Auf Wiedersehen. Bon Voyage. Goodbye."

He could feel their eyes on him as he headed for the door, pecan pie in hand. Could feel their concern, warm like flames on a cold winter's night. They were good people.

What a shame he couldn't say the same about Kinsey.

A tiny flicker of nerves prickled the base of his spine, and he shivered. Then he scowled. Screw Kinsey and his committee. He took a savage bite of pie.

Screw them all.

CHAPTER TWO

66"General Hammond," said Senator Kinsey, genial as a snake. He made no attempt to stand, just sat at the head of the Pentagon conference table as though he owned the room and the other people in it were his serfs. Kinsey would make a good Goa'uld. "Welcome back to Washington. And you, Colonel O'Neill." He sat back, fingers steepled. Fangs bared in a smile. "I must say, for a man whose questionable career is on the line you're looking remarkably relaxed."

Despite Hammond's presence, and everything he owed the man, O'Neill felt the adrenaline kick in. Fight or flight, that's how the body worked, and the day he ran from Kinsey was the day hell sent out for heaters. But before any lying cheating stinking political rat bastard got what was coming to him, Admiral Belweather cleared his throat.

"Senator—please. As Chairman of the Joint Chiefs I like to think that military personnel matters are my jurisdiction. A quaint notion, no doubt, but I'd appreciate it if you'd humor me."

Kinsey didn't acknowledge him. "Have a seat, gentlemen. You're late."

O'Neill exchanged a glance with General Hammond, who just tightened his lips. It was code for *Suck it up, Jack*. They were late because of traffic between Andrews and the Pentagon but there was no point trying to explain. Kinsey was looking for more ammunition and Belweather wasn't interested in irrelevant detail. The Navy's finest had a reputation for being task-oriented, no-nonsense and possessing zero patience for whiners.

So. Suck it up, Jack.

Once Hammond was seated, O'Neill slid into the next available chair and caught the sympathetic eye of Paul Davis, who was positioned as Belweather's right hand man. Possibly a friendly face, but he wasn't entirely sure. He hadn't made up his mind about Davis yet, though the major had seemed competent enough during the recent Replicator crisis. He wasn't a slick bastard like Samuels, that was for sure. But that didn't make him safe …

Admiral Belweather, fleshy face pink from too much recent sun, tapped his tidy fingernails on the buff manila folder before him. It was crisscrossed with blue-inked notes and stamped CLASSIFIED in red letters three inches high right across the top. Around the table the rest of the committee—a mix of military and civilian, three men, one woman, and O'Neill didn't know any of them, dammit—flipped open their own folders then once again rested impassive gazes on him and the general.

Hammond seemed unfazed. O'Neill hoped he did, too, but inside he was burning. Kinsey's stare was relentless and colder than any Antarctic glacier. His pale eyes were brimful of hate, and hope.

"General Hammond, you and—" Belweather began, but with a raised hand Kinsey cut him off.

"Admiral, the President has made it quite clear that I am the convenor of this investigation. Kindly wait until you're invited to comment."

Davis and the other three military types froze. Pink became red as Belweather flushed. Hammond sucked in some air, his dress jacket tight across his chest.

Oblivious, Kinsey continued. "General Hammond, this hearing has been convened in order to—"

To hell with *Suck it up, Jack.* O'Neill leaned forward, fists clenched on the table. "Hearing? Investigation? What crap are you trying to pull this time, Kinsey? Since when does a *politician*—" He spat the word like it was poison, ignoring Hammond's thrumming alarm beside him. "—investigate the actions of a sanctioned military operation? Correct me if I'm wrong, but you're not Chairman of the Congressional Oversight Committee any more. You don't—"

Belweather's hand slapped the table. "That's enough, Colonel O'Neill! Previous service to this nation does not give you permission to—"

He turned to the Admiral. "Due respect, sir, you've been Chairman of the Joint Chiefs for less than three months. *I've* been dealing with Kinsey for over two years. Whatever he says he wants to achieve from this hearing, you can bet your last little rowboat what he's *really* after is control of the SGC. And the last time he came within a whisker of that we were nearly wiped out by Apophis. I don't know what crap he's been spewing into your ear, or the President's ear for that matter, but you cannot give it a moment's credence. Put the safety of this country—this *planet*—into that man's hands and we might as well surrender to the Goa'uld right now."

Silence, explosive with repressed emotion. Davis's eyes were just about popped right out of his head. The other military reps—two Army colonels and a Marine major—stared at their folded hands as though their lives depended on the view. The civilian committee member was clearly owned by Kinsey; his beady gaze was stuck to the senator's face as though glued there.

"General Hammond," said the admiral, eyes slitted in warning, "I suggest you control your subordinate. This is the wrong place and the wrong time for an—interesting—career to end."

Kinsey was smiling again. "And the President wonders why I call into question Colonel O'Neill's fitness for duty."

Belweather's narrow gaze swung towards him. "We all wonder, Senator. Only a fool complains if his own rough handling of a gun results in a self-inflicted wound. And you don't strike me as a fool."

Under cover of Kinsey's sharp response, Hammond leaned close. "Jack … "

"Yes, sir," O'Neill muttered. "Sorry, sir."

His guts were so tight YoYo Ma could've used them to re-string his cello. He took a deep breath. Let it out. Across the table, Major Davis risked a tiny smile. Stupidly, it made him feel better. He turned to Belweather.

"I apologize, Admiral. That was uncalled for."

Belweather nodded. "It was. Let me make one thing abundantly clear to you, Colonel: attachment to an important, top-secret project does not make you invisible or protect you from the consequences of your actions. You are as answerable for your conduct as anyone in this room. And no impressive tally of war wounds or unlikely victories snatched from the jaws of defeat will ever change that. Not while I'm the Chairman. Is that understood, Colonel?"

Looked like Belweather's reputation was right. If he didn't dial it down, he was going to do more harm here than good. And George Hammond deserved better of him. O'Neill nodded. "Yes, sir. Sir, if I may speak candidly?"

Belweather snorted. "You've been circumspect to this point,

Colonel?"

"No, sir. I've been tactless." Releasing another deep breath, he met the admiral's frowning gaze. "Sir, whatever misgivings or disappointments you may have with regards to the Eurondan mission I want to make it absolutely clear that General Hammond bears no responsibility for its negative outcome. I—"

"Colonel O'Neill!" roared Hammond. "We have already had this conversation!"

He shifted in his chair to face Hammond's wrath. "Yes, General, I know. But all due respect, you're wrong. It was my call and I made it. And I'm not going to sit idly by while Kinsey uses my failure to nail your career to his mast. I will not—"

"*Speak another word until I give you leave to open your mouth!*" thundered Kinsey. On his feet now, all fire and brimstone. Moses in a three-thousand dollar suit. Fists planted on the conference table he leaned forward, alight with fury. "You are on *my* turf here, Colonel, and you will play by *my* rules. If you don't I have the President's full authority to punish you as I see fit and if you don't believe me I suggest you find a phone and ask him. Is that clear? You have permission to answer."

Permission? O'Neill couldn't trust himself to speak. God, he never should've come. He should've lied, told Hammond he had the 24-hour flu. Washington. Politics. He'd rather face a horde of screaming Jaffa with a worn-out slingshot, any day. He'd rather face Apophis. He didn't belong in this human jungle. He was a soldier. A warrior. Bloodshed was ugly, but at least it was honest. Simple. Kill or be killed. This was a quagmire, where friends were enemies and enemies never fought fair...

"Well, Colonel?" Kinsey demanded. "Have I made myself clear?"

O'Neill nodded. "Perfectly, Senator."

Beside him, Hammond fractionally relaxed. Fresh guilt stabbed. Damn. The last thing he wanted was to make George's difficult life more difficult. He had to keep a lid on things, no matter what provocation Kinsey used.

He was career Special Forces. He could do that.

"Good," said Kinsey. He straightened, but stayed standing, lording it over the rest of them. "Your effrontery, O'Neill, has expanded beyond sane comprehension. Just because you've had one or two serendipitous victories over a godless alien foe you seem to think you're invincible and beyond reproach. Somehow you've managed to hoodwink good men into turning blind eyes to your mistakes, your missteps and your military arrogance. Might makes right, that's your motto. You think that because you hold a gun you hold the rest of us hostage to your narrow understanding of the world. Well, Colonel, I'm here to tell you you're very wrong. You're not invincible or immune from censure and this administration will not be bullied by a man who looks upon orders as mere inconveniences!"

"Senator Kinscy, I really must protest!" said Hammond, firing up. "It's no secret you and Colonel O'Neill don't see eye to eye on some issues but—"

"*Some* issues?" Kinsey laughed. "General, we don't see eye to eye on *anything*. And that is because Colonel O'Neill's vision is skewed. When he looks in a mirror he sees a man without a master. A man answerable to no-one."

"He is answerable to me!"

Kinsey smiled. "I know."

It was a threat, and everyone in the room heard it. Hammond's chin lifted. "Senator, you're a busy man and so am I. Admiral Belweather is even busier. Why don't you just get to the point?"

"Certainly," said Kinsey. "Put at its simplest, the President of these United States, *your* Commander-in-Chief, General, has tasked me to uncover the truth of SG-1's mission to the planet Euronda. Colonel O'Neill, are you prepared, here and now, to answer for your actions?"

Admiral Belweather cleared his throat. "Senator Kinsey, this is an enquiry, not a court martial. You might consider moderating your approach."

"And you, Admiral, might consider recalling you're here by invitation," retorted Kinsey. "It would be unfortunate if I felt compelled to rescind it. Colonel O'Neill, you haven't answered my question."

O'Neill stared at the senator, abruptly off-balance. What the hell was going on here? Since when did Kinsey have this kind of influence? He'd been discredited after the near-miss with Apophis. Had lost some serious face. Something had happened since then. Something bad. While SG-1 was off saving the planet—again—someone had redecorated the corridors of power. Repainted them in Kinsey's colors. He glanced at Hammond, who nodded. *Let's just get this over with, Jack.*

Yes. Get it over with, get out of here, and find out who'd slipped Kinsey the keys to the castle. Then figure out a way to get them back before the bastard brought it crashing down round all their ears.

He made himself meet Kinsey's challenging glare. "I'm always ready to answer for my actions, Senator."

Kinsey sneered. "We'll see. Colonel O'Neill, having read your mission report there's really only one question to be asked."

"Then ask it already. Senator."

"The President wants to know—as do I—why one of the most potentially valuable allies in our war against the Goa'uld was not only rebuffed, but destroyed. Why their leader, with his incredible wealth of knowledge, was denied sanctuary from his enemies. Was in effect *murdered* by—"

The small stuffy Pentagon meeting room turned scarlet. Dimly aware of voices raised in protest, of Hammond's hand reaching for his arm, in vain, O'Neill surged to his feet. The chair crashed onto its side behind him.

"It wasn't murder, you sanctimonious sonofabitch! I warned him not to follow us through the 'gate. He knew about the iris. He didn't listen. He killed himself. I *did not* murder him!"

Kinsey's face was alight with glee, his eyes on fire with malice. "No? Then if not murder, what? An execution perhaps? Yes! That role suits you to perfection, doesn't it? The one and only Jack O'Neill: self-appointed judge—jury—and executioner!"

"Screw you, Kinsey! It was self-defence. I couldn't let him come through to the SGC. He was dangerous, he—"

"Dangerous? To us?" said Kinsey, pacing. "You mean he had a plan to destroy Earth? I don't recall reading that in your report, Colonel! As I recall he wanted to *help* Earth, he wanted to give us weapons and technology that would aid us in our fight against the Goa'uld! That is your purpose, Colonel, is it not? To procure weapons and technology that will help us defeat the barbarians at the gate *you* opened, who want to make us their slaves?"

God. Was the man really that much of an idiot? "If you read my report, Kinsey, you know why he was dangerous! He was a monster.

His father started that war and when his father died he kept it going, he slaughtered *thousands*, all in the name of white pride, he—"

"Thank you, Colonel," said Kinsey. He stopped pacing and rested his hands on the back of his chair. "I know what you claim were the circumstances on Euronda."

"What I *claim*?" Breathing heavily, O'Neill took a step back. It was that, or hit the bastard.

"Well, we've only got your word for it, haven't we?" said Kinsey, suavely.

"Fine! If you don't believe me, believe the rest of my team. Read *their* reports!"

Kinsey waved a negligent hand. "I have. I place no more faith in their version of events than I do in yours, O'Neill. SG-1 is a cult of personality. You've made sure of that. I have no doubt they'd lie for you at the drop of the proverbial hat. But if they are telling the truth, then in my estimation Major Carter, Dr. Jackson and the alien are as culpable as you over the loss of the Eurondan technology."

"Major Carter was following my orders. And Jackson? Kinsey, if Daniel hadn't opened his big mouth and argued with me till he was blue in the face we'd be in bed with Alar right this minute—and then God help us!"

"Yes," said Kinsey, unblinking. "Jackson's actions border on treason. And you showed yet more deplorable judgement in allowing yourself to be swayed by his namby-pamby, hand-wringing, soft-soaping, limp-wristed liberalism! The moment he challenged your authority he should've been ordered back to the SGC and his privileged status revoked. And then you should've finished negotiating the treaty with the Eurondans. As you were ordered to do. Failing that, you should've brought Alar back to Earth as a refugee and guest in good standing and allowed the elected officials of this brave nation to determine whether or not he was a fit individual with whom we could conduct business. But no. You took that decision upon yourself, O'Neill, just like you always do."

"You mean like I did when you closed down the SGC just as Apophis and his motherships were getting ready to burn this planet to cinders? Is that the deplorable judgement you're talking about?"

Kinsey snarled. "Must I remind you we wouldn't be having this conversation if you and your precious Dr. Jackson had left well enough alone? How many good men and women preceded President Alar into the grave, Colonel, all because of your Stargate? And how many more will follow them?"

O'Neill stared, incredulous. "God Almighty, Kinsey, could you be any more melodramatic? You stupid—"

Kinsey's face flooded crimson. "Do not take that tone with me, Colonel, or blaspheme in my presence!"

O'Neill moved round the table, past all the staring stone-silent witnesses, not caring he and Kinsey weren't alone. He was glad others were here to see the truth of the man stripped bare. His hands were fisted by his sides, aching to punch and pummel, to reduce the politician to pulp. He stopped in front of Kinsey and let the senator see that.

"You're a lying manipulative bastard, Kinsey. You know damned well—"

"There is only *one* liar in this room, Colonel, and I am looking at him!" said Kinsey, triumphant. "Your official report is a complete fabrication. You screwed up the mission to Euronda, you cost us the weapons and technology that would have given us victory over the Goa'uld *and* you're attempting to cover up the fact you killed an innocent man who could've born witness against you!"

"That is *not* true!"

Kinsey's eyebrows lifted. "No? So you're saying you're not a liar?"

"That's *exactly* what I'm saying!"

"Then you convict yourself with your own words. Because when it comes to falsifying official military records you're hardly a virgin. Are you? That first mission to Abydos..."

How fast could a heart beat before it burst? Or shattered its cage of ribs to bony shards? O'Neill felt as though he were standing somewhere outside his own body. Time slowed, thickened, like molasses on a winter morning. "The first Abydos mission is irrelevant."

"On the contrary!" Kinsey spat. "What we're seeing is a pattern of behavior that speaks to your total lack of fitness for holding command. You lied about detonating the bomb on Abydos and because you didn't follow orders Apophis came here!"

"I had good reason for what I did, innocent people were going to die, I made a judgement call to—"

"Your judgement, Colonel, was suspect to say the least! When you made that decision to disobey orders you were suffering from a suicidal depression brought on by guilt over the death of your son, a tragedy for which—"

"*You leave my son out of this*!"

"For which *you* were directly responsible—" continued Kinsey, remorseless. "You killed him as surely as if you pulled the trigger yourself and I for one *deplore*—"

Confusion. Voices shouting, hands grabbing, pulling him away from the man he had pinned to the wall. Kinsey. Pale eyes staring, fingers ineffectually tugging at the forearm threatening his throat, patrician face suffused with outraged fury. A desperate voice in his ear. "Back away, Colonel, please, please, for God's sake back away!"

It was Davis. O'Neill lowered his arm. Let himself be hustled backwards across the small conference room to hit the wall beside its curtained window. When he looked up Kinsey was in a chair, shaken, dumbstruck, his breathing irregular, his immaculate hair in disarray. He looked anything but suave. Hammond and Belweather flanked him, the other three military types stood to one side, shock showing through their rigorous façade of neutrality. Kinsey's civilian aide gibbered in a corner.

Davis's fingers were still anchored to his shoulder. "Colonel…"

"I'm all right," he said. His voice sounded very strange. "Let me go."

Davis hesitated, then loosened his grip. "Sir—"

Kinsey lurched to his feet, one shaking finger pointed. "I want O'Neill arrested. I want him court martialed. I want him in prison for the rest of his *life*!"

Admiral Belweather stepped closer. "Senator, you're upset. I suggest we adjourn this meeting until further notice. You have my word, Colonel O'Neill will be dealt with."

Something in Belweather's measured, deliberate tones breached Kinsey's fury, caught his attention and dragged his gaze sideways. "Your word, Admiral? I suppose I can trust it, can I?"

Belweather's lips thinned. "If it's good enough for the President, Senator, I assume it's good enough for you."

"Yes. Well." Kinsey tugged his jacket straight. Slicked his hair into place and became, once more, the consummate, urbane politician. "I'll expect a full report of action taken in this matter. Sooner rather than later, Admiral."

"Certainly, Senator," said Belweather. "My office will be in touch the moment a decision has been reached."

Kinsey's head came up. "No, Admiral. *You* will be in touch. By close of business today, with the details of Colonel O'Neill's preliminary hearing, or the first phone-call you receive tomorrow morning will be from the President, demanding your resignation as Chairman of the Joint Chiefs."

Belweather's expression didn't change. "Rest assured, Senator, you'll be kept apprised of developments. Now I'm sure you have a busy schedule lined up for the rest of the day. Please don't allow us to detain you any longer."

With a last, burning look Kinsey departed, his aide faithful at his heels. In his wake, silence.

General Hammond heaved a sigh. "Admiral, I—"

Belweather's hand came up. "Major Davis. Escort Colonel O'Neill to the staff room and remain with him there until you're relieved."

David nodded. "Yes, sir."

"Colonel O'Neill—"

O'Neill snapped to attention. "Sir."

"You will accompany Major Davis to the tea room and remain there until further notice. If you attempt to reinterpret these orders you will regret it. Understood?"

He couldn't bring himself to look at Hammond. "Yes, Admiral. Understood."

"Good. You're dismissed."

Davis opened the door for him, and closed it again once they were outside the conference room. The Pentagon corridor they stood in was clean and empty. Davis nodded. "Staff room's this way, Colonel."

"Thank you, Major."

They made the short walk in silence. Davis stood aside to let him enter, then closed and locked the door after them.

"Relax, Major," he said. "I'm not going to chase after Kinsey and finish the job."

Davis pulled a face. "Wouldn't blame you if you tried, sir." Then he straightened. "Sorry. I just thought you might like some privacy."

"That would involve you standing on the other side of the door, Davis."

"Ah. Yes. Sorry, Colonel."

He sighed. "It's all right."

The staff room was neat. Almost Spartan, as befitted a building crammed roof to basement with career military types. A sagging couch was pushed against the wall opposite the door. Suddenly very tired, O'Neill skirted the table and chairs and collapsed onto it. His head ached fiercely, and the last moments of his confrontation with Kinsey were rapidly taking on the unreal blurriness of a trip through the Stargate.

Davis cleared his throat. "Would you like a coffee, sir? Or a tea? There's some juice here too, if you'd prefer that."

He was standing at the open refrigerator, looking helpful. Looking nervous. Poor bastard. Bet the last thing he'd expected to do today was baby-sit a homicidal superior officer.

God Almighty. He'd tried to throttle Kinsey. Which meant, put bluntly, his checkered career was over. Kinsey had won. Maybe there'd be a court martial and maybe there wouldn't, but that didn't seem to matter much now. Either way, it was over.

The bastard brought up Charlie. *Charlie*. He'd deserved to have his windpipe crushed.

"Sir?"

O'Neill looked up. "I don't care. Whatever you're having, Major."

"Right. I'll make us some coffee, then," said Davis, looking relieved. "Would you prefer cream or milk with that?"

Hammond watched as Admiral Belweather nodded to the remaining personnel in the conference room. "That'll be all, people."

They left, quickly.

Belweather moved to the window, twitched aside the curtain and looked down to the gardens below. "That was unforgivable, General."

Hammond felt his stomach turn over. "Admiral—you need to

understand—Colonel O'Neill isn't the easiest officer I've ever commanded but he's probably the best. And Senator Kinsey—"

"It's Kinsey I'm talking about, George," said Belweather, and turned back from the window. "Using O'Neill's son like that, to score a cheap point." He shook his head, pink face creased with displeasure. "Unforgivable."

He perched on the edge of the table. "I did try to warn you, Reggie."

"Yes. You did. And it's not that I disbelieved you," said Belweather, grimacing. "But the President insisted that Kinsey head the investigation which meant my hands were tied. These days, George, I'm more politician than sailor."

"Serves you right for being a military genius, Mr. Chairman."

They exchanged swift, appreciative, self-mocking smiles. Then Belweather sobered. "But George. Unforgivably provoked or not, O'Neill's conduct is a court martial offence. I'm not sure we can save his bacon this time."

That had him on his feet. "Reggie, we have to. I owe Jack more than my life. If I stand by and let him be destroyed by pond scum like Kinsey I'll never be able to meet my own eyes in the mirror again."

Belweather didn't reply. Just nodded, frowning, and stared at the drab carpet. Then he said, his voice soft, "Do you think this Alar's death was murder?"

It was the one question he'd prayed no-one would ask him. Jack O'Neill had never asked it. He folded his arms across his chest. "Reggie..."

But Reggie Belweather wasn't a man to back down. "Do you think O'Neill made the wrong call?" he persisted. "Should we have done business with the Eurondan equivalent of the Third Reich?"

Another appallingly difficult question. One Hammond could, with extreme reluctance and no small measure of angst, answer. "Yes, Reggie. I think O'Neill was wrong. The United States does business daily with governments who hardly measure up to our standards of ethics and morality. It may be distasteful, but we don't have the luxury of looking too closely at the politics of the people who are willing to help us destroy the Goa'uld. We're at war. It's six billion of us... or them. I want it to be us."

"And so do I, George," said Belweather soberly. "So does the President. It's what Kinsey wants, too, though it kills me to say it."

Hammond shook his head. "Kinsey may well want that, Reggie, but it's not all he wants and it's not what he wants first. You can't trust him. You *mustn't* trust him, or give him what he wants more than anything: Jack O'Neill's scalp."

"George, George, don't you understand?" said Belweather, despairing. "I might not have a choice! Let's not forget O'Neill did physically attack the bastard."

Hammond slid off the edge of the table and squared his shoulders. "Admiral Belweather, I'm not the only one who owes Jack O'Neill his life. We *all* owe him our lives. Hell, we owe him the *planet*!"

"I know we do, General. And for that he will always be honored," said Belweather. His expression was sympathetic, but sympathy only stretched so far. "However he's still just a man, and he's still accountable, like Kinsey says. And George, by your own admission—this time, O'Neill made a mistake. What if it turns out he's guaranteed our destruction at the hands of the Goa'uld just because he had an inconvenient attack of conscience? What am I supposed to do about that? Or the fact he assaulted a United States Senator in front of witnesses? What am I supposed to do, George? What would *you* do, if you were me?"

Hammond sighed, and turned away. "I don't know, Reggie. God give me strength... but I just don't know."

After that, there wasn't much else to say. They parted company with assurances to keep in constant communication, and Hammond went to collect his errant subordinate.

"Thank you, Major," he said to Davis, dismissing the man.

Davis nodded, cast a final glance at Jack, and withdrew from the staff room. The door closed quietly behind him.

Standing at uneasy attention, hands behind his back, Jack stared without expression just past his weary general's left shoulder.

"Well, Colonel," Hammond said, and shoved his hands in his pockets. "For a smart man, that was a very, very dumb move."

A small nerve ticked beside Jack's eye. "Yes, sir."

"You know what this means, don't you?"

"That I should dust off my résumé, sir?"

Humor, humor, always humor. But this wasn't a laughing matter.

Hammond closed the distance between them. "It may yet come to that, Colonel!" he barked. Then, relenting, added more kindly, "But not if I've got anything to say about it."

Beneath Jack's practised, polished mask, some deep emotion swirled and shifted. "General, I'm sorry. I don't know what happened, I—"

"Hell, I do," he retorted. "Kinsey pushed your buttons and you went off like a damned Exocet missile." Despite all his best intentions, in the face of his maverick colonel's refusal to take a crisis seriously, just once, he felt his temper escape him. "*Dammit*, Jack! You just gave the bastard everything he's prayed for these last two years! On a silver platter, no less! What were you *thinking*?"

"I wasn't," said Jack, scowling. "And that would be the problem, wouldn't it?" He turned away, the heel of one hand pressed to his forehead as though attempting to contain some terrible pain. "I let him get to me. How did that happen? I spent four months in an Iraqi prison and I didn't tell them squat. Not about anything that mattered. How the *hell* did I let a weasel like Kinsey under my guard?"

It was a measure of the man's distress that he not only admitted the weakness, but that he'd voluntarily refer to one of the most brutal, sordid chapters of his pre-SGC career.

Clearly, any further dissection of this current debacle would have to wait.

Righteous anger extinguished, Hammond stepped closer. "Because you're tired, Jack," he said gently. "And what happened on Euronda has upset you more than you realize. This is my fault. I should've known something like this would happen."

Jack spun around. "*Your* fault? Bull! Sir. I'm the one who took a swing at Kinsey. I'm the one who lost control."

"And I'm the one who exposed you to his amoral machinations knowing—well. That you were still bothered by what happened on Euronda." He held up a hand, forestalling a furious protest. "Jack, please. It's just us here. There's no need for pretence. And I don't need to be a psychologist to know that killing Alar—allowing him to die or however you want to phrase it—isn't sitting well with you. Hell, it isn't sitting well with me, either. And before too long, it's something we're going to have to deal with properly. But for now—for right now—let's just get back home and see what we can do about saving your ass before Kinsey flushes it down the toilet, hmm? Can we do that, Jack?"

Rigid, resisting, bitterly resentful, Jack glared at the scuffed linoleum floor. Hating to be this vulnerable. Hating the need for a helping hand. Then he looked up. His eyes were unutterably tired.

"Yes, sir. We can do that."

Hammond nodded and smiled, offering a show of confidence he was far from feeling. "Good man. Then let's go."

CHAPTER THREE

"Oh my God," said Daniel blankly into the phone. "Uh—thanks, Paul. Really. I appreciate the heads-up. Bye."

Feeling totally thrown, he hung up the receiver and sat for a moment, just staring into space. Then he headed out of his office for Sam's lab. The doctor was in, doing something incomprehensible with an electron microscope and what looked like a sample of the weird green soil SG-8 had brought back from its exploration of P7G-112. There was no sign of Teal'c. Sometimes, for reasons known only to him, he lurked on the fringes of Sam's experiments. According to Sam he hardly said anything, just focused his powerful concentration on her and the task at hand. Apparently he'd said he was a wise warrior and an ignorant man and he owed it to his people to redress the imbalance in anticipation of the freedom to come.

Teal'c never stopped believing that one day, the Jaffa would be free. Doubt wasn't found in his dictionary—even though a lot of other, much longer words definitely were; sometimes he talked like a university professor. Once, when Jack complained, Teal'c had just smiled then said, "Enslaved Jaffa speak with their false god's tongue and utter only the words pleasing to it. Now I am free I speak with my own tongue the words that please me, and me alone."

Too often it was easy to forget that Teal'c was twice Jack's age, and then some. Jack had never complained again.

Daniel regretted the Jaffa's absence keenly; this wasn't the kind of news he wanted to announce twice.

Standing in Sam's open doorway, unnoticed, he took a moment just to enjoy her immersion in the work. Putting off the evil moment, true, but still...

Like him, she was a scientist at heart. It meant he understood her in a way he'd never, with all the good will in the world, understand Jack. She was as passionately in love with learning, with knowledge and the challenges of the unknown as he was himself and it bonded them as closely as any obscure warrior blood rites. Sam knew how it felt to be consumed by curiosity, overwhelmed with wonder, swallowed alive by the need to *know*. She understood that knowledge for its own sake was *important*. That not everything needed to relate to the concrete and touchable, the immediacy of the moment, the raw fundamentals of life and death.

Sure, in the grand scheme of things those matters were important. But they weren't the *most* important. They were, in fact, only important in that they allowed you to continue the journey of discovering the answers to life's infinite mysteries.

Mysteries that to him didn't include questions and answers like: Will it kill me? If it will, I'll kill it first. If it won't, it doesn't matter.

He'd more or less given up trying to expand Jack's intellectual horizons. The man was a far, far cry from dumb but he did redefine the concept of 'narrow focus' in a whole new and intimidating way.

And speaking of Jack... much as he wanted to, he couldn't put this off forever. "Hey, Sam," he said, stepping into the lab. "You got a minute?"

Eyes glued to the microscope viewer, she held up a finger. "Wait—wait—*yes*!" Then she straightened, her face alight with excitement and triumph. "I *knew* it! I knew my hunch was right."

Despite the grinding ache in his belly, Daniel had to grin. "Right about what?"

She flapped an indiscriminate, excited hand. "This!"

"And what is this? What are you doing, exactly?"

"What am I doing?" she echoed. She was close to dancing on the spot, something you didn't see every day. "I'm stealing Area 51's thunder... and I don't care." She snatched up the sealed beaker containing the green soil sample and waved it aloft like an Olympic gold medal. "This is not ordinary dirt, Daniel. This dirt contains traces of naquadah and an element not defined on the Periodic Table. In fact—and here's where things get *really* interesting—the only other reference to it in existence, as far as I know, is in the repository of knowledge we found on Earnest's planet. How do you like *them* apples?"

"Well—ah—"

"*That's* why the soil's green!" she crowed. "Because the naquadah and the—the—other stuff—have combined to create a brand new element! An element that has the most incredible potential properties! I can't wait to tell General Hammond when he gets back. He can tell those—those—*weasels* at the White House to stuff this in their pipes and smoke it." She paused. "Although if they did, I suspect it might blow them into a million pieces. So possibly not. But at least they won't be able to accuse us of not achieving anything! This could be one of the most significant discoveries the Stargate program has ever—"

Daniel swallowed an interruption. He wasn't Jack. He didn't have the heart to run roughshod over her enthusiasm. After a moment, though, Sam noticed he wasn't grabbing hold of her to dance a polka round the lab. She stopped burbling, put down the container of soil and crossed her arms.

"Okay. I know that face. What's wrong?"

He closed the lab door. "We have a problem."

"What kind of a problem?"

"Ah … a big one."

"Daniel!" She came round the front of her workbench. "Stop futzing and spit it out!"

He didn't want to spit it out. Once he said it, the problem became really *real*.

"*Daniel*."

Hands shoved in his pockets, Daniel chewed at his lip then sighed. "Okay. So here's the thing. Jack … assaulted Kinsey."

Her face went blank. "No way."

"Yes, way."

"No *way*. He's not that stupid!"

"No. Not stupid. Angry. Apparently Kinsey made a crack about Charlie."

"A crack?" she said, incredulous. "What kind of a crack?"

He grimaced. "Something along the lines of your son's dead and it's all your fault."

Sam looked as disbelievingly shocked as he felt. "*Kinsey* said that? No. Surely not even *Kinsey*— but *why*? And how do you know? Daniel, where are you getting this? Who's your source?"

"Major Davis," he said. "From the Office of the Joint Chiefs, remember?"

She turned away, still grappling with the enormity of the news. "Yes. Of course I remember. Oh my God."

"The good news is he's not in prison. He and Hammond are on their way back to the SGC now. But there'll be fallout, Sam. I doubt even Jack can attack a United States Senator and get away with it. Even if it is Kinsey."

She groaned. "Especially if it's Kinsey. The man's a Portuguese Man of War, he has tentacles that reach for miles. Anyone else's career would've been finished after that screw-up over Apophis — but Kinsey? He's just gone from strength to strength. I don't think I want to know how."

"Neither do I. Sam — I think this is bad. For Jack."

"No, really?" she snapped, then held up a hand. "Sorry. You're right. It is bad. It's very bad." Then she looked at him, her expression curious. "And Davis phoned you direct with a heads-up? I didn't realize you two were friends."

"We're not," said Daniel. "Not exactly."

Vivid memory assailed him: Jack, on the brink of gruesome death in a submarine over-run with Replicators, ordering him to fire the missiles. To kill him quickly. Cleanly. He'd hesitated, and Jack had told Davis to do it. But Davis held off, waiting for his okay. Between them, their hesitations had saved Jack and Teal'c. If they'd blown the sub five seconds sooner, Thor and Sam would've arrived too late to transport them out. Afterwards, he and Davis had exchanged complicated looks, and smiled, and gone their separate ways. Some moments — some connections — couldn't be put into words.

Sam said, "Well, whatever you are, thank God for it. At least we've got some warning."

"Yes, but — what can we do, Sam?" he said, collapsing onto the nearest stool. "If Jack really did attack Kinsey then his career is over, isn't it? Kinsey's not going to let it go. He's not the forgive and forget type."

Sam started pacing. "Hammond'll fight for him. He hates Kinsey too. And he's got a good relationship with the President. *God.*" She spun about. "The bastard actually threw Charlie's death in the colonel's face? Unbelievable!"

"And not to mention irrelevant. They were supposed to be talking about Euronda."

"For all it's any of Kinsey's business," she retorted, and fetched up against the bench. "He wasn't there, it wasn't his call. Damned

Monday morning quarter backer, that's all Kinsey is. The man couldn't begin to understand the complexities of that mission if you gave him a textbook and a dictionary."

Euronda, Euronda. A topic that redefined the term 'minefield' in new and unpleasant ways. Daniel crossed his arms and looked away. "Sam ... about Euronda ..."

"Daniel, no," she said sharply. "What's the point? It's over. Just let it *be* over, will you?"

From the look in her eyes she still hadn't come to terms with it either. "I know, I know," he said, placating. "I just—I'm worried, all right? About Jack. And what happened to Alar."

Sam knew exactly what he meant and resented him for mentioning it. "Daniel ..."

He hadn't got this far in a checkered career by giving up in the face of disapproval. "If Alar had pulled a gun on Jack, that would be okay. Self-defence. Part of the war. But he didn't. Alar asked for sanctuary and Jack denied it to him. And when he ordered the iris closed he—"

Sam held up her hands. "Daniel, I can't deal with that right now. Right now all I care about is making sure the colonel's career doesn't end up flushed down the toilet because of Robert Kinsey. Okay? Can we please just focus on that?"

Daniel couldn't know for sure, not before talking to Jack—and probably not even *after* talking to him—but he suspected the incident with Kinsey and what happened to Alar were intimately connected. Cause and effect. Action and reaction. Which meant Euronda wasn't over, and wouldn't be over, for any of them, until Alar's ghost was laid to rest.

But Sam wasn't ready to hear that. And shouting wouldn't get either of them very far. So he just nodded and said, "Sure, Sam. Let's focus on that. We should find Teal'c, tell him what's going on."

A wave of relief washed away her frown. "Yeah. Good idea. We should go do that."

As it happened, Teal'c was on his way to find them. They met at the Level 19 elevator. "General Hammond has returned," he said, with his customary bluntness. "He requests our presence in his office, at once."

"What about Colonel O'Neill?" said Sam. "Is he back too?"

"I did not see O'Neill."

"Right."

Teal'c's eyebrow lifted. "You appear distressed, Major Carter. Is something wrong?"

Sam dredged up a smile for him. "No more than most days. Let's go."

Hammond was in his office, still buttoned into his dress jacket and talking animatedly on the red phone. Seeing them through the window he waved them in. As they entered he was saying, "Thank you, Admiral. I can't tell you how much I appreciate this. Yes, I will. Yes. Yes. Good bye."

"You wanted to see us, sir?" said Sam, all military efficiency and severely neutral demeanor.

Hammond sat back in his chair and considered them for a long, critical moment. Then: "You know, don't you," he said. Sounding almost, strangely, relieved.

Sam's shoulders relaxed. "Ah—well—Daniel and I do, sir. Teal'c doesn't."

Hammond shook his head. "How the hell did you—" Then his hand came up. "Never mind. I don't want to know. I've got enough on my plate as it is."

"What is it I do not know?" said Teal'c.

Daniel glanced at him. "Jack attacked Senator Kinsey."

Teal'c's face stilled. "Indeed? Then Senator Kinsey is to blame."

"How would you know, Teal'c?" said Hammond. "You weren't there."

"My presence is irrelevant, General. I know O'Neill, and I know the Senator. Kinsey said or did something dishonorable, thus provoking O'Neill into action."

"Unforgivable provocation is no excuse for committing assault!" Hammond snapped. Then he shook his head. "Kinsey made an—ill advised—reference to the colonel's late son."

Daniel snorted. "He accused Jack of killing him."

"Then O'Neill was within his rights to attack," said Teal'c, shrugging. "On Chulak such a slur upon one's honor cannot be ignored."

"That's as may be, Teal'c," said Hammond. "But we're not on Chulak."

"No, we are not, General," said Teal'c. "Unfortunately."

Daniel exchanged a swift grin with Sam. Trust Teal'c. Even Hammond's tension eased, a little. He unbuttoned his jacket and let out a gusty sigh. "The point is, people, I've had no choice but to place Colonel O'Neill on administrative leave, pending a disciplinary enquiry. Which leaves you three flapping in the breeze, so to speak, until this—incident—is resolved, one way or another."

Daniel crossed his arms. "One way being Jack's removal from the SGC? The Air Force, even?"

Hammond frowned at the red phone. "I'm hoping it won't come to that, Doctor."

"For how long, sir?" said Sam. "Will we be at a loose end, I mean. We're scheduled to visit P5C-862 on Thursday."

"I know. I'm reassigning SG-6 to that mission."

"But sir—"

Hammond's hand came down hard on his desk. "Major, please. Believe me when I say I've had more than enough arguments for one day!"

"Sorry, sir."

Another sigh. "Not as sorry as I am, Major."

Daniel cleared his throat. "Ah—where's Jack now, if you don't mind me asking?"

"I dropped him at his place on the way back from Peterson," said Hammond. "With strict orders to stay put, at least for the time being." He pulled a face. "Of course whether he'll bother to *follow* those orders..." Abruptly aware he'd just committed the cardinal sin of criticizing a team leader to his team, Hammond sat up. "Anyway. That's where he is, Dr. Jackson."

"And Senator Kinsey, sir?" said Sam. "I understand he wasn't actually hurt during the incident?"

"Not unless you count his pride, Major. And with a man like Kinsey that can be fatal."

"For other people," Daniel added. "Sir, if we're not going to 862 after all, what is it you want us to do?"

The faintest glimmer of amusement lit Hammond's eyes. "You mean after you've run out of here and broken the local speed limits driving to Jack's place to see if he's all right?"

"Yes," said Teal'c. "After that."

"Well..." Hammond picked up a pencil and tapped it on the

desk. "I was thinking SG-1 is overdue for a little downtime. The last couple of months around here have been hectic, one way and another. So, Dr. Jackson, how would you fancy some time at those ruins SG-12 have found?"

Treacherously, Daniel felt a thrill of excitement. "Really? You'd really let me go and—"

"Your expertise would be invaluable. Major Lopez was saying just yesterday she could do with your input."

"Well, of course, General, if I'm needed—" He got a grip on his excitement. "But sir, I wouldn't feel right about going unless I knew Jack was—"

"Colonel O'Neill's situation won't be sorted out overnight," said Hammond. "I expect you'll have a good week, at least, to poke around those ruins." He turned to Teal'c. "This might be a good time for you to visit your son, Teal'c. If memory serves he's got a birthday coming up, hasn't he? I know the Jaffa don't celebrate birthdays, but even so . . . and while you're there, you can find out from Bra'tac any Goa'uld activities we should be keeping an eye on."

Teal'c looked pleased. "Indeed. But as Daniel Jackson says—"

"People," said the general, sweeping them with a serious look. "I'm not going to say this again. There is nothing any of you can do with regards to Colonel O'Neill's predicament. To be perfectly frank, the best action you can take is to make yourselves scarce for a while. There's a chance—it's slim, but it's there—that Senator Kinsey will use this incident to launch yet another investigation into SG-1's missions. Possibly the entire SGC. If he does try anything, my life will be a lot easier if I can put my hand on my heart and say you're off-world and unavailable for comment. Do I make myself clear?"

Sam nodded. "Yes, sir. Sir, where do you suggest I might best be deployed?"

"You could come ruin-exploring with me!" said Daniel, brightly. "You keep saying how you'd like to get your hands dirty with a real live archaeological dig. This is your chance." When she frowned he added, "You can't keep on stealing Area 51's thunder, Sam. We've got enough enemies to be going on with for now."

"I suppose," she said. "Sir?"

"It's a good idea, Dr. Jackson," said Hammond. "SG-1, your

assignments are hereby approved, starting immediately. And when you see Jack, please tell him I'll be in touch soon. And tell him—" He stopped. Sighed. "Tell him I'm sorry I yelled."

"We will, sir," said Sam, and led the way to the door. Reaching it, though, she paused and turned. "Sir ... can you fix this?"

For a long moment, Hammond didn't answer. Then he shrugged. "I don't know, Sam. But I'm sure as hell going to try."

Jack O'Neill had learned a long time ago, the *very* hard way, that there was no outrunning Charlie's monstrous death. It was a fact. A scar in his heart as gnarled and twisted as any he bore on his body. A pain that might sleep, but would never die. It had left him alone for some time now; it must be months since memory's cesspool had stirred.

And then along came Kinsey ...

Pounding the running track in the woods backing onto his long quiet street, ignoring the protests from his dicey knee, O'Neill felt the sick black hatred surge through him yet again. Saw again that smug, self-righteous, patrician face, heard the words no-one had the right to say, least of all Kinsey—

You killed him as surely as if you pulled the trigger yourself.

Wood pigeons startled skyward as O'Neill vented outraged fury in a wordless roar.

Exhausted, hurting, dripping sweat, he slowed, slowed some more, staggered to a stop. Leaning against the nearest tree he rested his head on his outstretched arm, panting. The sky was bleeding light, it'd be dusk soon. He should go back. It'd be too easy to turn an ankle out here at twilight, blow his knee, land himself in Janet Fraiser's infirmary where the politicians could find him.

Pushing away from the tree he started back the way he'd come, jogging gently this time, coaxing muscle and sinew into reluctant effort. Poor old battered body. First it was Iraqis and now it was aliens, poking him full of holes ...

Home at last, letting a hot shower drum and thrum and sluice away the sweat and stink of bitter memory, he released the last of his anger. Watched it swirl down the drain and wondered if his career wasn't swirling right along with it. The question was: did he care? The answer came back almost immediately: of course.

Which meant the next few days were going to be … interesting.

Comfortable in jeans and sweat-shirt, he was staring into the depths of his almost empty refrigerator, wondering what the hell to do about dinner, when the front door-bell rang. He didn't have to answer it to know who was standing on his doorstep.

He answered it anyway.

"Well, well, well," he said, surveying his visitors with a jaundiced eye. "Huey, Dewey and Louie. I take it you've heard."

Daniel sighed. "Uh-huh. So don't just stand there, Uncle Scrooge. Let us in. You don't even have to feed us — we brought pizza."

So they had. Three large boxes of it, safely cradled in Teal'c's arms, smelling deliciously of cheese and pepperoni and barbecue sauce. If ole Doc Fraiser were here she'd have a cholesterol fit on the spot. He stood back. "Fine. Come on in. Just don't expect me to entertain you, or anything."

"Do we ever?" said Daniel, and led the way.

Carter was carrying the beer, plus a bottle of something non-alcoholic for Teal'c. Well-trained after all this time, she headed straight for the refrigerator and put the drinks in the freezer section to recapture their chill. Teal'c deposited the pizza boxes on the kitchen table then rummaged in drawers till he found the paper napkins, paper plates and coasters. Daniel pulled down glasses from the cupboard, just in case someone had developed a sudden allergy to drinking out of the bottle.

After more than three years it was a comfortable routine and they hid behind it, all of them, steadfastly refusing to acknowledge the honking great Kinsey-shaped elephant squashed into the corner of the room.

Naturally it was Daniel who first mentioned the lurking pachyderm. Around a dripping slice of pizza he said, indistinctly, "General Hammond said to say he's sorry he yelled."

O'Neill reached for his second beer. Yelled? That was an understatement. Somewhere in the continental US of A Hammond's bellowing had triggered a seismograph, he'd lay money on it. "Uh huh."

"And that he'd call you soon. He didn't say what about but, you know, I'm guessing it's this whole Kinsey mess."

"Good guess."

"Jack…"

Daniel radiated concern the way Chernobyl radiated… all right, radiation. You could toast marshmallows on the warmth of his regard. It made slapping him down almost impossible. He sighed. "Daniel, I'm fine. It happened, it's over, it's time to move on."

Daniel smiled. "You don't seriously expect us to accept that, do you?"

"Why yes, Daniel, I seriously think I do."

"When your *career* is on the line?"

"Oh, please. You're exaggerating."

"And you're insulting my intelligence," Daniel retorted, flushed with more than beer. "Don't. What happened in Washington—it isn't just about you. If Kinsey gets you court martialed or cashiered or at the very least transferred to a weather station in Alaska what happens to the SGC? You're Hammond's right hand. He depends on you. What's he going to do if you're not around? What are we going to do? Didn't you think about that before you tried to take Kinsey's head off? Didn't you think at *all*?"

O'Neill sat back in his chair. Carter and Teal'c had their heads down, eating pizza like it was going cold. But listening, damn them. Dying of nosiness, just like Daniel, but perfectly happy for him to make the running. Chicken, was what they were.

Reaching for another slice himself, he took a bite, chewed, swallowed, and shrugged. "What do you expect me to say, Daniel?"

Daniel frowned. "Anything—except 'it's over, move on.' For one thing I want to know how it happened."

"I'm sure you do."

"And?"

"And what?"

Daniel slid his chair back and got to his feet. "And now is the perfect time to tell me! To tell us!"

Actually, now was the perfect time to stuff a napkin in Daniel's mouth and shove him out the front door. "Hey, guess what," O'Neill said, spuriously cheerful. "I came across this really neat saying the other day. You'll love it. It goes: Curiosity killed the cat. Or, possibly, the archaeologist. I'm not sure now. You know me, memory like a sieve…"

"Well, sieve is one word for it," said Daniel. His voice had taken on a dangerous edge. "I might choose—"

"Guys—" Abandoning pizza, Carter held up a hand. "Please. There's been enough violence for one day, don't you think?"

Daniel thunked against the sink, arms crossed, face pinched into a scowl. "I just want to know what happened."

"You already know what happened," she snapped. "Your good friend Paul phoned and told you, remember?"

Paul? As in Davis, Major, currently assigned to the Pentagon? O'Neill sat up, a slow burn that had nothing to do with the pizza-indigestion starting up beneath his ribs. "What the hell—"

"He was worried!" Daniel protested. "He really admires and respects Jack, he's a big fan of the Stargate program, and he—"

"Better not cross my path any time soon, the garrulous little—"

"*Cool it*!" said Carter, and banged her empty beer bottle on the table for emphasis. "Sir." She winced. "Sorry. But can we not get sidetracked by who said what to whom and why? Please?"

"Major Carter is correct," said Teal'c. "Do we not have bigger fish to pull out of the frypan?"

"Yes, Teal'c, we certainly do," she said, and flashed him a brief, grateful smile. Then she turned. "Sir..."

She never called him by his first name. Not any more. Even at times like this, when they were off-duty. In her head he no longer had a first name. Or maybe she'd just switched it out, scrubbed the 'Jack' and replaced it with 'sir'. Maybe she had a point. He didn't very often call her Sam. It was... safer... that way.

Pushing aside his irritation at Davis, he looked at her. "Carter?"

"Teal'c has a theory."

"He does?"

"I do?" said Teal'c. He looked moderately surprised to hear it.

Carter looked at Daniel. "Toss me another beer from the fridge, would you?" After he'd obliged, and she'd taken a good long swallow, she continued, "What you said in the car on the way over here, Teal'c. About Kinsey provoking the colonel on purpose. Forcing him to—" She hesitated.

"Do something really really stupid?" O'Neill finished for her.

"Well... yes."

"As opposed to just standing back and letting me be stupid all on my lonesome?"

"Sir—"

Teal'c leaned forward. "Kinsey is as wily as a Goa'uld, O'Neill, and you made him lose face. It is possible he engineered this morning's confrontation in order to create an excuse to have you removed from the SGC."

They were all looking at him. Worried for him. His team. His kids. "I know," he said. "I already thought of that." But too late. Only afterwards, on the largely silent flight back from Washington, as his mind replayed over and over again the morning's catastrophic events, did he see the game Kinsey might have been playing. "It's possible, but... I don't know. I think maybe things just got—out of hand."

"*Way* out of hand," said Daniel, snorting. Then he relented. "But I guess I can't blame you. I mean, what Kinsey said..."

"The man has no honor," said Teal'c. His expression was one of fastidious distaste.

Daniel pushed away from the sink and sat down again. "Jack, I'm sorry."

"Why? You're not the one who nearly snapped Kinsey's neck like a rotten twig."

"No... but if I hadn't stopped the Eurondan trade deal you wouldn't have been facing him in an enquiry, would you? And then this morning would never have happened."

True. But O'Neill was too tired, and too full of beer and pizza, for that conversation. And in his current frame of mind he'd more than likely say something to Daniel that was as unforgivable as Kinsey's accusation. Something that three years of hard-fought friendship might not withstand.

"Daniel. Like I said. It happened, it's over, it's time to move on."

Silence, while they all stared anywhere but at each other.

"General Hammond's stood us all down, while he tries to sort out this mess," said Carter, at last. "Daniel and I thought we'd go check out those ruins SG-12 found."

"And I will visit Ry'ac," said Teal'c.

"Provided you're okay with that," added Daniel. "I mean, we won't go anywhere if you don't want us to, Jack."

"Why wouldn't I want you to?" he said, surprised. "Visiting

Ry'ac's a great idea, Teal'c. You don't get to see him often enough. Of course you want to play in the dirt, Daniel, and as for you, Carter—actually, okay, you I don't get. I thought you'd jump at the chance to lock yourself into your lab and play Mad Scientist."

She shrugged. "You know what they say, sir. A change is as good as a vacation."

"Yes. Vacation," he said, nodding. "The way things turned out a while back we didn't actually get one, did we, what with me being shanghaied by Thor and so forth. So this is good. You three get to have some me-time."

"And you? What about you?" said Daniel.

He picked at a cooling slice of pizza. "Me? I get to … sleep. Yes. And read fishing magazines in lieu of the real thing. And pay the piper. That's what I get to do."

More silence, as they stared at each other not expressing any number of opinions that wouldn't change a damned thing and might very well start another round of fighting.

Carter stood. "We should go. It's been a long day, and Daniel and I have to pack for the dig."

"Yeah. All those little shovels and things," O'Neill said, and made himself smile at her. "Have fun."

When they were gone, the house felt very empty. He left the pizza cartons and beer bottles and dirty napkins to entertain themselves overnight—there was always tomorrow for cleaning up, and it wasn't like he had anything else to do—and went to bed. Lit by a shaft of moonlight, Charlie's photo smiled at him from the nightstand.

He fell asleep, looking at it.

CHAPTER FOUR

Living on Vorash, Jacob Carter decided, was like living in Albuquerque. Perfectly pleasant. Not enough green.

Comfortably curled in the back of his mind, Selmak chuckled. *As far as you're concerned, Jacob, were Vorash a veritable jungle still for you there would not be enough green.*

He grinned. What can I say? he retorted. I miss Seattle.

I thought you missed Seattle because of the rain.

I do. The rain is why it's green.

Selmak's sigh shivered through him. *Vorash might not be picturesque but at least it's safe. We haven't had to run for many months. I for one appreciate the downtime.*

Another grin. Selmak found his Tauri vocabulary a constant source of wonder and delight, and got a real kick out of tossing in Earthisms when conversing with fellow Tok'ra, just to see the looks on their faces. Being the oldest and wisest of the band meant never having to say sorry for showing off.

They were eating breakfast in the almost deserted communal dining hall. At least, he was eating—it was his turn—and Selmak was heroically not complaining about the blueberry pancakes with genuine Canadian maple syrup. God bless Sam. Sending care packages half-way across the galaxy to her poor old man. What a daughter.

Will she send more chocolate next time? said Selmak, hopefully.

What? he demanded. You've eaten it all? Again? When?

Last night. Amazing how a disembodied voice could sound so embarrassed. *You were asleep and I was working on our current problem. I was overcome by a sudden craving.*

Of course you were, he sighed. But did you have to eat it all? While I was sleeping? I like chocolate too, you know!

Sorry.

Jacob dribbled more syrup on his last pancake, feeling cranky. Sam's care packages weren't exactly on a weekly delivery schedule. It was a miracle she managed to send them at all. How she conned George into letting her have the 'gate-time to ship them, he'd never know. When he'd asked, the last time they caught up, she'd just grinned and changed the subject. But con George she did, thank God, and he loved her for it. Even when months went by between deliveries. But those long gaps meant he had to eke out their contents like a miser with a sockful of pennies. So when Selmak couldn't resist an attack of the midnight munchies...

Jacob, I said I was sorry!

And that was another thing. He couldn't even bitch about Selmak in the privacy of his own mind. Because that privacy no longer existed. Sheesh. If anyone had told him a couple of years ago that he'd be sharing his brain and body with an ancient alien masquerading as a do-gooding snake, eating meals on a timeshare plan, hell, doing *everything* with his own flesh and blood on a timeshare plan, he'd have laughed in their face then called for the men in white coats.

Yet here he was. No longer human, but Tok'ra. Destined to live a few hundred more years. Healed of cancer, arthritis, an incipient varicose vein and all the aches and pains a lifetime of combat had bequeathed him. Still Jacob, sort of. Still a father. Grandfather. Air Force general.

But at the same time so very, very much more.

Regrets, Jacob, after all this time?

You know the answer to that, he said.

Yes. But do you?

He didn't reply. Selmak knew the answer to that one, too. Pushing his emptied plate to one side, leaning back in his chair, Jacob looked around the dining hall. Quite often, whenever circumstances dictated that he spend any extended period of time on Vorash, he discovered in himself the crazy urge to run around with a tin of red paint and a paintbrush, just to change the changeless appearance of Tok'ra interior design. He didn't get it. They were smart enough to develop a crystal-based technology that could create entire city complexes underground... but every structure was the same. Identical floor plans, identical crystalline patterns... and always the same three boring colors.

I know, he said, before Selmak could comment. You wanted to set yourselves apart from the Goa'uld, with their greed for ostentatious display. But you know, it's been a few thousand years. I don't think the occasional splash of chartreuse is going to bring the Tok'ra civilization to its knees.

Tok'ra traditions are sacred, Selmak said firmly. *Hasn't your own Earth history shown you that once traditions are altered, even fractionally, they—*

"Jacob?"

He looked round, to see Martouf standing by the table's other, empty chair.

"Hey, Martouf. Help you with something?"

"Am I interrupting you?"

"No. Not really. Selmak and I were just having a Martha Stewart moment."

Martouf smiled. "I see."

It was the smile he smiled when he didn't have a clue what that very odd Jacob Carter was talking about, but didn't care to appear rude. Or ignorant.

"Sorry. Bad joke. What's up?"

Martouf sat. Casting a furtive glance around the room, to make sure the handful of other diners weren't paying them any attention, he said, "Per'sus wishes to see us in his private chamber."

"About our proposition?"

Martouf nodded. "I believe so."

Jacob smiled. He and Selmak had concocted the idea, deciding to push for a new and organized plan of attack against the Goa'uld. Knowing they needed support, they'd told Martouf. He agreed almost at once. His symbiote Lantash had taken a little more convincing, but was safely on board now.

The number of available hosts for Tok'ra symbiotes had reached a critical new low. This shortage, coupled with battle casualties and natural attrition, meant that after more than two millennia of warfare they were no closer to defeating the Goa'uld today than they'd been on the morning Egeria took a look around her and decided, *There has to be a better way*.

Something had to be done to find fresh hosts, so that the symbiotes currently existing in stasis could once more join the fight. The Tok'ra also needed to swell the ranks of human operatives, humans willing to join the bitter fight against the Goa'uld.

High Councillor Per'sus agreed with them. But he was newly

elected, still feeling his way through the dangerous labyrinth of Tok'ra politics. To flaunt another Earthism, he wasn't keen on rocking the boat so soon in his first term of office.

And yet... their numbers were dwindling.

Lantash said, with his typical abruptness, "*Per'sus must support our proposition. Stupid short-sighted self-interest is the hallmark of our unfortunate ancestry. If we do not take risks, if we do not trust our allies, we doom ourselves to extinction and give the galaxy to the Goa'uld.*"

"That is true," said Martouf, ever the calm voice of reasonable discourse. "But we cannot force Per'sus, or the rest of the Council, into acting faster than their natures allow. To do so would be to guarantee their refusal of our plan. We must coax, not coerce."

"*Martouf is right,*" said Selmak. "*Lantash, my old friend, we'll catch more flies with honey than with vinegar.*"

Martouf looked inwards for a moment, winced, then grinned. "No, Lantash, I'm not going to let you say that out loud. Jacob——"

"I know," he said. "I'm the ex-Earthling so it's up to me to convince Per'sus that the mission is viable, that Hammond will agree to it and that we're not going to waste Tok'ra lives on a wild goose chase." He rolled his eyes. "I'll do my best."

Martouf stood. "Then let us go. Per'sus is waiting."

Unlike the previous High Councillor, Garshaw, Per'sus had no taste for even the mildest private ostentation. His personal chamber contained no luxurious draped curtains, no jealously protected glass and ceramic vases, no tasselled cushions on the long, low benches that lined the crystal walls. His clothing was plain to the point of severity, in neutral shades of bone and sand. He wore no jewellery and kept his hair short and sleek. Yet despite the austerity, his air of command and authority was unmistakable.

His current host, Toba, was his third. It meant that by Tok'ra standards he was still young, but he made up for his youth with a keen intellect, boundless courage and a fierce dedication to the Tok'ra's primary goal: eradication of the Goa'uld. He and Selmak had been lovers, many decades earlier when each had shared different hosts. Passion was long dead but friendship remained. For himself Jacob liked the Tok'ra leader, quite aside from any of the shared memories he'd received from Selmak.

Some of which frankly he could've done without ... but that was a whole other ball of wax.

His expression troubled, Per'sus said, "*The mission you have proposed is fraught with danger. You all must know that.*"

Martouf said, even more humbly than usual, "We do. But Per'sus, it is my firm belief—and Lantash's, too—that unless we take this admittedly drastic action our future looks uncertain."

"*Lantash and Martouf both understate the facts,*" said Selmak. "*Per'sus, the Tok'ra have reached a crossroads. My blending with Jacob has convinced me beyond all possible dispute that unless we reach out to those who would join with us in the fight against the Goa'uld we will be defeated and the galaxy lost. The humans—the Tauri—call them what you will, are a brash and youthful race, it's true. But look who stands with them: the Asgard, the Nox, the Tollan. Can we allow our pride to blind us to their usefulness in this war?*"

Per'sus nodded. With one knee drawn up to his chest and his arms wrapped round it he looked like a student on leave from his studies. "*I do not deny the Earth humans have a part to play. But Selmak, I must temper your championship of them with the knowledge that your host is not unbiased. He was until recently one of them and it is his daughter in whom he wishes us to place most of our trust.*"

"Yes, a daughter," said Martouf, reproachfully, sitting so still and straight he looked to Jacob like a student, too—one who'd been summoned to the principal's office for a scolding, or worse. "But also a fierce warrior. A courageous woman who was once a host herself. Samantha spoke up for the Tok'ra to her own people and brought us Jacob in the first place, trusting only to the memories Jolinar left her that we ourselves could be trusted, not only with her father but with all the high secrets of her planet! High Councillor, the humans of Earth's Stargate Command are not the beaten, mindless Goa'uld slaves that we are used to. They are *all* free and dedicated warriors, unafraid to spill their blood in the cause we hold so dear. And for this plan to work, we need them."

Per'sus released a deep sigh and nodded at Martouf, acknowledging his passionate defence. "*Jacob,*" he said, turning, his expression still troubled. "*Firstly know this: your loyalty and commitment to our cause is not in question. But you have lived with us long enough now to know we are not a people who trust easily, or share hard-won secrets without careful deliberation. You have made it plain that you support this dangerous plan of attack against the Goa'uld and in principle I support it too. But can you accept my judgement that its greatest weakness lies in its reliance upon the humans of the SGC?"*

Selmak retreated, leaving the way clear for Jacob to speak. He stood, clasping his hands behind his back. Briefing senior officers always went better when he could think on his feet. "High Councillor Per'sus, I understand your reservations but I don't accept them. How can I? You're questioning the integrity and competence of my daughter, and of a man who's been my unswerving friend for decades. Not to mention the integrity and competence of three good people who risked their lives to rescue me and Selmak from Ne'tu when our goose wasn't just cooked, it was smouldering. Sam is in a unique position to help the Tok'ra, and George and the rest of her team will back her up if it's called for, without hesitation. Selmak is right. The Tok'ra aren't perfect or omnipotent, they're just ancient. You could stand to learn a trick or two from the new kids on the block."

Per'sus rested his shoulder blades against the hard crystal wall and considered him. *"They? You? Are you one of us, Jacob, or does your heart still bind you to Earth?"*

Selmak jumped in before Jacob could respond. *"Do not dismiss this proposal for the sake of two misplaced pronouns! At least allow us to broach the subject with General Hammond. It might be he will refuse Major Carter permission to participate. But if he is open to the idea—"*

He elbowed Selmak aside. "Per'sus, trust me. George Hammond wants to help us. Hell, he and his people keep offering to help us and we keep turning them down! It's starting to cause some major friction. If we keep slamming the door in their faces there's a good chance that when the time comes we really do need them, they won't pick up the phone. Do you want to risk that? Because I sure as hell don't! And I'd prefer it if we didn't keep on proving to the one or two skeptical humans at the SGC that we really are as arrogant and condescending as we appear!"

With Martouf too shocked to speak, Lantash was able to chip

in with his opinion. "*Jacob Carter is right. I find the SGC humans primitive, ill-disciplined and over-confident but they may yet serve a useful purpose. Garshaw is gone, Per'sus. The days of timidity and conservative attacks against the Goa'uld have gone with her. The time has come to strike hard against our ancient foe. This will be but the first blow.*"

"Wait a minute," said Jacob. "I never said they were primitive, ill-disciplined and—"

"*Enough,*" said Per'sus. "*I have heard your arguments. And while I am not entirely convinced that this plan will work, or that I can in turn convince the Council to support it, I agree that broaching it with Hammond of the SGC is the next logical step. Selmak, you and Jacob will go to him. You will speak with him and report back to me with his reply. You will not discuss the matter with anyone else until you have spoken with me. Is that clear?*"

Jacob answered for both of them. "Yes, High Councillor."

Per'sus stood. "*Then I thank you for your attendance.*"

In other words, the audience was over.

"You know, Martouf," said Jacob as they wandered through the corridors leading back to the complex's central work area, "when you get a minute you might try explaining to Lantash that he shouldn't go putting words in my mouth."

Martouf listened inwardly for a moment, then frowned. "Lantash says for you to—and I'm sorry, Jacob, but I have no idea what he means—'put a sock in it'."

Selmak sniggered. *Sorry, Jacob. He got that one from me. But of course I got it from you, so ... what is it you like to say? What goes around comes around?*

"Spare me," he said out loud. Then he patted Martouf's arm. "It's all right. You're not missing anything, trust me."

Martouf just smiled. "Did you wish me to accompany you to Earth, Jacob? I could ask Per'sus for leave to—"

"No. I'll be fine," he said. "But I appreciate the offer."

"Of course," Martouf said equably, hiding his disappointment like an Oscar-worthy actor. "Then please give Samantha my regards, when you see her."

Martouf always asked after Sam, if ever he missed a visit to the SGC. Did he know how his eyes lit up at the mention of her name?

Was he clear in his head who it was made his heart go pitter-pat? Jolinar, or Sam? Or maybe even both?

God save them all. *There* was a tangle a loving father didn't want to think about.

He nodded. "Sure. No problem."

Except it might be, one day. He and Sam had never talked about it. They always veered away from the subject at the last moment. Jolinar. Being a host. The memories you re-lived in glorious technicolor *and* surround sound, that weren't your own but felt so real they might as well be. Maybe, if George agreed to this new proposal, they'd get a chance to do just that.

After parting company with Martouf at the next corridor intersection, Jacob headed for his quarters. The time difference between Vorash and the continental USA meant he had nearly four hours to kill before he could 'gate through to the SGC. Which wasn't a bad thing. It gave him more time to refine his approach to George, who was going to need some careful handling over this one. George, not entirely without reason, wasn't who you'd ask to be president of the Tok'ra Fan Club just now. And of course Jack, who'd need to sign off on Sam's temporary re-assignment, wasn't likely to be sympathetic to the cause either. He could barely stand to be in the same zip code with a mature symbiote. Tok'ra or Goa'uld, it made no difference to Jack. They were all slimy snakeheads to him.

And given that he'd come within a mouse's fart of being Goa'ulded himself, by Hathor, well… you couldn't really blame him.

So. *Lots* of refining to do.

Hope you're okay to amuse yourself for a while, he said to Selmak. I've got some serious thinking ahead of me.

As have I, said Selmak, amusement glimmering in his voice. *About chocolate.*

It had just gone seven-thirty in the morning, and George Hammond was reviewing the first of the latest round of SG team psych evaluations when the alarm sounded in the 'gate room.

"Unscheduled off-world activation! General Hammond report to the control room, we have an unscheduled off-world activation!"

He tossed aside Dr. McKenzie's acerbic assessment of Major

Kasselman and hurried out of his office, pulling the door shut behind him. In the control room all the red alert lights were flashing, the 'gate room was crawling with marines like ants at a picnic and Sergeant Harriman was staring at the inbound computer as though everyone's lives depended on it. Which, he supposed, they did, when you got right down to it. Before he could catch himself he looked for Jack and the rest of SG-1, who were always first on the scene of a potential disaster. But of course Jack wasn't there, he was slowly but surely going out of his mind at home under virtual house arrest, and the rest of his team was scattered around the galaxy.

It didn't feel right, not having them there. Even when the control room was crammed to standing room only, if SG-1 wasn't there the place felt... empty.

"Report, Sergeant," he said, burying distress inside sharpness.

Harriman glanced at him. "No teams due back at this time, General. We're receiving a GDO signal..." He frowned at the computer screen, fingers tense on the keyboard. Then his face relaxed into a smile. "It's the Tok'ra."

"Fine," said Hammond. *Hell's bells. What do they want now?* "Open the iris." Then he hit the 'gate room intercom. "Stand down, people. It's a friendly."

The enormous iris guarding the Stargate contracted, spilling the wormhole's blue-white light onto every surface. A moment later the rippling energy of the event horizon parted, spitting out a spare, familiar figure in the odd-looking uniform Hammond thought he'd never get used to seeing. Not after nearly three decades of Air Force blue.

Despite his myriad worries, he grinned and waved. "Good morning, Jacob," he said into the intercom, as his old friend greeted those marines he knew who were still on standby around the 'gate ramp. "Come on up to my office. Shall I send to the commissary for some blueberry pancakes?"

Still chatting, Jacob gave him the thumbs up. Curiosity warring with shameful suspicion, leavened with simple pleasure at the chance of catching up with a friend he missed more than he liked to admit even to himself, Hammond returned to his office, tidied away the psych reports, asked the commissary to send him two servings of blueberry pancakes with extra maple syrup, and waited for that friend to join him… which Jacob did, some five minutes later, all boundless energy and breathtaking intensity.

Jacob greeted him with a swift hug. That much was immediately different about him, since he'd become… what he now was. The old—yes, say it, admit it—human Jacob Carter had resisted physical expressions of affection as though he—or everyone he met—was a second Typhoid Mary. To be embraced by him now with such casual ease was… unsettling. Not that Jacob loosening his armor was a bad thing, far from it. Just look at the difference it had made to Sam. But it was… creepy… knowing Jacob had changed because he'd, well, *changed*.

"How are you, Jacob?" he asked, waving his friend into a chair. "You look well. Better than well. Have the Tok'ra discovered the fountain of youth? Every time I see you it seems you look younger and younger."

"And every time I see you, George, you're a little bit balder and a whole lot more worried," replied Jacob, comfortably sprawling and blunt as ever. Nice to know that becoming a Tok'ra hadn't changed everything about him. "What's eating you this time? And don't say nothing because I'm the oldest wisest Tok'ra of them all and I see everything."

Hammond hid a sigh. The temptation to spill his guts was almost overwhelming. He had no-one else to talk to. Usually when he was facing SGC-related crises what he could say he said to Jack. Now, with that option eliminated… with Jack himself the cause of such concern…

But no. Maybe later, if Jacob had time to stay, he'd run this latest Kinsey encounter past him. For now it was more important to learn what had brought the Tok'ra back to Earth.

He flipped a dismissive hand. "No, Jacob, it's not nothing. Just politics. It can keep for a little while. I'm more interested to know why you're here. Not that I'm sorry to see you," he added hastily. "We don't see each other often enough as far as I'm concerned. But…"

Jacob grinned. "But you're wondering if it's a social call or if I've come waving the Tok'ra flag. Well, I'm sorry to say it's the latter, George. I've got a proposition for you, that I hope will end up doing both our people a whole lot of good. I—"

The office door opened, revealing an airman bearing a tray stacked with two covered plates, cutlery, napkins and a large bottle of maple syrup.

"On the desk is fine, Phillips," said Hammond. "Thank you." He hurriedly made more space. "I take it you haven't had breakfast yet, Jacob?"

"Actually I have," said his friend. "But you know me. I never say so no to blueberry pancakes."

As the door closed behind Phillips, Hammond grinned and passed over a plate. "I remember. I may be bald and worried, Jacob, but I'm not quite senile yet." Then he felt his grin fade, and he stared in alarm as Jacob suddenly stiffened, his expression frozen. "Jacob? Jacob, what's wrong? Are you in pain? Should I call the infirmary?"

"I know, but it's still my turn," said Jacob, his gaze somehow inwardly directed. Hammond relaxed; his friend was talking to the symbiote. The process never ceased to unsettle him. "I know I've already had blueberry pancakes today," said Jacob, sounding irritated. "But that was breakfast. And anyway, I never promised not to eat the same thing twice in one day. No, I didn't. Selmak, thanks to you I now have perfect recall, I'd remember if I promised—oh, God." His gaze had shifted outwards again. He shook his head. "George, I apologize. Talking to one's symbiote aloud is a beginner's mistake, I thought I'd beaten that bad habit." He pulled a face. "Selmak doesn't like blueberry pancakes. Or coffee. I've given up the coffee but I'll be damned if I give up blueberry pancakes too!"

Hammond chuckled. "Seems to me there's a whole lot about being a Tok'ra you haven't seen fit to tell me, Jacob Carter."

Like a defiant child Jacob slopped maple syrup all over one of his cooling pancakes, folded it in half, stuffed it into his mouth and swallowed. "George," he said, smearing stickiness from his chin with a napkin, "you have no damned idea!"

"Then one of these days you can fill me in. But right now I'm guessing you didn't come all this way to tell me Selmak doesn't care for pancakes and coffee. So. What is it you need?"

CHAPTER FIVE

"What I'm about to divulge, George, is our highest priority secret and most sensitive information," Jacob began, after a considerable pause. All traces of mischief and rueful embarrassment had vanished from his face.

"It won't leave this office, you have my word," Hammond replied. "I take it the Tok'ra need our help?"

Try as he might he couldn't quite keep a touch of sarcasm from his tone; clearly, he'd been spending too much time around Jack O'Neill.

Hearing it, Jacob frowned but didn't let himself be distracted. "We do," he said. "It nearly kills us to admit it—most of us still won't—but yes. We do."

We. Us. They were the wrong pronouns. Could Jacob really divide his loyalties so neatly? Hammond wondered. Successfully compartmentalise what was no longer his singular life?

With an effort he dispelled the discomfiting thought. "What kind of help?"

"When Earth joined the fight against the Goa'uld, it irrevocably altered the existing status-quo," said Jacob. "Unlike the Tok'ra, you attack the system lords head-on, killing them whenever you can. You foment rebellion amongst the Jaffa, turning them against their lords and masters. You've achieved results, but your gung-ho tactics are creating difficulties for us. There are consequences."

Hammond wasn't in the mood for being lectured. "War always has consequences, Jacob. Are you suggesting we should back down? Just when we're starting to make a serious dent in the system lords' stranglehold on the galaxy? Let's not forget the Tok'ra have benefited from our victories."

"I know," Jacob said quickly. "But your actions, your attitudes, are forcing the Tok'ra to re-evaluate how we do business."

"Really? Good," he retorted. "Because the sooner the galaxy is rid of the Goa'uld, the better off we'll all be."

Jacob nodded. "True. Except there's this old Earth saying, George, maybe you've heard of it? Softly, softly, catchee monkey. Since you've upped the ante in the war against the Goa'uld, and we've jumped on board for the ride, we've lost more people than in the previous twenty years, easily."

Stung, Hammond leaned across his desk. "And you know damned well I regret those dead Tok'ra as keenly as any lost member of the SGC!"

"George, please," sighed Jacob. "This isn't about who cares most for which fallen warrior. Or blaming you for the escalation in hostilities."

"No?" To his mind it was exactly what this was about. But getting into a fight with Jacob wouldn't help anybody. So he took a deep breath, throttled his temper, and said, reasonably, "Then why don't you cut to the chase, Jacob, and tell me what it *is* about."

With an impatient grunt Jacob pushed to his feet and began roaming the small office, vigorous and vital as a man in his twenties. "It's about survival, George. Our survival, as we wage war with the Goa'uld. A war that we started, remember, and have been waging for millennia. Bottom line? We can't sustain our current level of casualties indefinitely. Even the Tok'ra who aren't killed outright are dying sooner than necessary because of the strain of constantly healing their wounded hosts."

"I'm sorry to hear that, Jacob," Hammond said, meaning it. "You know that wasn't our intention when we took the fight to the system lords."

"Yes, but to be brutally frank, George, your intentions, good or bad, are fast becoming irrelevant." Jacob stopped roaming to stare at one of the framed purple heart commendations hanging on the wall. Over one shoulder he said, sounding pressured, "Elements of the Tok'ra Council are holding you responsible. If something isn't done soon I'm afraid our fragile alliance might not survive a hell of a lot longer."

Lord, lord. As if he didn't have enough to contend with. Folding his hands on the desk, mustering years of military discipline, Hammond said calmly, "All right. I'm listening. What is it you want me to do?"

Jacob turned, his expression strained. "We need the war to end, George, with victory for our side. To achieve that objective we have to finish what the SGC has started. We need more operatives in the field, helping to gather intel and destabilise the system lords. And we need to find more potential Tok'ra hosts."

Hammond sat back again, guts churning. The first point was something he could help with, maybe, but—"Hosts? Jacob, you know I can't—"

"Give me some credit. I'm not asking you to," said Jacob, still impatient. "At least not directly."

"Then how? Because there is no way I can go to the President and ask him—"

"It's true you can't supply the Tok'ra with humans from Earth willing to blend and strengthen our numbers," Jacob interrupted. "But you *can* help us find humans on other worlds who'd be willing to do it. You can help us convince them to join us in the fight for freedom from Goa'uld domination."

"By giving up their bodies to you for implantation?"

Jacob stared. "You make it sound like a fate worse than death."

Damn. With an effort, Hammond crushed his instinctive horror. "I thought the Tok'ra only recruited hosts from amongst the dying?"

"We did, George! And we were managing okay, too. But that was *before* Jack O'Neill killed Ra!"

"Ha! So you *do* blame us!"

Jacob's head lowered, and when he looked up again his face was subtly different. Jacob, but not Jacob. "*General Hammond,*" he said, his voice thrumming with strange harmonics. "*Please. Do not take this as a personal attack. We of the Tok'ra are aware of the debts owed to you and the warriors of Earth.*"

The symbiote, Selmak. Hammond couldn't hate the creature, not after it saved Jacob's life. But, like Jack, he couldn't bring himself to embrace it, either. Some things were just... unnatural. And two sentient beings sharing the same body, willingly or not, was one of them.

"Selmak, I appreciate the sentiment, but forgive me if I say that so far we haven't seen too much repayment of those debts. From where I sit, the Tok'ra are quick to ask for our help but very slow in returning the favor. Getting intelligence out of you is worse than getting blood from a stone."

"*I will not argue the point with you, General,*" Selmak replied.

"At least not today. Today we are here to talk of a specific way we can work together to hasten the downfall of the Goa'uld."

"I'm listening."

"What Jacob began to say is this: the humans we wish to recruit to our cause as hosts have no lives, if you define living as being free to choose your own path without fear of torture and death. You are aware that the system lords breed humans as humans breed cattle, for their ease and convenience?"

He nodded. "Yes, of course we are. It's an abomination."

"Indeed it is," Selmak agreed. *"One that with your help we hope to end. With that goal in mind, some of us have formulated a plan. We wish to infiltrate the slave populations of the system lords' breeding farms. To recruit not only young, strong Tok'ra hosts who will help prevent the dwindling of our numbers, but also human spies to work alongside Tok'ra operatives who have infiltrated Goa'uld strongholds. To sow dissent and discord amongst those upon whom the Goa'uld rely for their domination."*

"That," he said, after a moment, "is a very ambitious plan. Some might even call it aggressive."

Selmak's smile wasn't the same as Jacob's. It was thinner. More guarded. For Hammond, it was just another unwelcome reminder that life as he'd known it was dead and buried.

"More suited to the Tauri, you mean?" Selmak asked. *"Perhaps. But desperate times call for desperate measures, do they not?"*

It was one of Jacob's favorite sayings. Like Jack, he'd been one of the Air Force's mavericks. Getting the job done, but not always in the orthodox way. Suddenly suspicious, Hammond said, "Exactly who came up with this idea in the first place, Selmak? You? Another Tok'ra?"

"No. It was Jacob," said Selmak. *"But I agree with it, as do Martouf and Lantash, and our new High Councillor Per'sus. As much as many of our number might wish you Tauri had never involved yourselves in this fight, we cannot turn back the clock. Instead we must cut our suit to fit our cloth, and fight the war as it is, not as we wish it to be."*

"You say your new High Councillor is in favor of the plan? What of the rest of the Tok'ra Council?"

Selmak looked uncomfortable. *"They ... can be convinced."*

"Forgive me, Selmak, but you don't sound too confident of that."

"The Council isn't the problem, George," said Jacob, abruptly returning. "We can handle the Council. The problem is that the breeding farms we're talking about are guarded by Jaffa, who can sense the presence of a symbiote. Which frankly makes it too dangerous for any of us to blend in with the human population."

But not too dangerous for *us*, Hammond thought sourly. "Then why not choose an easier target?"

"Because the farms we've got in mind breed the most valuable slaves," said Jacob. "The most beautiful, physically perfect human specimens to be found outside of Hollywood. You know the Goa'uld. Big on appearances. They like to be surrounded by the best of the best. These humans are bred to be lotars, trusted system lord body slaves and other important personal attendants. There's no point infiltrating a bunch of farmers, they never get anywhere near the likes of Apophis or Heru'ur or Ba'al."

"That's true," Hammond conceded. "But why would any Goa'uld slave agree to do it? What you'll be asking of them is insanely dangerous."

"*Yes*," said Selmak. "*But it is my observation that humans, even those born into slavery, have a desire for freedom that transcends fear for personal safety. I believe that, given the chance, these unfortunate men and women will gladly fight to be rid of the monsters who enslave them.*"

Also true. Hammond sat back. "And when you've found your recruits? What then?"

"Then we take them back to Vorash and, like Selmak said, we train them as operatives," said Jacob. He grinned, briefly. "Think of it as our version of the French Resistance."

"All right," said Hammond, slowly. "I concede the plan has merit. But I'm still not entirely sure what it is you want from me."

Jacob returned to his chair. "Well, in a nutshell, George, I want Sam."

"To infiltrate one of these breeding farms and recruit potential spies for you?" he said, incredulous. "I don't think so, Jacob. I agree she'd look the part but she's one of the most valuable assets the SGC has, I can't—"

"I know," said Jacob. "And I wouldn't be asking you for her if I didn't think her participation was vital. But George, it is. We don't have anyone with her military experience and training, with knowledge of the Tok'ra, who won't be detected by the farm's Jaffa once they're on the inside. All our best operatives are Tok'ra."

"Then send in one of your human operatives to choose likely host candidates," Hammond suggested.

Jacob pushed to his feet and started roaming the office again. "That won't work. Selecting potential human hosts is a complicated process, with a lot of hoops to jump through. It's not like playing Pin the Tail on the Donkey. Getting it wrong has disastrous consequences. None of our human operatives has the skill or experience to do it. It's not their function. Only a Tok'ra can select a potential host."

"But Jacob—Sam's not a Tok'ra."

Jacob turned. "No. But she was host to Jolinar, and Jolinar was one of the best human recruiters we ever had. Sam's exposure to her memories, her experience, makes her unique. Because of her blending with Jolinar, without being consciously aware of how she knows what to look for Sam will be able to assess the human slaves she meets and choose the right people for us to recruit. It'll be almost instinctive for her. Not something she can explain, or teach to another human. Not in the time we have available."

Hammond watched his friend's restless pacing around the office. "Care to explain why we have to rush into this?"

The question earned him a sharp look. "*Our* politics," said Jacob, tersely. "The transition from Garshaw to Per'sus is turning out bumpier than we anticipated. Per'sus needs to put some impressive runs on the board—soon—to silence one or two troublemakers. If he doesn't…"

"And you're *absolutely* certain there's not a single human on Vorash who can do this instead of Sam?"

"Of course I'm certain! Would I be here if I wasn't certain? Humans are limited, George. They have their uses but—"

Silence, as they stared at each other across a sudden, unbearable gulf.

"I'm sorry," said Jacob, almost whispering. "I didn't mean that the way it sounded."

With some trouble, Hammond found his voice. "Are you sure?"

Suddenly looking very tired, Jacob sat down again. "George, please... you need to understand. Once a human has accepted a symbiote, once the process of blending is complete, you're... different. Changed. And you can't go back. You can't ever experience life the way you used to. Sometimes it's hard to remember how that life felt. How being alone in my mind, being *human*, felt."

Uncomfortable words. Hammond cleared his throat. "So... you no longer think of yourself as being human?"

"No," said Jacob simply. "Not quite."

"I see," he replied, and felt a shocking stab of loss, of grief... even though he'd always known it.

"George..." Jacob dredged up a smile. "I'm here because I need your help. Please. Help me. Help *us*."

Hammond sat back. "And if I do help you, Jacob? If I allow Sam to go on this mission for the Tok'ra? What's in it for the SGC?"

"The short answer? We'd owe you. Big time."

Despite his unease, Hammond smiled. "And the long answer?"

Jacob returned the smile. "We'd owe you. Big time. And both Selmak and I will make certain there's something substantial for you to collect."

Something substantial... "You mean, like a guarantee of shared intelligence?"

"For starters. Yes."

"Formalized by treaty?"

"Yes."

Hammond drummed his fingers on the desk. "Jacob, are you authorised to make me those kinds of promises?"

"I'm authorised to do whatever I can to see that the Tok'ra win this war against the Goa'uld."

And that was the Jacob he remembered. Obdurate, focused, bloody-minded in pursuit of a goal.

Scenting victory, Jacob leaned forward. "My word on it, George. You know it's good."

He certainly did. A guarantee of shared intelligence... now there was a prize worth winning. If only it didn't mean sending Sam into danger without her team as back-up...

A fresh thought jabbed Hammond like a pin. *What if she wasn't without her team*?

Jacob straightened. "George, I know that look. You've thought of something. What is it?"

He held up a silencing hand. Closed his eyes to better think through the idea. Cementing relations with the Tok'ra. Putting another spoke in the system lords' wheel. Pushing Jack O'Neill beyond the reach of his formidable enemies for an impeccable, unimpeachable cause…

He'd already stalled Kinsey for a week. He couldn't stall for much longer, the man was out for blood.

"Jacob," he said, opening his eyes. "I am inclined to grant your request. On one condition."

"What?" said Jacob warily.

"I don't just want to lend you Sam. I want to lend you all of SG-1."

"Why?"

Hammond frowned. "Let's just say… there are one or two troublemakers *I'd* like to silence."

"Yeah," said Jacob, shifting in his chair. "I need a little more information than that, George."

Succinctly, Hammond told him about Jack, and Kinsey, and Washington.

"Damn," said Jacob. "Not that I blame Jack, that was provocation above and beyond, but… damn."

Indeed. "Jack O'Neill may be a giant pain in the ass four days out of seven," said Hammond, "but six out of seven I like him and I need him seven out of seven and I'll be *damned* if I lose him because of Senator Robert Kinsey. If the request for his participation in this vital mission came from the office of the Tok'ra High Council itself…"

"I hear you," said Jacob. "Don't worry. Selmak and I will make sure the invitation to SG-1 is an offer the President can't refuse."

"*You have my word,*" added Selmak. "*As O'Neill protected Jacob and me from the scourge of Sokar, so shall we protect him from the tyranny of petty bureaucrats.*"

And with those words, Hammond felt the awful, impossible weight of Jack's clouded future lift from his shoulders. Suddenly he could breathe easily again, and realized just how hard breathing had been since that shocking scene at the Pentagon.

"Jacob ... we both know Jack's feelings about the Tok'ra. I'd like you to invite him to Vorash yourself. I know I could just order him to go, but he's feeling a bit confrontational at the moment. And he likes you. Do you mind?"

Jacob smiled. "You give him a hell of a lot of latitude, George."

"I know. But in the grand scheme of things, I figure he's earned it." Hammond opened his desk drawer, withdrew his car keys and tossed them over to Jacob. "Take my car."

Neatly catching the keys, Jacob stood. "Let me send a message back to Per'sus first. Get the ball rolling on our end."

"Good idea. I'll start laying the groundwork with the Chairman of the Joint Chiefs."

Jacob headed for the door. "You do that. Who is the Chairman now, anyway?"

"Reggie Belweather," Hammond said, reaching for the phone.

"No kidding!" said Jacob with a wide, pleased smile. "Rumblefish Reggie? Good for him. Tell him I said hello."

"I will."

As the door closed behind Jacob, Hammond called Jack and let him know to expect a VIP visitor within the next hour. Refused to say who: overworked generals needed to take their fun where they could find it, after all. Then he called the Chairman of the Joint Chiefs' private line.

"Reggie? George Hammond. Listen ... I think I've found us a way out of this O'Neill mess ..."

Selmak loved driving. *Such a primitive yet strangely satisfying mode of transport. And I like the smell. One day you must arrange for me to see Formula One up close and personal, Jacob.*

Sometimes Selmak made him laugh, and laugh ...

Jack O'Neill opened his front door wearing the kind of expression usually reserved for combatants of an opposing army. But scowling aggression was swiftly chased away by surprise and cautious pleasure when he saw who was gracing his doorstep.

"Jacob! What the hell are you doing here? Come in!"

He'd been to Jack's home only once before, during a rare and too-brief visit with Sam. Dropping her off for what she'd said was an important meeting, he'd discovered it was actually a pizza and sci-fi movie night and he'd been brought along under false pretences. He'd stayed, curious to know more about the man who'd risked his life on Ne'tu to save Sam Carter's father. The man who so often was responsible for keeping his little girl alive.

What he saw and heard that night confirmed his previous impressions. Daniel Jackson and the rebel Jaffa, Teal'c, clearly shared a close camaraderie with O'Neill. So did Sam. There was banter, laughter, good-natured insults exchanged four ways. His daughter called Jack sir and he called her Carter, but it was clear they were close. Comfortable. The team conversed in shorthand, started and finished each others' sentences, came damn close to telepathy at times. Four unlikely flowers growing in the same small pot, thriving, interdependent and complimentary—the way all the best teams worked.

He'd left Earth again not long after that night more confident in his daughter's happiness and safety than he'd been for a very long time.

A year and a bit later, Jack's place hadn't changed. Still obsessively tidy, sporting photographs of people the man never mentioned—including the son Kinsey had so recklessly and wickedly accused him of killing—with that strangely incongruous collection of medals and commendations still displayed over the mantelpiece.

"Make yourself comfortable. Can I get you a beer?" said Jack, waving him into the sunken living room.

"Sure," he said, and collapsed into an armchair.

There was the sound of a fridge door opening. The rattle and chink of glass bottles being pulled from a cardboard container. Moments later Jack joined him and handed over a gloriously cool bottle of ale. He threw himself onto the sofa opposite, cracked his own bottle's seal and held it up. "Cheers. Does Carter—Sam—know you're here?"

"On Earth?" Jacob said, returning the salute. "I don't think so. George said she's off-world at the moment."

"She is," said Jack, and took a deep swallow. "Futzing around in the dirt with Daniel on some ancient dig somewhere."

"Really?" Jacob let a cool mouthful of beer trickle down his throat. "Wouldn't you rather be with them, than hanging around here?"

Jack pulled a face. "Nah. I've tried and I've tried, but I just can't get excited about a bunch of mud brick houses that fell down four thousand years ago. As far as I'm concerned sloppy workmanship is nothing to celebrate."

He grinned, admiring the man's ability to camouflage his true feelings. "Then I guess that's a good thing, seeing as how you couldn't go even if you wanted to."

Beneath the clown's façade, something lethal stirred. "Sorry. Not sure what you mean there, Jacob."

"It's okay, Jack. George told me what happened."

The room's temperature dropped ten swift degrees. "Okay? Actually, Jacob, no. That's not okay."

"Come on, Jack," he said, reproving. "I had top level security clearance when you were still figuring out which end of a gun to point at the bad guys. All I mean is that I know about your current situation, and I'm here to make you an offer."

If he'd been anyone else Jacob had no doubt he'd have been thrown out of the house before finishing his last sentence. But because he was Sam Carter's father, Jack just sat there looking at him. "What kind of offer?" he said at last. "'Cause if it doesn't involve something that'll severely inconvenience Bob Kinsey I'm pretty sure I'm not interested."

Jacob had to laugh. "Funny you should put it that way …"

"Yeah. Hilarious," said Jack. No humor anywhere to be seen.

He sobered. "It's an offer that takes you out of Kinsey's firing line for a little while, Jack. With the added bonus of putting the boot into the Goa'uld's ass, and going a long way to shoring up the shaky alliance between Earth and the Tok'ra. So. Interested now?"

Jack finished his beer, taking his own sweet time about it. Then he sat for a little while longer, playing with the empty bottle. When he looked up again his eyes were cold and hard. "Tell me more."

Jacob told him. "Selmak's cleared the proposal with High Councillor Per'sus. George is squaring things away with Admiral Belweather and the President as we speak. It's up to you now, Jack. Are you on board, or aren't you?"

Jack put his beer bottle on the side-table with absolute precision. "I can think of three ways your plan could go belly-up."

"Only three?" Jacob said, eyebrows lifted. "I can think of five.

Selmak says there's six, but he won't tell me what I've missed. It amuses him to keep me guessing."

A shiver of distaste shimmered over Jack's face. "Three ways that don't include the fact I'm not too fond of the Tok'ra."

Let me talk with him, said Selmak.

I don't think that's wise, Jacob replied. We should take this one step at a time.

Please, Jacob. Let me talk.

All right, he sighed. But don't say I didn't warn you.

When he looked outward again, Jack was scowling. "See? That's what I mean. It's creepy."

"*My apologies, Colonel*," said Selmak. "*Unfortunately, since we have but one mouth between us, vocalizing our conversations is somewhat problematical.*"

Relegated to the back seat, Jacob watched as Jack did his best to disguise his unease. "I guess."

"*I wish you would agree to Jacob's proposal,*" said Selmak. "*Even though I know it was he you risked your life to save on Ne'tu, nevertheless you saved me too. I would greatly appreciate the chance to get to know you better. And, I confess, I would like you to know me. To discover for yourself that I am not the ogre you imagine me to be.*"

"I never said you were an ogre," Jack protested. "I'm sure you're a perfectly pleasant ... person."

"*For a snake,*" said Selmak.

Jacob felt himself grinning as Jack squirmed. "I'm sorry," he muttered. "I was busy saving the world, again, the day they held the Tok'ra Sensitivity Seminar."

"*My feelings are undamaged,*" said Selmak, utterly serene. "*Trust me, Colonel, I have been called far worse in my centuries of life.*"

"I'll bet."

"*Is it that you fear our plan has no hope of success?*"

Jack shook his head. "No. It's a good plan. Risky, but worth it if it comes off."

"*And still you hesitate. I'll articulate why, shall I?*" said Selmak gently. "*It is because you do not trust us. But trust grows out of familiarity, Colonel. And if you refuse to become familiar with us,*" *how can our two peoples hope to forge a true and lasting alliance? We are different, yes, but we have a fearful common enemy. Can you not find the courage within yourself to look past your fear and prejudice to the rewards of a possible friendship and mutual assistance?"*

Jacob held his breath. Selmak had just as good as accused Jack O'Neill of being a coward. *Not* the tactic he'd have recommended...

But Jack was smiling, his eyes no longer cold and hard but genuinely amused. "Sticks and stones, Selmak. If you think you can get to me that way, you're barking up the wrong tree."

Sticks and stones? Barking? What tree? said Selmak, bewildered.

Earthisms I don't use, Jacob replied. Thanks, Selmak. I'll take it from here.

Please do.

He said to Jack, "I might not have put it quite that way, but I agree Selmak's got a point. The Tok'ra aren't perfect, but neither are you. And if we don't find a way to see past our differences the Goa'uld will have won without firing another shot. Is that what you want?"

"You know it isn't," said Jack. Restless, he pushed to his feet and crossed to the French windows. Pulling aside the curtain he looked into his flowering garden. "Does Sam know about this yet?"

"No. Jack, we both know she'll go without you if she has to, but she'll be a lot more enthusiastic about this mission if she knows you're on board. Your whole team will be."

"I know," he said, not turning. "Why do you think I'm thinking twice?"

Jacob stood, then, and joined Jack at the window. Rested his hand on the man's shoulder, and was encouraged when it wasn't shrugged away. "It's a good plan, Jack. Risky, yes, but not unacceptably. And you need this, to give you some breathing space away from Kinsey, and Washington, and the idiots who don't know what they've got in you. So come on. What do you say? Are you in, or are you out?"

Jack stepped away, reclaiming his personal space. One hand

came up to scrub through his short, silvered hair.

"Okay," he said, and finally turned. Not smiling, still unhappy, but no longer downright angry. "Fine. I'm in." Then he muttered, under his breath, "As if I had a choice."

Grudging or not, it was a win. Jacob smiled, and nodded, and glanced at the ceiling. *Thank you, God.*

CHAPTER SIX

Like Earth, P8C-316 had a single yellow sun. It had grass and trees and flowers and insects, sweet smelling breezes, spectacular dawns ... and the most amazing ruins Daniel had seen since the lost city of Ur.

He sat cross-legged in the dirt in front of a tumbledown dwelling, surrounded by the tools of his profession, a cache of time-encrusted pottery shards and one unbroken, exquisitely glazed ceramic offering plate he'd rescued from under the home's collapsed mud bricks. Beneath the grime it gleamed crimson and ochre and lapis lazuli, so beautiful he was stung with tears. Holding the plate in careful, scraped and blistered fingers he felt so human, so humble, so connected to this long-dead community. And incredibly lucky, to be here. Touching this. Bringing the dead to life.

It had been too long.

Nearby, Sam worked in what remained of the dwelling's front yard, uncovering something she'd found. She didn't want to share until she'd made it look all neat and professional, she'd said. Hiding his amusement he'd nodded, one archaeologist to another, and wished her luck. SG-12 was spread over the rest of the dig, diligently revealing the ruined village's long-buried secrets. A handful of houses, a scattering of shops—some still, incredibly, sheltering unbroken clay jars sloshing with oil—what looked like a meeting hall, a grand, imposing temple. These buildings formed the heart of the community. On its outskirts, a cemetery. Half a kilometer beyond that, the Stargate.

He was becoming more convinced that the settlement's antecedents were Ancient Indian. Just yesterday he'd discovered what was almost certainly a possible proto-Buddha figure. Captain Brenda Faraday, however, wasn't convinced and said so. Emphatically. Vigorous conversation had ensued.

Still. It was all part of the fun, wasn't it? Toiling in dirt and debris through the day, sitting round the campfire at night eating MREs and tossing wild theories back and forth, dissecting competing explanations for the newest discoveries, never having to worry about being shut up, closed down, dismissed as a dreamer by someone who seriously thought *The Simpsons* was the apex of human cultural achievement...

Damn. And he'd promised himself he wasn't going to think about Jack.

He lifted his head and considered Sam, still industriously excavating. As always, looking like a whole new person, out of uniform. "I'm on vacation," she'd declared, with just a hint of defiance. "Technically, anyway. I'm going to wear jeans."

Major Lee, SG-12's team leader, had shrugged. "Wear what you like, Sam," he'd replied with a grin. "Just leave room for a weapon."

So she'd strapped on a shoulder holster to house her Beretta, and promptly pulled an eye-rolling face. "This is ridiculous," she'd muttered. "I feel like Jamesina Bond."

Holster abandoned within the first half-day of excavation, the gun was sitting on a rock near to her hand now. His own gun was in his tool kit; some habits were hard to break, even though the only living creature to disturb them in the last six days was something resembling a fox. Oh, yes. And the enormous flock of multi-colored birds that lived in the trees around their campsite. Birds who got out of bed at five a.m. and spent an hour telling each other at the tops of their raucous voices what they were going to do that day, flew away in a crashing of wings, then returned at dusk to spend another hour telling each other what it was they'd done.

Good thing Jack wasn't here, really. He'd have shot them all for sure by now. Or cut down the trees. Instant eviction, O'Neill style, with a bonus of firewood. Early mornings really weren't his thing.

On the whole, it was very... restful... without Jack. Odd, but restful. He kept expecting to hear that strident voice bellowing, "*Pack it up, Daniel! If you've seen one pile of ancient rubble you've seen them all! Don't you realize I'm missing a Burns retrospective?*"

Funny. Even when he wasn't here... he was here. Jack O'Neill's aura was pervasive, like indelible ink: once spilled on the psyche, never to be removed.

Daniel shook himself. He didn't want to think about Jack. About what might be happening to him back home. He refocused his attention on Sam instead.

For a brilliant astrophysicist she didn't make a bad archaeologist. He wasn't surprised. She had the kind of intuitive, multi-faceted intelligence that could turn its hand to just about anything. She was probably inventing a whole new strand of sub-atomic-quasi-quantum-ball of string-Stargate theory right now, while simultaneously uncovering the secrets of this village's past. Without elevating her heart rate by so much as a single beat.

With her long denim-clad legs folded neatly out of the way, blue cotton tee-shirt stained with sweat and smears of clay, blonde hair a little grubby, normally immaculate fingernails ragged and clogged with dirt, she looked... at peace. Released from the burdens they carried as members of SG-1, flagship team of Stargate Command. Intergalactic scourge of the system lords. Goa'uld Enemy Number 1, with a bullet. Or, in their case, a zat blast. The team nearly everybody else looked up to. Modelled themselves upon. Speculated about.

Behind their backs they were called 'The General's Darlings' by a handful of not nearly as *sotto voce* as they thought malcontents. Personnel who didn't appreciate not getting away with the stuff Jack and his team got away with at least once a week.

Fame wasn't anywhere near what it was cracked up to be.

Feeling his eyes upon her Sam looked up, excavation brush dangling from her fingers. Half-frowning, half-smiling she demanded, "What? Have I got dirt on my nose or something?"

Daniel grinned. "On your nose, your chin, the tips of your ears—" His gaze shifted downwards. "Your—"

"Okay, okay, I get the picture!" she retorted. "I'm a mess."

"Yes, you are. But in case you hadn't figured it out yet, making a mess is a big part of the fun."

She let the brush drop to the ground, sat on her heels and stretched the kinks out of her back and neck. He could hear the popping sounds as her spine released its tension. "It is," she agreed. "Daniel, I always knew you missed this, but I don't think I truly understood how much. Not till this week. You are more completely *you* here than you are anywhere else."

Reverently, he laid the glorious offering plate in the padded crate he'd prepared for it. "I know."

Now she was the one studying him, razor-sharp intellect putting him under the microscope of her regard. He concentrated on getting the offering plate centred just right. She said, "Daniel, can I ask you a question?" She sounded hesitant. Almost awkward, which was practically unheard of for Sam.

He nodded. "I guess."

"If you love it so much... if history—archaeology— this work... is so important to you and makes you so happy, why do you stay on SG-1? Hammond would give you any assignment you asked for. Hell, I bet he'd give you your own team of junior archaeologists if you asked him. No lurching from one near-death escape to the next. No injuries. No danger. Just... this." She gestured around them, at the peace and tranquillity of the village.

With the plate safely settled, Daniel rested his elbows on his knees and his chin in his hands and looked at her, unflinching. "You mean why do I stay when Sha're's dead, which means there's no more reason for me to go through the Stargate?"

She blinked. "Well... I don't think I'd have phrased it quite like *that*, but... all right. Yes."

"Because I believe I can make a difference," he said, shrugging. "That I have something valuable to contribute. To be honest, Sam, while I do love this work, passionately, it's something any well-trained archaeologist could do. But on SG-1 I believe I fulfil a function that perhaps nobody else can." *Putting the brakes on Jack O'Neill.* He let his gaze drop, then, and studied the fraying end of one bootlace, not saying out loud the thought that had been haunting him since the mission to Euronda. *At least, that's what I used to believe.*

"Well, you'll get no argument from me," said Sam, grinning. "SG-1 does need you. *I* need you. Us geeks have to hang together, you know?"

"Yeah," he said. "I know." Cautiously standing, he joined her and stood looking down at her painstaking excavation. "So what have you found here, anyway?"

She accepted the change of subject without argument, put her hands on her hips and looked with some pride at the result of her morning's hard work. "I'm not quite sure. I think there's a skeleton of something in here somewhere, but I haven't uncovered it yet."

"Can I give you a hand?"

"Sure."

He fetched his own excavation tools and in amicable silence, with interruptions for a little teacher-student back and forth, they completed the task of exposing the remains to the light.

"Wow," said Sam, staring. "Is that—it looks like a cat. It must have been somebody's pet, look, there's a jewelled collar round its neck. Are those rubies?"

Daniel peered more closely, hands braced on either side of the pathetic little grave so he didn't disturb the delicate, fleshless bones. "Yeah. I think so. Set in gold, it looks like. Alternated with a darker stone, might be sapphires."

Sam pointed. "And there. What's that? A clay tablet?"

Yes. Hardly breathing, he eased it out from between the cat's front paws—if it was a cat, it looked like a cat but there was something not exactly cat-like about the skull—and gently blew away the loosened dirt. The tablet was the size of a playing card, its inscription hauntingly familiar and drawn by what looked to his eye like a childish hand.

"Can you read it?" said Sam, leaning close.

He could feel the grin spreading across his face. "I think so. It seems to be a variation on Vedic Sanskrit..." Which meant he was most likely right, the figurine he'd found was of a proto-Buddha, even though the timeline didn't fit. Incredible. And now Faraday owed him fifty bucks...

"Well?" said Sam, and poked him in the knee. "What does it say?"

Haltingly he recited, softly, "*Here lies Agni*—Agni was an ancient Indian fire god—*beloved of*... I think it's *Panana. True friend. Stolen by*—God, what is that? *Stolen by*—I'm pretty sure it's—*the serpent's tooth*. Oh, it was bitten by a snake. Poor thing. *My tears will daily*—river? No. Water! *My tears will daily water his grave*."

Pleased with himself, he looked up—to see that Sam was crying. Not out loud. Silently. Tears welling and trickling, turning the dirt on her cheeks to mud. She flushed, and scrubbed them away. "Sorry. Sorry. Stupid, I'm being stupid."

She hardly ever cried. Not because she was unemotional—he knew her feelings were never far from the surface—but because the pressures of the job, being a woman in the military, forced her to keep them strictly strait-jacketed. And that kind of control became a habit, along with carrying guns and always assuming a worst case scenario in any situation.

He rested his hand on her shoulder and shook her, just a little bit. "Hey. No. You're right, it's sad. Panana, whoever she was, loved her pet and it died and she cried. A lot. Don't be ashamed of feeling her pain, Sam. That's why what we're doing here is important. We're rediscovering these people's humanity. Bringing their lives back to life. If you can't be touched by this then what is any of it for? What good are we doing out here? Why fight so hard to save the human race?"

Sam shrugged. "I guess." Then she shook her head. "No. You're right, of course." Contemplating the neatly composed curl of bones, she said, "I always wanted a cat. But Mark was allergic and we moved so often, from base to base. Dad said no."

She hardly ever talked of her childhood, or her brother. "Must've been tough."

Another shrug. "That's life. So, what do you want to do with Agni, here?"

"I'm not sure," he said. "Maybe remove the entire grave, preserve it somehow. I don't know. But until I make up my mind we should protect it from the elements."

"Good idea."

So he fetched a preservation kit from the campsite and they secured poor little Agni's grave. With that done, and the temperature steadily rising, they paused to drink from their canteens and bask in the glow of a job well done.

But then the question that had been nagging at the back of his mind for weeks now rose spectre-like before him ... and he knew he'd never have a better chance than right here, right now, to ask it. He cleared his throat. "So. I was thinking... can I ask *you* a question?"

Sam lowered her canteen. Kept her gaze pinned to it. "Tit for tat?"

"No. No, it's just... something I need to know, Sam. Need to understand."

She looked at him. "Then ask. But I don't guarantee you'll like the answer."

Which meant she knew, or at least suspected, what was haunting him. That was the trouble with being this close to another person. Spending so much time with them, learning to read them as fluently as any hieroglyphics. Since Sha're, sometimes he forgot it was a two-way street. Sam learning him, while he was learning her. She was warning him not to be surprised if she wasn't on his side this time. Undaunted, he continued.

"Why didn't you stop Jack from closing the iris, when you knew Alar would try to follow him to Earth?"

She answered his question with another question. "You agree with Kinsey, do you? You think it was murder? Or an execution?"

"I don't. I—"

She snapped the lid back onto her canteen. "Let me put it this way, then. Do you think Jack is a murderer?"

She almost never did that. Refer to Jack by name, instead of rank. Not even when he wasn't around. It was a measure of how strongly she felt. Her eyes were cool, calm, watchful. That scalpel intellect peeling back his layers, exposing his uncertain core. "No. Not a murderer. But he was angry, Sam. And you know what he's like when he's angry. He isn't … safe."

Her eyebrows lifted. "So, not murder? What, then? Manslaughter?"

God. He should've kept his big mouth shut. "Maybe. I honestly don't know. Just answer what I asked you. Please?"

She examined her canteen. "Why didn't I stop him from closing the iris?"

"You could have," he said. "And I was watching him, Sam. I think a part of him might have wanted you to. Maybe. But you did nothing. You said nothing. Why?"

"Because I didn't know what was coming through that wormhole, Daniel," she retorted, tossing the canteen aside. "It might have been Alar. It might have been a bomb. There was no way I could tell. Neither could the colonel. And Alar knew the iris was there. It was his choice. His gamble. And he lost."

It sounded good in theory. Could've been a bomb coming through, yeah, sure. Except she'd known it wasn't, and so had Jack. That conviction had been stark in his eyes, which never left Sam's face.

She said, "Anyway, I'm not the person you should be talking to about this, Daniel. If you have questions—reservations—you should talk to him."

"I can't," he said, after a moment. "I tried, but…" There'd been a short, sharp scene he didn't care to dwell on.

"Then give him more time. I think he's earned that much."

"He has. God, of course he has. I just… I need to work through this, okay? I need you to be a sounding board. Will you do that?"

She looked away, her jaw tightening. Tension thrumming through every long line of her body. All that lovely relaxation burned away. Curtly, she nodded. "All right. If you really want me to."

For a long, silent moment Daniel debated whether or not to keep talking. But he had to talk, or go mad, and Sam was the only one he could talk to. About this, anyway. Teal'c didn't see there was a problem. Alar was bad, Alar was dead. It was all good. Teal'c lived in a very… black and white world. Sometimes that was okay, other times it wasn't exactly helpful.

Like now.

He took a deep breath and let it out, incrementally. "When I first met Jack," he began, stringing thoughts together like beads on a wire, "I thought he was the most terrifying man I'd ever encountered. You know when people say things like: As hard as diamond. As cold as ice. As impenetrable as Fort Knox." Sam nodded. "Well, the Jack who went to Abydos that first time… he was all those clichés and then some. Basically, when he stepped through the 'gate he was a dead man walking."

Almost imperceptibly, a little of her chill thawed. "I know. But he's not like that now, thanks to you."

He shrugged. "Maybe. I don't know. He's never said as much. He's never said anything, really, about that time. He is different, these days. He never smiled *once*, that first mission. There wasn't a joke in sight. He can still be frightening, but he's not dead inside any more. And we can talk—sometimes—about things that matter. *Really* matter."

"So what's your problem?"

"My *problem* is that just when I think he's finally moved past his blind military pragmatism, the kind of mindset that says the end really does justify the means… something like Euronda happens and I feel like I'm looking at this total stranger all over again." Moodily, Daniel scraped his fingertips through the dirt. "Someone I'll never understand or communicate with in any meaningful way if I live to be a thousand. And I don't know if I can keep doing it, Sam. I get tired of fighting with him, you know? I just… I'm *tired*."

Her eyebrows lifted. "Then don't fight."

"Don't fight?" He stared at her, disbelieving, as though she'd suggested he should stop breathing. "When he's about to do something short-sighted? Something typically, pig-headedly Jack? How can I not fight?"

She sighed, and rubbed at a smear of dirt on her knee. "Okay, then fight. But then don't bitch about it afterwards. Especially," she added, pointedly, "since a lot of the time he agrees with you, eventually. Not always, I know, but then you're not always right. The thing is, he takes your advice. He did in Euronda. He sided with you against Alar. Okay, so you had to fight to get there. But wasn't it worth it? Isn't that what you were talking about, before? The job only you can do? Because Daniel, I don't know who else he'd listen to about stuff like that. There's no-one. Not even—" She stopped, her intent gaze flickering away, then back again. "He listens to you."

"I know, I know," he said, fists clenched, "but don't you see, Sam? This time he nearly didn't. He was willing to close his eyes to what the Eurondans were doing because he wanted their technology."

"Yeah, well, so did I."

"You think I didn't?" he demanded. "God, Sam. I'm as desperate to stop the Goa'uld as anyone. I wanted that technology—right up to the moment I realized we weren't getting the full story or asking the right questions about our new best friends. But Jack—even when he knew something was wrong, he fought me. And he did know, Sam. You know he did. He just didn't *want* to know because he was committed to procuring what the Eurondans offered us."

"It's our mission mandate, Daniel," she reminded him impatiently.

"That's not good enough!" he cried. "That's like saying, I was only following orders, Sam, and I'm *better* than that. So are you. And so is Jack!"

Her expression troubled, Sam pulled her knees up to chest. "So… what? Are you working your way up to leaving the team? Is this what it's all about, really?"

"No! No, of course not," he said, suddenly tired. "At least… I don't want to. It's just… it feels like we're dancing the same old dance over and over again. Me and Jack. And I'm sick of it. I find something incredibly important, something like these ruins, and he tells me I'm wasting his time. Or I point out the pitfalls of some plan he's making, try to get him to think outside his military training, just for a minute, God, for a *second*, and he slaps me down so hard, so fast, I practically get concussion."

She shrugged. "Maybe he thinks that when you do that, you're questioning his expertise, or his integrity, or—

"But I'm not!" he protested. "God, I'm not! I'm just trying to contribute a different point of view! Of course I don't question his expertise, he's the best soldier—warrior—we've got, I know that, but—"

"But sometimes it's hard to tell that you know it, Daniel," she said. "'Cause it's not what you say, it's the way you say it. Colonel O'Neill's devoted his whole life to the military. He sacrificed his family to it. Even before we discovered the Stargate, he'd come close to giving his life for his country more than once. You know that. Now he *has* given it for his country—for the planet—and it's sheer dumb luck the gift was returned unopened. So maybe when you get on your moral high horse and lecture him on how it's wrong for him to pick up his gun, what he hears is you telling him those sacrifices aren't worth squat."

Stunned, Daniel stared at her. "No. *No*, that's—is *that* what he thinks? Did he tell you that's what he thinks?"

She raised her hands. "Hey. I'm just the sounding board here, remember?"

"But it's not what I mean!"

"Then tell him what you do mean."

"God, doesn't he understand? I don't want him to make a mistake, do something he's going to regret, that'll haunt him for the rest of his life. *That's* why I challenge him!"

Sam touched his arm. "He realizes that, Daniel. But what *you* have to realize is that sometimes his decisions aren't wrong. They're just not the decisions *you'd* make."

He dropped his head into his hands. "I know. I know. I just—"

"You've worked with him a long time now, Daniel. Do you think he's going to stop being an Air Force Special Operations colonel any time soon?"

He sighed. "No."

"And what about you? Are you planning on giving up your career as a passionate, compassionate champion of the victimized, the voiceless, life's lonely discards?"

"No. Not really."

"Then Daniel, you need to find a way to make peace with him, don't you?" she said, relentlessly reasonable. "Or else you need to walk away."

He looked up. "I … don't want to walk away."

"Then make it work."

Just like that, huh? And when he was done, maybe he'd grab a few bottles of mineral water and turn them into a crisp Cabernet Sauvignon. Find the nearest beach and turn back the tide. Better yet, go walking on the—

There was a crackle of static and his radio, perched on a pile of mud bricks, burst into life. "Daniel? Daniel, come in. It's Lee. You and Sam have a visitor."

"Teal'c!" said Sam as they met at the campsite, and gave him a hug. "What are you doing here? Is everything okay with Ry'ac?"

Teal'c returned her impulsive embrace briefly, then stepped back. "Yes. My son has departed with Bra'tac and his fellow cadets on what I believe you would call a wilderness hike. He is happy, and growing like a weed."

Despite his lingering melancholy, Daniel laughed. "A weed? And you call yourself a doting father?"

"No, Daniel Jackson," Teal'c said impassively. "I call myself Teal'c."

Boom boom. The former Jaffa was a lot of things, but when it came to stand-up comedy Chris Rock didn't need to look over his shoulder. "Okay. So Ry'ac's blooming. And Bra'tac's well?"

"Master Bra'tac is indeed well."

"Okay. So that brings us back to: why are you here?"

"Let us sit," said Teal'c, indicating the camp stools.

Daniel and Sam exchanged glances, and sat. "Teal'c, you know you're making me nervous, right?" she said. "Is something wrong? Have they made a decision about Colonel O'Neill?"

"They have," said Teal'c. "But not in the way you fear. Your father is at the SGC, Major Carter. He has asked General Hammond to second SG-1 to the Tok'ra on Vorash, and General Hammond has agreed."

Daniel felt his jaw drop. "What? He's agreed? Don't we get a say? What is this, a game of pass the parcel?"

Teal'c considered him. "I am not familiar with that amusement."

Sam made a shushing motion with her hand. "What's the mission, Teal'c?"

"I do not know the details. General Hammond is waiting now to brief us."

"Well, do you have any idea how long this secondment is for?"

"I do not."

"I wonder why us," said Daniel. "I mean, it's no secret Jack's not a member of the Tok'ra fan club."

"I suspect," said Teal'c, with the faintest of smiles, "this has something to do with Senator Kinsey's attempts to gain his revenge upon O'Neill. It would seem SG-1 was specifically requested by the Tok'ra's new High Councillor after Jacob Carter met privately with General Hammond."

"Wow," said Sam, and chewed at her lip. "That's good intel-gathering there, Teal'c. I bet you dollars to donuts Dad and the General cooked this up between them to get the colonel out of the way till the dust's settled."

"And that sounds great, in theory," said Daniel. "I'm all for saving Jack from Kinsey. But you know what it means, don't you? We're going to be stuck on Vorash with Jack for who knows how long. He doesn't like the Tok'ra, he's going to know he's stuck there because of losing it in Washington and he's going to be in a filthy mood the whole time. It's a recipe for disaster! This secondment could set back the Earth-Tok'ra alliance by *decades*."

Teal'c shook his head. "I disagree, Daniel Jackson. I am confident O'Neill will do nothing to jeopardise the crucial alliance between Earth and the Tok'ra."

"Really?" said Daniel, surprised. "I'm not." Sam hit him. "Ouch," he added, and turned to her. "Look, Sam, you can hit me all you like but—"

"I'll do more than hit you, Daniel!" she snapped. "If you keep this up I'm going to take out my weapon and *shoot* you!"

He stared, impressed. "Wow. You sounded just like Jack, then."

"Good!"

"Look, guys," he said, sliding as far from Sam as he could get, "we have to face facts. Whatever this assignment involves, Jack's going to be an absolute pain in the ass about it and because he can't take out his frustrations on the Tok'ra, chances are he'll take them out on us."

Sam sighed. "Daniel..."

"Sam, you know him as well as I do. And because we're his team we'll have to grin and bear it. Indefinitely!"

After a moment, Teal'c nodded. "Daniel Jackson may have a point, Major Carter."

She nodded too. "I know."

They sat in silence, gloomily pondering the prospect of an absolute pain in the ass Jack O'Neill.

"But that doesn't matter," Daniel sighed, after a while. "Jack's always there when we need him. Now it's our turn to be there for him."

"Dammit," said Sam, and punched the arm of the camp stool. "That *bastard* Kinsey. This is all his fault. When is he going to leave us alone?"

"When he's dead," Daniel retorted. "Dead, decapitated, and buried at the crossroads with a stake through his heart."

"Indeed," said Teal'c, and stood. "We should depart."

With a pang, Daniel thought of the beautiful crimson, ochre and lapis lazuli plate. Of Agni, jewelled and sleeping in the grave. Of all the other treasures he'd hoped to find here. Would never find now. Sam's hand came to rest on his knee, and he looked at her.

"I'm sorry, Daniel," she said, her expression gentled. One minute threatening to shoot him, the next in complete sympathy with his disappointment. Nothing about friendship was easy or uncomplicated. Not even with someone as straightforward as Sam. "Truly. But there'll be other digs."

He nodded. "I know."

"For what it's worth, I had a really great time here, working with you," she added. "I learned a lot. I won't forget it."

He covered her hand with his, and tightened his fingers. "Me too."

And then it was time to go. So they went.

CHAPTER SEVEN

Martouf was waiting to greet them at the Vorash 'gate. It was late afternoon local time; the sinking sun cast long thin shadows and a rising wind whipped the loose, sandy soil into a frenzy. Sam fished out her sunglasses and slid them on, eyes gritty within moments of stepping out of the wormhole. Beside her, the colonel hunched his shoulders round his ears and muttered something she was better off not acknowledging.

"Colonel O'Neill," said Martouf, coming forward. "On behalf of High Councillor Per'sus, welcome once more to Vorash. The High Councillor regrets not being here to welcome you himself. He has been called away on urgent business elsewhere."

The colonel nodded. "Fine."

"When will he be back?" said her dad, sounding put out.

Martouf shrugged, seemingly not disturbed by the colonel's less than effusive response. "He does not know, Jacob. He has made it clear to the Council that we have his complete support and authority to act as we see fit in this current situation. He will contact us when and as often as his circumstances permit."

Behind his impassive surface, Sam thought Martouf looked… worried. But when he turned to her his face lit up, as usual, and that vivid, endearing smile dispelled his customary reserve. "Samantha."

She smiled back, acutely conscious of the colonel's dour presence at her shoulder. "Martouf. It's good to see you again."

"And you. And of course Dr. Jackson, and Teal'c," he added, nodding.

Teal'c bowed. "Greetings, Martouf."

Daniel said, "You know, since it looks like we'll be here for a while, here's an idea. Why don't we dispense with the formalities? Call me Daniel."

"Of course. Daniel," said Martouf.

"And I've got a better idea," said the colonel. "Why don't we get a move on? I'm freezing my butt off, if anyone's interested."

"You are right, colonel," said Martouf, unperturbed. Being two hundred and seventy-six years of age clearly had its advantages; lots and lots of time to perfect the old 'water off a duck's back' routine, for starters. "We should get to shelter. A storm approaches—and on Vorash, storms are not to be taken lightly." He indicated their solitary field remote expeditionary device. "These are the only supplies you brought with you?"

"That's right," said the colonel. "Why? Are you guys running low? You should've said something. We could've stopped off at a Wal-mart on the way."

Martouf's gaze flickered to her father, and back again. "No, Colonel. Our supplies are more than adequate. Please... if you would all like to come with me?"

"Sure," said the colonel. "Why not?" He waited for Martouf to lead the way, then followed. "Heel, F.R.E.D."

With a whine of its servers the heavily laden carrier lurched forward and trundled in his wake. Ages ago, after Daniel had accidentally permanently misplaced the fourth F.R.E.D. remote at a crucial moment, Sam had retrofitted the entire fleet with voice-activated control chips. She'd never admit it, but the self-imposed task had nearly defeated her. Cost her several nights' sleep and quite a lot of hair, from all the anguished pulling.

But that was okay. The alternative had been to watch the colonel dismember Daniel one muscle group at a time.

"Oh boy," Daniel said now, arms folded across his chest as they watched their intrepid leader kick his way through Vorash's sandy, grassless topsoil. "D'you think it's too late for me to change my mind?"

Her father shook his head. "It's all right, Daniel. I'll take care of it."

"Yeah... well... rather you than me, Jacob," said Daniel, and moved out, Teal'c at his side.

"Don't worry, kiddo," her father said, slinging an arm around Sam's shoulders. "He'll get over it. When he gets interested, or something tries to kill him."

If only it were that simple. Or certain... "Dad—"

His arm tightened. "Don't *worry*. You know my motto. Walk softly, carry a big stick—and make sure the other guy knows you'll use it."

"Yeah? Well, *his* motto is: It's only a flesh wound, come back you coward, I'll bite you to death." Seeing her father's blank expression, she elaborated. "Monty Python and the Holy Grail? The Black Knight? All his arms and legs cut off and he still won't give in? That's the colonel."

"I never understood Monty Python," her father said vaguely. "I guess you have to be British. Or strange. Sam, I promise I won't start anything I can't stop. And I know he's had a rough few weeks. But that's not the fault of anybody here and I'm not going to tolerate him disrespecting the people I live and work with. Any more than he'd tolerate me disrespecting the folk of the SGC. Okay?"

It was a fair point. "Okay. Just... be tactful, will you? Things really have been pretty awful."

"George said." His comforting hand rubbed up and down her arm. "I guess it's been pretty awful for all of you. We'll make some time to talk ..."

"Yeah. I'd like that. Maybe not right away. But soon."

"Whenever you're ready."

There'd been a time, not so very long ago, when they couldn't even say 'good morning' without a fight. Briefly, Sam let her head drop against him. "Thanks, Dad."

"No thanks needed, kiddo. It's my job."

She looked towards the encircling mountains. Their jagged peaks were capped with bellicose black clouds, and on the ever-rising wind the tang of snow and sleet. "Hey. There really is a storm coming. We'd better hurry."

He dropped a kiss on the top of her head. "That's my genius. Come on!"

Arm in arm they ran to catch up with the others, just like they'd run so many years ago in the Air Force picnic day three-legged Father-and-daughter races. Laughing, as though they hadn't a care in the world.

The underground Tok'ra complex was comfortably warm and depressingly homogenous. It'd drive her mad staying here for longer than a few months. She knew she'd end up doing something crazy, like running around with a paintbrush and a tin of paint, doing terrible things to the décor just to relieve its boredom.

She, the colonel, Daniel and Teal'c were each assigned small, boring but comfortable quarters in the residential wing of the base. After unpacking her meagre, functional belongings and stowing them in the trunks supplied for her use, she went to find her taciturn team leader.

He was sitting on his chamber's narrow bed, methodically checking a pile of spare ammo clips. Looking up as she tapped on the open door, he offered her a grimace masquerading as a smile. "Carter. Come in."

"Hey, sir," she said, and entered the lion's den. "Got everything you need? If not I can find Dad, or Martouf, ask them to—"

"I'm fine, Carter," he said. "How about you?"

"Yeah. I'm fine too." *Except that talking to you is like juggling live hand grenades while tap dancing on egg shells and how come I feel it's somehow my fault? Is Daniel right? Did you want me to stop you?* But she wasn't ready to ask that question. Wasn't sure she ever would be. Playing it safe, she added, "Just checking to see you had everything. Guess I'll go do the same for Daniel and Teal'c."

"Good idea."

She was nearly out the door when he said, "So… I guess I'm being a bit of a jerk."

She stopped. Turned. Eased back into the room and shoved her hands in her pockets. "Actually … yeah. You are. Sir."

"Oh."

He was surprised—had expected a soothing denial, probably. Well, he was barking up the wrong major. *Today the role of Dutifully Supportive Second in Command will be played by…* someone else. Someone who hadn't had her head bitten off a dozen times since returning with Daniel from P8C-316. So the colonel wasn't happy about this assignment? Well golly gee, neither was she, much. As far as she was concerned the only thing it had going for it was her father's involvement. Otherwise, all it meant was being taken away from a hundred important projects she had on the boil, back in her lab.

Now she was stuck indefinitely on Vorash, not a contender for Intergalactic Club Med status, and a couple of missions she'd really been looking forward to had been reassigned to other teams. Which came with the territory, but was still disappointing.

The colonel was staring at her. Waiting for some kind of response. An apology, most likely. Sam bit her lip, thinking furiously. *To hell with it*. "Sir, are we ever going to talk about what happened on Euronda? Or in the 'gate room, afterwards?"

He turned his attention back to the ammo clips. "Probably not."

"We should."

His lips tightened. "You get yourself a doctorate in psychobabble while I wasn't looking, Carter?"

"At the very least, you should talk to Daniel."

His busy fingers stilled. "Why?"

"Ask him, sir."

"Carter—"

Dangerously close to losing her temper, Sam held up her hands. "Sir—due respect, I'm not your Girl Friday go-between. Talk to Daniel."

The colonel looked up then, his expression formidable. She almost never took a tone with him, no matter what he dished out, and he really didn't like it when she did. Well, that was just too damned bad. Last time she looked she was a decorated Air Force officer, not a doormat. She held his hard gaze in silence. Not giving him an inch. Refusing to be intimidated.

Incredibly, he was the first to look away. "That'll be all, Major. Dismissed."

It was a cheap way of getting the last word. The fact that he took it told her, as if she didn't know already, that his reserves of emotional endurance were running perilously low.

"Yes, sir," she said quietly, and left him alone.

Sam didn't see him again until dinner. Like the personnel of the SGC, the Tok'ra ate in a large communal mess hall. Although here there was no chow line, no appetizing array of food kept warm in bain-maries, just a softly spoken collection of wait-staff who ferried full and emptied plates between the hall and what she assumed were the kitchens. Like everywhere else in the complex the artificially constructed environment was warm, and faintly scented with something floral.

She, Daniel and Teal'c were already seated at their commandeered table when the colonel walked in, more ruthlessly self-contained than ever. Only the merest tightening of the skin round his eyes suggested he found his surroundings distasteful. The other diners, all Tok'ra of course, inspected him under cover of their various conversations and the cheerful clattering of cutlery on plates. He had to be aware of the scrutiny, but nothing in his demeanor betrayed that. Look up 'poker face' in the dictionary, you'd find a photo of Jack O'Neill.

"Hey, Jack, over here," Daniel called, waving.

The colonel threaded his way through the hall's mostly occupied tables and slid into the chair Daniel pulled out for him. "Evening, campers," he said. Reaching for the jug of water that had been placed on the table, he poured himself a generous glassful.

"O'Neill."

"Sir."

"Jack."

He put down his almost emptied glass. "If you're waiting for Jacob or Martouf to join us, don't bother. We're on our own tonight."

Sam felt a stab of anxiety. "Why? What's happened?"

He shrugged. "There's something they had to do somewhere else. Jacob said it wouldn't take long, and they should be back by morning. He went to tell you, Carter, but apparently you were asleep. I said I'd be thrilled to be his Boy Friday go-between and pass on the message."

"What?" said Daniel, as she and the colonel just looked at each other. "Did I miss something?"

"No," she said at last. "It's nothing. A joke."

"Ha ha," the colonel added.

"You were asleep?" said Daniel, turning to her. "During daylight? That's not like you. Are you okay?"

"I'm fine. Just worn out by all that archaeology."

"Don't you mean bored comatose?" said the colonel.

"Not at all. I really enjoyed myself," she replied. "You should try it some time."

Daniel choked on his own glass of water, and Teal'c banged him so hard between the shoulder blades he nearly fell out of his chair. When he was upright and could speak again he gasped, "Jack on a dig? God, Sam! What did I *ever* do to you to deserve that?"

She was saved from answering by the arrival of a young woman wearing a brown Tok'ra tunic and a spotless apron. "Good evening, Colonel O'Neill, Major Carter, Dr. Jackson, Teal'c," she greeted them. "Welcome to Vorash. My name is Uthisbe. If you're ready to eat, Jacob has already provided the cooks with Tauri food for you. I believe it only needs heating, which will not take very long."

"Really? Uthisbe, did you say?" said the colonel. "Well, that's great, Uthisbe. We're all starving, so bring it on out."

She bowed. "Certainly."

The colonel watched Uthisbe as she disappeared through the swinging double doors at the rear of the hall. "Now that's something I wasn't expecting," he observed. "Being waited on by a Tok'ra."

"She is not a Tok'ra," said Teal'c.

"She isn't?"

"No."

"Carter?"

"Teal'c's right," she confirmed. "No symbiote. She's human, just like us."

The colonel shook his head. "No wonder we can't get any respect around here," he said, disgusted. "Servants and suitcases, that's all humans are to the Tok'ra."

She sighed. "Sir..."

He held up his hands. "I know. I know. I need to keep an open mind. Carter, my mind is always open. You hear that whistling sound? It's the wind, whipping through the space between my ears."

"Jack's not entirely wrong, you know," said Daniel. "We do have a few perception hurdles to leap over. Jacob's done a great job laying the foundations, but nobody can overcome a couple of thousand years of prejudice and preconceptions in a few months. Not even a race as advanced as the Tok'ra."

"Exactly," said the colonel. "Though when you say *advanced*— don't know what's so *advanced* about walking round with a snake in your head."

"I'm talking technologically," said Daniel, with an edge of impatience. "As you very well know."

The colonel pulled a face, then drummed his fingertips on the crystal-formed table. "So, boys and girl. Here we are on sunny Vorash. Except it's not so sunny. In fact it's a bit chilly. I may need to send home for a sweater. In the meantime, anyone got any thoughts about this mission Jacob's dreamed up for us?"

"I think it's inspired," said Sam.

"Not that you're *biased*, or anything," the colonel murmured.

"No sir, I'm not," she retorted. "Scientific method 101: evaluate the facts with complete objectivity. As Teal'c, Bra'tac and the rebel Jaffa movement have shown, destabilizing the system lords from within their own ranks is one of the most effective methods of defeating them. It's also a lot less dangerous, from our point of view. Every time we get into a pitched battle with loyal Jaffa, or someone like Apophis, we take major casualties and have to spend months and millions of dollars recouping our tactical strength. It's crazy. This way we have the potential to inflict enormous damage on the enemy without firing a shot. *And* it puts the Tok'ra in our debt. It's a win-win scenario, sir."

He stared at her. "And it doesn't bug you, having to use Jolinar to get the job done?"

She met his look without hesitation. Whatever she felt about using Jolinar—and she hadn't quite made up her mind about that—this wasn't the time or place to discuss it. "No, sir."

"Fine," he said, not quite frowning.

"Major Carter's analysis of the situation is correct," said Teal'c. "Do you not constantly complain, O'Neill, that we are given no access to the Tok'ra and their operations or intelligence?"

"I don't know about *constantly*..." said the colonel.

"I do," said Daniel. "But let's not dwell. The point is that as long as Garshaw was High Councillor the Tok'ra were never going to treat us as equals. After this, they will. And while I'm here I'll be able to start laying the groundwork for an official treaty. It's what I'm good at. Talking to people, and making them listen."

Sam held her breath as Daniel and the colonel locked gazes. Incredibly, again, it was the colonel who looked away first. "Yeah, I've noticed that. But—"

He broke off as Uthisbe and another waiter returned with their dinner: garden salad, spaghetti bolognaise, garlic bread and a bottle of Australian Merlot. After serving it, they withdrew.

Sam felt herself grinning like an idiot. "Oh my God. Dad must've raided the commissary supply room then got the base cooks to put a dinner together for us."

The colonel smiled back at her. "Go, Dad. The last time I ate Tok'ra rations my guts went on strike for a week."

She laughed. "Said the man who thinks beer and pizza form four of the five major food groups."

"And so they do, Carter, so they do," he said comfortably, refusing to be baited. "But only if the pizza is pepperoni. Now pass me the wine, will you? The bottle's staring at me."

By tacit consent they spoke no more about the impending mission. Used the meal-break to regroup, rediscover their rhythm, get back in the familiar, comfortable SG-1 groove.

After dinner they drifted to the Tok'ra's communal recreation area, where they found couches and board games and Tok'ra amusing themselves. In one corner of the hall a group of three women and two men sat in a circle playing a range of musical instruments: variations on a violin, recorders, guitar. The sound was pleasant, but felt... unformed. If they'd been on Earth, it'd be called jamming.

Leaving the rest of his team to fend for themselves, Daniel made a beeline for the musicians, his face alight with enthusiastic curiosity. The group welcomed him politely, but within a few minutes their reserve had melted and they were animatedly explaining their chosen instruments to him and encouraging him to have a go.

Watching, the colonel snorted. "There he goes again. Making instant best friends with everybody. He just can't help himself, can he?"

"Daniel Jackson has a pure heart," said Teal'c. "He possesses no defences. No agendas. He has no guile. He cares about people, all people, and wants the best for whomever he meets no matter who they are or even if they wish him harm."

"Teal'c's right," Sam said, smiling as Daniel tootled on one of the recorders. "Even when he screws up, like that time with Shyla, it's only because he cares. And it *is* because he cares that we've made a lot of the off-world friends we have today."

The colonel looked at her. "You had to mention Shyla, didn't you?"

"Sorry."

They made themselves comfortable on a couple of vacant couches and sat in amused silence, watching Daniel teach the Tok'ra musicians an old English folksong. Being an old English folksong it had to with witches, death and sex.

"God," said the colonel, listening to Daniel sing. "Where's the earplugs when you need them?"

"Oh, don't be mean," Sam said, wincing. "I've heard worse."

"So have I," said the colonel. "When I accidentally trod on a cat's tail. And on that note," he added standing, "I shall bid you good night."

She smiled up at him. "Good night, sir. Sleep well. Pleasant dreams."

Was it her imagination, or did he flinch? "Yeah. You too. See you both at breakfast."

"What time?"

He shuddered. "Half-past Oh God It's Way Too Early, or thereabouts. I don't know yet. When I find out I'll slip a note under your door."

"I'll make sure to look for it, sir."

"You do that, Carter." And as he walked away added, plaintively, "I just hope Jacob remembered to pack the Fruit Loops..."

At which point Daniel mercifully stopped singing, and beckoned her and Teal'c to join him. Which they did, with pleasure.

And a hey nonny nonny in the dingle and the dell.

The Tok'ra transport rings deposited O'Neill on Vorash's storm-scoured surface with a thud-thud-whoosh. Bitter cold lanced through his jacket and BDUs and into his flesh, reminding him sharply of other nights in another desert on a world far, far away.

Hey Jack. It could be worse. At least you're in one piece this time.

Vorash's single moon rode high in the black, starred sky. It was obesely full, colored a bold, deep golden yellow: what Charlie used to call an egg-yolk moon. The worst of the weather had passed; the cold, the crackle of ice underfoot and vestigial puddles of water were all that remained of its fury.

He took a few deep, lung-searing breaths, welcoming their bite and marvelling all over again how each world he visited smelled different. Smelled alien. This time ten years ago, if anyone had told him he'd be a seasoned intergalactic sightseer...

Pshaw. Do tell. Oh, really.

He started walking. Heading for nowhere in particular, just needing to move, to stir the sluggish blood, to regain that equilibrium the Eurondan mission had so wantonly disturbed.

Recent conversation, flotsam-like, floated to the surface of his mind. "*I don't give one good goddamn that you don't like the Tok'ra,*" Hammond had told him bluntly. "*This mission is your ticket out of trouble, Colonel, and you don't have the luxury of changing your mind. You're going to Vorash, do I make myself clear?*"

George Hammond didn't often pull rank, but when he did it was like being clobbered with a baseball bat the size of a California Redwood. "*Yes sir.*"

"*The President has expended a lot of political capital to save your ass from Kinsey,*" Hammond had added. "*And I used up a lot of favors convincing Admiral Belweather to convince him it was worth it. Do I need to tell you not to waste this second chance, Jack?*"

"*No sir,*" he'd answered, humbled. "*You absolutely do not.*"

Hammond had nodded, smiling fiercely. "*I'm pleased we understand each other. You dodged the bullet this time, Jack. Believe me when I say that given your—colorful—career it's unlikely you'll continue dodging them indefinitely—no matter how many more times you save the planet.*"

"*Yes sir.*"

"*Now you'd better get going. Jacob's waiting. And if you could avoid upsetting our Tok'ra allies I'm sure we'd all be very grateful.*"

Ouch. Hammond didn't often use sarcasm, either, but when he chose to...

"You don't have to worry, George," he promised the sparkling sky. "I won't let you down again, I swear it."

A faint noise behind him spun him about. Small in the distance—had he really walked so far?—the 'gate was powering up. He jogged gently back towards it, mindful of his gimpy knee. Fraiser would have his guts for garters if he blew it for a third time.

The inbound traveller was Martouf. They met halfway between the Stargate and the rings. "Hey."

Martouf frowned. "Colonel O'Neill. Is something the matter? Why have you left the complex?"

"Nothing's the matter," he said, tucking his cold-stung hands into his armpits. "Just… taking a constitutional. Where's Jacob?"

"Finalizing details. He will return in the morning."

When it came to revealing emotions, Martouf would give Teal'c a run for his money. "Everything okay?"

"It will be."

"This—new thing. Is it the same thing Per'sus is working on?"

Martouf hesitated, then nodded. "Yes."

"There. See?" he said, and clapped Martouf on the shoulder. "You told me something and your head didn't explode!"

"Colonel O'Neill…" Martouf sighed. "I find it quite curious that while you and your General Hammond see nothing untoward in restricting some areas and information when the Tok'ra visit the SGC, when we do the same you perceive our actions as untrustworthy and take offence. Why is this?"

"Why? Well—because when we do it, we know it's for a good reason. When you do it, we think you're trying to hide something," O'Neill said promptly, then replayed the words for his inner ear. Met Martouf's skeptical look, and shrugged. "Okay, so that didn't come out right. Martouf—"

"I understand, Colonel," Martouf said gravely. "The Tauri are long used to acting autonomously. So are the Tok'ra. Perhaps this joint endeavour will show us how we can work together for mutual profit, while still retaining our sovereignty and some secrets."

He nodded. "That's the plan, I guess. So. This other business…"

"If you are concerned the matter will impact our project, you need not be," Martouf replied with his trademark enigmatic smile. "The issues are unrelated."

To push or not to push, that was the question. And tonight, anyway, the answer was 'not'. "Good!" he said brightly. "Pleased to hear it." Martouf started walking again, and O'Neill fell in beside him. "Look. I'm glad I caught you. About earlier…"

"Yes?"

"If I was… you know… tetchy…"

"Tetchy?" Martouf frowned. "I'm afraid I do not know that word."

"Oh. Okay. Well, short-tempered, then. A little sarcastic. All right, I admit it, *rude*, I—"

"There is no need to apologize, Colonel. Or explain," said Martouf. "Jacob mentioned you have been under some stress lately."

Oh Jacob did, did he? Trampling his instinctive response, O'Neill said, "I see." It came out snippy.

"Jacob has a high regard for you, Colonel," said Martouf earnestly. "As do we all. Your willingness to risk everything to save him and Selmak has greatly endeared you to the Tok'ra."

Endeared him? *Really*? Cool. Wait till he told Carter … "Ah — good. Glad to be of service."

"Perhaps you should consider meditation to ease your stress levels," Martouf suggested. "Selmak is an expert in the practice; if you ask him I'm sure he would be glad to teach you."

Meditation lessons. From a snake. Right… "Thanks," he said. "I'll bear that in mind."

They reached the rings and transported back into the underground complex. "Please excuse me now, Colonel," Martouf said. "I have several reports to compose. Someone will wake you in time for breakfast, then afterwards escort you to the conference room that has been allocated for our purposes. Good night."

"Yeah. Okay. Good night."

After two wrong turns O'Neill made it back to his quarters. He shucked his clothes, showered in the miniscule en suite that appeared when he hit the designated button—creepy, but effective—then crawled into bed. Sleep hit him like a hammer… then, like a scalpel, dreams sliced his soul to ribbons.

Alar's desperate. Bloody. All that plausible suaveness obliterated, the arrogance, the smooth sleek self-assurance. His world is in flames. You lit the match. Nazi wannabes. The urge to control. Destroy. Expunge what you don't approve of. Is it genetic? Coded into human DNA?

Alar doesn't understand. He's genuinely bewildered. "It could've all been yours."

You look at him, feeling sick. "I wouldn't follow us if I were you…"

CHAPTER EIGHT

"The thing about dying," said Jacob, as he rolled the Goa'uld cargo ship through Vorash's ionosphere, "is that it really concentrates the mind. Don't you find it concentrates the mind, Jack?"

Hanging on for dear life to the sides of his seat as the star field beyond the tel'tac's view port spun lazily past, O'Neill spared Carter's insane father a sideways look.

"If you mean am I paying attention now, Jacob, the answer is yes! Absolutely! I am paying *strict* attention!"

Jacob righted the ship and released his hold on the bizarre Goa'uld controls. "No. That's not what I mean. What I mean is, imminent death really gets you thinking."

Cautiously, O'Neill let go of his seat. Somebody should introduce the concept of seatbelts to the snakeheads. Soon. "Well, Jacob, so far I've only died once, from a staff blast, and I didn't have time to think about anything. I was dead before I hit the ground."

Nudging the cargo ship into a stationary position above the planet, Jacob nodded. "Fair enough. But you nearly died in Antarctica, and that was a pretty drawn-out affair. You nearly aged to death from nanites, another prolonged journey—and incidentally, can I just say what the *hell* were you thinking? Unprotected sex on an alien planet with a woman you'd known for five minutes? *Not* one of your finest moments, Colonel."

What? "Ah—Jacob—"

"Then there was the time you nearly died pinned to the 'gate room wall," continued Jacob, ignoring him, "the time you nearly got sucked into a black hole, the time you nearly had your brain rewired by an Ancient database and—of course—the time you nearly gave your life in defence of the planet when Apophis attacked. And that's just since the SGC was formed. Before that there's the parachuting accident over Iraq, some unpleasantness in Central America, a couple of near-misses in Panama, your stint in Abu Ghraib, a little excitement in Lebanon… You know, that's a hell of a lot of 'nearly dieds', Jack. Do you expect me to believe not one of them got you pondering the mysteries of life and death?"

"Don't tell me. Let me guess," O'Neill said, when he could trust himself to speak without yelling. "You've read my file."

"Yes I have, Jack," said Jacob. "All four volumes. They were... fun."

He took refuge in sarcasm. "Glad you enjoyed yourself, Jacob. Maybe I should donate a copy to the Colorado Springs Municipal Library. Then *everyone* with a spare few hours can amuse themselves at my expense."

Jacob just smiled. "What? Did you think I *wasn't* going to investigate the credentials of the man responsible for the life of my only daughter?"

Hell. When you put it that way... "Jacob, I thought you were supposed to be teaching me how to fly a Goa'uld cargo ship, not... resurrecting the dead and buried past."

"I can do both," said Jacob, and pointed to one of the incomprehensible buttons on the dash. "That's the hyperspace window enabler," he said. "Push it, and you create the subspace conduit that allows the ship to travel multiple times faster than the speed of light. The trick is you have to plot your destination *before* you enable it, or you could end up anywhere. Inside a sun, even, which I wouldn't recommend. So, to plot your destination, you—"

"I don't need to know that," O'Neill said. "That's what your only daughter is for."

Jacob grinned. "And if Sam's otherwise occupied?"

"Then there's Teal'c."

"And if *he's* otherwise—"

"Jacob! Come on!"

"No, Jack, *you* come on," said Jacob. He wasn't grinning now. "Who do you think you're talking to, here?"

A short, sharp silence. Then: "Okay."

"Besides, what else is there for you to do?" asked Jacob, reasonably. "We're still waiting for a final mission greenlight from Per'sus. Sam's making sure she understands our recruiting requirements, Daniel's got his nose buried in Tok'ra archives and Teal'c's reviewing Jaffa protocols with the next operatives due to go undercover. It's not like you can *help* them."

Galling, but true. "I guess."

"Exactly." Jacob pointed at another bit of the tel'tac's control panel. One half of it was configured with the symbols found on a Stargate and its DHD, while the other half was a bunch of Goa'uld letters. "You don't have to do any calculating, as such. The onboard computer system, for want of a better term, will do that for you. All you need to do is punch in the co-ordinates of the Stargate closest to the location you're aiming for and the Goa'uld name of the planet or solar system you want, if they're not the same thing or the planet you want to reach doesn't have a 'gate. The computer does the rest."

"Jacob, I don't know the Goa'uld name for those things," he protested. "Hell, I only just found out what 'kree' means!"

"Don't worry," said Jacob. "I'll give you a list when we get back to Vorash. Learning it off by heart can be your homework."

"Homework. He wants to give me homework, no less," O'Neill complained to the stars beyond the tel'tac's window.

"For now, let's do an easy jump," said Jacob, again ignoring him. "Say to Earth, and back. You do remember the 'gate address for Earth?"

He gave the man a look. "Yes. That one I know."

Jacob slapped him on the shoulder. "Good. So. First of all, you punch in the Earth 'gate co-ordinates..."

Guided by Carter's incredibly irritating father, he jumped the cargo ship to a high synchronous orbit around home, slipped the tel'tac into top gear and had a little fun dodging satellites and space junk, then jumped back to Vorash. Despite himself he smiled, quietly pleased with the achievement.

"Good," said Jacob. "Now you make a jump on your own this time."

"Where to?"

"Your choice. But better make it another planet under Asgard Protection so we don't run into any Goa'uld."

The only one he could remember off the top of his head was Cimeria so he jumped them there, and back again, without a hitch.

"*Very* good," praised Jacob. "See? It's not hard once you get the hang of it. Now. Since we're out here having such a fun time, and it's just the two of us, I thought we could clear the air about a few things."

Oh. Right. O'Neill stared at him, not fooled at all. Whatever was coming was the *real* reason for this expedition. "Such as?"

"Mainly, your attitude to this mission. Even though you agreed to come, I get the distinct impression you're not in favor of it."

No, he really wasn't. "It doesn't matter what I think," he said. "It was Hammond's call, and he called in your favor."

"Yes, he did," said Jacob. "But we both know things'll go a lot more smoothly if you can put your hand on your heart and say you support what the Tok'ra are doing."

"And if I can't?"

Jacob sighed. "Jack, I mentioned dying before because it played a big part in my decision to accept Selmak and join the Tok'ra. Resume orbit around Vorash. We'll circle the block a few times before we start the next exercise."

With increasing confidence O'Neill punched the requisite control buttons and eased the cargo ship into a steady glide above and around the Tok'ra stronghold. Then he sat back and considered the man beside him. "Jacob, I get it. You were dying, and putting a snake in your head was the only way to save your life."

"Yeah, okay, you're going to have to stop calling Selmak a snake," said Jacob. "It's insulting and hurtful. How many times do you need to be told? The Tok'ra and the Goa'uld are *nothing* alike."

He snorted. "Apart from the whole invade your body and take over your brain part."

"There is *no* invasion!"

"Really?" he demanded. "Tell that to Sam! You weren't around, Jacob. You didn't see what having Jolinar stuck in her head against her will did to her! And the nightmares? Ask her about the nightmares, sometime. She used to wake up screaming. Crying. She—"

"*Jolinar was desperate,*" said Selmak. "*Fighting for her own life, and all the lives she was trying to save. She never would have taken Samantha Carter as a host if there had been an alternative course of action. And when it appeared certain that her choice would cost Samantha her life, she sacrificed her own to save her host. Is that the behavior of a Goa'uld?*"

He was too angry to get creeped out about the switch. The reminder that this was in fact a three-way conversation. "Forcing Carter to carry her in the first place was *exactly* the behavior of a Goa'uld!" he spat. "We've got a saying on Earth, Selmak. 'Blood will out.' You call yourselves Tok'ra and you claim you're nothing like the Goa'uld but you're the same species and when you're desperate enough you act just like them. How are we—humans—supposed to trust you when at any moment you can take us over against our will and there is *nothing* we can do to stop you?"

"*It's clear you take what happened to Major Carter very personally, Colonel O'Neill.*"

"Damn straight I take it personally! I saw what that Ashrak did to her because it wanted to kill Jolinar! I saw her dying in front of me! I sat with her in the infirmary three nights running because she was too afraid to go to sleep. Terrified of the dreams, the memories, Jolinar left in her head. Why would any sane person do that to themselves on purpose?"

"For one, because they're dying and they're not ready to go just yet," said Jacob, quietly. "But that's not the only reason. Jack, I understand your anger. So does Selmak. What Jolinar did was against our code. But like Selmak says, she was desperate. Are you going to sit there and tell me you've never done anything questionable out of desperation? Anything questionable at all?"

"That's dirty pool, Jacob. We're not talking about me."

Jacob shrugged. "And we're not talking about Sam, either. Do you think I'm happy she was put through an ordeal like that? You're a father. You know the answer. But this is bigger than my pain, or your pain, or even Sam's pain. This is about the survival of a people who might just hold the key to defeating the Goa'uld. Are you saying I should've *died*, rather than let Selmak heal me and in the process prolong his own incredibly valuable life? Seriously? Is that what you're saying?"

O'Neill slid out of the tel'tac's co-pilot's seat and walked away, as far as he could get. Brought up hard against a bulkhead he stopped, and leaned against it. "No. I'm not saying that."

"Sorry, Jack, but it sounds to me like you are," said Jacob. His voice was gentle. Reasonable. "Sounds to me like you want to stop any human from accepting a Tok'ra symbiote because you're not comfortable with the idea. That's hardly democratic. Can't you at least admit that maybe, just maybe, your entire view of the Tok'ra has been tainted by what happened to Sam?"

He turned back. "So maybe it is. First impressions and all that.

So what?"

"Well, for one thing, Sam's accepted what happened with Jolinar so maybe it's time you stopped being angry on her behalf," said Jacob. "You also need to accept that there are some people for whom the pros of blending with a Tok'ra symbiote far, far outweigh the cons."

"Well I'm not one of them!"

"Yes, I'm getting that, Jack."

He'd never understand Jacob, or the people like Jacob, not in a million years. "So you're saying you don't mind that you're different, now? That you aren't human any more? That doesn't bother you?"

Jacob took a moment to think about it. Then he said, gently smiling, "If I had become less than who I was, then yes. It would bother me. But Jack, I became so much more than plain old General Jacob Carter. And I have to tell you, I love the new me. I love my new life. I will be grateful to Sam forever, that I've embarked on such an incredible adventure. Selmak has given me… God. So much. We accept that becoming a host is not what you'd choose. But what gives you the right to stand in the way of those who *do* want it? Or at least might be willing to consider it. Who think that surrendering their individuality, their singular existence, could be a noble gesture? The best, perhaps the *only* way, they can fight against the Goa'uld? And in doing so, escape from slavery?"

"You call it escape, Jacob. I call it jumping from the frying pan into the fire."

"Jack, humans on a Goa'uld slave farm are treated worse than cattle!" said Jacob. "The Tok'ra want to offer them new lives. A way to fight for the freedom of all humans enslaved by the Goa'uld. Who are *you* to stand in the way of that chance?"

He felt like a butterfly, pinned wriggling and helpless to a cork board. "Okay. Okay," he said, goaded. "You've made your point. I don't have the right to make the decision for anyone else. I can only decide for myself."

Jacob nodded. "Good."

"*But*—" He held up a warning finger. "The Tok'ra have to practice full disclosure. You have to tell these potential hosts *exactly* what they're letting themselves in for. The bad as well as the good. They get to make a fully informed decision, Jacob, or I'll do my damndest to make sure they never get to hear what you're offering. And since you've read my file, you know that won't be pretty."

Jacob nodded. "I can live with that."

"What about Selmak? Can he live with it?"

"*He can.*"

"Good. Then I guess we've got a deal." Jacob leaned over and patted the other pilot's chair. "Come on. Take a seat, Colonel. We've still got work to do."

Four gruelling hours later, O'Neill found himself back on Vorash, in search of his team. He found Daniel first, huddled over a pile of notes and Tok'ra computer pad things in a corner of the recreation hall, which was otherwise empty. Geek-boy was listening to a digital tape machine and transcribing whatever it was he'd recorded in the swift, incomprehensible shorthand he used on archaeological digs. Focused like a laser, oblivious to his surroundings, he had that look on his face, the absorbed challenged hungry look that meant he was happy. Fulfilled. Doing what came naturally.

He stood by the table a full five minutes before Daniel realized he was there.

"Hey. Watcha doin'?" he said as Daniel looked up, startled.

Snatching the recorder's earwig free then hitting the pause button Daniel said, "Jack, it's incredible. I can't tell you—thank God we came—I'm learning so much. Tok'ra culture is amazing. It's actual living history, I am talking to people who witnessed events that occurred *hundreds* of years ago!"

He nodded. "Fancy that."

"Yes! I know!" said Daniel, breathless. "The perspective they offer on historical causalities, it's—it's—*unprecedented*! I really think I'll be able to help draft a truly meaningful Earth-Tok'ra treaty by the end of our stay here. So far I've only interviewed three Tok'ra and already I know more about their history, their customs, the way they think and how they view the world, what's important to their culture, than I've learned since we first encountered them. For instance—for instance—one of the reasons they're so wary about formalizing relations between us is their grasp of *consequences*. They worry that because our functional lifespan is so short—you know, the time between maturity and senility—that we can't understand the ripple effects of the decisions we make and actually, when you think about it, probably they've got a point. The thing is, the Tok'ra I *really* need to talk to is Selmak, he's kind of like a walking talking Encyclopaedia Britannica of the Tok'ra race, when do you think would be a good time to—"

O'Neill held up both hands, ready to stuff the tape recorder down Daniel's throat if that was what it took to stem the flood. "Whoa! Daniel! Chill! You're talking in chipmunk and I can only listen in human."

Daniel grinned, then pressed his thumb tips to his eyes. "Sorry. Guess I got a little carried away."

"Ya think?"

"So how was your day? Can you fly a Goa'uld cargo ship yet?"

He shoved his hands in his pockets. "Actually, I can."

"I'm impressed."

"So's Selmak."

Daniel started gathering his scattered notes together. "How are you doing with that, anyway?"

"What, being surrounded by sn—Tok'ra?" He shrugged. "I'm fine."

"Really?" said Daniel, with one of his swift, piercing looks. "Are you sure? I'm not just talking about the Tok'ra. I know you're pissed off about having to come here. It feels like running away."

Hell yeah, it felt like running away. Running from Kinsey, that sanctimonious rat bastard. And trust Daniel to get that. "I told you," he grunted. "I'm fine. What's not to love about Vorash? And the Tok'ra. They're not Goa'uld. They're anti-Goa'uld. Which is the point, I believe."

"Well," said Daniel, clearly not convinced, "if it helps at all, I think your dark cloud's got a seriously silver lining."

"I'll try to remember that. Daniel . . ."

"What?"

Against all expectation O'Neill felt his heart-rate increase. Felt an uncomfortable tightening in his gut. He had to fight not to look away from Daniel's curious face. "Carter seems to think we need to talk."

A shutter dropped behind Daniel's eyes, rendering them opaque.

Once upon a time the man had been as transparent as glass, incapable of shielding his thoughts, his feelings, from anyone. But that was before Apophis had stolen Sha're. Before he'd held her lifeless body in his arms. Before any number of other hurts had left him scarred in body and soul. He started putting the tops back on his scattered variety of pens.

"Really."

"Do you know what about?"

"I can guess."

"Well? Is she right? Is there something you wanted to say to me? About the Eurondan mission?"

Daniel shrugged. "Not really."

O'Neill's guts tightened further. Daniel had learned to mask his feelings from some people, yes, but not him. "Which means yes, but you don't think there's any point."

"I didn't say that."

"You didn't have to," he retorted. "Reading you is about as hard as getting through 'See Spot Run.'"

"Jack..." With a sigh, Daniel stopped stuffing pens back into their case. "Not now, okay? Let's just focus on this mission for now. We're making excellent progress, some really good things could come out of this. Let's not spoil it. At least not yet."

Spoil it? "Daniel, what the hell do you want from me? I apologized, didn't I? I admitted you were right and I was wrong and I made sure nobody like Kinsey could get their hands on Alar and start making deals that you couldn't live with. What else—"

Daniel started as though he'd been shot. "*What*? Are you saying you killed him for *me*?"

"*No*! I'm saying—hell, Daniel, I don't know what I'm saying!" O'Neill retorted, unnerved by the dreadful look in Daniel's eyes. "I just—"

Daniel shoved his chair backwards, and stood. "Jack, I don't want to do this. Euronda is done with. Nothing you or I say about it now can change what happened and frankly, I'm sick of thinking about it. We're here on Vorash to do some good. Let's talk about that, instead. Okay? Do you think we can do that?"

Searing, white-hot silence. Beyond the rec hall's open doorway a steady increase in foot-traffic, as off-duty Tok'ra operatives made their way to the mess hall, and dinner. Their passing conversations were jumbled, indistinct, but they sounded cheerful.

Subdued, stunned by a self-discovery he hadn't been expecting, O'Neill nodded. "Sure, Daniel. We can do that."

"Okay. Good." The relief in Daniel's voice was overwhelming. "I've got to go stow these notes. I'll see you in the mess hall, okay?"

"Yeah. Whatever."

Daniel departed. O'Neill stood alone in the Tok'ra recreation hall, lacking the will to move.

You killed him?

It was the first time Daniel had admitted he thought Alar had been killed on purpose. Not by accident, or through ignorance. On purpose. By him.

For me?

Oh, crap.

He'd lost his appetite but he went to dinner anyway. Carter was waxing rhapsodical about her day, and how much she'd gained from talking to some of the base's human operatives.

"Dad was right," she said. "About what I know from Jolinar, without realizing that I know it. When I was talking to them I could—I don't know—feel things about them. Tell which ones would make good hosts, and which ones wouldn't."

"How?" said Daniel. Inevitably, he looked fascinated.

"Beats me," said Carter, shrugging. "But I tested myself on a group of humans who've already been assessed as potential hosts. I was one hundred percent accurate. When the mission's a go and we're on the slave farm, I'll definitely be able to choose the best candidates for recruitment."

Even though it was good news, O'Neill frowned. It was galling to discover that Jacob was right. "You've changed your tune, haven't you?"

Surprised, she looked at him. "Sir?"

"Last time I looked you weren't too thrilled about having a snake in your head."

She flushed. "Jolinar was a long time ago. Since then I've got to know Martouf a lot better. And of course there's my dad. Besides, sir, it turns out I owe Jolinar a thing or two. Without her I wouldn't have saved Dad from Sokar ... and I couldn't participate in this mission."

Yeah. Right. Let's hear it for Jolinar. "Okay," he said.

With a last concerned glance, she turned to Teal'c. "What about you? How was your day?"

"Successful," said Teal'c. "I spent it describing the life of a typical Jaffa warrior to a group of Tok'ra operatives. Both Martouf and Aldwyn said afterwards they had gained much insight from my revelations." His eyes glimmered with dry amusement. "The Tok'ra are more used to killing Jaffa or giving them orders when they pretend to be Goa'ulds, than seeing us as potential allies."

"And they're treating you okay?" said Daniel. "I mean, nobody's giving you a hard time because you were Apophis's First Prime?"

For a moment Teal'c didn't answer. Then he released an almost imperceptible sigh. "There have been no active demonstrations of hostility, Daniel Jackson. Nevertheless I did sense, in some of the Tok'ra present, an air of tension. It is only to be expected. The Jaffa are sworn enemies of the Tok'ra, and have slaughtered thousands of them over the centuries. Trust between us can be built. It *must* be built, if we are to unite and defeat the Goa'uld. But trust is not built overnight. We must be patient. All of us."

O'Neill pulled a little face; that commentary had been directed right at him. "I'm beat," he said, standing. "I think I'll turn in."

They bade him goodnight, and he headed for his quarters with a detour via the communications room so he could give Hammond an update.

"*Jack, I was wondering when I'd hear from you,*" said the general through the audio-uplink to home. He wasn't even trying to hide his relief. "*Is everything okay?*"

"If you mean have I single-handedly dismantled the base and the cordial relations between the Tok'ra and the SGC, the answer's no, sir. Everything's fine."

"*That's not what I meant and you know it,*" said Hammond, reproving.

It was ridiculous, how cheered he felt just by hearing that brusque, familiar voice. "Yes, sir. Everything's fine, sir. How's life at your end?"

"*The same as you left it,*" said Hammond. "*Busy. When do you head out on Jacob's mission?*"

"Don't know yet. Apparently there's still some political in-fighting to sort out. But soon, I hope. The scenery here is kind of boring. Not enough green."

"*Hang in there, Colonel.*"

"Yes, sir." He took a deep, uncomfortable breath. "Sir—are there any developments with the Kinsey situation?"

"*Yes, as it happens.*" It sounded like Hammond was smiling. "*Senator Kinsey has a great deal more to worry about than you at the moment, Jack. Seems one of his trusted personal aides has been caught with a hand in the cookie jar. The press is having a field day.*"

"Gosh, sir. How sad for him."

"*Yes, I thought you'd be heartbroken,*" said Hammond, dryly. "*Colonel, I have to go. Is there anything you need?*"

"More food, sir," he said promptly. "Or Julia Childs, whichever is easier."

"*I take it Tok'ra cuisine isn't to your taste?*"

"They have cuisine?" He smiled. "We're fine, sir. Tell the President Daniel's got a good head start on the treaty."

"*He'll be pleased to hear it. Keep me apprised of your status, Colonel. Hammond out.*"

O'Neill disconnected the communications uplink and wandered the drearily all-alike corridors back to his quarters. There he sprawled on his bed and made notes in his own incomprehensible shorthand about intelligence sharing issues that Daniel needed to include in his preliminary treaty outlines.

They were good notes. Sharp observations. Relevant enquiries. Like a bear emerging from hibernation his command instincts were coming back to life. For the first time since Euronda he was feeling like a Special Ops expert again. Like *himself* again.

It was only just starting to dawn on him, how much Euronda had knocked the confidence that these days he took for granted. But now the fog was lifting.

It was about damn time.

Are you saying you killed him for me?

"Shut up, Daniel!" he said to the crystal walls. "Can't you see I'm working, here?"

Refusing to be sidetracked, he focused again on his notes.

CHAPTER NINE

Jacob called the mission briefing for an hour before lunch the following day. Now that the last minute political wranglings were over and the moment of truth was upon them, he could admit to a certain level of trepidation. He wasn't just risking his own life with this plan, he was risking Sam's and her team's, too. And Martouf's. Of course he'd spent a large chunk of his Air Force career risking other people's lives for the greater good... but he'd never liked doing it. That was just one advantage about being Tok'ra: he risked his own life, and Selmak's, and hardly ever anyone else's. He didn't relish this return to the good old days.

Your daughter chose this life, Selmak reminded him. *As did her companions, and Martouf. They are seasoned warriors. Focus your energy on success, Jacob, not on failure.*

I know, he replied. I will.

"Good afternoon," he greeted his team as they took their seats around the briefing table. "Let's get down to business, shall we? The breeding farm Martouf and I have selected as our target is one of the hundreds operated by the Goa'uld System Lord Yu, whom I believe SG-1 has already met. This particular farm is located on Panotek, a habitable moon orbiting a gas giant on the outskirts of Yu's territory."

He flipped a switch, activating a holographic projector. With a low-pitched hum a slowly rotating three-dimensional representation of the planet and its three moons appeared above the briefing table.

"The first thing to note is there's no 'gate access to this facility, which means we'll have to go in by ship.

"No Stargate?" said Daniel, frowning at the hologram. "Is that safe?"

"It's not *un*safe," Jacob said. "And the target is our best bet strategically. Panotek is located a long way from Yu's central administration centre. Goa'uld traffic is light."

"You mean he doesn't drop by once a week to visit and gloat?" said Jack.

"He doesn't drop by, period. Over the centuries Yu has conquered a vast area. Because of his empire's size, and since he frequently skirmishes with other system lords, he doesn't have time to administer it all himself. He's got a whole cadre of minor Goa'uld lordlings who take care of the day-to-day housekeeping chores."

"Like breeding humans," murmured Daniel. His face was screwed up in disgust.

Jacob nodded. "Exactly. And the lordling in charge of this sector is so busy trying to scheme his way into a position of real influence he doesn't have time to pay close attention to a single human slave farm."

Frowning, Jack said, "Okay. Sounds promising. What about the farm's security?"

"It's minimal. In fact, the lack of Stargate access *is* the security, pretty much. There's a small garrison of Jaffa stationed there, with a cargo ship and four gliders, and that's all."

"So how will you get us in?" said Sam. "They won't be expecting us. You don't think it'll make the Jaffa suspicious, us turning up on their doorstep out of the blue?"

"They're not paid to be suspicious. Or to question the orders of a Goa'uld. That's who I'll be impersonating when I deliver you into their tender care. Just another of Yu's lordlings doing his master's bidding."

"Deliver us as what?"

"Fresh blood, to prevent inbreeding."

"Actually, Jacob," said Jack, "it's not the getting in part I'm worried about. It's the getting out again. Especially if we're leaving with some new friends."

"That is true," said Martouf. "A successful withdrawal is likely to be challenging."

Jack turned to Teal'c. "He's got a lovely turn of phrase, hasn't he? 'Likely to be challenging'. I wonder what that means, exactly?"

"It means," said Jacob, before Jack could really warm to his theme, "that to a certain extent we're going to have to play it by ear."

"But if we just vanish into thin air," said Sam, "with or without other slaves, won't that create a huge panic?"

"It might," said Martouf, "in a sector controlled by a different lordling. We chose this particular farm in part because the lordling who rules it has in the past allowed ambition to override his feudal obligations."

"Four years ago," Jacob added, "a plague broke out on the farm. Choulai covered it up rather than admit to Yu he let over thirty slaves die needlessly."

Daniel cleared his throat. "And you know this how?"

"We have excellent intelligence."

"So, Jacob, you're sending us into a *plague* zone?" said Jack.

"Of course not," he snapped. "The disease has long since been eradicated."

Jack's expression was skeptical. "According to your excellent intelligence."

"That's right."

"And you're banking this Choulai character will just fiddle the books so Yu never knows he's got cattle rustlers?"

"Actually, sir," said Sam, "it's not an unreasonable assumption. Not if he's determined to keep a clean record and provided we're only talking about a handful of individuals. Covering up the loss of a few slaves wouldn't be too hard. I'm betting that humans die all the time on these farms. Accidents. Childbirth. Illness."

"It is even possible that the Jaffa in charge might lie to save themselves from retribution for incompetence," added Teal'c. "It would not be the first time."

Jack turned to Teal'c. "Really?"

Teal'c nodded. "Yes."

"Cool. Nice to know that 'covering your ass' is a universal constant."

"So Jacob," said Daniel. "These breeding farms. How are they set up, exactly?"

"For the most part as regular farms, actually," he said. "They're almost completely self-sustaining. The humans raise a variety of crops and livestock, to feed themselves and other parts of Yu's empire—"

"And in their spare time they raise little babies," said Daniel, fingers tight around his unused pen, "which grow up to become slaves. Great. Am I the only one here who feels like puking?"

"No, Daniel, you're not," said Jack, forestalling other comments.

"But before you start getting any radical ideas, here's the deal. No matter what we find when we get onto this moon, no matter how offended your sensibilities are by this whole slave farm thing, we *do not* rock the boat. This *is not* a rescue mission. We *are not* going there to free the slaves. We have a single objective: to recruit hosts and spies for the Tok'ra. That's it. Are you reading me, Kunta Kinte?"

Daniel blinked. "Jack?"

Jacob exchanged a look with Martouf, then considered the others. As usual, Teal'c's expression was inscrutable. Sam was frowning, her gaze lowered, the muscles in her jaw tense. Jack leaned forward across the table, pointed finger jabbing.

"You know what I'm talking about, Daniel. Once we're in place there will be no arguing. There will be no passionate speeches about the rights of man. There will be no heated debate on the ethics of leaving tiny babies to grow up as Goa'uld slaves. *This* time we're going in with our eyes open. *This* time we know exactly what we're letting ourselves in for. *This* time if you cross me it will be for the last time. Do you get it now? Or do I have to draw you a map?"

Electric silence. Then Daniel shook his head. "No. You've made yourself perfectly clear."

Jack sat back. "Good."

Jacob cleared his throat. "Okay," he continued, because they still had stuff to get through, "what we don't want to do is hang around longer than absolutely necessary. Once you're part of the slave population you'll mingle, you'll chat, you'll identify the people most open to questioning the Goa'uld and taking direct action against them, so that Sam can assess their suitability for recruitment."

"What's our operational timeframe?" said Sam.

"A week, max. First time out I want to play things safe. At the end of seven days, or sooner if you get lucky, Martouf and I will pull you and any volunteers out of there."

"But we must make one thing clear," Martouf added. "Only those slaves willing to risk their lives for the Tok'ra will be taken off Panotek. And you cannot promise them freedom as an incentive to gain their co-operation. They must first prove their worthiness by expressing a desire to fight the Goa'uld."

"And what will you two be doing while we're fomenting rebellion?" said Jack.

"Martouf and I will be standing by ready to scoop and run at the first sign of trouble," Jacob replied. "Either in cloaked orbit, or somewhere safe on the ground. You'll all have Tok'ra communicators. We'll never be out of touch."

Teal'c frowned. "I wish to once again state my objection to not being included on this mission."

"Sorry, Teal'c," said Jacob. "I've weighed the pros and cons a dozen times, but I think it's just too risky. If the worst happened and we fell into enemy hands we could bluff our way out, but you'd be recognized as the First Prime who defied Apophis. That nifty gold brand of yours is as good as your name in flashing neon lights and it doesn't rub off."

"See?" Jack murmured. "That'll teach you to be famous." Then he sighed. "I hate to say it, but Jacob's right. This is one time your defiance of Apophis won't be a rallying cry to the troops. You need to sit this one out, Teal'c."

After a moment, Teal'c nodded. "Very well. I will not speak of this again."

"And that about wraps it up," Jacob said. "Anyone have a que—"

"I do," said Daniel, raising a finger. "The slaves we—" He pulled a face. "*Recruit*. They'll be given Tok'ra symbiotes and sent back in to spy on Yu or some other Goa'uld, yes?"

"Some will become Tok'ra," said Martouf. "Others will remain human and be placed on another slave farm to recruit among the humans there."

"Go back to being slaves, in other words."

"Yes. But it will be their choice, Daniel," Martouf said solemnly.

"And what happens if it turns out they aren't suitable as hosts and don't want to be spy slaves? Or they *are* suitable hosts but don't want a symbiote. What happens to them then?"

Jacob swallowed a sigh. He was starting to see where Jack was coming from. "Daniel, don't worry. We've got a range of options we're considering. Let's not get ahead of ourselves, shall we?"

"Yeah," said Daniel. He didn't sound convinced. Just temporarily silenced. "Okay."

"Good. So now we can move onto the next phase of the mission."

"Next phase?" said Jack delicately, after a pause. "Jacob, all the hairs just stood up on the back of my neck."

He pulled a face. "I'm sorry. I didn't think there was any point getting into the fine print before I had to. We've got some costuming issues to sort out—Yu's slaves don't generally wear combat fatigues—and then there's the matter of the brands."

Jack's eyebrows shot up. "*Brands*?"

"All of Yu's human slaves are branded shortly after birth," Martouf explained. "It is a common Goa'uld practice. You will all be branded with his device, painlessly, so as not to arouse suspicions. Once the mission is complete we will reverse the procedure."

Jack slapped the table. "Hey, Marty! D'you happen to remember what I said to you that time back in the SGC? You know? About *surprises*?"

"Blame me, Jack," said Jacob. "I wanted to keep this low key till I was sure it'd happen."

Jack turned to Teal'c. "I'm assuming that as a former First Prime you knew about this? Why didn't you say something?"

Teal'c shrugged. "I thought you knew, O'Neill. At least your procedure will be painless. It was not so for me, or for the human slaves you will encounter."

"Gee," said Sam, no happier than Jack. "That's comforting. Where are we supposed to be getting this little souvenir, anyway? 'Cause if we're talking anywhere below the belt you can—"

"The back of the shoulder is a common location," said Martouf. "I am sorry, Samantha. I truthfully had no idea this would be a matter of concern for you."

"Hey, no, don't give it another thought," said Jack. "We *love* to mutilate ourselves in the name of duty."

Jacob looked at his daughter. "Sam…"

She glared. "Don't you 'Sam' me, Dad. You should've told us."

"I did. Just now, when it became germane to the mission. Hey, kiddo," he added, as she continued to glare. "You say you want me to treat you like just another warrior? Okay. Fine. This is me, treating you like just another warrior."

She subsided, very close to pouting, just as she'd pouted as a teenager. He could've hugged her.

"Carter?" said Jack. Clearly inviting her opinion. Her refusal.

She drummed her fingers on the briefing table. "You're absolutely sure it's non-permanent, Dad?"

He crossed his heart. "I swear."

She let out a gusty sigh, rolling her eyes, then looked at Jack. "Hey, it can't be as bad as wearing that stupid head-dress for the Shavedai."

They exchanged swift, private smiles. Jack looked at Daniel. "How about you?"

Daniel shrugged. "Whatever."

"*Daniel*—"

"What? There's no need to bite my head off, Jack. Jacob says we need a brand then fine. We need a brand."

Jack hesitated, thought about saying something else, then changed his mind. "So, Jacob, is that it? Is that the only surprise you've got in store?"

"The only surprise I know about? Yes, Jack. But I can't guarantee there won't be more down the track."

"Of course you can't. Where's the fun in that?" Jack retorted. He let his head drop, then looked up. "So... is that it? We get branded, we get costumed, we head out?"

"Yeah. That's pretty much it. So if there aren't any more questions I suggest we break for lunch and meet up at the infirmary in an hour's time. We'll get the medical stuff taken care of, find you some appropriate clothing and then take off. The cargo ship is prepped and waiting."

"*Medical stuff*," said Jack, still unimpressed. "Gotta love those Tok'ra euphemisms."

Just as George had told him, the best way to handle Jack O'Neill in this mood was to develop sudden deafness. "*Are* there any other questions?"

Sam shook her head. "Not from me."

"Daniel?"

Another headshake. "No."

Jacob switched off the hologram. "Okay then. See you in an hour."

Without another word Daniel shoved his chair back and left the room. Sam and Jack stared after him. "Dammit," Jack muttered, and pushed to his feet.

"You did bite him pretty hard, sir," said Sam.

Jack turned on her. "Because I'm not interested in a repeat of our last mission, Carter. I want to make sure we're all on the same page this time. Do you have a problem with that?"

She sighed. "No, sir."

"Pleased to hear it."

"Maybe I should go talk to him, sir."

"Carter—"

"Please."

For a long moment Jack looked at her, his expression cold and set. Then it thawed a little, and he nodded. "Fine."

"Thank you," she said, and went after Daniel.

Jacob looked at Jack. "Is this going to be a problem, Colonel?"

"No," Jack said. "No problem at all."

"Are you sure? Because once you and your team are in place the margin for error will be practically non-existent. If Daniel isn't totally on board then—"

"He's on board, Jacob."

"Perhaps you should speak to Daniel Jackson yourself, O'Neill," Teal'c said reluctantly. "If he should once more allow his heart to rule his head, even with good cause…"

"The consequences could be fatal," said Martouf. "For the Earth-Tok'ra alliance, as well as us."

"Sorry, Jack. I'm with Teal'c on this," said Jacob. "You're Daniel's team leader. I'd feel a lot more relaxed if you made absolutely certain he knows what he's getting himself into with this mission, and that none of us can afford him losing sight of the big picture."

For a long time Jack stared at the floor. Then he nodded. "Sure," he said, looking up. "No sweat. I'll sort it out."

Sam just missed stopping Daniel from ringing to Vorash's surface. Dancing with impatience she waited for the device to return, then followed him up.

The wind was busy again, gusting sand-laden across the barren landscape. Running to catch him, wincing as her exposed face was scoured with grit, she shouted, "Daniel! Daniel, wait!"

For a moment she thought he was going to ignore her. Then he slowed, stopped and turned. Behind his glasses his eyes were hurt. Angry. "If you've come out here to defend him, Sam, don't bother. I don't want to hear it."

She stepped back, stung, all her good intentions, her sympathy for his inevitable misgivings, evaporating in the face of his intransigence. "What do you want to hear, then? That he's wrong because he's Jack O'Neill? Is that your default position now, Daniel?"

"No!"

"Then what?"

"Sam..." His clenched fists lifted. "I'm not a military robot, okay? I never have been, and if Jack thinks he can turn me into one he's deluding himself."

"Nobody's asking you to be a robot, Daniel!" she snapped, and wrapped her arms around her ribs. She should've grabbed a jacket. "But we're not a symposium of random academics debating the latest theory! We're SG-1, a team, and as a team we need to follow the same game plan. We need to know we've got each other's backs!"

His head came up as though she'd struck him. "When have I *ever* not had your back?"

She looked at him steadily. "Do you really want me to answer that?"

"Oh here we go," he said, and turned away. "You'll never let me forget it, will you? How many more times do I have to apologize for Shyla, Sam? Put my life on the line for you before you let that one go?"

"That's not fair, Daniel," she said. "I have *never* thrown Shyla in your face. Not once. None of us have, and you know it. But since you bring it up—admit it. *Sometimes* you let your heart rule your head and *sometimes* that's been a problem for the rest of us."

"And sometimes it's been the only thing that's saved us," he retorted. "*You* admit *that*."

"I do! God, Daniel, how many times have I gone to bat for you with the colonel?"

"Then why won't you take my side this time?"

"Because this time *your* side is the *wrong* side!" she shouted. "It's his job to make sure you understand the ground rules, Daniel."

"Fine! But that doesn't mean he has to jump down my throat,

does it?"

"Maybe! You do have a habit of marching to your own drum, you know! And you made it pretty clear back there you aren't happy about the idea of Goa'uld slave breeding farms."

He turned on her. "Are you?"

"Of course not! But that isn't the point," she said, and on a deep breath made an effort to moderate her tone. "Daniel, what the hell is going on? You've known from the start what this mission's aims are: infiltration and recruitment. It was *never* about liberating the slaves."

He shrugged. "I know," he said, his voice unsteady. "I guess it's just... until now there was a chance the mission wouldn't happen. Until now, I could push the cold hard facts to the back of my mind. Focus on other things, like drafting this Earth-Tok'ra treaty. But now we have a go and I can't pretend any more. I can't —" He stopped. Frowned. "Oh, God. I can't do this, either."

She turned. It was the colonel, jacket collar turned up, trudging through the whipping wind towards them. He looked... resigned. All his anger dissolved, or at least safely leashed. Somehow, between the briefing room and the surface, he'd found his way to understanding. Solid and imposing by his side, seemingly oblivious to the flying sand, Teal'c.

"It's okay, Carter," the colonel said, joining them. "I've got it."

With an anguished glance at Teal'c, she stepped back.

All of the colonel's focus was on Daniel. "You didn't think it through, did you," he said quietly. His voice was remarkably... kind.

Daniel opened his mouth. Closed it. Shook his head. "No."

"That was stupid."

"Yes, I guess it was."

The colonel's eyebrows lifted. "You *guess*?"

Daniel held up his hands. "All right. Yes. It was stupid."

She flicked another glance at Teal'c, who returned it without revealing a thing, then looked at Daniel and the colonel as they looked at each other in frustrated, baffled silence.

They'd never had an easy relationship. Probably they never would. But something tied them, some weird chemistry she'd never understand. She doubted they understood it, either. But it glued them together, kept them in mutual orbit when so often, too often, they opposed each other like boxers in the ring.

The colonel sighed. "Do you understand my position, Daniel?"

"Yes," said Daniel. "Always. But do you understand mine?"

"Yeah. For once, I do. Trust me, I'm not looking forward to infiltrating a Goa'uld slave farm any more than you are. I think the whole idea sucks."

"Then why agree to do it?"

"*Because*, you idiot," the colonel said, with his typical tact, "it might just be the first step along the road to destroying *all* Goa'uld slave farms. Not just one of Yu's hundreds. Do you *get* that, Daniel? Do you get it's not about winning one battle, it's about winning the whole damned war?"

Daniel's arms moved in a gesture that mirrored his strangled feelings. "*Yes*, Jack. I *get* that. I just…"

The colonel stepped forward, and briefly rested a hand on Daniel's tense shoulder. "I know. Daniel, I know. And I'm sorry. I wish there was another way. And I wish I could say it was okay for you to sit this one out, no harm, no foul. But the truth is we're going to need you. It kills me to say it, but I think we'll fail without you."

This time when Sam glanced at Teal'c, he nodded. So she risked adding her two cents' worth. "He's right, Daniel. You have a gift for inspiring trust. The colonel and I, we might be able to protect them. But you're the one who can reach them."

"If your positions were reversed, Daniel Jackson," said Teal'c. "If you were a slave on a Goa'uld breeding farm. Would you not wish for someone who could give you a chance to strike back at your oppressors?"

Reluctantly, Daniel nodded. "I guess."

"Every time I engage in battle with the Goa'uld," said Teal'c, his voice heavy with regret, "I kill my brother Jaffa. Jaffa I do not know, who might well burn for freedom as I burned whilst still a slave to Apophis. Every time, I wish that I could save them. Offer them the freedom the Tauri have given me. I cannot. So I must hope—I must *believe*—that my actions will one day lead to freedom for all my people. For the sons and daughters of the Jaffa I have fought, and killed, never knowing if they would have joined me had I been able to ask."

The colonel said, "Daniel. I won't lie. This mission's going to be rough. Not just on you, on all of us. You think Carter doesn't want to save those people? You think *I* don't? Of course we do. And leaving them behind will be hell. But it'll be worth it in the long run."

"You're certain of that?"

"*Yes*. Daniel, I want you with us. But only if you can promise me you'll stay focused on the objective, no matter what. Because I meant what I said before. If you change your tune half-way through it really will be over."

"If I say no," said Daniel, after a long silence. "If I say I can't trust myself not to … you know. What happens then?"

The colonel shrugged. "Carter and I'll go anyway. There's a lot at stake."

"You'll go. Even though you think you'll fail without me?"

The merest hint of a smile touched the colonel's lips. "I may have been exaggerating. A bit. You know me, always running my mouth."

Daniel's smile was equally ghostlike. "Yeah. It's what I've always admired about you, Jack. Your loquacity."

"*Are* you saying you can't trust yourself?"

"I'm saying…" Daniel shoved his hands in his pockets. "I'm saying this sucks, all right? I'm saying it's not fair, nobody should be bred into slavery, there should be a way to save them all. Even though … I know … there isn't."

The colonel nodded. "Amen. Which means we do what we can, where and when we can, and we pray that in the long run it'll be enough. So, Daniel. Are you in, or are you out?"

Sam held her breath. This was it. This was the moment. If Daniel agreed to come they'd muddle through their differences somehow, just like they always did. But if he said no…

"Fine. I'm in," said Daniel. "And I'll do my absolute level best to be a good little soldier. But I'm *not* wearing pink, okay?" He folded his arms to underscore the point. "Pink is not my color. And I'm not keen on the idea of prancing around half-naked, either. I mean, I've seen how the Goa'uld dress their slaves, you know? I'm an archaeologist, not an escapee from Chippendales. No pink, and no skimpy bolero-type tops. Are we clear?"

The colonel came as close to grinning as he ever did. "As crystal.

Don't worry, Daniel. Carter can wear the skimpy bolero. In fact I think she'd look totally *fetching* in a skimpy bolero. Don't you?"

They all looked at her: the colonel, Daniel, Teal'c. The guys. Waiting, just waiting, for an outraged feminist response. She shrugged.

"Not fetching. Hot. I would look *hot* in a skimpy bolero. And for your information? I was *born* to wear pink."

Smothering a wide smile, she turned and headed for the transport ring platform, leaving them speechless in her wake.

CHAPTER TEN

"Papa! Papa, come quick! Jaffa!" Boaz dropped his hoe amongst the corn rows, guts clenching with sudden fear. Jaffa? Why? The next culling was months away. None of the women were due to give birth this week. Nobody was sick, or injured beyond healing, so there was no need for a killing. Why else would Hol'c and his underlings leave the comfort of their palace and come down to the village in the hot sun? What could they want?

Wiping a sleeve across his face he stepped out of the cornfield and waited for his son Mikah to reach him. Tall and beautiful and still only nine, five years before he'd be culled, the thought of his boy's taking like the sharpest knife buried in his bowels.

"Hol'c sends for you, Papa," Mikah panted, his bare chest sticky with dirt and sweat. Like some of the other grown children he'd been at work in the shucking house. "A Goa'uld is here, with strangers."

It frightened Boaz, putting Mikah to work with the long-bladed shucking knives, but he couldn't play favorites. Every child took its turn in the shucking house; it was the rule. But there were no cuts on Mikah's bare arms, so he was safe. Relief flooded him: blemished slaves were unacceptable to the god, and met no happy end.

"Goa'uld?" he said, letting Mikah take his callused hand and tug him along the rutted path between the cornfields, back to the village. "What Goa'uld? Not Lord Choulai, you mean?" Curious faces peered as they hurried by, but nobody stopped working. Nobody was so foolish.

"No, a different one. Hol'c is afraid of him," Mikah whispered.

Hol'c? Afraid? "And who are the strangers?"

"Humans. New slaves."

"Ah." Boaz felt his twisting guts relax. So this was nothing more dangerous than fresh blood. A nuisance, to be sure. Fresh blood always upset the community's balance. Sometimes Lord Choulai decreed a man should leave his woman and mate with someone new. Or a woman bear the children of a new man. Nobody protested, at least not out loud, when such decrees were made. Protesters were punished. But still there were tears and sometimes raised fists, in private, where the Jaffa would not see.

But in the end, they did as they were told. How could they do otherwise? Disobedience was death.

"Tell me of the new slaves, Mikah," he said, as they jogged towards the distant village buildings.

"Two men and a woman," said Mikah. His dark curls bounced as he ran. "They have good faces. Strong bodies. They'll work their share hard. The woman looks kind." Mikah's gaze flickered upwards. "Maybe the Goa'uld will give her to you, Papa. Then you won't be lonely."

He'd had no permanent mate since Nona died in childbirth last season, and the baby with her. She'd been given him in place of Mikah's mother, who'd been lost to plague with all but one of his other children in that bad, bad time nobody talked about. Nona's sire Ferek had blamed him for the young woman's death, but then Ferek had never been right in the head. Ferek's last two get had been disfigured by birthmarks so when he raised ruckus over Nona, Hol'c had him plowed into the barley field as fertiliser, his bones to mix with hers and the child's.

He missed Nona. He even missed Ferek, for all his troublesome ways.

"Maybe the Goa'uld will," he said, patting Mikahs's head, and wondered if that were true. He'd be pleased if it was. Five of the farm's women would birth his get sometime before season's turn, but that wasn't the same as a familiar warm woman beside him, night after night.

He and Mikah jogged on, past green wheat and grubby sheep and soon enough reached the village centre where sometimes men were killed like bullocks, or women stripped and whipped for bearing ugly babies, and children chained and taken away, their faraway fates never disclosed to the silently grieving. Where the tall golden statue of Yu, their great god, stood in splendor, a constant reminder of his might.

Attended by two underlings, Hol'c stood before the statue, waiting with the unknown Goa'uld lord. He was sweating in his Jaffa armor, staff weapon in one hand, fire-brand in the other. Hol'c liked to use the fire-brand on the human slaves everyone knew he thought of as his. He loved the flames that poured from their eyes and mouths as they screamed their torment, punishment for crimes large and small. There was no saying what could provoke his wrath. Sometimes a slave's only crime was to stand too near when the hurting mood was on him.

Kneeling on the brick-paved ground before Hol'c and the unknown Goa'uld were the three new slaves. Two men, one woman. As he and Mikah approached, walking now, Boaz looked them over closely. All were dressed in fine silk tunics and trousers, green and crimson and clear sky blue. Breeding farm slaves were never gifted with such finery. It was a puzzle.

Mikah was right, though; the woman's face was kind. Beautiful too, of course. He felt himself stir, seeing her, and hoped she'd be his reward for all the good get he'd already sired, and the many babies yet unborn. The younger man was also beautiful. He would do well mated with Diera, once she was emptied of her current get. But that was Lord Choulai's decision. Humans did not choose their own mates. The older man was plain of face but his body was strong, and tall, and comely. Though his hair was turning silver he must still have vigor. For his life's sake, he'd better. If not he'd soon join Ferek in the barley field. But if he was still a man, then mated with the right woman his get would be beautiful in face and form and so prove pleasing to Lord Yu, God of Gods, Mightiest of the Mighty.

Upon reaching the waiting group he and Mikah threw themselves to the ground, face first, and waited for permission to rise.

"*Stand*," said the Goa'uld who wasn't Lord Choulai. "*And answer my questions.*"

He and Mikah scrambled to their feet and bowed. "My lord," he said. "My life is yours."

This Goa'uld lord was tall, and losing his hair. Even though he was dressed in gold and turquoise magnificence he was not beautiful. Boaz marvelled. It was the first time he'd ever seen a servant of Yu who was not perfect in face and form. He felt his knees tremble. What power did this Goa'uld have, then, that he could serve Yu and not be beautiful?

No wonder Hol'c was sweating.

The Goa'uld's eyes flashed white fire. "*I am Lord Rebec, servant of our god Yu. The Jaffa Hol'c tells me you are Boaz, senior human in this place. Is this so?*"

"My lord, I am Boaz, head slave of this village. Property of Yu, the grand and glorious."

"*The child?*"

"This child is my son Mikah, property of our god."

Lord Rebec nodded, satisfied. "*Here is more of Yu's property, Boaz. The woman is Serena. The men are Joseph and David. All three are highly valued by our god. Yu decrees Serena and Joseph be mated together, and David be put to a woman of this village. Where are your empty women, that I might assess their suitability?*"

He felt a surge of pride. The humans here served their god well. "My lord, we have no empty women of breeding age."

Lord Rebec frowned. "*I see. Hol'c?*"

The Jaffa stepped forward, chin pressed to his chest in respect. "My lord?"

Lord Rebec bestowed on him a chilly smile. "*Our god is well satisfied with this farm. The property Lord Choulai breeds here is pleasing to his eye. When the women who survive childbirth are ready to be mated, Lord Choulai will choose the one best suited for David.*"

"Yes, my lord. Thank you, my lord."

"*Continue your stewardship here, Hol'c,*" said Lord Rebec. "*My report to our god will reflect your good service to him.*"

"Thank you, my lord," said Hol'c. His voice was puffed with self-congratulation. "I live to serve our god Yu."

"*And provided all continues here undisturbed, you will continue to do so,*" said Lord Rebec, eyes flashing once more. "*I will be watching.*"

The warning was subtle, but not lost on Hol'c. The Jaffa's fingers tightened into fists, then relaxed. "My lord."

So, this Goa'uld Lord Rebec was sent to oversee the overseers? That had never happened before. Boaz felt curiosity stir, and swiftly crushed it. Humans did not survive curiosity. Or at least, not for long.

Lord Rebec touched a crystal on his wrist-band. "*Our god Yu wishes my visit here to remain shrouded in mystery, Hol'c. To disobey his will—*"

"My lord!" cried Hol'c, and dropped to one knee before cold

Lord Rebec. "I serve the god, as do my Jaffa! All glory to the great god Yu, Mighty and Everlasting!"

Lord Rebec nodded, and stepped away. "*Until my next visit, Hol'c, which will be soon. Glory to the great god Yu, Mighty and Everlasting.*" He touched another crystal on his wrist-guard. Moments later a ship's transporter rings descended upon him, and he was taken from them in a burst of blinding blue-white light.

Because it was safe now, Hol'c laughed, and turned to his Jaffa. "See how I am noticed and blessed? This farm pleases our god!" The other Jaffa nodded and smiled. "*Boaz!*"

He bowed. "Sir?"

"Tell these *humans*—" One by one, he slapped the bowed heads of the new slaves. "— *why* it is that this farm pleases Mighty and Everlasting Yu!"

Boaz felt his heart sink. Poor new blood. They had no idea what Hol'c was like ... but they were about to learn.

"Sir, this farm breeds beautiful humans. This farm is a place of peace and perfect obedience to the great god Yu, whose will is made known to us by Jaffa Master Hol'c. Jaffa Master Hol'c is the voice and the hand of Yu in this place, and we serve him as we serve the god."

"Tell these humans, Boaz, what happens to slaves who forget these truths."

"Sir, the wind in the storm season is the howls of the humans who forget these truths."

Hol'c unclipped his fire-brand from his belt and touched the switch in its handle. The sound as it sprang to life was loud in the silence. Boaz felt all the muscles of his body tighten, and sweat break out on his brow. Beside him, Mikah swallowed a whimper. He wanted to hold his son, to shield him from Holc's cruelty.

He couldn't.

The slave with silver hair, the one Lord Rebec had called Joseph, looked up. Boaz felt a thrill of shocked surprise. The slave Joseph's face was full of defiance. In his eyes, anger and a grim endurance. It was not a face to be found on many slaves, and never more than once. Slaves who defied were slaves who died.

Or so was his experience.

Hol'c said, savoring the moment, "Perfect obedience is the only acceptable behavior from a slave. A slave who is not perfectly obedient is swiftly punished. Like this."

With the flat of his booted foot he pushed the woman Serena face-first to the ground. Then he pressed the fire-brand between her shoulder blades and watched, smiling, as she convulsed in pain. As she tried, and failed, to muffle her screams.

Holc's Jaffa were laughing, just as they always laughed when they or Hol'c punished a human. On either side of the screaming woman Joseph and David knelt in perfect obedience. Joseph's face, like David's, was blank now. Boaz frowned. Had he imagined its ferocity, a moment ago?

The woman Serena lost her wits, falling silent. Hol'c next touched the fire-brand to David and then, when he too was mercifully delivered from torment, finally to Joseph.

Joseph didn't scream.

At last it was over. Hol'c clipped the fire-brand back to his belt and said, "You are excused from fieldwork the rest of the day, Boaz. When the new blood wakes, explain to them the rules of this farm. They will share your roof until there is time to build new dwellings for them. Joseph and Serena are to mate from this night forth, tell them. Tell them she will quicken with his get by one month's end or both will be punished."

He bowed. "Sir."

Hol'c frowned down at Joseph, unmoving. "He is strong. Lord Rebec chose wisely."

Boaz watched him and his Jaffa walk away until they were gone from sight, then he turned to his son. "You'd best return to the shucking house, Mikah. There's hours of work light left yet."

"But I want to help you with—"

He slapped his son lightly on the rump. "You heard Hol'c. I am to see to the new blood. You can spread the word of their coming, in the shucking house and when you water the others in the fields, since it's your turn this moon."

Mikah sighed. "Yes, Papa," he said, and disconsolately trudged to do his duty.

The new blood was starting to stir. Boaz dropped to a crouch and rested a gentle hand on David's shoulder. "Move slowly," he advised. "Your body obeys you again and the worst of the pain is gone, but the fire-brand's flame lingers."

"I know," said David. "The fire-brand and I are old... friends." Accepting a helping hand, once he was sitting upright he turned to the woman. "Serena? You okay?" he said as she, too, slowly sat up.

Even when narrowed with the aftermath of pain, her eyes were wondrous. "Yeah," she said, and scrubbed dirt from her face. "Terrific. What happened to the bit about us coming to no harm?"

"There is no permanent harm from a fire-brand," said Boaz. "Only pain."

The man Joseph rolled over. "Crap," he said vaguely, forearm shading his eyes. "How much do I hate those things?"

"You okay, Joseph?" said Daniel. "Don't sit up too fast."

"Who's sitting up?" said Joseph. Turning his head, he touched the woman on her bare ankle. "Serena?"

"I'm fine... Joseph," she said.

Boaz stared. They were so easy with one another. And there was warmth in their voices that spoke of some affection. "You are not strangers?"

Joseph grunted. "Sure we're strangers. But it was a long trip from—where did we come from, Serena?"

"Farms on the other side of Yu's empire," she said. "I'm sorry—did I hear you say your name was Boaz?"

He nodded. Her voice... it was like warm honey. Strangely accented, like the men's. But beautiful, as she was beautiful. Regret welled, that she was already spoken to Joseph. "Yes. I am Boaz."

"And you're the—the village head man?"

"I am the man who has sired the most get," he said. "So I am the man who keeps order, and makes certain the things that must be done are done."

David said, "That Jaffa—the one with the fire-brand—"

"Hol'c."

"Yeah. Him. He said something about us building homes? How?"

Turning a little, he pointed to the brick-yard. "With the spare bricks, and hay for thatching. Did you not do this on the breeding farms you came from?"

With another grunt, Joseph sat up at last. "Yeah, well, the thing is, Boaz, we weren't on those farms for very long before we got sent here. We come from other planets in Yu's empire. Planets where humans don't live as breeding stock or build their own homes."

Puzzled, he stared at them. "I know of these other planets. They are where our get are sent after the culling. But you were born on breeding farms, so—"

"No," said David. "We weren't. We were born in a place where humans are not ruled by Jaffa, or the Goa'uld."

He laughed. "There are no places where humans are not ruled by the god and his servants."

"Yes, Boaz," said Serena. Her eyes were soft, and very sorry. "There are."

How could he disbelieve her? His laughter died. "Then speak not of them!" he hissed. "If Hol'c should hear you he will kill you and anyone who has heard your words. Not even Lord Rebec could save you."

The new blood exchanged looks. Then Joseph nodded. "Sure. Sorry, Boaz. Didn't mean to alarm you."

They were the strangest humans he'd ever met. "If you are strong enough to stand now we should go to the storehouse, so you might be clothed for working."

Joseph looked down at his jewelled green sleeveless tunic and trousers. "Too gaudy? Y'know, I kind of thought so."

Boaz rose from his crouch. He didn't understand this man, or like him. He was too different. In this place, being different was dangerous. In his bones he knew these new humans meant trouble for the village, and his mouth soured.

"It is clear from your clothing you are not humans who worked in fields with crops and animals, as we do here," he said. "Perhaps that's why you are strange."

One by one, the new humans stood. "It's one explanation," Joseph muttered.

Serena gave him a sharp look. "I'm sorry if we make you uneasy, Boaz," she said. "This is all very new to us. Until recently we were in service to Goa'ulds like Lord Rebec."

"Yes," said David, brushing the dirt from his crimson tunic. "But our lords displeased the god Yu, and so we were sent here. To serve in a different way."

"Here, David, there is only one way to serve our god," Boaz said severely. "And those who fail in that service are punished."

"Don't tell me," said Joseph. "Let me guess. They die."

"Of course they die, Joseph," he replied. "What use is a human that cannot serve?" He stepped back, one arm held wide. "The storehouse is this way."

They followed him in silence from the village centre to the workhouse. Reaching it, Boaz opened the door and led the new blood inside. As well as being used to keep such clothing as was not needed at the moment, the storehouse was where some of the farm's women worked as seamstresses, mending work clothes that were damaged but not beyond repair or sewing new work clothes to replace those that could not be salvaged. Upstairs, above the large work-tables where the women stitched and cut and kept close eye on the small children assigned to such tasks as sweeping and folding and gathering odds and ends, were the looms. More women worked at them now, the air beneath the workhouse roof clacked and rattled and hummed to the flying shuttles as they turned sheep wool into fine cloth for Yu and his many many lords in service. The place smelled of lanolin and fresh dyes and, faintly, of old urine.

No woman or child stopped working as Boaz and the new blood entered, of course. Only Hol'c and his Jaffa could stop a human working. And he could, if he was about Yu's business. But a woman could work and feed her eyes at the same time; all the women mending and stitching at the work-tables looked and looked at the three new humans. The children looked too, and their piping little voices fell silent, even as they scurried to their tasks.

Boaz pointed. "You, Rusha. To me."

Rusha's belly was only just rounding now, small and shy like a melon beneath its leaves. She put aside her shears and the knobby blue roughspun she was cutting, and came to him. "Boaz."

"Here are Serena and David and Joseph," he said, indicating each in turn. "Come to breed for Yu's glory. They need work clothes."

"Of course." She smiled at the new blood. "This way."

As she led them to the far side of the workhouse, where all the spare clothes, shoes and belts were stacked neatly by size on shelves, he busied himself with inspecting the work done that day. But even as he spoke with the other women, he kept part of his attention on the newcomers.

"These should fit," said Rusha, handing out shirts and trousers to the men, a shirt and a skirt to Serena. "Try them for size, and if they suit then I can give you more."

"Try them... here?" said Serena, sounding uncertain. "In the open? Is there nowhere to undress in private?"

"In private?" said Rusha, mystified. "No."

"Suck it up, Serena," said Joseph. He sounded almost... amused. "We won't peek if you don't."

Serena made a soft sound of scorn. "Me? What would I peek at, Joseph?"

Then came the slithering sound of silk, soft exhalations and little grunts, as the new humans shed their fine skins to become no finer than any breeding farm human.

When they were done, their silk tunics folded and put away, and their feet were laced into proper working shoes, plain leather belts about their waists, Boaz turned. He'd wanted to turn before that, to glimpse from the corner of his eye the strong sweeping line of Serena's back, the lithe length of her thigh from hip to knee, but that would be wrong. She wasn't his to look at. She was Joseph's.

Rusha was pulling more clothes down from the shelves and piling them into the newcomers' arms. "That should be enough," she said at last, once they each had two more sets of work clothing. "Wait here, and I will fetch you a bitty bag each."

"Bitty bag?" said David.

"You know," said Rusha, mystified again. "Comb. Razor. Small things in a bag."

"Of course," said Serena. "Thank you, Rusha. We'd appreciate that."

When they were given their bitty bags, and had inspected them to make sure all they needed was there, he ordered Rusha back to cutting the roughspun and led the new blood out of the workhouse, down the widest village road to his home. Inside it was cool and quiet. With Nona and her baby dead, with his other get dead as well, or culled, with only Mikah left, the house was always quiet. Or so it had been. Until the new blood's own homes were built there would be noise again.

How strange.

"You'll be here," he said to Joseph and Serena, opening the door to the room that until that morning had been his.

"It looks occupied," said Serena. "Is this yours?"

"It is the room with the mating bed," he said. "I have no mate. The room is yours."

"Ah…" Joseph cleared his throat. "You know, Boaz. About this whole 'mating' thing. I was thinking maybe Serena and I could kind of wait on that for a while. You know. Since we only just met…"

He stepped back and looked this Joseph up and down. "You are a stupid man," he said, not hiding his contempt. "And if you are not plowed into the barley field before the moon grows fat I shall be most surprised."

Joseph's eyes turned cold. "Stupid? Really? Gosh. Been a while since I was called that."

"I think what Boaz means," said David, "is that since Lord Rebec decreed you and Serena should mate, then there's not really any question of waiting."

"Ah. Yes," said Joseph, his eyes still chilly. "Lord Rebec. Bless him."

"Look, s—*Joseph*," said Serena, and laid her hand on her mate's arm. "I know this is difficult but we are sworn to obey Lord Rebec, servant of Mighty and Everlasting Yu. And if we resist our fate we will only make things hard for Boaz, who has shown us nothing but kindness."

"Exactly," said David. "So… you know. Just close your eyes, Joseph, and think of the Empire."

Watching them, Boaz again was struck by the feeling there were words being spoken that he couldn't hear. Some strange communication passing from look to look as the three newcomers considered each other.

Then Joseph sighed. "Yes. Of course. Boaz, I apologize. This is still all very new to us. Please… be patient."

"Put your clothes and bitty bags away," he said. "As I show David where he is to sleep."

He gave David the room Mikah's older brother had slept in. Tayt, his only other unculled get to survive the plague, had gone in the cull before last, brave and beautiful as Mikah was growing to be. He felt his heart pinch and turned his thoughts, swiftly. There was no profit in thinking of Tayt, or looking ahead to Mikah's leaving.

With the newcomers assigned their rooms, he took them outside again to show them the meeting hall where most slaves gathered for the morning and evening meals, the long bath-house where they washed the sweat and dirt of labor from their bodies, the fields and the crops, the livestock, the laundry, the kitchens, the smithies, the brick yard, the horse barns, the poultry runs, the threshing sheds, the silos. The holding barns where all those things created for the god Yu were stored as they waited for collection by his servants, every thin moon.

Last of all he took them to the slaughter yard, where the air was rank with blood and death, and black flies clotted the landscape. A few nervous sheep huddled in a pen nearby. From inside the main slaughter shed came the sound of frightened cattle bellowing, and the hollow thudding of poleaxes against horned heads.

"We eat nothing we have not grown or killed ourselves," he said. "And all men here must serve their turn in providing meat for the table." Reaching over the side of the sheep pen to the knife-box hanging there, he withdrew a sharp blade and tossed it at Joseph. "All men."

He expected Joseph to fumble the blade. Drop it, maybe even cut himself. But Joseph plucked the knife from the stinking air without looking to see where his fingers reached. Without speaking he rested his other hand on the pen's top railing and vaulted over it, landing lightly on the balls of his feet.

"Joseph?" said Serena. She sounded uncertain. Worried, even. David touched her briefly on the shoulder. Leaned close and whispered something.

Joseph ignored her. Moving swiftly, surely, he separated one sheep from the rest. Snared it in a single movement, lifting and twisting so it landed on its rump between his waiting knees, which clamped like a vice against its agitated ribs. His empty hand cupped the sheep's jaw, cutting off its distressed bleating, stretching the neck taut and blinding the beast against his belly. His other hand drew the sharp knife blade across the sheep's throat, slicing deep and sure through windpipe, veins and artery. Scarlet blood sprayed in a pumping arc. The sheep convulsed once, thin legs shuddering, and died.

Joseph wiped the bloody knife clean on the sheep's fleece, slid the blade through his belt, and hoisted the carcass over one shoulder.

Blood dripped down his back. Keeping the carcass neatly balanced, he let himself out of the pen through its gate, and took the dead sheep over to the dressing-bench on the far side of the slaughter yard. There he pierced its hocks with the awl, strung it up over the wooden gut pail, and eviscerated it. As the carcass's remaining blood drained out of the severed neck vessels, he finished the job by skinning it.

When he was done he tossed the bloody sheep-hide onto the nearest empty rack, sluiced his face and hands clean under the waiting pump, then rejoined them. With very great care, he put the knife back in its box on the fence. His work clothes were soaked scarlet in many places.

Beneath its light brown tan, David's face was shocked. "Ah—Joseph? Where the hell did you learn to do that?"

Joseph's eyes were colder than ever. "Does it matter?"

Boaz didn't like the man, but he could respect him. "It was well done."

"I don't—I've never—Boaz, do you want *me* to do that?" said David. He sounded horrified.

"This is a big farm," said Joseph. "I'd say Boaz could think of twenty jobs off the top of his head you could do that don't include butchery."

It was true. He'd lied, before. Wanting to test Joseph. Or punish him. Or both. Not every male slave took a turn in the slaughter yard. Not every male slave could stomach the work. Like David, they turned sickly at the sight of blood, at the stench of death. All they could kill with comfort were cobs of corn, and rows of wheat and barley.

Joseph was a strange, wrong man. His face had blazed defiance as Hol'c prepared to use the fire-brand. Though it burned, and burned, he did not scream. He killed the sheep as though killing was his service. He held himself like a god.

Boaz felt a worm of fear twist in the pit of his belly. What was this human doing here? Why had he been sent? Surely Yu must *know* this man was different? Dangerous?

Serena said, "Boaz? Am I expected to slaughter sheep?"

He shook his head, tore his gaze away from Joseph and found some ease in her beautiful face. "No. Women weave and sew, tend children and the fields. Husband the livestock. They mend clothes and clean them in the laundry. They cook. Can you cook?"

"Yes, Boaz," she said. Her taut expression relaxed in a smile. "I'm a very good cook."

"I can cook too," said David. "In fact, I can cook better than Serena."

He frowned. "Men do not cook."

"Really? No. No, of course they don't," said David. "What was I thinking. Well, okay, then give me another job. Anything. So long as it's not..." He gestured at the butchered sheep. "That." He brightened. "I like horses. Can I help look after the horses? Or the goats, maybe? I get on well with goats."

"Since it takes one to know one..." said Joseph, under his breath.

As Serena swallowed a laugh Boaz said, "You can start with the goats."

"And don't we have to build ourselves houses?" said Joseph.

"In time," he said. "When men can be spared from the fields. House-building is a job for many hands. You have my home as shelter, for the time being."

"Yes," said Joseph. "And your bed to sleep in. How could I forget?"

Ignoring that, Boaz crossed to the big bell that hung by the slaughter shed door and dinged it until a man came out. His leather apron was slicked wet crimson, and he had a clotted cleaver in one hand.

"Yes, Boaz?"

He pointed. "Here is a butchered sheep, Dayn. Take it to the smokehouse, send a boy out to dress the hide, and another to wheel the guts to the fertiliser pit."

Dayn's gaze flicked to the sheep, the hide, the newcomers and back again. "Yes, Boaz."

"New blood," he said, answering Dayn's unasked question. "You may spread the word."

Dayn nodded. "A fine woman."

"She's spoken to the silver-head," he said curtly. "Joseph. Be about your business, Dayn."

Dayn stepped back inside, and he returned to the new blood.

"Come," he said. "We are almost finished. All that remains is the babyhouse. I will take you there now, but first Joseph must change and his bloody clothes be put to the laundry."

"Babyhouse?" said Serena. "I don't know what—"

"You will see," he said, and chivvied them back into the road. "Quickly, no more idle chatter. The light fades, and we must be done before the evening meal."

Without giving them a chance to question further he hurried on, and they fell into step behind him.

CHAPTER ELEVEN

The god Yu decreed that human children could be useful once they had reached their fifth sunseason. All the get five sunseasons and older, like Mikah, were put to work with the other slaves, assigned tasks that did not overtax their childish minds and bodies. But the get still younger than five stayed their days in the babyhouse. It was the largest building in the village, with rooms for eating and rooms for sleeping and rooms where the older children could play. A large fenced enclosure at the back meant there was sunshine and fresh air in safety, too. Some women worked all their time in the babyhouse, as caretakers and birthseers, but there was also an ever-changing list of women and girls who worked there a shorter time to learn about babies and their birthing, the most sacred work a human could perform for the god Yu.

Boaz led the new blood into the enormous hall where the babies cooed and cried and kicked and crawled after woven hay balls rolled across the wooden floor by giggling nursemaids. Some lay in arms, nursing at the breast. Some wriggled on padded mats, inspecting their tiny toes. Some laughed, and some slept. The air was ripe with the sounds and smells of babies.

"Oh my God," said Serena softly. "*Look* at them all …"

Boaz nodded, full of pride. "Our current crop of get stands at two hundred and eighty. Almost half of them you see here, for they are not yet walking. When the last ripened woman gives birth our number will swell to over three hundred."

"And that's good, is it?" said Joseph. His voice sounded strange. Tight and small and trapped in his throat.

He nodded. "It is very good. Lord Choulai says there is no breeding farm to match us for beauty and vitality of get. For the last three sunseasons we have lost only two in every ten babies. Lord Choulai says we serve the god Yu better than any other farm. He says he is proud of our service to the god."

"Well hey," said Joseph, still in that odd little voice. "Let's hear it for Lord Choulai."

"Joseph," said David. His tone was a warning. "We live to serve our god."

"Boaz, do any of your children live here?" said Serena.

"No," he said, after a difficult moment. "My youngest get died. Of the living, only Mikah remains unculled."

Her hand rested on his arm, briefly. "I'm so sorry. And you have no mate?"

Memory tormented him with an image of Marise, copper-haired and supple in her beauty. "She died. So did the one assigned to me after her. I must wait now, for Lord Choulai to find me another woman of breeding age."

"I'm sorry," said David. "That must be very difficult."

There was genuine feeling in the man David's voice. In his eyes, too. A memory of pain. "It is the way of things," he said, making his own voice rough. Softness was a danger, here. "Best you get used to it, quickly. Leave behind the worlds you came from. You are on a farm now, and all that matters is this." He nodded at the babies, and the women tending them, then looked at Serena. "You like children?"

A shadow of sadness flitted over her face. "Very much."

"Good. That is a good and proper thing," he said, nodding. "How many have you birthed already?"

"What?" She looked up at him, her eyes wide. "Birthed? Ah — none. Not yet."

"*None*?" he echoed, astonished, then lowered his voice to a fierce whisper. "Are you not fertile, Serena? If you are not fertile Hol'c will put you down!"

"Kill me, you mean?"

"Yes! Why have you not delivered babies unto the god Yu? That is a woman slave's first duty!"

She looked at Joseph, then David, then cast her gaze to the floor. Her cheeks were pink with discomfort. "My lord did not permit me. He said I was not comely enough to breed."

"Oh," he said, and swallowed. It was unthinkable to criticise one of the mighty god Yu's servants, but ... "I am surprised." He looked at Joseph. "And you? Have you sired get for our great god?"

Joseph's face went very still, very hard. Then it relaxed. "A son."

Only one? That was not good. "He is beautiful?"

"He was."

"He is dead?" Boaz clenched his hands. "A defect?"

"An accident."

He didn't know whether to feel relieved, or sorry. "No more than one?"

Joseph looked at him. "After his death I served a different lord. He decreed me too ugly for breeding."

That was not surprising. He turned to David. "And you?"

"Ah—I was a scribe, Boaz," said David. "My lord believed that breeding would overtax my strength and weaken my mind."

"A scribe?"

"Yes. I worked with words. Does no-one here read or write?"

"We have numbers," he said dismissively. "We have no use for reading or writing. That is a Jaffa secret. Serena—"

"Yes?" she said, her fine skin pale again, her embarrassment past.

"I have changed my mind. You will not cook. You will work here, in the babyhouse, and learn all of babies and birthing you need to know before your time. Joseph must quicken you soon, and after that the days will fly."

Serena lowered her head. "I serve the great god Yu," she murmured. "Whatever task you assign me I will perform to the best of my ability."

Boaz ached to touch her, but here stood Joseph, her mate, and he was the head man and the women were watching, despite the babies. "I know you will," he said, smiling. He looked at the men, and let his smile vanish. "You all will. For if you don't I must tell Hol'c, who will tell Lord Choulai, and if you are very lucky you will be punished to blood and weeping."

From outside the babyhouse came the loud clang-clang-clang of the meeting hall bell. As one, Serena, Joseph and David spun about to face the room's large double doors. They were alert, poised for some kind of swift action.

"It is the signal for day's end," he explained, and watched as their faces lost their tension, and their hands came to rest by their sides. "Now everyone ceases their labor, cleans their body in the bath-house, and at the next bell gathers in the meeting hall. That is where I will take you now. There is always much work to be done to prepare for nightmeal. You can help the others until it's time to eat. I must mingle with the returning workers."

Joseph had turned back, and was once more staring at the babies. "Yeah," he said. "Whatever. Let's just get the hell out of here."

Boaz didn't really need to mingle. He learned what he needed to learn of every day's work at the end of nightmeal, when the chosen group leaders stood to make him their reports. But he liked to snatch a moment with Mikah whenever he could, under pretence of head man's business. Leaving the new blood at the meeting hall, in the care of the cooks and servers, he hurried down to the shucking house where the children and the men tasked to guide and guard them streamed out into the dusking street.

"Papa!" his son cried, face lighting with his glorious smile. "I shucked three bushels all myself, Papa! Even though I had to water the workers in the fields! And look!" He held out his hands. "Not a single cut from the shucking knife!"

Boaz caught Mikah to him in a fierce embrace. "So it should be."

"I spread word of the newcomers, Papa," Mikah confided, as they joined the flow of workers heading to the bath-house. "Will I see them again at nightmeal? There were so many questions I could not answer. What are they like? Which lords did they serve before coming here? Did they know any of our culled get? Are you sorry Lord Rebec put the woman to the old man? He is an old man, Papa. His hair is all silver! Have I seen a man with silver hair before, Papa? I can't remember a man with silver hair."

"Hush, Mikah. You talk too much," he scolded, half his attention on the passing men and women who heard Mikah's prattle and slowed a little, to hear him answer. He hurried them on with a lowering look. "It is not for me to question Lord Rebec's choice. Never speak of it again. As for Joseph, yes. His hair is silver. He has more years than most men here. But he is strong and he will work, as we work, for the glory of the god."

"Do you know where they came from, Papa?" said Mikah, as they reached the bath-house and took their places in line to wait their turn for a stall. "Their clothes were almost as fine as a Goa'uld's."

"Their clothes mean nothing, Mikah. They are humans. Slaves. No better than we are, even if they did serve great Goa'uld lords. That was far away, and nothing to do with us. They are breeders and farmers for the god Yu, now, just like us. Like us they will wear roughspun and their fine clothes will sit in the storehouse gathering dust."

"Yes, Papa," sighed Mikah, and glanced up. "I like the woman's face, Papa," he whispered. "I am sorry she won't be yours."

Boaz let his hand smooth Mikah's riotous curls. "Hush," he said again, but not harshly. He was sorry, too.

After the cleansing they walked in their shifts back home to put on clean clothes. Dressed again, Boaz cleared his trunk of his belongings and put them in the room that Tayt had slept in. Lit the lamps in the window and the hall, collected the walking lamp and tinder for lighting it, then went with Mikah to the meeting hall.

Serena, David and Joseph were just laying the last of the wooden plates on the trestle tables when he arrived. They saw him and stopped, uncertain. He looked to Curjin, chief cook of the meeting hall. "Ring the summons to nightmeal, Curjin," he said.

As Curjin nodded and went outside, he beckoned the new blood over. "I sit there," he told them, pointing to the trestle table at the top of the hall, closest to the kitchen. His hand bell, bright with polish, rested by his plate, bowl and cutlery. "At the head man's table. My son sits with me, and every night those I choose to speak with over nightmeal. You will sit with me tonight, your first night. In the morning, at firstmeal, you will mingle with the others."

"And this is your son?" said Serena, nodding at Mikah. "I remember him from before. When we arrived."

"Yes," he said, and did not try to hide his pride and pleasure. "This is Mikah."

"Pleased to meet you, Mikah," she said. "I'm Serena. This is Joseph, and this is David."

"Papa says you come from worlds far away," said Mikah, eyes shining with excitement. "He says you served great lords, Goa'uld who serve the god. One day *I* will serve a great lord, I know it. Perhaps I will even serve the god himself! He has human servants, Lord Choulai says. And Lord Choulai must know. He is beloved of Yu."

As Joseph opened his mouth, Serena fixed him with a stare. "Don't, Joseph."

Joseph returned her look with one of his own, critical and reassuring at the same time, then dropped to a crouch before Mikah. "I still serve a great lord, Mikah," he said. "Every day I do his bidding. It pleases me that I do this. That's why I'm here. And while I'm here, I'll do whatever it takes to see that his wishes are fulfilled."

"Of course," said Mikah, puzzled. "That is what humans do. They obey the wishes of their great lords. The wishes of the Goa'uld, who rule the universe."

To Boaz's great surprise, some deep and painful feeling washed over Joseph's face. He reached out a hand, and touched it to Mikah's cheek. "Yeah. It feels that way sometimes, I know."

Outside the hall, Curjin clanged and clanged the bell, and the first of the villagers entered the hall hungry for nightmeal. Their faces were curious, their gazes lingering on the new blood, but of course they did not approach or speak. They would not, until their head man gave them leave.

Boaz dropped his hand to Mikah's shoulder, easing him away from Joseph. "Come," he said. "We must sit. Nightmeal will be served soon."

So in silence they sat, waiting for the hall to fill. Even as he inspected each entering worker, he also watched Mikah trying not to stare at the old man with silver hair. Watched a smile creep into Joseph's stern eyes, aware of Mikah's interest. When the last villager arrived and took her place, he stood and rang his hand bell.

"Here are three newcomers," he announced, once all the chattering tongues had stilled. "Serena and Joseph, mated by Lord Rebec, servant of Yu the Mighty and Everlasting. And David, unmated as yet. Serena will work in the babyhouse. David will tend the goats with the children. Joseph will help me prepare the fallow fields for planting the coldseason crops. Let us pray." He bowed his head, and held wide his hands. "We gather together in the sight of our god Yu, Mighty and Everlasting. Our blood is his. Our bodies are his. We serve him without reservation, for his glory and gratification. Great god, hear our prayer. Fill our seed with life and quicken our wombs, that we may deliver to you the most precious harvest of all."

"Great god, hear our prayer," the villagers replied in a gusty sigh.

Then it was time to eat.

"Fill your bellies well," Boaz advised, as the servers brought them boiled corn, roasted fowl, goat stew, buttered potatoes, steaming honeyed carrots and peas, plump and greenly shining. "Tomorrow you will rise before the sun and labor until the dusk, with only a break for water."

"What?" said Joseph, as another server filled his mug with ale. "No lunch?"

He frowned. "What is lunch?"

"A meal eaten in the middle of the day," said David.

"The day is for working," he said. "Before and after day is for eating. Only babies eat a midmeal. Come. Fill your bellies. If you do not eat you will grow weak and if you are weak not only will you fail to quicken get, most likely you will not work hard enough. Hol'c has a remedy for humans who do not work hard enough. I doubt you will like it."

Joseph made a face. "You heard the man, David, Serena. Eat."

There was no more talking after that, just the sounds of knife and fork against plate. When the food was eaten and the ale drunk, Serena said, "What happens now, Boaz? What do you do in the evenings?"

Boaz shrugged. "Sometimes there is singing. Sometimes there is dancing. Sometimes there are games. You three will go home, now. You and Joseph must mate, and—"

"Now?" said Joseph, startled. "Ah—Boaz—"

Was the man stupid after all? "She must ripen within a month, Joseph," he said, impatient. "If she does not, Hol'c might decide she's infertile and put her down instead of giving her another mate. You he *will* put down. I know Hol'c. He will look at your silver hair and the lines on your face and he will say you are withered, your seed leached of life. He will say you are only good for fertiliser."

Joseph smirked. "Lord Rebec might disagree."

"Lord Rebec is not master of this farm. This farm lies in Lord Choulai's domain and he scarcely comes here," Boaz retorted, flooded with frustrated fury. "He relies on Jaffa Master Hol'c to tell him what he needs to know. Hol'c is the true lord here, Joseph. Not Lord Choulai." Then, abruptly horrified, he remembered Mikah.

Snatching his wide-eyed son's ear between his fingers, he twisted. "But you did not hear me say that, Mikah," he whispered fiercely. "That is secret head man's knowledge and if you speak it elsewhere the god will know and he will strike you down!"

As Mikah whimpered, Joseph leaned close. "You're hurting him, Boaz. Let him go."

Boaz turned, his spine prickling. Joseph spoke softly, but in his voice was a killing coldness. His eyes were slits of rage.

"Joseph..." said David. He sounded afraid.

Serena put her hand on Joseph's arm. "Please," she said. Then she looked at him. "Boaz, let Mikah go. I'm sure he knows how to hold his tongue. We all do. The last thing any of us wants is trouble."

"But you will have it, Serena!" he said, and released Mikah's ear. "You are too bold for humans, on these strange worlds you've come from you've somehow forgotten your places! Death is only ever a whisper away, here. Holc's word is law and he strikes without mercy. If I do not guide you, if you do not *listen*, and *obey* me, you will die. Others might die because of you. I am head man. Every life you see here—" He gestured at the crowded trestle tables, at the men and the women and the children, eating and drinking and laughing. "—*every* life is in my hands. How can I make you understand that?"

"You don't have to," said Joseph. He looked even older, now, and very tired. "We understand already." He flicked a glance at Serena, and at David. "Don't we?"

"Yes," said David. "Of course. Boaz, we want to help you, not hurt you."

Boaz gave them all his hardest look. "You can help by doing what you're told," he said, then held out his hand to his son. Mikah's fingers wrapped tight around it. "You will go home now. Joseph and Serena will mate, and David will sleep. I must stay here, and be told of the day's work for the god. I will see you again in the morning."

Without further speech Joseph pushed back his chair and stood. Serena and David followed him. As they filed out of the meeting hall, watched by hundreds of curious gazes, Boaz turned to his son.

Mikah's eyes shone with tears. "I'm sorry, Papa," he whispered. "I didn't mean to anger you."

"You didn't," he said, and kissed Mikah's hand. "I promise. You are a good boy. I was angry at Joseph."

"He is a strange human, Papa," said Mikah. "I don't understand him."

"You don't have to," he replied. "You stay away from him, Mikah. He'll end his days in the barley field with Ferek, and I'll not have you plowed there with him."

Mikah nodded. "Yes, Papa."

With that settled, Boaz stood and picked up his hand bell. With its silver echoes dying around him and all the villagers falling silent he declared, "Now shall I hear the deeds done this day in the name of Yu, the Mighty and Everlasting!"

As Tomlan stood, to give an accounting of the smithing works, he felt himself smile with relief.

For the next while, at least, he could forget all about newcomers, and the trouble they dragged in their wake.

The moon was bright enough to comfortably see by. Unspeaking, they made their way back to Boaz's house—their house—and let themselves in. Oil lamps burned, pooling the space beneath the thatched roof with warm, friendly light.

O'Neill closed the door behind them. Fell against it, palms pressed flat to his face, and said, muffled, "Jesus Christ Almighty." He dragged his hands down and stared at the rest of his team. "And I mean that with absolute sincerity."

It was a sparse bare box of a house. Nearly all bedrooms. With communal bathing facilities and a communal eating hall, what else was left? Just this little bit in the front here, with four wooden chairs and a table. Daniel sat down, and Carter followed his example.

She looked sick. "Did you see all the *babies*?" she whispered. "All the pregnant women? Some of them were practically children themselves, thirteen, fourteen. It's so *wicked*." She pressed trembling fingers to her mouth. "If I'd known Yu was responsible for this—"

"Get a grip, Carter," O'Neill said. "You knew what we were heading into."

"No, she didn't," said Daniel. He looked just as sick. "None of us did. Not really. This place is like the worst nightmares of the pre-Civil War South. It's the most degrading kind of exploitation. And somehow the fact they're well-fed, well-dressed, well-housed—in a crazy way it makes what's happening here even more repugnant."

"What's *repugnant*," said Carter, "is that it's clear they think they're serving a loving god."

O'Neill was feeling pretty sick himself. Sick, and furious, and itching for a fight. "Hey. Both of you. Stay focused. Boaz is right about one thing—that bastard Hol'c is bad news." He felt his skin shiver at the memory of the fire-brand. Saw the same memory skitter over Carter's face, and Daniel's.

"Did you see there isn't a cemetery here?" said Daniel. "Does that mean what I'm really, *really* scared to think it means?"

"You heard Boaz," he said. "If I don't watch my step Hol'c will kill me and have me plowed into the barley field. So yes, Daniel. I'm pretty sure it means what you think it means."

Carter dragged her fingers through her hair. "God. This place is a *nightmare*."

He pushed away from the door. "Yes. It is. But it's not our problem. We're here to do a job, get out with our skins intact and then work our asses off to see that this place, and all the places like it, are put out of business permanently."

"And how long will that take?" said Daniel. "Years. Decades, maybe, with this plan the Tok'ra have dreamed up. And in the meantime..."

"In the meantime, Daniel, unless you happen to stumble across a magic wand on one of your precious archaeological digs, the Tok'ra's plan is the plan we're stuck with," he retorted. "Now that's enough. I don't want to have this conversation again. How are you coping without your glasses?"

Daniel shrugged. "Okay. It's not like I'll have a lot of reading to do while we're here."

"Good. Did you both manage to palm your Tok'ra communicators okay?"

"In my bitty bag," said Carter.

"Mine too," said Daniel.

"And I'm three for three," he said, smiling without humor. "I should call Jacob. Someone better keep an eye out, just in case Boaz and Mikah come back." He ducked into the bedroom Boaz had assigned him and Carter, tried not to look at the double bed, and retrieved his communicator. "Hey, Jacob, you there?" he said, wandering out again. Carter had positioned herself by the window, and was keeping an eye on the street. "Jacob, come in."

A faint mushy hiss, then: "*Jack? Thank God, Martouf and I were starting to worry. You all right? Sam? Daniel?*"

"Oh, we're all peachy," he said. "You know, this is some seriously deep stinking crap you've landed us in here, Jacob!"

"*Come on, Jack,*" said Jacob, after a short pause. "*You didn't think you were taking a break at the local Goa'uld Club Med, did you?*"

He felt a surge of anger. "Exactly how long have the Tok'ra known these—these—*places* existed? And why the *hell* haven't you done something about them before now?"

"*Do what, Jack?*" said Jacob. "*There's nothing we can do, any more than the United States can ride in to every crappy dictatorship on Earth and liberate the local downtrodden masses. This is the way it is, my friend. This is how the Goa'uld play the game. How they've played it for thousands of years.*"

"*Yes!* Because you've *let* them!"

Through the static, the sound of Jacob's sigh. "*Jack, we can argue Tok'ra foreign policy all you want once this mission's over. But first it has to be over. How are you situated?*"

"We're living in the head man's house, for now," he said. "The three of us. And oh—yes—your daughter and I have been ordered to *mate*, thank you so *very* much!"

"*I had to make sure at least two of you were together at consistent times,*" said Jacob. "*Don't worry, Jack. You know I trust you.*"

As Carter made an incoherent sound of outrage, O'Neill glared at the communicator. "Jacob, I swear to God, when this is over I am going to punch you on the nose!"

Jacob laughed. "*Let me talk to Sam.*"

He tossed Carter the communicator then dropped into the nearest empty chair and pulled a face at Daniel as she said, "And when *he's* punched you on the nose, Dad, then it'll be *my* turn!"

"*I'm sorry, sweetheart,*" said Jacob. "*We're on a tight schedule, we can't afford to waste time with delayed communications.*"

"Dad…" Her voice hitched. "It's really awful here."

A long silence. "*I know,*" said Jacob. "*I'm sorry about that, too. But at least we're doing something about it now, Sam. It may take time… it may take generations… but at least we're doing some-*

thing."

"I'm worried it's going to take us longer than a week to get past these people's defences, past their—their brainwashing," she said. "They're terrified of that Jaffa, Hol'c, with good reason. And they absolutely believe that Yu is their god. I don't see how we can undo that in a week."

"*Well, Sam, maybe you can't,*" said Jacob. "*Maybe all you can do is plant the seeds of doubt, and leave it to someone else to reap the harvest at a later date. I don't know. This is as much a fact-finding mission as anything else. You knew that going in.*"

"Yeah? Well now I know the kind of life these people are living and I'm not so sure I can just wash my hands of them and walk away!"

Another Jacob sigh, shorter and sharper this time. "*Let me talk to Jack again.*"

Carter's eyes were too bright as she handed back the communicator. "I'm turning in," she said shortly. "You and Dad go on having a nice chat."

"Yeah, Jacob," he said, as their bedroom door banged shut behind her. "Don't worry, she's okay. We're just feeling a bit ... tetchy. Our visit started with a spot of torture and it's been downhill from there."

"*Torture?*" The communicator's mush couldn't hide Jacob's alarm. "*After I ringed up, you mean? My God, Jack—*"

"We're fine, we're fine," he said quickly, regretting the impulse to shake Jacob up a bit. Indulge in a little payback. "It was ... pretty minor. Just Hol'c letting us know who's boss. Listen, I'd better go, Boaz could come back any minute. We'll try and call you every night. There won't be much hope through the day—sounds like we'll be noses to the grindstone from sunup to sundown. And it's too dangerous to keep the communicators on us. Will you and Martouf be all right up there?"

"*We're fine. We've got supplies and there's no traffic, radio or ship. You worry about you, okay? Look, Jack, I know it's only been a few hours but do you think there's a chance you'll be able to reach anyone there? Make any kind of meaningful contact?*"

O'Neill thought of Boaz. Of Mikah. "Maybe. But it's too soon to say. Call you tomorrow night, Jacob. O'Neill out."

He slipped the communicator into his pocket and rested his folded arms on the table. Daniel said, "I get the feeling this is going to be the longest hardest week of our lives. And I'm not talking about the daily chores."

He pulled a face. "Sorry you came?"

"Bitterly," said Daniel, and he wasn't joking. He looked lost. Stricken. The way he'd looked after Sha're was taken. "The only way to make any of this right is to leave, now, come back with a hundred Goa'uld cargo ships and take every last person back home with us."

Pressing his fingertips against his eyes, O'Neill said, warningly, "Daniel..."

Daniel sighed. "We can't. I know. And even if we could, we'd only be saving—how many people live here, do you think?"

"Including the babies?" He shrugged, and lowered his hands. "Five, six hundred."

"And that's just one farm, owned by just one system lord. Multiply that by all the system lords out there and—" Daniel shook his head. "It's days like this I find myself actually agreeing with Kinsey. Wishing I'd never helped Catherine open the damned Stargate."

"Because ignorance is bliss?" O'Neill said, and sat back. "Bull. You might feel better but this would still be happening. Now that we know, at least we're trying to stop it."

Daniel's expression was despairing. "How can we stop it? It's too big to stop. It's systemic. Endemic. It's a cancer and we don't have nearly enough drugs to kill it."

He pushed himself to his feet. "That's probably what they told Abraham Lincoln," he said, heading for his bedroom. "Lucky for the rest of us Lincoln didn't listen."

"Jack..."

He stopped, hand on the doorknob. Turned. "Daniel?"

Without his glasses, Daniel's face looked naked. "Be careful with Boaz. You scare him. And you fascinate Mikah. That's a dangerous combination."

He smiled, just a little. "I'll bear that in mind, Dr. Freud."

"Jack!"

He bit back an oath. "*What?*"

His expression anxious, Daniel nodded at the closed bedroom

door. "Are you okay? With that?"

"Get some sleep, Daniel," he said, no longer smiling. "We've got an early start."

"You don't have to tiptoe," said Carter's voice in the bedroom's dense darkness. "I'm still awake."

He pushed the door till the latch clicked shut. "There's no lamp in here?"

"Couldn't find the matches."

Inching his way forward till he bumped the bed, he sat down on its very edge. "It's all right, Carter. I'll take the floor. Just chuck me a pillow and a blanket."

"And if Boaz decides to look in on us at some point?" she said. "I wouldn't put it past him, he's obsessed with making babies. And I don't think he was kidding about Hol'c, sir. Do you?"

He heaved a heavy sigh. "No."

There came the sound of blankets being pulled back. "Come on. There's no point delaying the inevitable. You're just going to get cold, sitting there."

"Yeah," he said. "I suppose I am." He kicked off his shoes, slid beneath the covers and let his head drop onto the pillow. It felt strange, lying next to a woman after so long. Huh. How long had it been, anyway? Not since Kinthea . . . or Antarctica. That had been Carter, too.

God. Don't think about Antarctica, or Kinthea. Don't think, full stop.

"What's that?" she whispered.

He listened. "The front door," he whispered back. "Boaz. And Mikah."

She made a small sound in her throat. "Pity we don't have a headboard," she muttered. "We could bang it, suggestively. That'd keep him happy."

"We could bounce, instead," he muttered back.

"And moan," she replied, then rolled over to muffle a giggle in her own pillow.

He swatted the nearest bit of her he could reach. "Shhh! *Shhh!*"

Paralysed with silent hysterics, they listened to Boaz and Mikah retire to their own rooms.

"Oh, God," she said, when it was safe to speak. "I knew I should've stayed at the Pentagon."

He snorted. "I should've stayed retired."

"Huh," she said, and shifted a little away from him. "Coulda, woulda, shoulda."

He tried not to care that her hip no longer touched his. The darkness was absolute, pressing him flat to the mattress like an enormous velvet hand.

"You know," she said, after a little while. "This could be worse."

He rolled his head on the pillow, even though he couldn't see her. "You're joking, right?"

"No, I'm not joking."

"Carter, how could this *possibly* be worse?"

He felt her shrug. "There could be ice."

Again, the danger of hysterics. "There could be Daniel."

"And Teal'c."

"There were four in the bed," he warbled softly, "and the colonel said—"

She dug her elbow in his side, shaking with repressed laughter. "Stop it! *Stop* it!"

"I've stopped! I've stopped!" He dropped a forearm over his face. "Okay. That's it. Serious now. We need to sleep." He took a deep breath. Let it out. "Good night ... Serena."

"Good night, Joseph."

On cue, together: "Good night, John Boy."

More muffled laughter. A slow sinking into quiet. Then:

"God, Jack," she said, her voice small and lost in the darkness. "All the poor babies ..."

He wanted to hold her hand. He didn't dare.

"I know, Sam," he whispered. "But we'll save them. Somehow, we'll save them."

Silence. And finally, sleep.

CHAPTER TWELVE

It turned out, O'Neill discovered the next day, that preparing the fallow fields meant plowing in troughs and troughs of rotted down animal guts, heads and sundry other parts, smashed up bones and food scraps from the daily meals. But no dead humans, at least not this time. Not that he could see, anyway. And he made sure to look, because he'd accepted Boaz hadn't been blowing smoke when he said it was what the Goa'uld and their Jaffa henchmen did around here to troublesome humans.

After less than a day in this hellhole he knew, more completely, more *intimately* than ever before, just what evils the Goa'uld were capable of committing.

Field preparation was filthy, stinking work. Back-breaking. Nauseating. After three hours of solid labor he stopped, just for a moment, to scratch at the damned brand on the back of his shoulder and wipe his sweaty face with his forearm. His blistered hands were smarting abominably.

"I don't get it," he said to Boaz, toiling beside him. "You're the head man. You could assign yourself to any job. Why pick this one?"

"Keep working," said Boaz. "Hol'c will come soon. Every day he inspects us to make sure we work hard for the god's glory. If he sees you not working, he will hurt you."

Even dirty and runnelled with sweat, with flies crawling on his face, he was one of the most extraordinarily good-looking men O'Neill had ever seen. Tall, golden, built like some Greek god brought to life. Compared with him, GQ cover models were plain. All the men here made them look plain. And the women? Hugh Heffner would think he'd died and gone to heaven. The least attractive slave on this moon would own Earth's catwalks, its fashion shows, Hollywood. Being here was like living in the middle of a Vanity Fair photo shoot.

Man, did I wander onto the wrong sound-stage or what?

It was creepy. For countless generations these humans had been selectively bred for beauty so Yu would be surrounded by humans pleasing to his alien eyes. Nirrti had done the same to Kinthea's people. Ra, too; those poor kids he'd surrounded himself with were all perfect. Probably they all did it, every last Goa'uld system lord in the galaxy.

He'd never get used to it. Never stop hating it. If he died fighting it, well, like Bra'tac said. Today I die well.

Stretching out his tight neck muscles O'Neill said, wryly, "And if Hol'c did hurt me I get the feeling that wouldn't bother you much."

"If it was only you that Hol'c hurt, Joseph?" Boaz said, his expression grim. "No. It would not bother me at all. But Hol'c would hurt me too, for allowing you to stop working. Hol'c would hurt everyone working here now, for your sin."

O'Neill looked at the score of other men scattered around the ten acre field, slaving away under the hot sun, methodically grinding blood and guts into the rich brown soil, making it even richer for the glory of a rotten corrupt sonofabitch snakehead. None of them was close enough to overhear their conversation. Good. Because he hated this place worse than anywhere he'd been in his life, even Abu Ghraib, and that was saying something.

It was time to get Jacob's Tok'ra Resistance on the road.

"Fair enough." Swallowing a groan, he bent again to his gross task. "So you're keeping an eye on me, is that it?"

"Of course," said Boaz. "There is something not right about you, Joseph. You don't belong here."

He snorted. "You can say that again." His stomach rolled, protesting the stench of decomposing entrails. "Boaz… how many children have you sired? Do you know?"

Boaz didn't answer. Just picked up his two empty wooden pails and walked back to the nearest wagon to fetch more muck from the fly-smothered tubs it carried. He filled the pails with blood and guts, brought them back, and methodically dripped the stinking slop further along the furrow. Then he put the newly emptied pails aside, and continued to mulch the stuff into the clotted earth.

"I have sired twenty-seven get," he said, not looking up. "Two a year without fail." His expression clouded. "Twenty-seven living, that is. Not all survived. Thirty-four when the dead ones are counted."

Thirty-four? God. He must have started when he was still a kid, practically. No older than fourteen, fifteen tops. He looked around thirty now, at least in Earth years.

"How does that work?"

Boaz shot him a look from under his extravagant eyelashes. "You have sired a son, Joseph. You have mated Serena. You know how it works."

"No," he said, impatient, as he kept on with his own hoeing. "Not that. I meant ... twenty-seven kids. That's a hell of a lot. Is that all you've ever done? Make babies and work in the fields? You've never served the Goa'uld in other ways?"

Boaz shrugged. "Like other males I was put to a woman the year before I reached culling age, so Lord Choulai might see I was fertile and could breed true. The child was beautiful. Lord Choulai decreed I should not be culled, but stay here on the farm to sire more get. My sire was culled instead. He was old, older than you, even, and his eyes were not good."

Something in Boaz's face—a memory, an echo of pain—told O'Neill that this time *culled* was just another word for *killed*. He didn't pursue it. Raking over old wounds wasn't going to help him bond with this man and anyway, he really didn't want to know the details.

He'd have enough to forget about this damned place as it was.

"So ... you were born here? You've never lived anywhere else?"

Boaz shook his head. "I have never lived anywhere else."

Or experienced anything other than brutality and fear and rutting like a bull to make babies, slaves, for the use of a parasitic life-form that no sane God in the universe should allow to live. O'Neill let that sink in for a while, and relieved his feelings by smashing more clods of dirt to smithereens.

"What about Mikah?" he said at last, when he could trust himself to speak without screaming obscenities.

Boaz tensed, then relaxed. "What about him?"

"If he breeds true—" He felt his mouth twist, saying the vile words. "Will he stay here to sire more children?"

"No. Only one male of each bloodline is permitted on a farm," said Boaz, after the briefest hesitation. "If he breeds true he will be sent elsewhere. To another farm. Or, if he is honored, into some other service for the god first before siring his share of get."

Some other service like being taken as host for one of Yu's larval offspring, maybe, or a symbiote destined to become another Lord Choulai. Did Boaz even know that happened? Was *anyone* here aware of the Goa'uld's true nature? O'Neill really wanted to know, but it was too soon to raise that thorny subject. Revealing the truth about the Goa'uld was a conversation for another day. A day when Boaz wasn't holding a potentially deadly weapon.

Of course, there was another alternative. Mikah could stay to take Boaz's place here, and soon after that some slave Boaz once called a friend could be plowing *his* pulped flesh and bones into a fallow field. *God.*

Then an even less palatable possibility occurred to him. "But what if your son doesn't breed true, Boaz? What happens to him then?"

Boaz shot him a sharper look. "He will breed true. All my get breed true, boy and girl alike. Mine is the strongest, purest bloodline on this farm."

Jesus Christ, the man sounded *proud* of it. "And that's good, is it?" he said, roiling with baffled anger. "That's something to throw a parade for?"

Boaz was equally baffled. "Parade? Joseph, you use words that have no meaning. Stop talking and work. I have the power to punish you. Must I punish you?"

He bit back words Boaz would understand all too well. "No, massah," he said instead. "Sorry, massah."

And got back to work. When his own pails were empty again he trudged to the wagon, refilled them, and trudged unevenly back again.

Boaz was watching him. "You are limping," he accused, his expression stern.

O'Neill considered his gimpy knee. It was giving him hell. Just wait till he got home and had words with Janet Fraiser... "Yeah. So?"

"You must not let Hol'c see you limping."

"Don't tell me, let me guess," he sighed. "He'd hurt me?"

"He'd kill you," Boaz said starkly.

He straightened, slowly, ignoring his back's pained shrieking.

"And again I wonder: what do you care?"

Boaz's fingers tightened, loosened, tightened, on the handle of his hoe. "I do not have to like you, Joseph, to value your life," he said at last. "And a killing upsets the village."

"Well, Boaz, God forbid I should upset anyone," he said, and pressed a fist against his howling right sacro-iliac. "Why would Hol'c kill me?"

Boaz looked at him as though he was an idiot. "Limping is weakness. Weakness is not allowed. You might be defective. You might breed a defective child."

Right. Of course. All hail the mighty gene pool. He nodded. "Okay. Fine. I get the message: no limping."

Boaz gestured at his hoe. "Now back to work."

More guts. More sweat. More aching muscles and ripening blisters. Time dragged on. There really was no lunch. Hollow, hungry, parched, he toiled beside Boaz in silence and tried to think of another way to reach this unreachable man. To fulfil his mission here. Mikah appeared, a wooden yoke weighing down his shoulders. Suspended on each side a bucket of water with a cup attached.

O'Neill watched Boaz smile at the boy and stop himself from touching him, ruffling his hair, giving him a swift hug. In his eyes a blaze of love and pride ... and buried beneath that, fear. The kind of fear only a parent experienced, or understood. The fear that sprang to life the moment you saw your child for the first time: squalling, bloody, helpless. A tiny scrap of humanity that wouldn't exist if it wasn't for you. It never went away, that fear. It just grew, as your child grew. With every passing day, week, month, year, the fear sank its claws deeper in your heart and soul.

Because you'd given the universe a hostage. Something it could take away from you without warning or appeal. If you were bad. Or careless. If you didn't love enough.

Charlie.

Blindly O'Neill took the cup of water Mikah offered him, and poured it down his sand-dry throat. In his ears, his hammering heart.

"I passed Hol'c, Papa," Mikah said, readjusting the weight of the yoke across his shoulders. "One field away yet. He wasn't using his fire-brand, so maybe his mood is good today."

"Maybe it is, Mikah," Boaz agreed. "So don't you do anything to change that. Hurry and water the other men, and be on your way. You still have corn to shuck."

Mikah flashed him a cheeky grin. "*Four* bushels, I'll make it!"

Boaz laughed. "You boast? And shall I beat you if the boast falls flat on the ground?"

Mikah just chuckled, and went to water the other men.

O'Neill watched Boaz watch Mikah walk away, another Greek god in the growing. "He's a fine boy."

Caught unawares, Boaz smiled. "Very fine." Then he frowned. "And not your concern. Get back to work."

He was sick of work. Work wasn't getting his mission any closer to completion. "I'll bet all those other boys you sired were fine, too, Boaz. And the girls. Don't you ever wonder about them, the ones you saw taken from here? Worry about them? Don't you want to see your sons and daughters again? Know they're okay? That they're happy?"

Boaz's expression was once more baffled. "They are no longer my concern. They serve the god."

"And what about Mikah? Will you say the same about him, after he's taken from you too? Disappeared somewhere to serve the god?"

A spasm of pain flickered over Boaz's face. "We will not talk about Mikah."

O'Neill stepped closer. This was it. Mikah was Boaz's weak spot, the key to breaking the man, he could smell it. "You're scared sick for him, Boaz. It's written all over you. You love that boy, the way any good man loves his son. You don't want him culled. You don't want him sent away in chains, into slavery somewhere in Yu's empire where you'll never see him again. Admit it. This is *wrong*. All of it's wrong, you know that in your bones. He's your son and you want to save him. But you don't know how."

Boaz's face drained of color as his eyes blazed with terror, and rage. "Be silent, Joseph!" he commanded, knuckles white around the handle of his hoe. "I will excuse you this once for you are new here and you do not understand! But if you speak of this again I will tell Hol'c and he will kill you. Do you understand me? Say you understand!"

Damn. O'Neill swallowed other, less harmless curses. Too hard, too fast. He was letting this place get to him. Releasing a sharp breath he stepped back and held up his hands, letting his hoe drop. Lowered his gaze. Submit, submit. Don't challenge the top dog. Show him your belly. Let him know you know he's boss.

"Sorry, Boaz," he said, very quietly. "You're right. I'm new here and I don't understand. I was wrong to speak. I won't do it again."

After a glaring moment, Boaz nodded. "Very well." His gaze shifted and a grim smile touched his lips. "Now get back to work. Hol'c is coming. If he sees you idly standing he'll use his fire-brand on you ... and I won't say a word to stop him."

O'Neill turned. Yes, there was Hol'c. Striding towards them from the far side of the plowed field as though he owned the world.

Ignoring his back, his knee, his blisters and his sunburn, O'Neill picked up his hoe and went back to work ... and hoped Carter and Daniel were having better luck.

With a smile plastered to her aching face Sam thought, grimly, *I'm going to do it. I really am. Five seconds after I lay eyes on my father again I am going to punch him on the nose.*

She was sitting on the grass outside the babyhouse, under a shady tree. The kindest of breezes rustled the blue-tinged leaves, ruffled her hair. Stirred sweet floral scents from the scattered flower beds. Jewel-bright butterflies flirted with nothing. There were children everywhere she looked. Vigorous, vocal and apparently happy. Too young, still, to know how to be anything else. All of them were sure-fire winners of any Baby Beautiful competition they entered.

Sitting with her were three of the women currently assigned to working in the babyhouse. Qualah looked to be in her late twenties, and well into her third trimester. Berez was maybe a year or two younger, her pregnancy barely showing. Even so, she was nursing a baby. It wasn't hers. Some women, she'd been told without the slightest hint of horror, were kept in milk all the time in case another woman should dry up without warning.

She was trying very hard not to think about that. Or what happened to the women whose bodies, protesting an endless cycle of conception, gestation and birth, simply shut down and ceased to function.

The third woman in their group wasn't even a woman. Not really. Tima could only have been sixteen but she was nursing her fourth child now. Two of her other babies, both toddlers, were around here somewhere. The oldest lived with their father, Tima's mate before last.

She'd heard it all, chapter and verse, and could barely keep from screaming. How no woman could bear more than two children to the same man. How the Lord Choulai was very careful about selecting which man should quicken which woman. How he always selected just the right combinations to ensure maximum beauty and grace.

It was the most revolting kind of eugenics. It was Alar and his horrible Eurondan followers all over again, obsessed with purity and control. What she couldn't understand was these women's *complacency*. They were so calm, so accepting, so unquestioning of what was being done to them. And while yes, she knew it all came down to environment and brainwashing and never knowing anything different… what about the human spirit? Surely it was natural to rail against this barbaric treatment? Where were the fighters, the protesters, the rebels?

You know where they are, she answered herself, and felt a pricking of tears. *Plowed into the barley field. Silenced. Murdered.*

Which was why she was here. To speak for them. Rebel for them. To put a stop to this Goa'uld-inspired evil.

"… but if he *doesn't* quicken you within the month," Qualah continued, comfortably oblivious, "then perhaps Lord Choulai will take you from Joseph and give you to *Boaz*!" She sighed, and rubbed her plump hands together. The equally plump baby slung in the hammocked skirt between her knees giggled, and pumped its own little hands with glee. "Boaz sires the most beautiful children. And this Joseph you've been given—he's not what *I* would call a man to sire beautiful children. Strong, yes. And tall. But you are so *very* beautiful, Serena. You should have a beautiful man."

"Not that we question the wisdom of the Lord Choulai," added Berez, hastily, and poked Qualah in the shoulder. She looked afraid. "Lord Choulai is beloved of the god, and must know what is best."

"Except I was given to Joseph by Lord Rebec," Sam said. *Who is so going to get punched on the nose.* "Lord Choulai had nothing to do with it."

Berez nodded. "Yes. I see. And this Lord Rebec did not know Boaz was here, and available."

"You might be given to David," said Tima, wincing as the baby suckling at her breast snuffled and grunted with his eagerness. "He is beautiful too."

If I hear the word 'beautiful' one more time I'm going to scream.

"Well, possibly," Sam said, inwardly boggled by the thought. "But it's a bit early to be worrying about all that. I was only given to Joseph yesterday."

Qualah laughed and dug Berez with her elbow. "This Tima, she just wants Boaz for herself!" she scoffed. "I've watched her making eyes at Boaz since she was a child."

Berez nodded, chortling, and Tima pouted. Sam kept on smiling, because it was smile or fall into a foaming fit. Qualah hadn't trusted her with a baby to hold, yet. The last thing she wanted was a baby to hold. If she held a baby she'd fall in love with it, and there was no way the colonel would let her take it home. Probably he'd bite her head right off just for asking.

"Boaz says," Qualah murmured, her expression sympathetic, "your lord before Choulai would not let you breed. So sad. You must be happy to join us here, Serena, knowing your life will from now on be filled with babies."

It wasn't something she'd let herself think about. Marriage. Children. Engaged to Jonah there'd been the expectation, of course. The assumption that one day, down the track, she'd become a mother. But then that relationship blew up in her face, messier than the Texas Chainsaw Massacre, and after that it was work, work, work at the Pentagon. Followed by Excuse me, you want me to do *what*? Travel through a wormhole to the other side of the *galaxy*?

Are you *kidding*? Of *course* I'm on board! Where do I sign?

There were married people on other SG teams. She didn't understand how they could do it. Not that she was judging, that wasn't her place. But to leave a husband, a wife, children… and step through the Stargate. Yes, yes, married military personnel served on active duty in a dozen hotspots round the world. Always had, always would.

But this was different. This was serving on other *planets*.

And anyway. When did she have time to date? And how could she possibly get involved with someone in any meaningful fashion when she wasn't allowed to explain how she'd come home from a hard day's monitoring deep space telemetry with a staff weapon burn, or someone else's memories downloaded into her brain, or the remnants of a Neanderthal retrovirus still percolating in her bloodstream, or a weird blistery scald mark in the middle of her forehead where an evil alien parasitical life-form had tried turning her brain into scrambled eggs...

Sam blinked, and emerged from profitless speculation to find Qualah, Berez and Tima staring at her expectantly. Dear God, they were so... so... she had to say it: *beautiful*. And exquisite. And perfect. Luminous. They made the celebrated beauties of home—women like Catherine Zeta Jones, Charlize Theron, Halle Berry—look, well, not plain. Never plain. But... ordinary. Or... not so *extra*ordinary.

It was creepy.

Qualah said, "Serena? Did you not hear me?"

"I'm so sorry, I didn't," she apologized. "I was... daydreaming."

Berez laughed. "Of babies. It is good for women to think of babies."

Yes, but she wasn't here to think of babies. She was here to do a job, one far more difficult and complicated than any of them had anticipated. On a deep breath she tried to access the part of herself that had somehow become Jolinar, so it could help her assess these women as potential hosts. She'd done it on Vorash, she could do it here.

The trick was not to try too hard...

"Berez, isn't it difficult?" she said, and rested her fingers on the woman's bare arm. Physical contact seemed to help her subconscious read the subject. "Giving up your babies to Lord Choulai?"

"They are not babies when Lord Choulai takes them," said Berez. "They are grown and ready to serve the god Yu, Mighty and Everlasting."

"All right, but still. Don't you find it wrenching, to see them taken away? Don't you wish you could keep them, see them grow into young men and women?"

Tima, her sculptured face pulled into a frown, shifted her nursing son from one breast to the other. Qualah and Berez exchanged uneasy glances. Tima said, fussing with the baby, "We serve our Lord Choulai without question."

Berez was staring at the scattered playing children, her gaze fierce, as though searching for one child in particular. "What we might wish for, Serena, doesn't matter," she said, her voice distant and cool. "You come to us from far away. There you served our god as he desired in a manner unknown to us. But now you are here, and here you serve him with the babies of your body. It is your duty to give them to the god when he sends for them. Not once, not twice, but all the times you bear a child. The women who cannot accept that do not live long or happily."

"I understand that," Sam said. With an effort, she hid a surge of excitement as the part of her that remained Jolinar stirred softly, like a breeze. This Berez could be a potential recruit. She had strength and fire. The kind of mental flavor the Tok'ra were seeking. "I do. But I can't help wondering… are you all really as indifferent as you seem? I can understand how the men might not feel the loss so deeply. Men can love their children but they aren't mothers. It's not the same. Maybe it should be, but it isn't. You three are mothers. *Are* you indifferent?"

"What does it matter how we feel?" said Tima, roughly. "The babies are taken whether we cry or we laugh. And if we cry, Hol'c hurts us. Lord Choulai hurts us. It's better for us if we don't feel anything at all."

"You will learn this," said Berez. "Sooner or later. For your sake, Serena, learn it sooner. Whether it is by Joseph or some other man you will soon quicken and bear your first child and before you know it, that child will be taken. As will the other children you've birthed in the meantime. Accustom yourself… or pay the price."

"You must not say more," said Qualah. The warm friendliness had died out of her face; now her magnificent green eyes were cold and suspicious. "You insult the god when you question his desires. We were born to serve him, Serena. Those who will not serve must die. Is that what *you* desire?"

The woman was serious. "No," Sam said fervently. "I don't want to die. I want to serve. I was only curious. I meant no harm."

Moving awkwardly, hampered by her large belly, Qualah scooped up her drowsy baby from its skirt-hammock and lumbered to her feet. "It is time to prepare the children's midmeal. You will assist me, Serena and Tima. Berez, see that the children out here are calmed and ready for their food."

The cosy gossip was over. Sam, Berez and Tima stood too. Hiding her frustration and annoyance, Sam watched Qualah march back towards the babyhouse with Tima by her side.

Berez looked at her. "Be careful. If Hol'c suspects you are not peaceful in your duty, you will be punished. Or killed."

"Even if I'm pregnant?"

"Once the baby is born," said Berez. "If you have quickened. Don't think your beauty will save you. Here, beauty is common-place. Obedience is prized highest of all. And Hol'c is easily offended. There is no profit in weeping for what cannot be changed, Serena."

"And if it could be changed, Berez?" she replied. Wondering, *what would this woman say if she knew I've killed more Hol'cs than she can count? That I could kill Boaz or any man here with my bare hands? That everything she believes to be true is a lie*? "If it could be changed ... would you want to change it?"

Deep in Berez's clear blue eyes, a killing flame. "*Yes*," she whispered. Then she drew back. "But if you tell anyone I said so, I will kill you myself."

From the babyhouse, Qualah's imperious cry. "Serena! Join us now!"

Berez was holding a baby, so a hug was out of the question. Sam squeezed her shoulder instead. Her instincts were correct; Berez was definitely a candidate for the Tok'ra. "I won't tell a soul, I promise," she whispered. "I just want you to know ... you're not alone."

"*Serena!*"

She turned. "Coming, Qualah!"

And with a last, swift smile at Berez, whose face had gone still and frowning, she jogged back to the babyhouse. Suddenly, unexpectedly, filled with hope.

Maybe they weren't wasting their time here after all.

"And so," said Daniel, "Jack grabbed his axe and he chopped and he chopped and he chopped that beanstalk all the way through. And the giant fell down, down, down and he hit the ground and he died. Splat."

There was a silence as his audience sat and thought about that for a while. Eventually one young girl poked him in the knee and said, "But you said the giant was a hundred times bigger than Jack."

"Yes, Sallah, I did say that," he agreed. "Which means ... can you guess what it means?"

Padra, a year older than Sallah, gave a scornful hoot. "It means this is a made up story," she said, witheringly. "It never happened."

The rest of Daniel's audience snickered and giggled. Little shoves. Sly pinches. Sallah looked ready to cry. "True. It is a made up story," Daniel said quickly, forestalling catastrophe. "But even made up stories can mean something important. So ... what does this one mean, do you think?"

Sallah sniffed. "Maybe—maybe that big people don't always have to win?"

He grinned. "Exactly. That's exactly right, Sallah. Big people—powerful people—people you might think you can never defeat? They can be defeated."

Baen, at twelve the oldest in the group, said, "David, we're supposed to be picking stones and minding the goats. If Hol'c finds us sitting around listening to stupid made up stories we'll get into trouble."

At the mention of Hol'c's name the other children's faces pinched tight with terror. With little cries they scrambled to their feet and looked at him, fearful, accusing, as though he'd somehow let them down.

Slowly, Daniel unfolded his crossed legs and knelt before them. "We have been picking stones and minding the goats all day," he said gently. "I was tired. I needed to rest. So did you. The goats are still here, and so are the stones."

"And so is Hol'c," said Baen. "You're new, David. You don't understand."

"Trust me," said Daniel grimly, and pushed to his feet. "When it comes to the Jaffa I understand everything." He dusted his hands up and down the front of his shirt, then reached out and patted Sallah on the head. "I'm rested now, and so are you. Baen is right. We should get back to work."

Sallah tugged at his sleeve. "Why are you here with us, David?

Men don't mind the goats. That's child work."

"Ah, but you see, Sallah, I'm not like other men. I'm a scribe. I've spent my life working with words, not knives and hoes and axes. Boaz thinks this is the safest place for me. Looking after you, and the goats, and picking up the rocks and stones that work their way to the pasture's surface."

Sallah had a smile to warm the dead. It lit her face now as she said, "I'm glad Boaz thinks that." And she danced away to join the other children.

Daniel smiled after her, then got back to collecting the damned rocks and stones.

Goats being goats, the animals were happy to thrive on tough pickings. They were pastured daily some distance from the village and its surrounding rich fields and growing crops. Maybe a mile, a mile and a half. Out here the land wasn't so intensively cultivated. It was hot, but not unbearably so. The work was steady, but not too taxing. The children, a dozen of them, were scrappy little buggers. Daniel was reminded of Abydos. Of Skaara and his friends, squabbling and scuffling and turning chores into an excuse for laughter and play. With the spectre of Ra gone they had learned the meaning of freedom.

Ra. One down, only a few hundred more to go. As Jack would say, giant killer in his own right: a piece of cake...

Abydos. One small planet that had shaken itself free of Goa'uld shackles. Once upon a time his home. The home, the family, he'd never thought to have.

Don't, Daniel told himself sharply. *Abydos is the past. Sha're is the past. And Skaara. Kasuf. All of them, the past.*

The pain faded, slowly. He shook himself, bent to picking up more stones and gradually became aware he was being watched.

"Your face is sad, David," said Sallah, her small hands full of rocks. She had a look of Sha're about her; dark hair, dark eyes. That smile. "Don't you like to be here with us?"

He took the rocks from her and placed them on top of the tall pile they'd collected already. Nearby, two young buck goats got into an argument over a scrawny thistle. He watched them until he could trust his voice not to frighten the child.

"I like you, Sallah," he said, and touched her petal cheek with his finger. "And your friends. But I wish we all were somewhere else."

The vanquished buck gave one last toss of its head—*I never wanted it anyway, so there*—and trotted off to find another thistle. Sallah said, puzzled, "Where else could we be? I am too young to serve the god, and you serve him here already."

He felt his heart hitch. She was what—seven? eight?—and she made him feel like an adolescent. The wickedness of this place would destroy him, if he let it. *Get in, do the job, get out. Stay detached. Stay focused. It's not a rescue mission, Daniel.*

It sounded so simple, in theory...

"Listen!" said Sallah, and tugged at his hand. "The night bell, can you hear it?"

He turned his head. Yes. There, on the breeze. A faint clang-clang-clang from the village. Scattered over the rest of the pasture, picking up rocks, the other children heard it too.

"We must go back now," said Sallah. All day long she'd been lecturing him. Guiding him. Pointing out his myriad errors. The older boys, led by Baen, had dismissed him within minutes as a lightweight. But it seemed that Sallah had adopted him.

I wonder if Jack would notice an extra, short team member.

Baen came over now, loping easily like some young hunting cat. "That was the bell, David."

"I know," he said. "I heard it. Time to gather the goats and chivvy them home to the village. I'll take the ones with two legs, you can take the rest."

A grudging smile quirked the boy's lips. "Ha!"

We have to get them all out of here, Daniel decided, as he took Sallah's hand and began to round up the scattered children. *I really don't care what Jack says. I don't. I don't. We cannot leave these people behind.*

He didn't know how, but he'd convince Jack of that if it was the last thing he did.

CHAPTER THIRTEEN

Daniel was just finishing up his rag-and-bucket ablutions in the communal bath-house when he heard the familiar, deadly sound of staff weapons discharging.

"Assemble, slaves!" a harsh voice shouted. "Hol'c commands an inspection!"

Cries of consternation echoed up and down the bath-house. Doors, banging. Feet, both bare and shod, running. A collection of roughspun shifts had been left hanging on rows of pegs outside the cubicles, for after bathing. Grabbing one that looked like it'd fit, Daniel hauled it over his head, shoved his feet back into his shoes, and joined the anxious flood of humans heading for the village centre.

Hol'c was there, with all his Jaffa. He ruled a garrison of twenty. As Jacob had said, not a large contingent... but then it didn't need to be. Not when the humans were unarmed and long-since browbeaten into obedience and the Jaffa had staff weapons and zat guns and firebrands to enforce their absolute unconquerable will.

Jostled and pressed into line, Daniel looked for Jack or Sam. Ah. There she was, with a group of other women. He shoved as close to her as he could get without drawing the wrong sort of attention to himself. She was dressed in clean clothes. Her hair was wet, and a line of soap bubbles was drying on her cheek. He risked a little wave; she saw him, and nodded, but didn't wave back. She was closer to the Jaffa than he was, and therefore in more danger.

Where's Jack? he mouthed at her.

She shrugged. *Don't know*.

He kept on looking, fighting to see past heads and shoulders on every side. Then Hol'c shot his staff weapon into the air and the villagers' low murmuring stopped as though guillotined. The twenty Jaffa formed a formidable line behind their leader, staff weapons at the ready.

"Come forth, Boaz!" Hol'c commanded. "Your god's beloved servant would speak to you."

In Daniel's experience, Jaffa were bred for speed and skill and trainability, not generally for looks, but even amongst his own kind, not measured against the outrageous beauty of the slaves he guarded, Hol'c must have been counted ugly. Of middling height only—he'd barely reach Teal'c's shoulder—he had too much muscle laid over a spindly frame. Small eyes, slitted with bad temper. Feral, like a rabid dog's. His pallid skin was seamed and pocked as though from some disease his symbiote had struggled to vanquish. And there hung about him, like a marsh miasma, an air of power unbridled. Cruelty unchecked.

No wonder Sallah and the other children had whimpered at the mention of his name.

On the far side of the village centre the gathered slaves shuffled apart, and a moment later Boaz stepped clear. Trailing him was Mikah and behind Mikah—of course—was Jack. He was shirtless; his bare chest and arms were thickly smeared with dirt and blood and muck. He looked exhausted. Angry. Looked too as though he wanted to limp, and was fighting the urge. After four years Daniel knew to a hairsbreadth how much trouble Jack's knee was giving him on any given day.

After ten hours toiling without cease in the fields, the knee was clearly misbehaving.

For a moment it seemed as though Mikah was going to face Hol'c alongside his father, but Jack's fingers caught the boy's shirt and held him fast. He bent down, whispering something. Mikah's set face eased, just a fraction. He nodded. Jack loosened his grasp but kept his hand where it was.

Boaz reached Hol'c and flung himself to the ground. Kneeling, supporting himself on either side with his outstretched hands, he folded himself forward till his forehead was touching the dirt. Held himself there till his muscles were visibly quivering.

"Rise, slave," said Hol'c.

Boaz unfolded himself and regained his feet. "Master Hol'c. How may I serve?"

Hol'c was shorter than Boaz, but what he lacked in height he more than made up for with menace. He unhooked the fire-brand from his belt and stroked it like a plucked flower down the side of Boaz's face.

"Your get. Mikah. He has stolen from our god. From Yu, Mighty and Everlasting."

A single tremor ran through Boaz's body. His head jerked, as though instinct would have him turn to his son and self-preservation stopped him. "Master Hol'c?" His voice sounded sick, and pale.

"He was seen," said Hol'c. "He took a corn cob from the shucking house."

"It is my fault, Master Hol'c," said Boaz. "I have failed to teach him proper reverence for our god."

"Yes, Boaz," said Hol'c. The fire-brand stopped stroking and came to rest in the hollow of Boaz's throat, where sweat pooled and a pulse of fright beat in time with his frantic heart. "You have failed. But it's your get that will pay the price."

"Please, Master Hol'c," whispered Boaz. Even so, his voice carried across the village centre. "Punish me."

"*No!*" cried Mikah, and bolted forward before Jack could stop him. "*I* took the corn cob, Master Hol'c! *I* sinned against our god. Punish *me!*"

Hol'c swung his staff weapon, knocking Mikah hard to the ground. Daniel bit his tongue as he saw Jack react, arms reaching out to grab the boy. Then, incredibly, he stopped. Remembering, hopefully, that they couldn't afford to blow their cover. Not when their Tok'ra communicators were back in Boaz's house and they couldn't call Jacob for an emergency ring-out.

Hol'c loomed over Boaz's son. "Where is the corn you stole?"

Mikah's hand crept inside his shirt and pulled out a stunted, withered cob of corn. "It has weevils, Master Hol'c," he said, his eyes wide with trepidation. "It would've been thrown away. I wanted to make a doll. For Serena's baby, the one that will come after Joseph has quickened her."

Daniel looked at Sam. Saw that Jack was looking at her too, as though he'd always known where she was. Sam's hand was pressed to her mouth and her eyes were horrified.

Hol'c leaned down and glared into Mikah's scared white face. "Nothing is thrown away, slave boy. Weevilled corn goes to animal feed or fertilizes the fields. You stole from our god. Now pay the price."

The fire-brand swung from Boaz's throat to Mikah's belly.

Hol'c's sure finger flipped the switch. And Mikah was screaming, screaming, scarlet fire bursting from his mouth and eyes. All around the village centre the gathered humans turned away, clutching at the other children old enough to gather with them. Some wailed. Some wept. Others cried out to the great golden statue, "Forgive us, god, forgive us, Yu!"

Boaz stared at his writhing son as though his life was over. Tears were pouring down his cheeks.

"*Sonofabitch*!" Jack shouted, and threw himself at Mikah, or Hol'c, it was hard to say which. Twenty Jaffa staff weapons hummed into life and swung towards him.

As one, Daniel and Sam shouted: "*Joseph! No*!"

Jack stopped, hands fisted and raised. "He's just a kid," he said over Mikah's keening. "Leave him alone, you Jaffa bastard!"

Hol'c laughed. Jerked the fire-brand away from Mikah and planted it against Jack's chest. Jack crashed to the ground, shuddering, convulsing. Hol'c laughed harder. Leaned on the fire-brand as though he wanted to press it through Jack's flesh and bone and into the dirt beneath him.

Probably he did.

After an age he pulled it away and said, snarling, "You are valued by our god, Joseph. If you were not I would kill you now." He turned to Boaz. "This one is punished for defiance. Your get is punished for theft." He rammed the fire-brand into Boaz's belly and watched him fall and writhe and scream for long moments, then pulled the instrument away. "And you are punished for letting it happen. Next time I will not be so lenient. Next time I will not let you live."

Gasping, trembling, Boaz dragged himself to his knees. "Master Hol'c is merciful," he choked. "I will not fail him or our god again."

Hol'c raised the fire-brand above his head. "It is done. Finish your day, slaves, and remember what you have seen!"

As the gathered villagers began to withdraw, silent and shaken, Boaz looked at Jack. "What of this one, Master Hol'c?"

Hol'c spat. "Leave it where it lies."

"And my get?"

Mikah was stirring, sniffling a little. One hand reached towards the sound of his father's voice. Hol'c nudged him with a booted foot;

not quite a kick, but almost.

"Take it with you."

Hol'c and his Jaffa withdrew. As soon as it was safe, Daniel rushed to Boaz, who'd gathered Mikah in his arms and was holding him close.

"Boaz! Is he all right?"

Sam joined them, dropping to a crouch. "Boaz, I'm so sorry," she said, her voice unsteady. "I had no idea he'd do something so foolish for me."

Still kneeling, Boaz smoothed the tumbled hair from Mikah's face. "It's not your fault, Serena."

Beside them Jack sprawled insensible. Sam pressed a hand to his face then looked at the charred mark on his chest. "Boaz..."

"You heard Hol'c," said Boaz. "Joseph must stay here."

"For how long?"

"Till he regains his senses and strength enough to crawl away."

Daniel touched her arm. "It's okay. I'll stay with him."

"No," said Boaz. "It will be time for nightmeal soon. We must eat, then I must hear the day's progress. This is how the god decrees I order our lives. I cannot disobey him and neither can you."

"But Boaz, Joseph's hurt," Sam protested. "Because he—"

"*No, Serena!*" In a single swift movement Boaz stood, his son drowsy in his arms. For all he was smeared with filth, like Jack, and tear-tracks marred his perfectly sculpted cheeks, his authority was complete. "Mikah has bathed and dressed, and so have you. Take him to the meeting hall and wait there with the others until it's time to eat. I must bathe and dress. You, David, must dress. In this village we do not eat unwashed, or clothed in our bath shifts. That is to show disrespect to the god."

"A god who sanctions the torture of children," Sam spat.

Boaz's arms tightened. "Mikah was wrong. He is punished. It is over."

Daniel bent down, took her by the elbow and made her stand. "Serena—we must respect the god," he said sharply. Thinking, *not you too, not you, don't tell me I'm the only one who's got his act together.* "We must remember why we're here!"

She flinched and pulled her arm free. He watched his words reach her, watched her gather her scattered emotions and use her strict military training to button them down tight. Her gaze flicked downwards once, to Jack, who was yet to move. Then she nodded. "I am corrected, David," she said softly. "We must respect the god."

Mikah was fully awake now. Boaz set him on his feet, hands bracing his shoulders till it was clear the boy could stand alone. "Mikah, you were wrong to take the corn cob."

Beneath his golden tan, Mikah's skin was pale. In his eyes, a shadow of pain. "Yes, Papa."

"If I had discovered your theft I would have punished you. But Hol'c has punished you, and that is enough." Boaz bent and retrieved the stolen corn cob and gave it back to his son. "Tomorrow morning you will feed this to the hogs, Mikah," he said, his face stern. "Before five witnesses. Then you will return here—" He pointed to the golden statue. "—and you will kneel to the god three hours, forsaking firstmeal."

"You said he'd been punished enough," protested Sam.

"Kneeling to the god is not punishment," said Boaz curtly. "It's penance. The god will see him kneel. The god will feel his hunger. The god will know his heart is pure once more. Now go. Curjin will be ringing the bell very soon."

Sam held out her hand. "Come on, Mikah," she said, and smiled at the boy. "Let's show everyone we're still best friends."

They started towards the meeting hall. Boaz said, abruptly, "Mikah. Who was it saw you take the corn cob?"

Mikah stopped and turned. "I think it was Jenc, Papa."

Daniel saw some dark emotion flick across Boaz's face. "Jenc. I see. Go on, Mikah."

"Who's Jenc?" he asked, as Sam led the boy away.

"A villager."

No kidding. "An enemy?" he prompted.

"He wanted Mikah's mother. The god gave her to me."

"Oh," he said. "Right. Say no more."

"He did not have to tell Hol'c about the corn cob," said Boaz. His voice was tight, his expression full of pain. "He could have taken it from Mikah and put it in the hog pile and warned me in private that Mikah had strayed."

"But he wanted Mikah's mother, so . . ."

Boaz pressed his fingers to his eyes for a moment, hard. Then he straightened his bowed shoulders. "Go dress yourself, David. And take a lesson from what has happened here today. Only your Lord Rebec saved Joseph from death. He might not save him again. And if Joseph should raise his voice to Hol'c a second time... then he is too stupid to save."

On that note, Boaz headed for the bath-house.

Daniel glared after him. Wanted to shout, *Stupid? Stupid? He tried to protect your son, you miserable ungrateful bastard, while you just knelt there and let that Jaffa burn him!*

But he didn't. There had been enough unwise actions taken today. Instead he dropped to one knee beside Jack, who still wasn't stirring. The prolonged nerve-wracking assault of the fire-brand on top of a day's back-breaking slog in the fields had wrung him out.

"Jack, Jack, what are we going to do with you?" he murmured. "Start following your own orders, will you? Or we're all going to be in trouble."

It killed him to leave Jack lying there, stinking and blood-smeared and flinching still, intermittently, from the fire-brand. But Boaz had spoken and must be obeyed.

He hurried back to the house, pulled off his bath-shift, pulled on fresh shirt and trousers... then stopped. Jack had said it was too dangerous for them to carry their Tok'ra communicators, but he was starting to think it was too dangerous not to. If this afternoon's little disaster had really got out of hand, if it looked as though Hol'c was going to *kill* Jack...

He fished his communicator out of his bitty bag, shoved it deep in his trouser pocket and immediately felt better. Unlike Jack and Sam, he'd drawn no attention to himself and he had no plans to change that. He was the softy scribe who couldn't be trusted with a knife, after all. The chances of Hol'c strip-searching him had to be slim to none. And with a communicator in his pocket he could probably save them all if things went bad again.

But he didn't think he'd mention it to Jack. The mood Jack was in, he wouldn't take kindly to contradiction. And he wouldn't tell Sam, either. For all he knew she talked in her sleep.

Ha! Wait till he told Teal'c about *that* one. Jack and Sam, bunked in the same bed and ordered to procreate for the glory of Yu. Teal'c would laugh for a week...

God. I miss Teal'c.

He toyed with the idea of giving Jacob a quick call before going back to the meeting hall for nightmeal, but decided against it. That was Jack's prerogative. No point stirring him up unnecessarily. When he finally came to he'd be pissed enough without anyone throwing fuel on the fire.

Daniel heard the front door open and bang shut. It was Boaz, returning to dress. When he was done they lit the house lamps and returned to the meeting hall together. They walked past Jack, still lying in the village centre, abandoned like road kill. Boaz didn't even spare him a glance.

Bastard.

Daniel and Sam sat at different trestles this time, mingling with the villagers. Mikah sat with his father and some of the women from the babyhouse at the head trestle. The mood in the hall was subdued, appetites half-hearted. Last night there'd been laughter and joking and a swirling of energy beneath the high roof. Tonight voices were low, gestures circumspect. The older children at their special trestles stared at each other with frightened eyes. Their wide gazes skittered to Mikah and away again and they spoke to each other in whispers.

When the meal was over and the plates cleared away, Boaz rang his hand bell and called for the day's accounting. One by one a villager from each task group stood and recited the work achieved that day for the glory of the god.

After hearing from the storehouse, the smithy, the slaughterhouse and the kiln-shop, a woman from the babyhouse rose to speak.

"All the babies and small children thrive," she said. "The quickened women thrive. No births today. Perhaps tomorrow. Three children stood for the first time today. Five took their first steps. Four spoke their first words. New blood Serena joined us and shows promise, though she still has much to learn."

"Thank you, Qualah," said Boaz. "Your service honours the god. Who now speaks for the poultry-sheds?"

When it was Daniel's turn he flicked a smile at Sallah, sitting with Baen and the others at their trestle. "Today we collected many stones from the goat pasture," he told the attentive villagers. "Baen and

Sallah helped free a goat that had tangled itself in brambles. Ochek, Tor and Bron stopped several snake holes and killed one snake. All the children worked hard for our god Yu, Mighty and Everlasting. I thank you, Boaz, for allowing me the chance to learn how I can best serve him. For a scribe has no purpose here … yet you have given me purpose."

"Your service honours the god, David," said Boaz. For the first time since he'd entered the hall, his face lost some of its tension. "You may sit. Lastly, we will hear the report from the shucking house."

It seemed to Daniel that everyone held their breath. All eyes turned to one man, who slowly stood at the back of the hall and turned to face Boaz. His skin was a dark copper, his hair deep auburn.

"In the shucking house today," he said in a rich, melting baritone, "we finished shucking the last ripe corn and took it to the drying house. It will be ready in time for the next collection."

"Good news, Jenc," said Boaz, his voice light and even. "And is that all you did in the shucking house today?"

Daniel looked for Sam, and exchanged uneasy looks with her. If Jenc confessed he'd reported Mikah to Hol'c, what would the villagers do? And if he didn't, what would Boaz do? What was Jenc's game here—to strike back for a petty, personal grudge, or to cause a wider rift and perhaps see Boaz's authority publicly challenged?

Jenc held Boaz's gaze. Held it—held it—and broke. Staring at the floor he said, "That is all."

Boaz nodded. "Your service today has honored our god. All service today has honored our god. Today we are reminded, most humbly, that not one of us may disrespect the god and go unpunished." His hand rested, briefly, on Mikah's bowed head. "Now let us set our trestles to one side and make merry, in celebration of all the good service done to our god this day."

Under cover of bustling activity, Daniel took Sam to one side and said, "Hey. Are you okay?"

Her lips trembled, just for a moment, and her jaw clenched. Then she nodded, control restored. "Fine. You?"

"I nearly had a heart attack when the kids killed that snake," he said. "They snuck up behind me and draped it round my neck. It's a wonder you didn't hear my scream in the babyhouse."

She managed a small, tight smile. "Kids will be kids." Then she flicked a look at Mikah. "He seems okay. I guess they're used to it. Being brutally punished on a whim."

"Is that something you get used to?" he wondered, and shook his head. "Listen. I'm going to sneak out of here in a few minutes. Make sure our fearless leader got back to the house in one piece."

"I'll come too."

"No. You'd better stay. You're a lot more conspicuous than I am. Have a dance with Boaz. Not that he deserves it. Ja—Joseph—copped what was owing to Mikah but the way he's acting—"

"He got a bad fright," Sam said. "And he had to watch that bastard Hol'c hurt his child. Listen—I don't suppose you managed to sound out anyone on the chances of—"

"Yes. All the goats have volunteered to join us."

She laughed, this time. "Yeah. Okay."

"How about you? Any prospects?"

Sam turned her head, just a little, and nodded fractionally towards a stunning blond who was organizing Sallah and her friends into some kind of a leap-frogging contest. "Berez," she murmured. "She's a definite possibility. If I can only talk to her without Qualah hovering in the background."

"Try," he said. "I don't want to leave this place without something concrete to show for it."

She touched his arm. "Believe me, neither do I."

They both turned, then, at the sound of drums, tambourine and triangles. The village band, striking up their brand of music to chase the day's demons away.

"Incredible, isn't it?" he said, touched almost to tears. "The resilience of the human spirit. That's why we'll win here, you know. That's why the Goa'uld will be defeated. Because humans were born to be free and deep down, no matter how beaten we are, no matter how frightened, we know it."

Sam surprised him, then, by folding him to her in a swift, fierce hug. By whispering in his ear, "Go see Jack. Make sure he's all right."

She hardly ever hugged him. She never called Jack 'Jack'. Not any more. It told Daniel just how upset she was. How deeply this place was affecting her.

He hugged her back. "Going now. Hang in there, Sam. We'll win this one. We have to."

Nobody noticed him slip out of the hall; the need to wipe out the aftermath of violence and terror with desperate frivolity was overwhelming and universally human. Jack was no longer lying unconscious in the village centre. Daniel checked the bath-house but Jack wasn't there, either. So he went back to Boaz's house... and found him in the bedroom. Hiding in the eldritch shadows cast by a single lamp.

When the bedroom door opened Jack took one look and said, "Piss off, Daniel."

In between waking and coming back here he'd found the strength to wash; he no longer stank like an abattoir or looked like an extra from a cheap splatter film. But he still looked bad. Chalky beneath a gloss of sunburn, and with some bleakly unpleasant thought or feeling in his eyes.

Daniel kicked the door shut behind him and sat on the floor. There was no chair, and sitting on the bed was out of the question. He didn't feel the least bit intimidated by sitting below Jack's line of sight. He'd stopped being intimidated by Jack years ago.

"Yeah," he said, and folded his arms on his pulled-up knees. "Like that's going to happen." He glanced at the ceiling. "Have you checked in with Jacob?"

"Yes."

"Is he still okay?"

Jack glowered. "Well, he and Martouf don't want to kill each other yet, so what does that tell you?"

Mostly, that Jacob and Martouf weren't Jack and Daniel. He let his head tip back until it rested against the door and, frowning, marshalled his thoughts. Then he recited, with meticulous accuracy: *"No matter what we find when we get onto this moon, no matter how offended your sensibilities are by this whole slave farm thing, we do not rock the boat. This is not a rescue mission. We are not going there to free the slaves. We have a single objective: to recruit hosts and spies for the Tok'ra."* He smiled, brightly. "There's more. Wanna hear? After *that* you said—"

"I swear to God, Daniel, I swear to *God*," Jack interrupted, conversationally. "If you don't stop with the photographic memory routine *right now* I'll shoot you."

Daniel thought about that. "Actually," he said, after a moment, "it's really more like perfect audio recall. And you can't shoot me, Jack. You don't have a gun."

Jack's glare was baleful in the extreme. "Daniel, there's a smithy here. I'll *make* one. And *then* I'll shoot you."

Daniel sighed. "Jack, what the hell is going on with you? First it was attacking Kinsey in the Pentagon in front of the Chairman of the Joint Chiefs and sundry other witnesses. Now it's nearly getting yourself killed, practically blowing your cover—and mine, and Sam's, incidentally—when you must be one of the most experienced behind-enemy-lines operatives in the US military."

"Gosh, Daniel, who knows?" said Jack, with his trademark excoriating sarcasm. "Maybe I'm just having a bad day."

Another sigh. "Jack, please. Don't treat me like an idiot. Something is going on. You are the most emotionally detached person serving in the SGC. They call you Iceman O'Neill when they think you can't hear them."

A muscle twitched in Jack's face. "They think wrong."

"My *point*," he said, sharply, "is that you are not me. Except lately you are. And to be perfectly frank, Jack, you're scaring me. Iceman O'Neill I can handle. I've met him before. But Exploding Volcano O'Neill? Not enjoying his company so much. He's a loose cannon. He's going to get us into trouble. He's not someone I want leading my team."

"It's *my* team, Daniel. And I'll lead it however I see fit."

"Yes, but you're not fit, are you?" he pointed out. "You're still hung up on what happened in Euronda. Okay. In the interests of full disclosure, so am I. But this is neither the time nor the place to get into that, Jack. We have bigger problems on our plate. More important fish to fry. And why is it that *I'm* the one having to tell *you* that?"

Jack looked at him with the kind of icy disdain that froze other SGC personnel solid. "I am not hung up on what happened in Euronda."

Daniel snorted. "Yeah. Right. And *I'm* not an archaeologist."

Another freezing look. "Daniel, drop it."

"Drop it," he said, scathing. "What am I? A dog? Okay. Maybe this *is* the perfect time to get into Euronda. You're not usually a captive audience, so what the hey. I'll summarize for you, shall I? You were wrong, I was right, it pisses you off."

"Want a newsflash?" Jack retorted. "You're right again. This isn't the time or place, Daniel."

"Why isn't it? You're always saying I insert inappropriate personal commentary into every conversation. Why break the habit of a lifetime?"

Jack stared at him. "I don't say that."

"Yes, you do."

"No, I don't."

"You do."

"I don't."

"Jack, you do."

"Daniel, *I don't*!"

Daniel thought for a moment. "Okay. Maybe you don't. But you think it."

"Which *isn't* the same as saying it!"

"Oh, so you do admit you think it?"

"*Daniel*!"

He smiled. "Gotcha."

They stared at each other in rueful, irritated, mutually baffled silence. Jack was the first to look away. "I apologized for being wrong in Euronda."

"I know. But that doesn't stop you from being pissed."

"Yeah. Okay. I'm pissed," said Jack, and looked back at him. "Do you want to know *why* I'm pissed?"

Ah! Progress. "Please."

"I'm pissed, Daniel, because I'm still waiting for an apology from you."

He felt his heart thud, hard. "I don't owe you an apology for Euronda. I was right to ask questions. I was right to say slow down. I was right to halt you in your tracks and make you look at what you were doing."

Jack nodded. "Yes. You were. I'm not pissed about what you did, Daniel, I'm pissed about how you did it. About how you always do it. You question my judgement and my authority regardless of who's listening. And when you do that you undermine my leadership in front of people who have to believe that I am strong. That we're strong. A single united front."

"Jack, I had to over-ride you in front of Alar! You wouldn't listen to me, you—"

"Oh, please," said Jack, derisive. "When have I *ever* not listened to you, Daniel? When have I *ever* not taken a leap of faith when you've asked me to? I have trusted you over and over and over again. And all I ask in return is that you show me a little respect. I have *never* said don't disagree with me. What I *have* said, more than once, is disagree with me by all means … just do it in *private*. But you never do. And you don't even see it's a problem. *That* is why I'm pissed at you, Daniel. Because at the end of the day *you're* the one who's arrogant. *You're* the one who won't get off his moral high horse. *You're* the one who has to be right all the time, no matter what it costs. Or who you hurt."

It was like being gut-punched. Zat-blasted. Kicked in the balls. "That is *not* true."

Jack looked away. "Okay. Whatever."

It *wasn't* true. He didn't ride a moral high horse, he just spoke up about the things that mattered, the inconvenient complicated truths the military just loved to ignore. "Jack—"

Jack closed his eyes. "I'm tired, Daniel. Don't let the door hit your ass on the way out."

He hadn't come in here for this. To be raked over the coals when he'd clearly been in the right. He'd come to talk about the *end* of the Eurondan mission. Those final moments in the 'gateroom whose echoing reverberations were putting the team in danger now. "Jack, we have to talk about Alar." He got up. Couldn't finish this conversation sitting down. "About how what happened—how he died—*why* he died. It's eating you alive from the inside out and compromising you and—"

"Daniel, I don't *have* to do anything!" Jack retorted, glaring. "I *especially* don't have to talk about Alar."

"Yes, you do," he insisted. "Because what happened to him is making you short-tempered and unpredictable and so long as my life depends on you in this crappy place I want you to—"

"And what *I* want, Daniel," said Jack, moving with the speed of a striking snake, off the bed and into his face, "is for you to *shut the hell up!*"

Heart pounding, Daniel lifted his hands and took a step back. Bump, right into the door. "Okay, Jack. I hear you. I'm listening. I'm shutting the hell up."

Slowly, too slowly, the murderous rage drained out of Jack's face. He released a shuddering sigh then with a painful, visible effort, shifted his thoughts in a different direction. "How did you make out today? Did you find any potential candidates for the Tok'ra?"

Daniel let out his own unsteady breath. He was fairly certain the joke about the goats would go down like a lead balloon just now. "Not yet. Sam has."

Jack flicked him an acid look. "Then I suggest you get your ass into gear, Daniel. We're running out of time and so are these people."

"Yes. Yes, I know."

"I need some air," said Jack, abruptly. Pushing him aside, he opened the door and stalked out of the bedroom. A moment later came the sound of the house's front door opening and slamming shut.

"Okay," said Daniel to the empty room. "That went well."

And then he gave in to the promptings of his trembling knees and sat down hard on the bed.

Oh, God. Oh God, he prayed, meaning it more than usual. *Help him, please. And then help us to get out of this mess alive.*

CHAPTER FOURTEEN

Boaz let the games and dancing go on longer than normal, that night. After the horror in the village centre the people needed healing. Laughter, merriment, a surcease of toil; they were the best healers of a hurt spirit.

And spirits were always hurt hardest when Hol'c punished a child.

Seated at his head man's trestle he watched the people—his people—slowly rediscover laughter. Watched Jenc, playing his drum, and wondered if the man was sorry, now, for letting the old spite, the nursed grudge, overwhelm his better judgement. They hadn't spoken. They wouldn't speak. What could Jenc say that he'd believe? It was an accident? I didn't know?

Mikah was playing tag with the other older children, darting around and between the adults. He seemed no worse for his punishment. Stealing a corn cob? What a foolish thing to do...

His gaze drifted to Serena, who was being taught a new dance by Berez, and he felt his lips twist in a wry, self-mocking smile. If Mikah was foolish for stealing a corn cob then how much more foolish was Mikah's father, falling in love with another man's mate?

Falling in love with anyone. To love someone on a breeding farm was a curse, not a comfort. No man with any sense loved the woman he mated... or the babies born of that union.

I am a man of no sense whatsoever.

Worse still, he was not even mated with Serena. Might never be mated with her. She was Joseph's, at least for now, even though Joseph gave no sign of wanting her. Was the man *blind*, then? Touched in the head? Who could see Serena, and not be moved to wanting her?

Joseph.

He was too tired to think of Joseph.

Serena was dancing with Mikah now, showing off her brand new skill. Mikah was laughing. He hadn't laughed like that since his mother died. Serena would make a good mother. Qualah had told him, taking him aside after dinner, that the new woman had a clear heart for babies. He'd thanked her, swamped with relief. There were some women whose bodies quickened but not their hearts. Those women Lord Choulai disposed of into the ground for fear they'd contaminate the bloodlines.

Boaz looked around the meeting hall. The people were tiring. Children had dropped to the floor in corners and were drowsing on each other's slumped shoulders. It was late, and time for bed. Dawn came too soon as it was.

He stood and rang his hand bell. It was all he needed to do; the music stopped, instruments were returned to the trunks against the wall. The trestles were put back in their places, ready for breakfast. Sleepy children were roused to stand, or picked up and carried. The hall emptied until only Mikah and Serena remained.

He lit a walking lamp for them, doused the hall's lamps, and closed its doors behind them. Serena held Mikah's left hand. He took Mikah's right and together they headed back to the house.

"David did not stay long in the hall tonight," he said. "He should stay longer next time."

Serena looked at him over the top of Mikah's drooping head. "You didn't stop him leaving."

"He is new. I know that can be difficult but even so, he must stay longer tomorrow. If Hol'c suspects he might be trouble..."

"He was worried about Joseph," she said. "I'm sure he will stay longer tomorrow."

"And what of you, Serena?" he asked after a moment. "Are you worried for Joseph?"

Even with the burning lamp it was hard to see her expression. "Yes," she said simply. "I'm very worried."

"Do you love him?"

"*What*?" Now she sounded shocked. Flustered. "Boaz, I hardly know him."

"That is true."

"No," she said. "No, of course I don't love him."

"Good," he replied, staring straight ahead. "Love your babies if you must, Serena, while you have them. Love no-one else. That is how you'll survive this place."

"Is that how *you* survive?"

"It is."

"I'm sorry," she said. "It sounds so … cold."

He looked at her then, as she turned her head to look at him. "It is," he said. And said nothing else, during the rest of the walk home.

David had not gone to bed. He was sitting at the table waiting for them. He too looked worried. "You didn't see Joseph out there, did you?" he greeted them as they entered the house.

"What?" Serena said sharply. "Are you saying he hasn't—"

"No, no," said David. "Sorry. He was here when I got back, but then he left."

Now she was frowning. Apprehensive. "David, you didn't—"

"No. Not exactly. Well, sort of," said David. "You know."

Boaz stared from him to Serena. Not for the first time he had the strange feeling a different conversation was going on between these two, one he couldn't hear. Or begin to understand.

It made him uneasy all over again.

"David …" Serena sounded impatient, yet resigned.

David shrugged. "He said he needed some air."

Mikah, almost sleeping on his feet, frowned and said muzzily, "There's air in here, David."

"Not that kind of air, Mikah," Serena said, distractedly. "I'd better go find him. Boaz—"

"No," Boaz said, and made his voice quite final. "I am head man, and this is my house. I will find him. You will all three go to bed now. After today there can be no lateness to the meeting hall for firstmeal. Our god has been angered enough."

For a moment Serena looked as though she'd argue. Then she sighed. "Yes. You're right, Boaz." Bending, she dropped a swift kiss to the top of Mikah's head. "Sleep tight, Mikah. Don't let the bed bugs bite. David—"

David smiled at her. "I know. I know. Softly softly catchee monkey."

She just shook her head, smiled at him, and went into the bedroom she shared with Joseph.

"Good night, Boaz," David said, pushing to his feet. "Good night, Mikah."

"Good night," Boaz replied to David's retreating back, then

kissed his son's curls himself. "Go to bed, Mikah."

"Yes, Papa," said Mikah, and did as he was told.

Boaz took a small clay pot of salve from the cupboard by the window, checked to see there was enough oil still burning in the walking lamp, then went outside to find troublesome Joseph.

He didn't have to look far. The man was sitting on the ground behind the house, his back propped against the mud-brick wall. Silent. Unnervingly still. Eyes closed. Hands neatly folded. Boaz stopped three paces away, the walking lamp dangling by his side.

"*Sonofabitch*," he said. "That word is unfamiliar. What does it mean?"

"It means," said Joseph, not opening his eyes, "that I don't like Hol'c very much."

He'd washed his hair as well as his body. Dressed in clean clothing so the burn from Hol'c's fire-brand was hidden. Boaz took the clay salve-pot from his pocket and placed it on the ground by Joseph's knee. Then he stepped back again and waited to see what would happen.

After the longest time, his eyelids still closed, Joseph said, "A present? For me? You shouldn't have."

"It is salve, for the fire-brand burn you bear," he said. "Is that a present? I don't know that word, either."

Joseph opened his eyes. "Boaz, there's too damned much you don't know."

Boaz put down the walking lamp and dropped to the ground. "Then isn't it time you told me, Joseph? Who are you? Where are you from? No slave would do what you did for Mikah today. I am his father and *I* did not—" His voice broke. Shame and rage and pain and resentment welled without warning, unstoppable. He was weeping. Sobbing. Rocking back and forth like a woman whose get has just been taken.

And then, to his great surprise, Joseph's hand came to rest on his shoulder and Joseph's voice, so gentle it was unrecognizable, was saying, "Easy, Boaz. Easy, there. It's okay. It's okay."

The last man's hand to touch him in comfort had been his father's, moments before Hol'c's staff blast killed him. Joseph's kindness now, reminding him, was more than he could bear. He pulled away, gathering to himself the tatters of his self-control. Sucking in great lungfuls of the cool night air he forced his grief and tears and impotent rage back deep inside, where they belonged. Where Hol'c would never see them.

Joseph said, his voice still gentle, "I could tell you all the things you don't know, Boaz. The question is, do you want me to? Because there's no going back, after. And if you try to betray me to Hol'c I'll kill you. If you believe nothing else I say, believe that."

Boaz believed it. He remembered Joseph's face, that first day in the village centre. That first day? It was only two days ago… yet somehow it felt like another life entirely.

"I want to know," he said. "I have to know. I am head man of this village. The humans here are in my care. If you have come to hurt them then *I* will kill *you*. Myself. No need for Hol'c."

Joseph's teeth bared in a smile. "I didn't come to hurt you or your people, Boaz. I came to help."

"Why? We need no help."

"No?" said Joseph, his voice cold and hard again. "So that wasn't your son being tortured today? Those aren't your people being plowed into the dirt? This place isn't your prison? I see. My mistake. Guess I was imagining it."

"You are just a human," Boaz said, his voice very small. "How can you help?"

"I can help because I'm a human who knows the truth about the Goa'uld," said Joseph. "The Jaffa. This whole stinking lousy set up."

Now he was confused. "Truth? What truth? The Goa'uld are gods, Joseph. Yu is *our* god. That is the truth."

Joseph took a deep, harsh breath and hissed it out between his teeth. "Boaz, the Goa'uld aren't gods. They are life forms, the way humans are life forms. But they don't look like us, they look like snakes, and they live by stealing our bodies and taking over our minds. They wear us the way we wear clothes and they care as much for our well-being as we care about the feelings of our *boots*."

There was a roaring in his ears. A dreadful sensation of falling. "No," he said faintly. "You're lying. The god Yu is our god, Mighty and Everlasting. He—"

"Mighty?" said Joseph, sneering. "Yeah. Okay. Mighty *egos*, I'll give you that. But Everlasting? Not so much. Let's see…" He pulled a face. "So far me and my people have killed the gods Ra, Apophis, Seth and Hathor. Hathor I did personally, with my bare hands, and boy I gotta tell ya, it felt good. I've also killed a lot of Jaffa, Boaz. In fact I've killed so many Jaffa I lost count a couple of years ago."

All his bones had turned to butter. "You killed a god with your bare hands?"

Joseph shook him. "Boaz, you're not listening! They're *not gods*. And we weren't born to be their slaves. What's happening on this breeding farm is an abomination. It has to stop. And we can stop it, you and me. Together. We can stop it here. We can stop it everywhere. We can destroy every last damned breeding farm and all the Goa'uld bastards who own them. How does that sound? Do you like that idea? 'Cause I do. I like it a *lot*."

"I think I must be dreaming," Boaz said at last. "Yes. I am dreaming."

"And did you dream Mikah on his back screaming while Hol'c rammed that fire-brand into his belly?" said Joseph, cruelly. "Did you dream your other children, taken away in chains, or your father dying so you could take his place here?"

"No—Joseph—you must be quiet, you must—"

In the lamp-light Joseph's face was frightening. "Do you want to save Mikah, Boaz? Do you want to see him grow up healthy, and happy, and free? Do you? Then *help* me! I can make that happen! But I can't do it alone."

Defy the god? Escape this farm? It was impossible and Joseph was mad. Boaz scrambled to his feet. "I think you are ill, Joseph. I think Hol'c's punishment has upset your mind. I will excuse you from work tomorrow. You will rest. Sleep. You will get better. You must get better. If you don't, Hol'c will make us plow you into the fallow field. You risked your life for Mikah. I'll save you if I can, for that. But you must *never* speak of this again. I will forget you ever said it."

Joseph growled something under his breath and stood. "I should've known better," he muttered. "I'm no good at this crap." He looked up. "Boaz, come inside. There's more you need to hear."

Yes. Definitely, Joseph was mad. Boaz let the man chivvy him into the house. Stood back, torn between alarm and dismay, as he banged on the door of the bedroom he shared with Serena.

"Carter, get out here!"

"Joseph," he protested. "Stop. Your brain is fevered, you must—"

Joseph ignored him, and went to David's door. "Yo, Daniel! Up and at 'em! It's touchy feely time!"

Serena came out of the bedroom, alarmed. "Joseph? What's wrong? What—"

Joseph waved his hand impatiently at the table and chairs. "You can cut the undercover crap, Carter. Take a seat. Boaz, sit next to her. *Daniel*!"

David joined them, blinking. "Ah, Joseph…?"

"Oh my God," said Serena, groping for a chair. "You told him."

"Yeah," said Joseph, smiling grimly, and leaned against the window-frame. "I told him."

Still standing, David crossed his arms. "Told him what? Told him *everything*?"

"Everything he needs to know. Yeah."

Serena stared at David, then at Joseph. "Oh my God, sir, what were you *thinking*? Dad specifically said—"

"To hell with what Dad said, Carter," Joseph retorted. "It's my call and I'm calling it. Dad wants spies and hosts to fight against the Goa'uld? Fine. So do I. But he's not going to get them by pussy-footing around. There's no time. In case you haven't noticed, these people have a sword hanging over their heads. Its name is Hol'c and he can torture them—kill them, even—with impunity whenever he damn well pleases."

"Yes, Joseph, we noticed," David said, his voice calm and careful. Clearly he too realized that Joseph had gone mad. "But barging ahead like a bull in a china shop—"

"Daniel, trust me," said Joseph. "I can do finesse when I have to. One of the top behind-enemy-lines operatives, remember? But Boaz is a resource and we need him on our side. We don't have time to tiptoe through the tulips. Carter?"

"Yes?" said Serena.

"What does your finely tuned Tok'ra sense tell you about ole Boaz here? You think he's got what it takes to join the team?"

Serena gave Joseph a sharp look, then closed her eyes. A strange expression crossed her face, uncertain and seeking and touched with pain. After some time she opened her eyes. "Yes, sir. I think he does."

Joseph nodded. "Good. Now, I've told him the truth about the Goa'uld but he doesn't believe me."

"Gosh," murmured David, looking at Serena. "That's surprising."

"*Daniel*!"

Serena turned and reached out her hand. "Boaz. I'm so sorry. Please. Sit down and we'll try to explain."

Boaz looked at her outstretched hand for long moments, then took it and sat beside her. He had never felt so uncertain, so dizzy, in all his life. "Joseph says the Goa'uld are not gods," he whispered.

"Not Joseph," said Joseph. "Jack. Jack O'Neill. Colonel. United States Air Force. Planet Earth." He pointed. "That's Daniel Jackson. This is Major Carter."

Noise, noise, the words were nothing but noise. Boaz looked again to Serena, his heart pounding so hard it was painful. "Serena—please—"

"Actually, it's Samantha," she said, her voice and face apologetic. "But mostly people call me Sam." Her gaze flickered. "Or Carter. But Sam is fine."

He shook his head. "I don't understand. I don't understand. Have we *all* gone mad?"

She took his other hand and held him fast with cool, strong fingers. Looked into his face, a small smile curving her lips. And as he looked back at her, he saw something... change. Shift. Something behind her eyes. She was still Serena, but suddenly she was something—someone—else as well. Suddenly he could see in her face what he'd seen in Joseph's—Jack's—in the village centre when they first arrived. Some clear, cold, sharp purpose. No soft feminine energy, nurturing and warm, now; just a blazing ferocity of will and mind. He knew then without asking, without being told, that Samantha could kill him as swiftly and easily as Jack could.

He felt sweat break out all over his body.

David—Daniel?—came and dropped to a crouch beside Sam's chair. "Boaz, listen to me. Jack told you the truth. The Goa'uld are not gods. I know they seem so but it's all lies and trickery. We can prove it, if you'll let us."

But they *were* gods, they *were*… "He said he has *killed* them…"

Daniel nodded. "Yes. We all have."

"It can't be," he whispered. "The god Yu is our *god*…"

"Why would we lie to you, Boaz?" Daniel asked gently. "What purpose would that serve?"

What purpose? None he could imagine. "Boaz," said Sam, and in her face was such compassion and strength he could barely breathe. "It's the truth. I swear it on my life."

His world was fracturing like a dropped clay urn and he was powerless to stop it. He could feel his tears, welling again. "But my children… my sons and my daughters… I sent them away, I told them to *rejoice*, they were going to serve the *god*…"

Daniel nodded. "That was the lie, Boaz. But you can't blame yourself for it. How could you know? From the moment you were born you've been lied to. Nothing you did or believed before today is your fault, I promise."

"But after today, Boaz?" said Jack, stepping forward. "What happens then, *that's* on you. If you don't help us you're helping the Goa'uld. If you don't help us you're not a slave any more. You're a slave-master."

Boaz looked into Jack's harsh and unforgiving face. "If I don't help you, you'll kill me."

Daniel leapt up. "*Jack?*"

"Daniel?"

"You can't seriously—"

"Really, Daniel? Can't I?"

Boaz held his breath. Sam released him and stood in one swift move. "Ah, guys? Chill. We don't have time for pissing contests."

Jack snapped his white-hot glare away from Daniel and burned her with it, instead. "*Excuse* me, Major?"

Her chin lifted defiantly. "Sorry. But I had to get your attention. Sir, you're right about one thing: as head man of the village Boaz can help me work out who's most likely to be on board with the plan. Whether or not it was a smart move to tell him is moot. It's done. So let's just finish what you've started and get the hell out of here, shall we?"

Slowly, so slowly, Jack's anger cooled. His posture relaxed.

"Actually, Carter, I didn't get past the whole 'the Goa'uld aren't gods' bit. Wanted to save something for you to do."

She gave him a look. "Gee. Thanks." She turned. "Boaz…"

"Who is Lord Rebec?" Boaz asked. "His eyes flashed fire. Is he a Goa'uld?"

"Not exactly," said Sam. "We'll explain about him later. Boaz, it's clear to us that you love Mikah very much and that you don't want him to live the rest of his life as a slave. Can you think of any other humans here who feel the same way about their children? I know you've never discussed it, I know probably most of you have never even dared to *think* it … but sometimes we know things about people without ever having to ask." She smiled. "The way I knew you were a good man the moment we met."

Daniel sat in a chair. "The reason we're asking, Boaz, is because we need help in fighting the Goa'uld."

Boaz nodded. "Jos—Jack said. But how can we leave here? Where would we go? How would we fight them? They—they may not be gods—" He stopped, as the fear of saying such words aloud threatened to blank his mind. Then he took a deep breath and continued. "They may not be gods, Daniel, but they are still very powerful."

"Yes they are," Daniel agreed. "But powerful or not they can be fought. Their evil can be stopped. If you agree to help us, we'll take you—and whoever else wants to come—far away from here to a place where you'll learn how to fight them. How to stop them. How to make sure no more children are taken from their parents and cruelly treated for the rest of their lives."

"Papa!" said Mikah's small and frightened voice behind them. "Papa, I'll go! I'll fight the Goa'uld! I'll kill them, Papa, and all the Jaffa too! I don't want you to send me away, I don't want to be a slave!"

Boaz staggered to his feet and spun around. "*Mikah!* What are you doing? You're supposed to be *asleep*!"

Jack walked past him, past all of them, and went to Mikah. He dropped to the floor and rested both hands lightly on the boy's shoulders. "How long have you been listening, Mikah?" His voice was quiet. Almost—tender. It was a father's voice. But *he* was Mikah's father…

"It's all right, Boaz," Daniel whispered, and touched his knee. "Mikah's safe."

Boaz sank back to his chair, to wait and watch.

"You woke me up when you called for David. I mean, Daniel," Mikah said. "I've been listening since then."

Jack nodded. "And you want to fight the Goa'uld."

Mikah's lower lip trembled. "Yes. I'll go with you to fight the Goa'uld but only if you promise not to hurt my Papa. Would you really hurt him, Joseph? You tried to stop Hol'c hurting me. Why would you do that, then hurt my Papa?"

Boaz felt his throat close tight. He watched Jack flinch, and heard him whisper, "Jesus wept." Then Jack put his arms around Mikah and held him tight. "I'm not going to hurt your Papa," he said, his voice unsteady. With a grunt he pushed to his feet, Mikah still in his arms. "Nobody's going to hurt your Papa. Or you. We're here to make sure of that."

Boaz held out his arms and took his son back from the man who had absolutely meant to kill him if he didn't do as he was asked . . . or told. The boy was too big now for lap-talk, but he needed the contact as much as Mikah did.

He looked at the newcomers' faces, each one in turn. "The Goa'uld are not gods," he said slowly. Waited for the stabbing fear to subside and said again, with more strength, "The Goa'uld are not gods."

Sam smiled her heartbreaking smile. "You keep on saying that, Boaz. Say it as many times as you need to until it doesn't scare you any more. Until you believe it without hesitation. The Goa'uld are not gods."

"Are there any gods at all?" he wondered. "Does any great power care what becomes of us?"

"Well," she said, "some people think so. Some people believe there's *a* god. A supreme being. A power of good in the universe."

"Do you believe it?"

She nodded. "I do."

"Then I'll believe it, too."

"And me," said Mikah.

"So Boaz," Jack said briskly, "you can talk comparative religion with Daniel when this is over, it's right up his alley, but for now we need to focus. Which of the villagers would join a fight against the Goa'uld?"

Boaz frowned, thinking. "I cannot say for certain, Jack. You must understand—whatever we might think we never question the god aloud. Defiance is death."

Mikah made a rude noise. "Jenc wouldn't join you. Jenc would run to Hol'c if you asked him to fight."

Boaz tightened his arms. "Mikah's right. Jenc must not suspect a thing."

"I doubt Qualah would join us either," said Sam. "Or Tima. But I know Berez would."

"Berez?" He was shocked. "Berez questioned the go—the Goa'uld?"

Sam shrugged. "Not in so many words. It's hard to explain, Boaz. I just have a sense about these things. And when I hinted I wasn't happy about children going into slavery she didn't argue. She was upset at the idea of hers being sent away."

"Perhaps that's the key," said Daniel. "Jack reached you, Boaz, because of Mikah. Sam's reached this Berez through her children. Maybe that's the approach we should be taking. Targeting the parents upset about losing their children to the Goa'uld."

Jack made an impatient sound. "Daniel, that's all of them."

"Well, can you think of a better opening?" Daniel retorted. "I mean, we're new here. It's kind of a natural question to ask, isn't it?"

Jack rubbed his face. "Yeah. I guess."

"And at least it's more subtle than, 'Hey I was just wondering, has it ever occurred to you that the Goa'uld aren't gods?'"

"Okay, Daniel, you've made your point!" said Jack. His voice was dangerous again; Mikah flinched, and Boaz tightened his arms protectively.

Daniel seemed unaffected. "So if that's the approach we're going to take," he said, sounding perfectly cheerful, "I guess that means you'll need to assign me somewhere else tomorrow, Boaz. I doubt very much if the goats have an opinion about the Goa'uld."

"Speaking of tomorrow," said Jack, "it's late. Time to hit the hay."

Mikah giggled drowsily. "Why? Was it bad?"

"It's an expression," said Jack, briefly smiling. "It means get some rest. We've only got a few days before we have to get out of here and we need to stay on our toes."

Sam tugged Mikah's curls. "*That* means stay alert," she said. "And be *very* careful about what we say outside this house. Do you understand, Mikah?"

Solemnly Mikah nodded. "I understand, Sam."

"Because our lives depend on all of us keeping this a secret."

"I know that, Sam," said Mikah. "I know what Hol'c will do if he finds out we know the Goa'uld are not gods."

She leaned forward and kissed his forehead. Her eyes were very bright. "Good boy. And don't forget—I'm only Sam here, in the house. Outside I'm still Serena."

"Yes. And he's Joseph, and he's David," said Mikah, pointing. "I won't forget. I promise."

Boaz stood, Mikah in his arms. "Nor will I."

"Thank you, Boaz," said Daniel. "We know you're afraid. We know we're asking you for an incredible leap of faith. But it will be worth it, I swear."

There was no guile in this man. No cold killing hardness, as he'd seen in Jack. In Sam. In this man's eyes were warmth and compassion and a deep well of sorrow.

"Good night," he said, Mikah's head on his shoulder. "I will wake you in the morning." And he took his son to bed. Covered him in blankets, kissed his cheek and said, his voice unsteady, "Sleep now, Mikah. And dream of freedom."

Then he retired to his own room, blew out the lamp and lay in the darkness.

The Goa'uld are not gods.

Never once in his life had he thought to question the divinity of Yu. Even when his heart was breaking, when he denied his anguish at the loss of Tayt and all the children culled before him, buried that pain in work or making more babies, he had never thought, *Yu is no god and this is wrong*. Never. It was not safe to think such things.

But I believe them now because in my heart I know them to be true.

Did he? Or did he only *want* them to be true?

And did the difference matter? These strangers, these humans who had never been slaves, they said they could stop the hurting and the culling. They said they could make the god—the Goa'uld—Yu pay. Make Hol'c pay, and his cruel Jaffa.

It was enough.

The Goa'uld are not gods.

As the door to Boaz's room closed, Daniel let out a gust of air from his aching lungs.

"*Dammit*, Jack. You took one hell of a risk!"

Jack shrugged. "Not really." Then he disappeared into his bedroom, came out again with his Tok'ra communicator and added, "I had the situation covered."

He looked at Sam. She raised an eyebrow. He waited a moment till he could trust himself then said, with immense care, "You were serious? If Boaz had tried something you'd have killed him. Just like that."

Jack was wearing his 'Special Forces face'. The one that meant he was in no mood for arguments or taking prisoners.

"Yes, Daniel," he said, his voice clipped and neutral, with the merest hint of warning. "Just like that. And you know it. So why are we having this conversation?"

These were the times Daniel remembered that much of Jack remained a mystery. Perhaps, when it came to throats and knives and slitting, there wasn't so much difference between a sheep and a man. If it had to be done then it was done, efficiently and humanely. Sometimes it was almost impossible to reconcile those two stark sides of his difficult friend: the Jack who'd invited cruel punishment to save a child from torture, and the other Jack who was prepared to kill that same child's father if it came to a choice between him and the team.

Jack's expression had changed again. It was impatiently understanding now. "Daniel. Stop brooding. It didn't happen, let's move on." He flicked on his communicator. "Jacob. Jacob, it's Jack. Do you read?"

A buzzing hum, then: "*Colonel O'Neill? This is Martouf. Jacob is sleeping. Do you have a report?*"

Jack rolled his eyes at Sam, who grinned and shrugged. "Yes, Martouf, I have a report. It's ten bells and all is well."

"*I'm sorry?*" said Martouf, after a puzzled pause. "*Why are there bells? Is it not night in the village?*"

"Never mind," said Jack. "When Jacob wakes up, tell him we've made some progress."

"*That is good to hear, Colonel.*"

"It is, isn't it? So that's it from me. But you guys might want to stand by the radio and keep the engine running; could be we'll need to make a fast getaway in the next day or so."

"*A fast getaway,*" said Martouf. Now he sounded resigned. "*I will tell Jacob.*"

"You do that, Marty. O'Neill out." He clicked off the communicator, shaking his head. "The Tok'ra should hold a raffle and raise some money so they can buy that guy a clue."

"Be fair," said Sam. "You do it on purpose, just to confuse him."

A small spark of amusement glinted in Jack's eyes. "You say that like it's a *bad* thing, Carter."

Sam pulled a face at him, and he pulled one back. Daniel made sure his own expression stayed studiously blank.

Sam said, only a little hesitant, "Daniel's right, sir. You took an awful risk."

"Yeah. And it paid off. Even if Boaz can't help you finger any more likely spies-in-training, at least we've got him and Mikah to take with us. Berez too. That's not bad for a couple of days' work."

"And there's the baby Berez is wet-nursing."

Jack frowned. "It's not hers?"

"No. Her first child died. She's pregnant again, though."

"Yeah…" Jack said, sounding reluctant. "About that…"

She sat up. "Sir, I doubt she'll leave it behind!"

"She might not have a choice."

"But *sir*—"

"Hey!" he said, one hand sharply lifted. "If you can think of a way to winkle a screaming baby out from under that Qualah's nose, Carter, good luck to you. But I'm telling you right now, and if I have to make it a direct order I will: babies in swaddling clothes not directly related to a recruit can't be our top priority. Because our mission here is—" He turned. "Daniel, what's our mission here?"

Daniel favored Jack with his most innocent face. "Sorry. I forget." Which earned him a look fit to incinerate asbestos, but that was too bad. It wasn't wise to let Jack have things all his own way.

Sam was chewing a thumbnail. "Sir, what if Berez will only come with us if—"

"Carter!" said Jack, exasperated. "Worry about it when it happens, not before."

She sighed. "Yes, sir."

"You two should hit the sack," he added. "Tomorrow's going to be a busy day."

"What about you?"

"Me?" Jack hooked out a chair with his foot and sat on it. "I had a long nap already. Think I'll stay up a while and... pare my fingernails."

Daniel exchanged a meaningful look with Sam. "You mean you want to stand guard in case Boaz isn't as shattered as he looked, or on our side as much as we think," he said, and felt his guts tighten.

"You suspect he was playing us?" said Sam. "That he might try and sneak out once we're asleep and tell Hol'c who we are and why we're here?"

Jack shrugged. "Thinking's your department, Carter. I'm just the muscle."

Desperately, Daniel tried to lighten the suddenly tense mood. "Hey. If she's the brain and you're the brawn, what does that make me?"

Jack smiled, not altogether kindly. "The pain in the ass. Now go to bed, both of you. That *is* an order."

There was no point in arguing. They went to bed.

Boaz woke them in the morning. Calm, resolute, committed. "I thought of what you said all night," he told them, as they prepared to leave for firstmeal. "I haven't changed my mind."

"Good," said Jack, and patted him on the shoulder. "Then it's game on. So let's do it."

CHAPTER FIFTEEN

Thank God for Tok'ra subspace communication technology, thought Jacob, as he waited for someone to fetch George Hammond to the phone. Beyond the cloaked cargo ship's window, the stars continued their twinkling undisturbed. The gas giant continued its slow self-immolation. Panotek and its other two moons continued orbiting without comment. It was very much a case of same old, same old.

Just the way he liked it.

A crackling hum, caused by interference from the gas giant, then George's voice filled the flight deck. *"Jacob! It's about time, I was starting to worry. What's your status?"*

"My status, George, is near-terminal boredom. There's not a lot to do out here. And there's only so many times I can listen to Selmak's jokes before they stop being funny."

George chuckled. *"I can imagine."*

"Sorry if you've been worrying, my friend, but I did warn you I'd only make contact if I had something to report. We may be parked in the ass-end of Yu's empire but I still don't like taking unnecessary risks. Slim or not, there's always a chance our transmissions could be picked up."

"I know, Jacob, I know," said George, apologetic. *"I'm just not very good at sitting on the sidelines."*

"Then I guess you should've thought twice about accepting that promotion."

"So I take it there's good news?" said George, refusing the bait. Sounding hopeful, even through the static.

"Well, there's news," he said. "How good it is remains to be seen. We heard from Jack last night. He says they're making progress."

"And that's it?" said George. *"That's all he said?"*

"Martouf took the message. It was a typical O'Neill communiqué—short on details, long on obscurity. Personally, I think he just likes twisting Martouf's tail."

"Then you tell him from me I'll be the one doing the tail-twisting if he doesn't provide a complete update the next time he contacts

you!"

That made Jacob laugh. "Be fair, George. He's got to keep it cryptic."

A crackly, static-ridden sigh. "*I'm just worried about them, Jacob. Are you sure you're in a position to get them out of there fast if anything goes wrong?*"

Jacob hesitated, debating whether or not it was worth worrying George with stuff he couldn't fix sitting in the SGC. Then he considered how pissed he'd be if someone withheld information from him in a misguided attempt to spare his feelings.

"Honestly, George? Conditions aren't ideal, but we're coping. This whole mission's a tightrope walk, you know that."

"*I don't much care for the sound of that, Jacob.*"

"I don't much care for it either, George, but it is what it is. We're doing our best."

"*I know you are,*" said George. "*And you say they're making progress? Does that mean they've found some candidates for you?*"

"I'm guessing that's what it means," he said. "I'll know more tonight hopefully, once I've spoken to Jack."

"*And you'll make sure to speak with him yourself this time? No more cryptic messages via Martouf?*"

"Don't worry, George, I'll get all the skinny."

"*And you'll contact me as soon as you can, to keep me apprised? Kinsey's pressuring the President again, wanting to know if Jack's so-called emergency secondment was really an emergency after all. I swear, Jacob, the man's like a case of athlete's foot. Just when you think you're rid of him ...*"

"I'll contact you the moment I know *anything,*" he promised. "What time is it there?"

"*Fifteen-twenty.*"

Jacob checked his flight deck chronometer and did a quick mental calculation. "Okay. Expect to hear from me around 0700 tomorrow, your time."

"*Good. And Jacob—when you speak to Jack—tell him we're thinking of them here and we're looking forward to seeing them home again, safe and sound.*"

"Will do, George. Jacob out."

He disconnected the subspace communicator and sat back, smil-

ing. Good old George. There wasn't a better man in the service to
have at your back, or at your front for that matter. He inspired the
kind of loyalty the Kinseys of this galaxy could only dream about.
The kind of loyalty Jack O'Neill inspired.

No wonder Kinsey hated them.

Selmak said, *You did a fine job fooling the general, Jacob, but
don't think you can fool me. You're worried.*

Of course I'm worried, he replied. That's my little girl down
there. Being treated like a piece of meat because *I* asked her to get
involved. What father wouldn't be worried?

She chose this life, Jacob.

Because she wanted to please me.

*She didn't join the Stargate program to please you. She did that
to please herself.*

Hey, he said. Worrying is a father's prerogative.

You're not just worried about Samantha. There's something else.

No, there's not.

Jacob, please. I know you. What is—

"I don't know!" he snapped. "Nothing I can put my finger on.
Now quit nagging me, would you?"

"Nagging you?" said Martouf, bemused, emerging from the
cargo hold where they'd set up their camp-beds. "When was I nagging you?"

Jacob shifted round in the pilot's seat. "Not you. Selmak."

"Ah." His brief smile fading, Martouf began a series of complicated and painful-looking stretches. "Has there been more word
from SG-1?"

"No, but I've updated George Hammond. He's starting to get
antsy." Shifting to face front again, Jacob frowned at the surface of
the distant moon. "And he's not the only one."

Martouf lowered himself into a split position that would've turned
Rudolf Nureyev green with envy. Resting his forehead on his leg
he said, slightly muffled, "Samantha is a formidable warrior, Jacob.
And she has been in far more dangerous situations than this."

Jacob stifled an impatient sigh. Martouf would never admit it but
he was worried for Sam too. "I know."

"In addition, she has Colonel O'Neill watching her back. He will
not let any harm come to her. Indeed, I have observed he is quick to

put himself in danger to protect her."

"I know that, too." And he did. In fact, it was something he kept meaning to talk to Sam about. Because he had some nasty suspicions in that department ... a strong hunch there were things brewing beneath the surface of her professional relationship with Jack that could get messy if everyone involved wasn't extremely careful.

"So really," said Martouf, encouragingly, "there is very little to worry about. Yours and Selmak's choice of a preliminary target has proven most worthy."

Maybe. But Jacob was in a worrying mood. He felt uneasy. Prickled with nerves. He couldn't explain why; the feeling wasn't rational. It was a familiar sensation, one he'd experienced many times, in conflicts throughout his military career on a number of different continents. Well. Planets, now.

He'd learned the hard way not to ignore it.

"What are you doing?" said Martouf, on his feet again and holding a perfectly balanced one-legged stand, his left leg folded behind him.

"Running a long-range sensor sweep," he said, his fingers dancing across the control panel.

"Why?"

"Do I need a reason?" he said, as the skin between his shoulder blades crawled and twitched. "I'm bored. It'll kill some time."

Slowly Martouf put his left foot on the ground. "*Jacob*," said Lantash, sounding more than ever like an irascible schoolmaster. "*Is there cause for concern*?"

"I don't know," he said, checking the sensor readouts. "Nothing's showing up, and I've sent the sweep out to a full parsec. I've just got this feeling that—"

Far below, on Panotek's green surface, a sudden flame blossomed.

"What was that?" said Martouf, leaping forward to the co-pilot's chair. "Where did it come from?" Now he was checking the sensors too, fingers blurred with speed. "An explosion. Very large. Not in the village, but nearby. And I am picking up Goa'uld al-kesh! Three of them. Jacob, take us closer!"

He was already on it, swooping the tel'tac in a huge nose-dive towards Panotek—the village—Sam. "Martouf, what are you reading?"

"Nothing," said Martouf, gaze fixed to the sensor display panels, his fingers still dancing. "Except—" He looked across, his normally tranquil face vivid with alarm. "—traces of naquadah-enhanced Goa'uld plasma weaponry. Jacob, this must be a—"

"*Jacob! Jacob, can you read me? Jacob, are you there?*" a breathless, desperate voice burst from the control console's speakers. "*Jacob, it's Daniel, do you read me? Come in!*"

Relief and terror flooded through him. Behind Daniel's shouting were the sounds of men and women screaming, engines roaring, staff weapons firing.

He slammed the comm-button. "Daniel, it's Jacob! What the *hell* is happening down there?"

The sound of Jacob's voice was such a relief Daniel almost sobbed aloud as he crouched in the cornfield like a terrified mouse. Along the corn-rows on either side of him men, women and children ran screaming for their lives, chased by Jaffa with staff weapons and zat guns. The air was thick with choking smoke; the bastards had set the cornfield on fire to flush out their prey. He heard the electric whine of a zat-gun discharge two rows over, and the pained exclamation of the woman it struck. The thud as her fleeing body hit the ground.

"*Daniel, for God's sake answer me! What's going on?*"

There were Jaffa all around him now, thrashing through the corn crop, but he had to risk being overhead. Shoving himself amongst the stalks, rolling himself into a ball, he pressed the communicator against his lips and whispered, "Jacob, help! We're under attack. Heru'ur's Jaffa have stormed the village and blown up Hol'c's palace. We're being over-run!"

"*Heru'ur?*" said Jacob, incredulous. "*Are you sure?*"

He'd seen the Jaffas' forehead brands. "Positive."

"*No, it can't be, he and Yu have a treaty!*"

"Well don't look now but I'd say it's been broken!" Daniel said as loudly as he dared. "Jacob, we can't get captured, we'll be recognized for sure! Come get us, quick!"

"*Where's Sam? Where's Jack?*"

"I have no idea!"

"Well, where are you?"

"Hiding in the cornfield!"

"What can you see from your position?"

"Lots and lots and lots of corn!"

"Can we ring you out of there?"

Oh, if only. "No—I don't think so. Not without putting you in danger or getting me shot by a Jaffa."

A moment's pause, which lasted forever. *"Okay, Daniel,"* Jacob said. He sounded stressed. *"Get the hell out of the cornfield. Find a secure location with a clear line of sight to the rest of the village then call me back and tell me what's happening!"*

"But Jacob —*Jacob*—"

No answer. Daniel stared at the communicator, some small detached part of his brain noticing that his hand was cut, and bleeding, and had developed an impressive tremor. It hurt a lot, too, but that was the least of his worries. He shoved the communicator back in his pocket.

Get the hell out.

Easier said than done. God. If only Teal'c was here.

Find a clear line of sight.

Yes, but where? The whole damned place was on a plain, where the hell could he go that would give him a decent view of the—

"Jaffa *kree!*" a loud voice bellowed way too close behind him. The sound of corn stalks smashing beneath way too many armored feet. More screaming. A child's keening cry. "Jaffa rok'nor alcash-la—tedek kree!"

No, no, not tedek, Daniel thought wildly. *I'm* tedek!

They were heading straight for him. Time to go.

He bounced to his feet and started running, blindly at first, caring only that it was 'away'. Then his brain kicked in and he remembered the bath-house, the enormous drums holding the water that fed down into each bathing cubicle. If he managed to climb on top of those—they were tall—they'd give him good line of sight. He might even spot Jack, or Sam...

A dreadful wave of fear crashed through him.

Please God, let them be safe. Please God, don't let them be captured.

Please God, don't let me be captured...

With the Jaffa pounding behind him, with villagers still fleeing those Jaffa and the flames on either side, running in front of him,
screaming and falling, with his ragged breaths searing like fire, he
veered to the left and out of the cornfield, towards the village centre.
As he ran he thought of Mikah. Of Sallah and her friends in the goat
pasture. Of the little ones in the babyhouse. All of them so innocent,
so vulnerable.

Please God, keep the children safe.

Gasping, heaving, he staggered free of the corn rows and into
the open. He had to stop, he had no choice, he needed to get his
bearings...

What he saw punched the air from his lungs like a sledgeham-
mer: squatting on the grass between himself and the village was a
Goa'uld al'kesh, heavily armed and four times larger than a tel'tac,
easily; scores of Heru'ur's Jaffa; and huge piles of villagers, unconscious, being picked up and slung into the ship like sides of slaughtered beef. More villagers, these ones conscious, being herded inside
at the point of menacing staff weapons.

It was a *raid*. They were being *rustled*, like *cattle*.

He turned on his heel to run the other way, to find another route
back to the bath-house. A huge Jaffa crashed out of the cornfield in
front of him. He had time to gasp—turn back—

—and to fall, as a wicked close-range zat-blast caught him
between the shoulder blades and catapulted him face-first into
oblivion.

Boaz's first thought as the enemy Jaffa stormed his village was
of Mikah. He'd assigned his son to work in the poultry barns
today—collecting, cleaning and grading the eggs, checking for
sick or dead birds, feeding, sweeping. Mikah had offered to help
Joseph—Jack—in the slaughterhouse but he'd forbidden that. Not
only for the blood and the muck and the pathetic squeals of dying
beasts, but because Mikah's shining eyes looked upon the man with
awe, and curiosity, and a growing respect.

While Jack looked at Mikah with... hunger.

So. It was a relationship he could not—would not—allow to
fester. Let Joseph—Jack—breed himself another son, if a son was
what he wanted.

Mikah belonged to *him*.

The enemy Jaffa were shouting. Shooting. Burning. As head man he should've thought of the villagers, called for calm, made sure they offered no resistance, discovered who was behind this terrible attack—

All he could think of was his precious son.

Breathless, terrified, Boaz ran for the poultry barns, evading capture, escaping the desperate clutches of men and women who howled to him for help.

"Mikah!" he called out, almost winded. "Mikah, where are you?"

His son stood at the entrance to the main barn. He held a basket. He was throwing eggs at an approaching enemy Jaffa.

"Mikah!" he shouted. "Mikah, *no!*"

"No more slaves, Papa!" Mikah shouted back. "No more hurting! Humans should be *free!*" He threw another egg; it burst yellow and dripping in the Jaffa's face.

The Jaffa shot Mikah right in the heart.

"*Mikah!*" Boaz screamed as his little boy fell, eggs cascading from the basket to smash on the ground. He started running. The Jaffa turned and shot aga—

"We don't dare contact Vorash," said Martouf, as they hovered in their cloaked cargo ship above the slagged and smoking ruins of Hol'c's palace. They'd counted twelve dead Jaffa in the charred forecourt; chances were the rest had been incinerated inside the building, along with their human servants.

"I know," Jacob agreed. "At this range they're almost guaranteed to notice a subspace communication." He punched the flight console, furious. "How the hell did this happen? We've got four—no, *five*—operatives inside Heru'ur's circle of Goa'uld underlings. How the *hell* could this happen without us being warned?"

"I do not know," said Martouf. "Jacob, I hope this attack does not presage another major conflict between Yu and Heru'ur. We cannot afford to lose more operatives."

They'd lost three the last time these two Goa'uld had butted heads. One had been a very dear friend to Selmak; his symbiote's grief had made Jacob ill for weeks.

"We should have a fly round," he said, fretting. "See how many of Heru'ur's Jaffa we're up against." See if we can find Sam, or Jack, or Daniel.

Oh, God. *Sam*.

"Is that wise?" said Martouf. "Should we not wait until Dr. Jackson gives us some idea of the attackers' strength? With no defences but our speed and manoeuvrability—"

"It's been ten minutes, Martouf, how long did you have in mind?"

"Control your emotions, Jacob," Lantash snapped. *"Do you really want to bump into an al'kesh as we 'fly round' cloaked but incapable of returning fire? There is more at stake here than the life of one human."*

He's right," said Selmak. *Insensitive, but right. I know you're worried. So am I. But we can't help Sam now. We must wait to see what eventuates. With luck events will turn in our favor and we'll be able to rescue her undetected.*

Jacob nodded. I know, he acknowledged. "I know," he said again, to Lantash. Then glared at the comm-console and muttered, as the fear knocked his heart into his ribs, "For God's sake, Daniel. What are you doing? *Call* me!"

"It is unlikely Heru'ur's Jaffa will return here. Perhaps we should assume a higher altitude," suggested Martouf. "It will afford us a better line of sight."

Of course it would. And he should've thought of that. Lantash was right: he was letting his emotions get in the way. With a grunt Jacob hit the controls, sending the tel'tac shooting hundreds of metres higher into the air.

The view was not reassuring.

Homes and workshops and crops on fire. Cows, goats and sheep milling hysterically through the village or lying in bloody heaps on the ground. A great flood of water from ruptured holding tanks on the roof of a partially flattened building. And people. Scores of them, running, doubtless screaming, some senseless in the mud, as Heru'ur's Jaffa hunted them down, rounded them up, herded them towards an al'kesh landed directly in the village centre. Yu's golden statue lay broken on its side.

How the hell did we let this happen?

His fingers itched to hit the comm-console. Call Daniel. Make sure he was okay. Find out where Sam was. Jack. Find out if they were safe or … But if Daniel was hiding, an incoming transmission might betray his position. He had no choice. He had to wait.

In the name of God and all that's holy. How the hell did we let this happen?

The minute he saw the Goa'uld al'kesh uncloak and blow Hol'c and his minions to a fiery hell, O'Neill knew they were screwed. Had no idea what was happening, only that they were screwed. To the wall and without mercy.

He'd been working in the slaughterhouse. Not the assignment of his choice, not by a long shot, but one of the experienced slaughtermen had tripped that morning on his way to firstmeal and sprained his wrist.

Slaughtering stock wasn't a job for everyone. A certain knack was involved, and a strong stomach, and an ability to kill swiftly with a measure of rough kindness. Boaz had looked at him, his eyes full of questions and challenge. O'Neill nodded, knowing he had no choice.

"Joseph shall take Filip's place in the slaughterhouse till he is healed," Boaz pronounced, as he assigned the day's tasks. "Joseph is a skilled slaughterman, with much experience in killing."

And wasn't that the perfect double-edged compliment.

He'd just finished jointing a goat when the cries of alarm from outside alerted him to disaster. Instinct had him slipping two of the smallest boning knives into the pocket of his bloodstained leather apron before he abandoned his business with the unfortunate goat and went to see what the trouble was.

The sound of Hol'c's palace exploding into smithereens almost burst his eardrums. The sight of the uncloaked al'kesh sent him sprinting for the babyhouse, and Carter.

He never reached her.

Another al'kesh uncloaked right in front of him. He tried to spin, to run. His knee howled a protest and buckled, surrendering … and he was smashed from behind with the butt of a staff weapon. Time passed in a kaleidoscope of shouting, crying, the familiar clank-clank of Jaffa armor. Dazed, he felt someone grab him by the wrists. Drag him across the ground, to the ship's lowered loading ramp. There were already villagers crammed inside it, unconscious or weeping or silent with fear. He was dumped on top of someone else and kicked in the guts for good measure. Retching, head spinning, he rolled off his human mattress and tried to see what was going on. Tried to get to his feet, grope for a knife, kill at least one Jaffa bastard before they killed him ...

Another staff weapon struck his head. As reality receded, and with it his wits, he remembered Jacob sitting safely invisible above them and his Tok'ra communicator, just as safe in his bitty bag on the bed.

Dammit it, Jack, he thought, despair like a tidal wave rising, rising. *You should've let Teal'c come.* Then, *Daniel.* And lastly, *Sam.*

From a long way away, he heard Alar laughing.

Oh, God, oh, God, the babies were crying. "Run faster, Berez!" Sam gasped. There was an al'kesh on the ground behind them, and way too many Jaffa. "Run faster, Qualah!"

"What's happening, what's happening?" Qualah wailed, the stupid woman, when she needed her air for getting away.

"I don't know! Shut up and *run*!"

Three babies between them, heavy as hell. Somehow the Jaffa hadn't caught them when they'd caught nearly everyone else. Sam risked a backwards glance. No, they were still unchased. It was a miracle. God, where was the colonel? Where was Daniel? Boaz? Mikah? What the hell was *happening*?

They reached the rear door of Boaz's house, flung themselves inside and kicked the door shut after. One awful, heart-stopping moment, thinking *are there Jaffa in here waiting*?

They were alone. She thrust the baby she'd grabbed at Berez, dashed into the bedroom and snatched her Tok'ra communicator from her bitty bag. She nearly broke it in half, turning it on.

"Dad! Dad, are you there? Dad, come in!"

"Sam? Sam! Oh, thank God. Where are you?"

She fell against the bedroom's doorframe, shaking so hard she nearly dropped the damned communicator. Berez and Qualah were staring, terrified, but she didn't have time to care.

"In Boaz's house. Dad, get us out of here! We're under attack!"

"I know. I'm coming. Leave this link open, we'll home in on your signal. How many with you?"

"Two women, three babies."

"Jack and Daniel?"

She flinched. "I don't know. Dad, hurry. We don't have long, the Jaffa are bound to find us!"

"On my way, sweetheart. Hang tight."

She shoved the communicator into her pocket and turned to the staring women. "Keep hold of the babies. Get to the back door. In a moment we're going outside so someone can take us to safety."

"Who are you?" demanded Qualah. "Where do you come from? Are you a traitor to our Lord Chou—"

"Be quiet, Qualah!" Berez shouted. "What does it matter who she is? She's taking us to safety!"

God bless Berez. Nice to know she'd been right about the woman. In her pocket, the communicator shrilled. *"Sam! Get outside! There are Jaffa all around you, we'll be coming in hot!"*

Jaffa all around them? God. *I want Teal'c.*

She hustled the women and babies to the house's back door and flung it open. Practically shoved them through it and into the open, to see six Jaffa with staff weapons and zat-guns at the ready. The tallest one shouted. "Halt, humans! You are now the property of our god Heru'ur!"

What the hell? *Heru'ur?* Sam pushed the women behind her, the babies in their arms screaming blue bloody murder. She didn't have time to care about them either, poor little mites.

"Stay close to me, you two," she hissed at Berez and Qualah. "Any second—any second—"

She looked to the sky. A roar, a ripple, and there was her father, she could see him through the tel'tac viewport. Heru'ur's Jaffa stopped, spiked to the ground with amazement. Giving them the spare seconds they needed.

The rings rushed down with a glorious whoosh. Blue-white light. The bizarre sensation of being, and not being, within the same heart-beat.

Then reality returned and they were safe in the tel'tac and her father was shouting, *"Go! Go! Go!"*

She could hear staff weapon blasts impacting on the shields as they screamed away into the empty sky.

"*Sam!*"

It was her wonderful father. She threw her arms around him, felt his arms close hard around her.

"Thanks, Dad," she whispered. "Great timing. Now let's go get the guys."

He loosened his suffocating grip and held her at arm's length. His expression was anguished. "We can't, Sam. I have no idea where they are and I can't risk this ship against that much Jaffa firepower. I'm sorry."

She felt her throat close, and had to wait a moment before she could speak. "Dad, we can't leave them down there! Daniel was in the cornfield, the colonel was in the slaughterhouse. Please. We have to go back."

His hand cupped her cheek. His eyes were dark. Sorrowful. "Listen to me, Sam," he said, his voice low, the bearer of bad tidings. "I managed to raise Daniel on his communicator. He was going to find a better vantage point and call me back but it's been over twenty minutes and we've had no word. It's a good bet he's already captured. Jack, too. There's no way you, me and Martouf on our own can stage a rescue. Not in an unarmed tel'tac."

To hell with bad tidings. She was in no mood for bad tidings. Rule Number One of the O'Neill Survival Handbook: Never. Say. Die.

"Dad, we can't just *leave* them, we can't abandon them to Heru'ur! Heru'ur *knows* us! God knows what he'll do to them if they're discovered among the villagers! We have to find them. Boaz and Mikah, too. They want to fight the Goa'uld."

"Sam," her father said gently. "Of *course* we're going to find Jack and Daniel. Your two recruits, as well. We just can't do it now."

She wanted to hit him, hard, to pound him with her fists until he did what she wanted. "If we don't do it now we might never do it at all!"

"That's not true," he said sharply. "We have operatives in Heru'ur's hierarchy. As soon as we can we'll make contact with them. Find out where Jack, Daniel and the others have been taken. *Then* we'll come up with a rescue plan."

She pulled away from him, fury over-riding her fear. "If you've got operatives undercover in Heru'ur's empire then why the hell didn't they warn you of this attack? Why did they let it happen in the first place, didn't they know we were *here*?"

From the flight deck, Martouf's calm and measured voice. "No, Samantha, they did not. Information about ongoing missions is kept strictly secret from our undercover operatives, in the event they are discovered and for whatever reason cannot self-terminate. It would be disastrous if they could be made to divulge what they know."

Of course. Of course. Hell. She was out of control, letting her fears dictate her actions. The colonel would bite her head off if he could hear her now. *God, Sam, stop being such a girl.* She took a moment to breathe, just breathe, and regain her equilibrium.

"I get that, Martouf," she said, when she was her soldier-self again. "What I *don't* get is why you chose this farm in the first place when you knew it could be *raided*!"

"Sam, we didn't know," her father said. Now he sounded hurt. "Do you think I'd have risked you if I thought this moon could be raided? Heru'ur and Yu have a non-aggression treaty. At least they did. Obviously, Heru'ur has broken it."

"And none of your undercover operatives knew?"

"Clearly not. Or they would've sent word."

"Would they?" The words came out far more bitterly than she'd intended. Right now she didn't care. She was starting to think the colonel had the right idea. Never trust a snake...

"Sam..." Her father rested his hand on her shoulder. "Please. Let's save the recriminations for later, okay? We've got more important things to worry about." His gaze shifted, past her to the women and the crying babies behind her. "So. Are you going to introduce me to your friends?"

He was right, again. Dammit.

She turned. Pointed. "This is Berez. This is Qualah. I'll introduce you to the babies later. We were in the babyhouse when the Jaffa attacked."

"Okay," said her father. Smiling now, summoning all his considerable charm. "Ladies. Welcome. My name is Jacob, and I'm Sam's father. I'm sorry you've had such an alarming morning and I wish I could offer you somewhere comfortable to collect your thoughts. But as you can see..." He indicated the spartan cargo hold with its makeshift beds. "We're not exactly five-star."

From the look on Qualah's face, speech was beyond her. But Berez stepped forward, still jiggling her grizzly infants, and said, frowning, "She told us her name was Serena."

"I lied, Berez," Sam said. "I'm sorry."

"You're not a slave."

"Far from it. I belong to a group who want to end human slavery."

Berez's chin lifted and her eyes lit with a fervor that burned her fear and exhaustion to ash. "I want to end it too. How can I help?"

"Your third recruit, Sam?" her father said, smiling. "Way to go, kid."

"Jacob!" Martouf called. "The al'kesh are moving!"

As her father joined him, Sam turned to Berez. "I know you have questions. I'll answer them later, I promise. For now, please, you and Qualah just stay back here and mind the children."

"We are safe now?" said Qualah. She looked ready to drop from fear and exhaustion.

"You're safe. And whatever happens, you'll never be slaves again."

Berez nodded, tears filling her eyes. "I like your father, Serena. He has a good face."

"Yeah," Sam said, backing away. "I like him too. He has a *great* face."

Turning away, she wiped the women and children from her mind and hurried onto the flight deck.

After transporting her, the women and the babies aboard, Martouf had shot the re-cloaked tel'tac into a low orbit round Panotek. Below them, oblivious to their presence, two of the three Goa'uld raiders sat silently waiting. As she watched, the third approached from the moon's surface and joined the others.

"They still have not seen us," said Martouf. "Our cloak is holding." His hand reached out. "I will see if we can intercept their communica—"

"No," said her father, grabbing Martouf's wrist. "We're too close. If they pick up a glitch and realize we're on top of them, listening—"

Helpless, they could do nothing but observe as the three armed ships, loaded with stolen humans, broke from their holding pattern and eased away. Three pin-points of purple light blossomed as each one opened a hyperspace window. The al'kesh accelerated.

Going ... going ... gone.

"It's not over, Sam," her father said, his hands hard on her shoulders. "I promise you, kiddo. It's far from over."

Martouf said, "We should return to the surface, Jacob. Rescue any humans Heru'ur's Jaffa failed to capture or kill."

"Good idea," her father said. "Especially since there's a chance Jack and Daniel are among them. Or Sam's other recruits."

So they returned to the village centre. Martouf stayed on the tel'tac while Sam and her father ringed down. They found twelve survivors huddled in the ruins of the meeting hall, most of them injured, all of them mute with shock and pain. The colonel and Daniel weren't among them. Neither were Boaz or Mikah.

"We should search the whole settlement, Dad," said Sam. "They could be hiding anywhere."

"We'll split up," said her father. "I'll check the fields, you check the buildings and workhouses. Keep your communicator on and let's make it fast. I don't want to hang around here any longer than we have to."

The babyhouse had been emptied of children. Sam found six dead women there; they'd been trying to protect the infants. Swallowing nausea, banishing grief, she kept on looking.

Her communicator clicked. "*How's it going, Sam?*"

"Nothing but bodies so far, Dad."

"*Same here.*"

Heavy-hearted, wracked with fear, she kept on looking. Every time she found another man's body she had to nerve herself to turn it over. Steel herself for the unbearable. In her head a never-ending chant: *Please don't be dead, guys. Please don't be dead.*

She reached the poultry barns. Found Boaz and Mikah.

"Oh, God," she whispered, and didn't try to stop the tears. "Oh, *damn* ..."

Leaving them was hard but she was running out of time. Done with shouting through the fields and the crops, her father joined her and they finished searching the village's houses and barns and work sheds.

The colonel and Daniel were nowhere to be found. Dead or alive.

"I'm sorry, kiddo," her father said, holding her close. "But I promise: we'll find them."

They couldn't bury Heru'ur's victims. Sooner or later Lord Choulai would come, to find out why Hol'c had ceased communications. If he found buried bodies instead of rotting flesh, questions would be raised. And they couldn't afford Goa'uld questions.

Together they freed all the animals still penned in barns and yards and paddocks. The livestock could fend for itself. Then they returned to the tel'tac, taking the twelve shell-shocked survivors with them.

"Okay, Martouf," said her father, sliding into the co-pilot's seat. "Let's get the hell out of here."

Sam sat with Berez and Qualah and the other refugees on the floor of the crowded cargo hold. Eyes closed, numb and drained, she held the sleeping baby Berez had pushed into her arms.

Somewhere ... *somewhere* ... the colonel and Daniel waited.

Hang in there guys. I'm coming. I'm coming.

CHAPTER SIXTEEN

Jittery with nerves and impatience, George Hammond stood at the base of the 'gate ramp and stared at the tranquil blue surface of the wormhole, his face still tingling from the aftermath of its event horizon's violent blooming.

Come on, come on, come on...

The shimmering puddle rippled and parted, and there they were at last: Jacob, Sam, Teal'c and Martouf. Sam was out of uniform, dressed in roughspun skirt and blouse. Physically she looked unhurt, but her face was tight with tension. So was Teal'c's—not something you saw every day. Stepping through the 'gate behind them came two of the most extraordinarily beautiful women Hammond had ever seen in his life. Both were pregnant. Accompanying the women came two more Tok'ra, operatives he'd never met, each guiding an anti-grav sled. From inside the sleds, the wails of indignant babies.

Wonderful. Now I'm starting up a nursery.

"I'm sorry, George," said Jacob, quietly, as the wormhole dispersed with its familiar whooshing, sucking sound. "The mission just blew up in our faces."

He was furious, and made no bones about letting Jacob see it. "We'll discuss this in the briefing room. Dr. Fraiser?"

Janet Fraiser stepped forward. "Sir?"

"See to our... guests."

"Yes, sir."

Sam turned to the apprehensive women she'd brought back to Earth with her. "Berez, Qualah, this is Janet. She's a very good friend of mine and she loves babies. She understands everything about healing and she's going to take really good care of you and the children. So you go with her now and I'll come see you as soon as I can."

"Hi there," said Dr. Fraiser, coming forward with her trademark dazzling smile. "I'll just bet both of you are dying to get off your feet."

"It's okay, I promise," said Sam, as the women looked to her, dazed and uncertain. "You're safe. Choulai will never find you here."

As the med team came forward to usher the women and the Tok'ra with the crying grav sleds out of the 'gate room and down to the infirmary, the doctor touched Sam on the shoulder.

"And I want to see you, too," she murmured. "Just as soon as you're finished with the general."

Sam nodded. "I'll try, Janet."

Dr. Fraiser raised her eyebrows. "It wasn't a suggestion, Major."

"She'll report to you before she leaves, Doctor," Hammond said briskly. "You have my word. Now—the briefing room. I want to know what happened."

It was a grim story, quickly told.

"And you had absolutely no idea Heru'ur was planning this raid," he said, when Jacob had finished talking.

"George," said Jacob, looking pained.

"The President is going to ask me, Jacob," he said. "So I have to ask you."

Jacob lifted his hands. "I know. I know."

He was in no mood to be placated. "The Tok'ra should have mentioned the possibility of a raid when this mission was originally suggested."

"We did not deem its mention necessary," said Martouf. "The treaty between Yu and Heru'ur—"

"Isn't worth the papyrus it was written on now, is it?" Hammond snapped. "Excuse me if I seem a little put out, Martouf, but once again it's *my* people in the line of fire because *your* people asked for our help. From where I sit it's beginning to look like standard Tok'ra operating procedure."

"Trust me, George," said Jacob. "We're no happier about this than you are."

"Well, I'm relieved to hear that! Now what are your people doing to get *my* people home safe?"

Sam leaned forward across the table. She looked exhausted. "Sir, Daniel may still have his communicator. We're waiting for him to make contact. Obviously it's too dangerous for us to try contacting him."

"And Colonel O'Neill? Does he have his communicator?"

"I don't know," she said, then shook her head. "I don't think so. We weren't supposed to be carrying them on us at all, in case we were searched by a Jaffa. But you know Daniel. Orders are things that happen to other people."

"For which we should be profoundly grateful," said Teal'c. His gaze was a molten glower. "If he is still alive, and if the communicator is still in his possession, it may be our only hope of finding him and O'Neill."

"I have no intention of assuming they're anything *but* alive," Hammond said firmly. "We are talking rescue, people, not recovery. And most certainly not abandonment." He looked at Jacob. "What about your spies in Heru'ur's ranks? What can they tell you?"

Jacob looked uncomfortable. "Nothing. At least not yet. Getting word to them is a delicate, dangerous operation. I've started several balls rolling, George, but I can't tell you when we'll hear anything. I hate to say it, but our best bet right now is Daniel. If he manages to make contact—"

"Don't your communicators contain signal-lock technology? A way to trace their position?"

"Yes, but only if they are activated," said Martouf. "And not over a vast distance. We would need to be in the vicinity of his location to pinpoint his exact whereabouts."

Hammond took a moment to think, resting his gaze on his folded hands. "All right," he said at last, looking up. "Best case scenario. We hear from Dr. Jackson or one of your operatives. Our people are alive and haven't been identified as members of SG-1. How do we get them home again?"

"If they are to be rescued from within Heru'ur's empire, General Hammond, it must be by the forces of the SGC," said Martouf. "The Tok'ra cannot risk large numbers of personnel on such a dangerous mission. Its chances of success are not high."

Hammond looked at the man, just looked at him. Until he looked away. "I should be surprised to hear that," he said. "But somehow, I'm not. Jacob—"

"I'm sorry, George. Martouf's right," said Jacob. "We're spread thinner than Saran Wrap as it is. But we'll give you all the assistance we can. Transport, if it's needed. Intelligence. Mission planning. And you know I'm with you, you know I'll do whatever it takes to get Jack and Daniel away from Heru'ur."

"As will I," said Martouf. "General Hammond, please do not mistake my reserve for indifference. I have nothing but respect and admiration for the Tauri—Colonel O'Neill and Dr. Jackson in particular. I will not abandon them to a Goa'uld. You have my word."

Slowly, he nodded. "So. It's a waiting game."

"Yes, sir," said Sam. "And while we're waiting, we'll put together a range of rescue options for your approval. Which means I'd like to do the waiting on Vorash. Take advantage of Tok'ra intelligence on Heru'ur's operations. Plus it means we'll be on the spot should Daniel or a Tok'ra operative make contact."

"Agreed, Major. I want you on point with the planning. In the meantime I'll see that SG teams 2, 4, 5 and 11 are prepped and ready for a go on your signal."

A little of the strain eased from her face. "Yes, sir."

"Good. Then as soon as you're given a clean bill of health by Dr. Fraiser, you and Teal'c will return to Vorash with your father and Martouf. Are there any questions?"

There were no questions, so Hammond dismissed them. But at the doorway, once the others had left the room, Jacob paused and turned back.

"George…"

Still seated, he looked up to meet the apprehensive gaze of his oldest friend in the service. "It's ironic, isn't it, Jacob? I pulled strings and twisted arms and called in favors to save Jack from Robert Kinsey… and in doing so, I delivered him into the hands of a Goa'uld who equally has no cause to love him."

Jacob stepped closer. "It's not your fault, George. And it's not mine, either. It's just one of the risks we take when we step through that damned Stargate. Jack knew that. So did Daniel."

Hammond allowed himself a very small and unpleasant smile. "Careful, Jacob. You're using the past tense."

Jacob slammed the door behind him.

Janet was still busy with the babies when Sam presented herself for inspection. So she took a seat on an empty bed, trying to ignore her aches and pains and the ocean of worry churning inside her.

Teal'c had insisted on coming to the infirmary with her, and she didn't try to dissuade him. She appreciated the company. Right now the two of them *were* SG-1. Without Teal'c she'd really be alone.

It was a horrible thought.

Seated on a chair beside her bed he said, as sombre as she'd ever seen him, "I feel most..." He searched for a word. "Helpless, Major Carter. It is a strange sensation. I am not prepared to endure it for long."

Sam dredged up a smile for him. "I feel the same way, believe me."

"I have been feeling this way since you departed Vorash for Yu's breeding farm." He frowned. "I should not have permitted myself to be persuaded to stay behind."

"I'm with you there," she agreed. "And I'm sorry. I've had so much other stuff on my mind I haven't stopped to think how you must be feeling."

"By 'other stuff', you are referring to O'Neill's difficulty in reconciling the events on Euronda?"

"Yeah. He and Daniel are back to tap-dancing on eggshells around each other."

"I see."

Sam sighed. "They didn't let it get in the way of the mission but the tension's there, Teal'c. Under the surface. It's like waiting for a really big bad storm to break. But they'll get through it," she added, with far more confidence than she felt. "They always do."

"Indeed."

Provided they were still alive to get through it. But she wasn't going to say that aloud. Saying that aloud would be tantamount to giving up on them. She brushed Teal'c's arm with her fingers, instead. "I'm sorry. I should've spoken up about you not coming with us."

His hand covered hers. "It seemed a wise decision at the time."

"Yeah. Maybe. But God, I wish you'd been there. You could've evened the odds." Brutal as blood spatter, the image of Boaz and Mikah's bodies, sprawled in ugly death... "We made friends there, kind of. The head man and his little boy. Heru'ur's Jaffa killed them."

"Hey, Sam!" said Janet brightly, sweeping into the room. "There you are. Teal'c, you want to give us some privacy? This won't take long."

As Teal'c withdrew, Janet whipped the curtain round the bed then took a moment to give her a hard once-over look. "So. I hear things went to hell in a hand basket."

"Yeah," she managed. *Boaz. Mikah.* "Just a little bit."

With a sigh, Janet put an arm around her shoulders and squeezed. "You know it's not your fault, right? That you escaped, and they didn't? You know it was just dumb luck, the way the cookie crumbled, the chips falling where they fell? Sam? Tell me you know it's not your fault."

"It just all happened so *fast*... one minute I was playing pat-a-cake with a three year old girl, then the doors were blowing in and there were Jaffa and—and—we had no warning—we had no weapons—there was nothing I could do but *run*—"

"Shh, shh, I know," said Janet, soothing. "But you're okay? You're not injured?"

"No, no, I'm fine, I'm just tired, the colonel's a really bad sleeper *and* he hogs the bed, I—"

"Sam," said Janet, delicately. "Is there something you need to tell me?"

She felt her face heating. "Damn. I wasn't going to say anything about that. Um. Look. Janet. It's not what you think. Nothing... happened. We just got stuck sharing a bed. In our clothes. I even kept my socks on. All perfectly innocent. And our little secret, okay?"

"Hmm," said Janet, and looked at the enclosing curtain. "Hey, Teal'c. You still out there?"

"I am."

"Did you hear any of that?"

"I did not."

"Good. Let's keep it that way."

Sam was torn between laughter and anger. "Janet, God, none of this is *funny*!"

Janet picked up her wrist and pressed cool fingers to its pulse point. "Adrenaline fatigue, Sam," she said quietly. "I know you know the drill. If you don't unwind you're going to burn out, and how will that help the colonel or Daniel?"

She was right. It wouldn't. And it wouldn't bring back Boaz or Mikah. "How are Berez and Qualah? The babies?"

Janet smiled. "Everyone's fine, Sam. Now hush a while and let me do my thing, so you and Teal'c can go do yours."

It was a good idea. She hushed, and let Janet work.

Hang in there guys. We're coming. We're coming.

On regaining his senses, Daniel discovered two important things. He wasn't dead... and he still had the communicator. On the downside, his cut hand hurt like hell and insisted on dribbling. He was squashed in the back of a Goa'uld al'kesh with several hundred crying, wailing, terrified humans of assorted ages. And as far as he could tell, none of them was Jack or Sam. Not that he wanted Jack or Sam to be captured. He just didn't want to be captured alone.

Which still didn't sound right, but what the hey. In the immortal words of Jack O'Neill: he was having a bad, *bad* day.

Please God, please, let them have escaped.

The other good thing was there weren't any Jaffa squashed in here with them. Well, naturally. Catch a Jaffa flying coach. He wondered if Boaz or Mikah were in here with him but nobody he was squished with knew where they were, and he couldn't see them anywhere. When he called out their names they didn't answer.

In his overcrowded and post-zat blast haze, it felt as though the ride through hyperspace went on forever. He drifted in and out of consciousness and didn't try to fight that; it was a relief to escape the stench of fear and sweat and bodily wastes. The gut-churning sounds of misery, unbridled. He was vividly reminded of photos he'd seen depicting railway cars crammed with Jews on their way to Dachau, Auschwitz, Sobibor.

The analogy was uncomfortably close for comfort.

He knew he should be thinking of escape. And he would be, if he had the first idea of where to begin. But he was an archaeologist, for God's sake, not Harry Houdini. Not Jack O'Neill, career military expert and survivor extraordinaire.

God. I wish Jack was here.

It occurred to him, as he drifted in and out of his current revolting reality, that it was perhaps the merest smidgin hypocritical, maybe, the way he looked on Jack as his very own personal Swiss Army knife. Handy for picking locks, prying the tops off stubborn drink bottles and... oh yes, slitting the occasional enemy throat.

Otherwise to be folded up neatly and put away where he wouldn't slice any accidental fingers.

I have trusted you over and over and over again. And all I ask in return is that you show me a little respect. I have never said don't disagree with me. What I have said, more than once, is disagree with me by all means ... just do it in private. But you never do. And you don't even see it's a problem.

The words reverberated inside his skull, courtesy of that damned inconvenient perfect audio recall. And now, at last, as he found himself in the direst of dire straits, he could finally admit it.

Jack was right.

Pride: it was his besetting sin. He liked to tell himself it was integrity. Perseverance. The courage to hold fast in the face of adversity. And yes, sometimes it was. Mostly, it was. But other times it was nothing but good old fashioned stubbornness and pride, bolstering his ego, giving him permission to cross the line. To fool himself into believing that because he was morally in the right he didn't have to concern himself with the position or feelings of the individual he'd placed squarely in the wrong.

These days, usually, that individual was Jack.

But what gutted him breathless now, even more than the unpalatable truth or the stinking atmosphere in this temporary prison, was the fact that Jack had said it. Jack never—well, almost never—made inappropriate personal comments. In fact, he practically never made appropriate ones. Jack was the kind of man who really did believe that actions spoke louder than words.

Hey, I killed the bastard who was trying to kill you, what else do you need? Flowers?

For him to articulate, with such devastating bluntness, in sentences longer than five words—hell, in sentences, full stop—the depth and breadth of his hurt, his disappointment...

Without any warning the al'kesh shuddered, decelerating. The other captives cried out in fear, or pain, or both. Some started pushing at the rear doors, at the walls, all rational thought abandoned.

"It's all right!" he shouted. "Don't be frightened, we're just slowing to sub-light. We'll probably be landing soon. Don't panic. Stay calm. Or people will be hurt."

But they wouldn't listen. Just when he thought he'd be trampled himself, smeared to red jelly by mindless mob terror, the rear doors of the ship opened, admitting fading afternoon light, warm air and a phantom promise of freedom.

"Humans, be silent!" roared an enormous Jaffa, and punctuated the order with a staff weapon blast above their heads.

Silence fell like an ax.

"Humans," the Jaffa bellowed, "You are now the property of our great god Heru'ur, held in trust for him by Lord Anatapas. I am Va'ton, the lord's First Prime. Glory to Heru'ur and his beloved Lord Anatapas! Glory to Heru'ur and his beloved Lord Anatapas! Glory to Heru'ur and—"

Raggedly, weakly, Yu's former humans took up the insistent chant. Repeated it more loudly, more fervently, as Va'ton and his Jaffa poked and prodded and menaced them out of the al'kesh, into a courtyard, then a massive stone building, and finally down a long, dark stone staircase to cages deep underground.

Treading carefully, one hand pressed protectively over his pocket and the Tok'ra communicator hidden there, Daniel went with them ... just one more faceless human in the crowd.

Dedra, loyal servant to Lord Anatapas and to the great god Heru'ur, known elsewhere as Leith of the Tok'ra, watched as one by one the returned al'kesh disgorged their stolen cargo into the fortress courtyard, and was dismayed.

She'd been told of the raid on Yu's breeding farm only after the al'kesh had left. Too late to try and use her meagre influence to stop the madness before it began. She'd protested anyway.

"My lord Anatapas, why would you do this? Against Heru'ur's wishes? His treaty with Yu *forbids*—"

"You forget yourself, Dedra!" Anatapas had snarled. Like so many Goa'uld he was gloriously handsome. Irredeemably degenerate. Ruthless, and cruel. "I serve Heru'ur with every breath. Yu's minions have raided us three times in the last star cycle. Heru'ur does battle with Cronos therefore *I* have punished Yu for him. Yu thought to keep these humans hidden, his most prized and valuable crop. Now they will serve Heru'ur—and Yu will never know. But *we* will know. *We* will flaunt them under his nose when next the system lords meet in treaty. And so will Yu be punished for trespassing in the empire of Heru'ur! And the god Heru'ur will reward me!"

He was mad, of course. Crazed with ambition, another predictable Goa'uld trait.

All those poor humans. Pretty cattle, nothing more.

She'd have to tell the Tok'ra. If Yu discovered the identity of the thieves who'd raided his slave farm it might have grave repercussions for the galaxy's balance of power. The Goa'uld were so easily offended; there could be all-out war between Yu and Heru'ur over this.

Leith kept her Tok'ra subspace communicator hidden beneath a loosened flagstone under the rug in her chamber. For nearly one whole Vorash year she'd lived in Anatapas' fortress, located on a small planet within Heru'ur's empire. In all that time she'd never been suspected. Never had trouble making her regular reports. She hoped now, fervently, that her luck would continue to hold.

Behind her closed door, tucked into her chamber's small bathing alcove, she opened a secure channel and contacted home.

"Vorash. Vorash this is Leith, requesting communications. Vorash, this is Leith."

Long, heart-pounding seconds of silence. Then: "*Leith, this is Vorash. A moment, please.*"

She knew that voice. Her heart constricted with a dreadful wave of homesickness. "Anise? Why must I wait, I don't have long, I—"

"*Leith, this is Aldwyn. Listen carefully. Heru'ur's forces have raided one of Yu's slave farms. They—*"

"I know! It's why I'm calling! It was Anatapas. The stolen slaves are here, on Elekba. If Yu finds out it was Anatapas acting for Heru'ur, he—"

"*Listen, Leith!*" said Aldwyn sharply. He sounded odd. Alarmed. Aldwyn was never alarmed. Her heart-rate soared. "*Humans of the Tauri were on that slave farm. Members of SG-1. Jacob and Martouf rescued Major Carter but believe Colonel O'Neill and Daniel Jackson were captured in the raid. Do you understand?*"

Leith felt her mouth suck dry with fright. All the Goa'uld knew of SG-1. If Anatapas discovered he held them captive... "Yes, Aldwyn. Of course."

"*Can you mingle with the slaves at all? Find O'Neill and Jackson*" *without revealing yourself to the Goa'uld?"*

"Possibly. I'm not certain. Anatapas trusts no-one. He suspects the birds of conspiring to thwart his service to Heru'ur."

Aldwyn sighed. *"We think Jackson has a Tok'ra communicator. He knows we have operatives spying on Heru'ur. He might try to send a distress call. If he does, do your best to answer it. Let him know who you are."*

"And if he is recognized? He'll reveal my presence, he—"

"Leith, we are standing by to extract O'Neill and Jackson, if they are there. We'll bring you out as well. But first you must confirm they are prisoners of Anatapas and warn them to draw no attention to themselves or attempt escape on their own. Do you understand?"

Oh yes, she understood. She understood that her dangerous life had just become infinitely more so. "I understand, Aldwyn," she said, subdued. "I will contact you again when the chance presents itself, and I will do my best to find the Tauri humans."

She ended the transmission. Returned her transmitter to its secret home in the floor, and took her small hand-held communicator from its hiding place in the wainscoting by the window. It had a silent alarm function for covert operations; she activated that, and tucked the whole thing into her bodice.

For once, having large breasts was coming in handy.

We must take care, said her symbiote, Moradh. *Or this situation will rapidly deteriorate.*

Moradh had a knack for stating the obvious. I know, she replied. Are you ready?

Always.

She checked herself in the mirror, to make sure none of her inner turmoil was reflected in her demeanor. It wasn't. Her eyes were calm, her mouth relaxed. Her face wore its usual haughty mask of Goa'uld superiority. Excellent. The hour for dinner was almost upon them, and all the Goa'uld residing here were expected to attend the feast.

She adjusted her fine brocade skirts and swept from the chamber. The human slave in the corridor outside prostrated itself as she passed. She ignored it, as any Goa'uld would, her mind racing with thoughts.

O'Neill and Jackson of SG-1 in the slave pens deep below the fortress of Anatapas.

Could her day get any worse?

Daniel couldn't be certain, but he thought there were three cages in total filled with humans from Yu's farm. Jack or Sam weren't in his cage, so they had to be in one or both of the remaining two.

They had to be. He'd decided any other possibility was ... well ... impossible. Unthinkable. And not not *not* true. Because they'd escaped.

Oh God. What if they didn't?

What he *really* wanted to do was stand up and shout their names at the top of his lungs until one of them heard him and shouted back. And he'd have done it, too, if it weren't for the Jaffa guards prowling the place like panthers in search of their next good meal.

So if they *were* here he'd find them tomorrow, once the humans had been let outside for some exercise. The Jaffa had to let them out, right? They hadn't been stolen from Yu's farm just to rot underground in these cages, had they?

Yeah. Okay. That would be something else he wasn't going to think about.

So the plan was: survive the night. In the morning hook up with his missing team mates in the clean fresh air. And in the meantime ...

Contact the Tok'ra, you idiot.

Because Jacob knew he was alive. Jacob knew he had a communicator. And Jacob, being unable to rescue him or anyone else in his eensy teensy unarmed tel'tac, must have hotfooted it home to Vorash, raised the alarm, and told every last Tok'ra spy who was spying on Heru'ur to keep an ear out for a call from one ever-so-slightly panicked Doctor Daniel Jackson.

Unless of course Jacob *had* managed to rescue Jack and Sam and believed him to be dead or unsalvageable. Or been blown out of the sky by one of the al'keshs' plasma cannons ... in which case he really was alone.

Oh, God.

Just like Sam, he thought too much.

Exhausted, Daniel slumped against the wall in a corner of the cage and tried to get some sleep. He was roused from his stupor an

indeterminate time later by the arrival of food. Well. Stuff impersonating food. He was unpleasantly reminded of the slops they'd been
fed on the prison planet Hadante.

Surprisingly, thoughts of Hadante cheered him up. He'd made
it out of that hell hole. He'd make it out of this one, too. Just see if
he didn't.

Except, his treacherous inner Daniel reminded him, *then you had
Jack, Sam, Teal'c and Linea on your side.*

Daniel, shut the hell up, he told himself. And realized that now,
with the Jaffa guards occupied with feeding time at the zoo and his
fellow cage-mates likewise food-focused, for themselves and the
children penned in with them, he could maybe possibly whisper
'help' into his Tok'ra communicator and nobody would notice. Of
course he had no idea what the range was on one of these things;
probably Jacob had mentioned it at some point but when briefings
got military and technical he tended to tune out. A communicator
like this one had reached Teal'c in orbit above Ne'tu, and even further away than that. It had to be worth a try.

Huddling as far into his corner as he could reach, presenting his
back to the rest of the cage's occupants under guise of eating his
disgusting dinner in private, he fished the communicator out of his
pocket, turned his face to the wall and did indeed call for help.

Called once. Called twice. Called thrice and a fourth time for the
dregs of luck.

And just as he was about to give up and turn the damned thing
off… somebody answered.

"This is Leith of the Tok'ra."

For a moment he couldn't speak, the shock and relief and sheer
disbelief of hearing a friendly voice, no matter how soft and hard to
decipher, was overwhelming.

"Oh, thank God," he said at last, barely moving his lips. "Where
are you? Can you get me out here?"

*"I reside in the fortress above you. You must be strong. You will
be rescued but it could take time. Do nothing to reveal yourself. I am
known here as Dedra. I will come for you when I can."*

"What about the others, Leith? Colonel O'Neill and Major Carter,
do you know—"

But the Tok'ra was gone. With trembling fingers Daniel put the communicator back in his pocket. Covered his face with his hands, breathing hard.

Somebody touched his leg, and he jerked around. It was Sallah, from the goat field. God, he hadn't seen her, hadn't realized she was here. She was a child, he hadn't been looking at the children.

"Don't be afraid, David," she said. She was smeared and filthy, her lovely face marred by a swollen bruise. "The great god Yu, Mighty and Everlasting, will save us. You'll see. He will come, and we'll go home."

"Where's your mother, Sallah?" he whispered. "Where's your father?"

Her thin shoulders lifted in a shrug. "They died in the sickness, seasons ago. I live with Dusha, but I can't find her."

She was so young, and helpless. Daniel put his arm around her, felt her sag against his side. Her head drooped to his shoulder.

"Probably she's in one of the other cages," he told her. "We'll find her in the morning, Sallah. Okay? Until then, try to sleep."

She was sleeping already, worn out by her ordeal.

After speaking with Dedra, Leith, whatever her name was, he was too keyed up to sleep. So he sat with his back to the wall, with his arm around Sallah, and waited for tomorrow. For rescue.

Daniel Jackson's call for help had come during the evening banquet's second course. Leith's communicator's silent alarm was heat activated. It sat in her bodice like a burning coal; she could scarcely keep from squirming.

"My lord Anatapas," Moradh murmured. It had to be Moradh; when in the Goa'uld's presence, one spoke as a Goa'uld. "Your servant requests leave to withdraw momentarily."

Anatapas had stared at her, his deep-set eyes avaricious. Then he jerked his head at the banquet hall's door. "Go."

"Thank you, my lord," said Moradh, and sank out of sight. Walking when she wanted to run, Leith slipped out to the corridor then let herself onto one of the fortress's fourth floor balconies. Answering the call from her communicator, she spoke for the first time with Daniel Jackson of the infamous Tauri warriors SG-1.

He'd sounded young. And ordinary. And scared. Not the stuff of legend ... or a man to frighten the Goa'uld.

Nevertheless he was feared and hated by the system lords and held in high affection by Selmak. So possibly his day had been less than inspiring, also.

She tucked the communicator back in her bodice, her mind a maelstrom of thought and conjecture.

If she approached Anatapas and begged for a boon, for a slave from among the new arrivals... Anatapas desired her. She could see it in his eyes but had never allowed him access. That might have to change. She might have to lower herself to consorting with a Goa'uld, just a little, in order to achieve her objective.

Yes. She could surrender to him then ask for a gift as a token of his appreciation. She'd have to flatter him to vomiting point, of course. And pretend his attentions were welcome. Pleasurable. Addictive. Pretend she'd just been too shy, too awed, too disbelieving that such a great lord could truly be interested in her...

Yes. She could do that. She and Moradh would hate it. But she could do it.

O'Neill and Jackson must not be discovered.

The decision made, her distaste buried deep inside, for later perusal, she stepped from the balcony back into the corridor...

... and was confronted by Lord Anatapas himself. He was smiling. His eyes lit from within, a burst of heat and power.

"Enjoying some fresh air, Dedra?"

Leith swept him the lowest of curtseys, making sure all her cleavage was displayed. "My lord, yes," Moradh answered for them. "I was overcome by the warmth of the feasting hall. The... warmth of your regard."

"Indeed?" said Anatapas. Bending down, he placed a finger beneath her chin and raised her, inexorably, to her feet. "You value my regard, Dedra?"

"Most highly, my lord."

"If that is so, Dedra, explain this."

He snapped his fingers and the Goa'uld lordling Rabek stepped out of hiding, her long range Tok'ra communicator dangling from his hand.

She felt herself flush as hot as Abydos. As cold as the moons of Vexitilia.

"An unknown tel'tac was seen at the raided slave farm, Dedra.

If that is your name," said Anatapas, his voice trebled with rage. "Part of a communication was intercepted between the tel'tac and someone on the ground. I have deemed the communication to be Tok'ra. We have suspected you are Tok'ra for some time now. I alerted Heru'ur to your... suspicious... behaviors and he told me to watch you closely. I did. Then a Tok'ra spy was caught aboard the god Kotosh's own personal ha'tak, some little time ago. It spoke at length before it died." He laughed. "So much for Tok'ra fortitude. It said one of my servants served not our system lord. When Heru'ur told me, I knew it had spoken of you. But I had no proof... till now."

Leith felt her insides twist in anguish. Felt Moradh's anguished echo. Irrilain. Was it Irrilain who'd spied on Kotosh? Had he been caught, and failed to commit suicide in time? And did the High Council know? Operatives were often out of contact for extended periods...

Anatapas said, "I have been monitoring subspace communications, Dedra, since receiving Heru'ur's warning. We found this device in your chamber. It is of Tok'ra origin. We know you called the Tok'ra after the raiders returned today. Were I to strip you naked, I would find a smaller Tok'ra device about your person. A device you were using just moments ago, on the balcony. And were I to inspect the slave pens below this fortress... I think I might find another. Who were you talking to, Dedra? A human co-conspirator? One of your fellow Tok'ra? Who?"

Leith felt her spine stiffen. Her head come up. Her racing heart settle to a more bearable rhythm. Moradh stepped back, and she spoke as herself.

"No-one. I talked to no-one."

Anatapas stroked his fingers down her cheek. Plunged them into the bodice of her dress and withdrew her small communicator. His perfect lips curved into a perfect smile.

"You are lying. But that's no matter. I will find the person on the other end of this device, Dedra. They are here... now... below our feet. And when I do, you will both beg for a mercy that will never be shown."

CHAPTER SEVENTEEN

*D*amn and damn and damn his damn crap knee. To hell and gone, and back again.

Swallowing a grunt of discomfort, O'Neill shifted position on his cage's cold stone floor. The chill seeping up from the unprotected flagstones had sharp teeth; it tore at his strained anterior cruciate ligament like a starving dog.

If his knee hadn't stopped him, he might've got away.

Had anyone else got away? Carter? Daniel? Mikah? Boaz?

He had no way of knowing. His al'kesh had been the last unloaded, all the other humans were locked out of sight in their cages when he was locked into his. He didn't dare risk calling their names, either; Heru'ur's Jaffa stood guard outside.

God. Not knowing was a bitch.

He thought of his Tok'ra communicator, back in Boaz's house, and could easily have wept... if he'd been the weeping type. He wasn't.

You haven't got the damned thing, Jack. Deal with it and move on.

The cage wasn't tiny but it wasn't a penthouse at the Ritz, either. Designed to hold a hundred, a hundred and fifty humans, tops. Right now it held closer to two hundred, and even though a bunch of them were children conditions were still uncomfortably close.

He wondered, briefly, what had happened to the farm's babies then decided he didn't want to know.

His internal clock, finely calibrated over years of Black Ops work, told him that five hours had passed since they'd been shoved into these pens. Chances were it was dark outside now. It was still light in here, though. Torches guttered shadows over the blank stone walls and stank up the air with their smoke.

He leaned his head against the wall behind him. He needed to sleep, to recoup some energy so he could face whatever the universe threw at him next. Provided Jacob and Martouf hadn't been discovered and blown out of the sky *please, God, please God* chances were good—okay, fair—that some kind of rescue was imminent. The Tok'ra had ways of findings things out. They might never *share* the information, but they usually had it.

And if anyone could make them cough it up it was General George Hammond. As sure as God made little green apples, Hammond wouldn't leave any of his people stranded here. The smartest thing to do right now was stay low. Unnoticed. Completely unremarked.

If Carter was here somewhere, he knew she'd be okay. She'd know to keep her head down. Play it cool. If Daniel was here...

God. If you're here, Daniel, no matter what happens don't do anything stupid. And for crying out loud keep your big mouth shut.

Clearly SG-1 had been caught up in some kind of pissing contest between Yu and Heru'ur. Funny how the Tok'ra had let *that* fact slip their minds.

Yeah. Freakin' hilarious.

He'd never heard of this Goa'uld Lord Anatapas. Obviously he was one of Heru'ur's minions. Well, with a bit of luck snaky Lord Anatapas had never heard of him either. Or Carter. Or Daniel. Of course he'd have heard of the Tok'ra... but there was no reason for Anatapas to suspect a Tok'ra presence amongst these stolen humans.

Keep flying under the radar, Jack, and you just might make it home for The Simpsons.

God. He hoped Carter and Daniel were okay... and far away from here.

Selfishly, he did wish Teal'c was here. Having Teal'c in the trenches with him was like having a twin, only bigger and stronger and even less likely than he was himself to care about alien rights, interesting cave paintings and whether or not what they did in the here-and-now might affect someone sixteen generations down the track.

But he didn't have Teal'c. He didn't have his Tok'ra communicator. He didn't have a gun or even the small boning knives any more, because the Jaffa had stripped him of the bloodstained leather apron. In short he was deep in *me, myself and I* territory and if he didn't stop fretting about that he was going to erode the inner barricades he'd built over more than a decade of Special Forces work...

And that might well prove fatal.

Get a grip, Jack. You've been here before. And with any luck you'll be here again. Or at least you'll get the chance to avoid being here again. Just stay cool, and don't screw up.

Beyond the overcrowded cage, a stirring. Jaffa voices, babbling in Jaffa. His cage was closest to the doors of the underground prison complex; he heard one of the Jaffa say, "Kree! How can we serve you, Lord Anatapas?"

So... the snakehead had come to pay a visit. Couldn't resist the urge to gloat. Typical. God, they were so pathetic.

As the other occupants of his cage stirred and muttered and whimpered in fright, O'Neill managed to get himself back on his feet. Even though he'd made sure to position himself right at the back, where the Jaffa couldn't easily see him, he still had a decent line of sight to the cage's iron door.

Which opened with a jingling of keys to admit the enormous Jaffa Va'ton. He was armed with a staff weapon and accompanied by a swanky, slimy, over-dressed, over-coiffed, over-*everythinged* individual with glowing white-hot eyes.

The prisoners fell silent, cowed by the presence of a god, and pressed as far away from him as they could get.

"I am Lord Anatapas, beloved servant of the god Heru'ur," the snakehead announced. He looked at the Jaffa, and nodded. Va'ton shot dead the nearest five humans. Two of them were children.

Sonofabitch!

The bodies hit the floor. The other humans started shrieking, crying. Howled for Yu to save their lives. The Jaffa flipped his staff weapon up and discharged it over their heads. Smoke. Sparks. The eye-searing stink of melted rock. Silence fell, broken only by a woman's terrible weeping.

Heart pounding, bile scalding his throat, O'Neill stared at the Goa'uld. God, to be an X-Man, to freeze the bastard solid or burst him into flame or cook him alive from the inside out!

The Goa'uld ignored the murdered humans at his feet. "I speak to the Tok'ra," he said, his voice bloated with malice. "Your agent Dedra, sent to spy on Heru'ur, has confirmed your presence. She was caught talking to you on her communicator. Surrender yourself, Tok'ra, or I will kill more of these humans."

What? He didn't *have* a communicator...

Oh, crap. It had to be Daniel. Carter would never have disobeyed his order to leave their communicators in Boaz's house. In Daniel's world, orders were just suggestions. He was here, somewhere. He'd managed to make contact with a Tok'ra operative inside this bastard's fortress... and now their cover was blown to hell.

Anatapas had him, which was bad enough. But if he got his hands on Daniel too...

Bite the bullet, Daniel. Keep your damned head down ...

Anatapas looked again to his hulking First Prime. Va'ton swung his staff weapon—hit the switch—plasma surged, waiting to fire—

"*No!*" O'Neill shouted, and shoved his way forward, cursing the brushfire in his knee. Cursing the Goa'uld. Cursing God. "Don't shoot! *Don't shoot!*"

He made it to the front of the crowd, just, and sprawled without dignity at the Goa'uld's feet. Va'ton bent down and hauled him upright, almost yanking his arm from its shoulder socket.

Anatapas considered him. "You have no symbiote. You are not Tok'ra."

The staff weapon charged, swung—

"I am! I am! I'm a human Tok'ra! Swear to God. Mine, not yours. I work for the Tok'ra. Don't kill anyone else. I'm the guy you're after. I wish I wasn't, but there you go. I am."

The Goa'uld's heavy eyelids drooped to half-mast. "Prove it," he drawled. "Give me your Tok'ra communicator."

Crap. "I threw it away. I got scared you'd discover me and I threw it away."

Anatapas curled his lip in disgust. "Kill it," he said to his tame mass-murderer. "And then kill two more. The true Tok'ra is in here somewhere. I will flush it out if I have to kill every last slave in this place."

"*Wait!*" O'Neill shouted, as Va'ton took aim. "Okay! You win! I'm not a Tok'ra!" He took a deep, shuddering breath and let it out slowly. *God help me, God help me, you'd better be sending the cavalry, George ...* "I'm Jack O'Neill of SG-1. Possibly you've heard of me, from such popular shows as *Killing Apophis 2*."

Silence; the kind that sent cold shivers down a person's spine. The Goa'uld's eyes flashed. "Jack O'Neill?" He was practically purring. "SG-1 of the Tauri?"

"One and the same." O'Neill forced a smile. "Ah, fame. Ain't it sweet?"

"And what were you doing on Lord Yu's slave farm, O'Neill of the Tauri?" demanded Anatapas, stepping close.

He shrugged. "Oh, you know. A bit of this, a bit of that. Some sight-seeing. A little souvenir shopping."

The Goa'uld ignored that. "Where is the rest of SG-1?"

"Kicking some snaky snakehead Goa'uld butt on the other side of the galaxy. Haven't seem 'em for weeks."

The Goa'uld's eyes narrowed. "I do not believe you."

He risked another shrug. "You might as well. It's the truth."

Anatapas hit him, hard enough that he saw stars. *"Where is the rest of SG-1?"*

He spat blood. "Go screw yourself," he suggested, savagely. "Which I guess you can do more easily than most. I *told* you already. I'm flying solo!"

"You lie," said Anatapas. "The Goa'uld know you work as a team." He whirled in a flurry of silk brocade skirts and stepped out into the wide corridor between the cages. "I have O'Neill, Tauri SG-1!" he shouted, his thrumming voice bouncing from wall to wall. "Now I want the rest of you! Surrender yourselves or I will kill these humans one by one until you obey my command or they are *all* dead!"

"You stupid bastard, I'm on my own!" O'Neill shouted, launching himself at the cage's open door, and Anatapas. Va'ton swung a fist, knocking him to the floor.

"Jaffa, kill another one!" Anatapas ordered. "Make it a child!"

"You *bastard*—"

"My lord, my lord!" a new voice shouted. "My lord, you must come! The god Heru'ur commands your presence!"

Head ringing, the flesh over his cheek-bone split from the Jaffa's blow and rapidly swelling, O'Neill slowly sat up.

Anatapas raised his hand, halting Va'ton, and waited for the new Jaffa to join him. "Heru'ur calls?"

The Jaffa plunged to one knee. "My lord, he does. He summons you to him and commands you take no further action against the captured Tok'ra until you both have spoken."

"You *told* him?"

The Jaffa went pale. "My lord, he asked."

Anatapas nodded, curtly. "Very well. Tell Heru'ur I come this instant."

"My lord," said the Jaffa, and ran out.

Anatapas turned to his First Prime. "Take the Tauri and put him with the Tok'ra. Fair Dedra can tell him what pleasures await if he refuses to co-operate."

O'Neill scrambled to his feet before Va'ton could try ripping off his other arm. "Since when do the Goa'uld care about co-operation?"

Anatapas smiled. "When the other system lords learn it is Heru'ur who possesses SG-1 they will choke on their envy and ire. He will wish to display you as a trophy... *after* you have revealed to us all your secrets. But if you do not co-operate we will torture you... for longer than your puny intellect can imagine. The choice is yours."

As Va'ton dragged him away down the corridor, to whatever new cell and horrors awaited, O'Neill thought he caught a glimpse of Daniel. Just a blurred impression from the corner of his eye, as he was hauled past the other cages.

Hang in there, Daniel, he tried to signal. *You know help's coming. It's coming. It has to.*

Daniel knew the situation had plummeted from bad to worse when he heard the staff blasts, and the screaming. It meant people were dead, and their murders hurt like a knife-thrust through his heart. Sallah whimpered, hiding her face in his chest.

Soon after that he heard a furious, despairing, familiar voice shout: "No! Don't shoot! *Don't shoot!*"

Damn. It was Jack.

Chaotic emotions cascaded through him. Flooding relief, that he wasn't alone. Shame, that he could be so small. Fear, because he had no idea what was coming next.

His guts churned. He felt light-headed. He gave Sallah to someone else to hold and clawed to his feet. All the humans in the cage with him were silent, eyes wide, faces chalky-white with terror and shock. They knew what those sounds meant as well as he did. After life on the slave farm, probably better. They looked at each other, but not at him. Time passed, and they waited to hear more staff blasts. The ugly sounds of death. Would Jack's be among them? And what about Sam? Was she with him? Was she here at all? If so, she was keeping silent. He should keep silent too. That was their game plane, the standard M.O.

But how could he do that if people were dying? Jack hadn't...

Without conscious volition, prompted by four years of training with Jack, and Teal'c, and Sam, and Hammond, with everyone who'd done their damndest to drum some military pragmatism into him, he pulled out the communicator and shoved it into his bowl of uneaten slops. It sank to the bottom without a trace. Then he shoved the bowl away with his foot, into a collection of other slop-filled bowls.

Nobody noticed, not even Sallah. And nobody could connect that bowl to him, now. Maybe, just maybe, he was safe. At least for a little while—provided Jack could convince whoever was shooting that he was here on his own. Until Jacob and Teal'c and maybe—hopefully—*please God*—Sam came to save them.

They had to be coming. They *had* to.

A Goa'uld's voice sounded in the passageway, in the space between the cages. Mellifluous. Cadenced. Ripe with menace.

"I have O'Neill, Tauri SG-1. Now I want the rest of you! Surrender yourselves or I will kill these humans one by one until you obey my command or they are *all* dead!"

More dreadful silence. If Sam was here she was following orders. Daniel dithered. He should too, but the people... the children...

Then a shouting Jaffa, he couldn't hear what was said. Taking a risk, having no choice, he eased his way to the front of the cage and stood off to one side, hiding most of his body, letting himself see just enough. Just a little bit, through the bars.

The Goa'uld's First Prime Va'ton marched past the cage, dragging Jack with him.

Jack was limping, badly. Blood from a cut over his cheek-bone smeared his face. His eyes were wild and rage ruled every muscle: O'Neill on the warpath.

Their gazes met briefly, and then he was gone.

Shaken, sweating, cold to the bone, Daniel pushed his way back to the rear of the cage. Slid down the wall to the floor. Pulled his knees to his chest, crossed his arms over them and buried his face, so no-one would see.

Oh, God. Oh, God. I don't know what to do. Sha're, can you hear me, sweetheart? Tell me what to do ...

Her'ur's face in the long-range communication device was chilly and displeased.

"*It is fortunate for you, Anatapas, that you have both a Tok'ra and a Tauri within your possession. If that were not the case you would be dead now, for breaking my treaty with Yu. It is also fortunate Yu's grasp is weakening and he cannot afford to engage me in battle while he attempts to wrest back stolen territory from Ba'al.*"

Anatapas shivered. "My god is merciful."

"*Your god wants to know of the booty you took from Yu.*"

"Slaves, Heru'ur. The most beautiful bred in all of Yu's empire. Adults, children and infants. The infants have been sent to your farm on Banto. They will know only your greatness." He hesitated. Should he mention the five dead humans now cooling in their cage far below his feet? Doubtless Heru'ur would be angered by their loss. But he'd be more than angered if that truth was withheld.

Heru'ur said, "*Tell me all, Anatapas. You know I will find out.*"

"My god is truly omniscient," he admitted, and got down on both knees. "It was necessary for me to kill five slaves in order to bring forth O'Neill from hiding. It might be necessary to kill more, so his evil companions can be unmasked."

"*No,*" snapped Heru'ur. "*I would have the use of these beautiful slaves. Find another way.*"

Anatapas touched his forehead to the floor. Heru'ur was unpredictable. Appeasement, abasement: they were the only sure paths to success. "As my god commands. When will my god return to inspect his new property?"

"*Soon.*"

"And the Tok'ra, my lord?"

"*Have you taken away its suicide pill?*"

"Of course, my lord."

"*Hold it in close confinement, along with O'Neill and any other Tauri you uncover. But conduct no interrogations of them.*" Heru'ur smiled. "*That pleasure I reserve for myself.*"

"Of course, Heru'ur. My lord..." He hesitated, then continued. "My lord, is it possible to send back one of your warships to help protect my fortress? We may be the victim of attack."

"*By whom? The Tok'ra? They do not rescue their own.*" Heru'ur glowered. "*And the Tauri do not know O'Neill is captured. Do they?*"

Anatapas thought of the mysterious tel'tac that escaped from Panotek, that he'd neglected to mention to Heru'ur. If Heru'ur knew he'd been so careless...

He must keep that secret a little longer. "No, my lord," he said faintly. "They cannot know."

"*Then why do you ask for a warship? Are you a coward, Anatapas? Incapable of serving me with competence?*"

Heru'ur's rage was palpable. "No, no, my lord," Anatapas whispered. "I misspoke myself. We are in no danger. I serve you loyally and well. I am your truest believer."

"*Set extra Jaffa at the chappa'ai,*" said Heru'ur, dismissive. "*If you must fear your own shadow.*"

"Yes, my lord. My lord is wise."

"*And slow to forgive,*" said Heru'ur. "*You would be wise too, remembering that.*"

As if he could forget. Slowly, Anatapas straightened, daring to breathe again. "My lord, how goes the battle with Cronos?"

Heru'ur laughed. "*How do you think? Am I not the greatest of all the system lords?*"

"You are, Heru'ur. Our hearts hunger without you. We look to your coming."

"*It will not be long.*"

And Heru'ur was gone.

Anatapas released a hard-held breath. He had to locate O'Neill's companions. Success in that would protect him from previous mistakes.

A pity he could not use the other humans. *Find another way.* He would, and quickly. He had no intention of failing Heru'ur again.

As prison cells went he'd been in worse, O'Neill decided. True, this one was small and damned chilly. The single guttering torch shed some light, but no appreciable heat. Four stone walls, a stone floor, a stone ceiling, an unbreachable door and no windows, but at least the company was easy on the eyes. Leith—not Dedra, that was her hated *Goa'uld* name—looked to be about thirty in human years. Who knew how old she really was? Like every Tok'ra he'd ever met, barring Jacob, she was lusciously good-looking.

It was another thing the Tok'ra had in common with the Goa'uld, though you'd never get them to admit it. They liked nice clothes.

Oooh. Did he think clothes? He meant... hosts.

Leith said, sounding disinterested, "If it concerns you, Jacob managed to rescue his daughter."

Thank God, thank God. Carter was safe. Just as important, it meant the SGC cavalry was coming. "It concerns me."

"You should not have surrendered, O'Neill," she added, mildly scolding.

"I had to. That snakehead bastard knew *someone* had spoken to you. And he was killing people. Killing *children*. He wasn't going to stop until he got what he wanted. What did you expect me to do? Sit on my ass with my fingers crossed hoping he'd get bored and give up?"

Her eyes flashed, once. "*And how many more will die, do you think, once the Goa'uld wring from you everything you know about Earth? About us? Your noble defence of those slaves will prove expensive.*"

He didn't quite repress his distaste. "Ah. Right. And who am I speaking with now?"

"That was Moradh," said Leith. "My symbiote."

"Yeah, well, you can tell *Moradh* I know how to keep my mouth shut," he said emphatically. "Besides. We won't have long to wait, dollars to donuts there's a rescue mission on the way as we speak. All we have to do is sit tight and not panic."

Do you hear me, Daniel? Sit tight and do not panic.

Leith looked at him, her eyes pitying. "O'Neill, every Tok'ra operative knows when he or she goes undercover... if something goes wrong we are on our own. The Tok'ra do not expend time or resources on hopeless attempts at rescue."

"Yeah? Well, that would be one of the *many* points on which our sides part company," he retorted. "See, at the SGC we have this little saying. 'Leave no man behind'. We borrowed it from the Rangers.

Oh, and we changed it a bit—actually, what we say is 'Leave no *person* behind'—Carter would kick my ass if I forgot to clarify that— and what it means, Leith, and Moradh if you're eavesdropping, is that when you send your people into harm's way you don't *leave* them there when the crap hits the fan."

"*Another noble sentiment,*" said Moradh, sounding snippy. "*It would be interesting to know how many people have died while attempting these daring rescues. And how those rescued feel, having cost the lives of their friends.*"

It was a sore point. "Hey. *Ladies.* It so happens I have been left behind and let me tell you, it *sucks.* I've also risked my life on rescue missions. We have another saying, see: What goes around, comes around. I save you, you save the next guy ... it all comes out in the wash. Yeah. Sure. Sometimes a rescuer becomes a casualty and *that* sucks too. But we would rather take that risk than leave one of our own in a place like this. Call us crazy ... but it's a big part of being human."

For a long time, neither Leith nor Moradh answered him. Then Leith said, very quietly, "For your sake, Colonel, I hope that is true. I hope your people do save you from Heru'ur."

"Save *us,*" he said. "You Tok'ra may drive us little humans nuts but we're not going to leave you here on the strength of it."

"Colonel, by the time your people get here—*if* they get here—there will be no-one but yourself and your friend to rescue."

"You're talking *suicide* now?" he demanded. "Uh-uh. That is *not* going to happen. You are *not* going to chew on some damned cyanide pill or whatever it is you people use!"

"I know," said Leith. "Anatapas found my capsule. But Moradh has devised another way." A shadow of apprehension chased across her face. "It will not be ... pleasant. But we have no choice. The Tok'ra must be protected."

She was serious. Even though touchy-feely really wasn't his thing, O'Neill grabbed both her hands and held them. They felt cold and fragile. "Leith. Moradh. *Listen* to me. We're getting rescued. Okay, between now and then things might turn a bit ugly but who cares? We'll survive it. The point is, we stay alive until my people get here. You got that? *We stay alive.*"

"You are overconfident, O'Neill. It is one of the Tauri's greatest failings. What if Heru'ur implants you with a Goa'uld?" Gently, she withdrew her hands. "If you think you can survive that, human, you are sadly mistaken."

Sudden flashback, wickedly unwelcome. Hathor's larval Goa'uld, trying to take him over. Scrabbling around inside his body, wrapping itself around his spine. Pain like being shot in slow motion. The snake's mind battering at him, like he was a locked door and it was trying to break in. But it had never taken a host before; it wasn't certain what to do. All instinct, no finesse.

"You see?" said Leith, watching his face. "There are worse things than dying."

An icy sweat slicked the skin between his shoulder blades. "Have they got any Goa'uld symbiotes here?"

She shook her head. "None that are ready to take a host. But Heru'ur can find one."

"Yeah, well, Heru'ur's not around, and at the risk of sounding like a broken record *we are getting rescued*. There is no call for anyone to be committing suicide!"

"I can kill you, if you'd like," she said, ignoring him. "It will be quick. Painless. Death will ensure you are neither turned into a Goa'uld nor tortured until you reveal all you can about the Tauri and the Tok'ra."

O'Neill shuffled away from her, quick damn smart. "Are you out of your *mind*?"

Now her expression was brooding. "Perhaps I should kill you whether you want me to or not. There is much at stake for the Tok'ra and I have a duty to protect us. Even from our allies."

He held up a warning finger. "You stay the hell away from me! I have *no intention* of dying here."

She fell silent, abstracted in the way that he'd come to recognise in Jacob meant host and symbiote were having a private conversation.

He thought perhaps he was having another very bad dream. If his damned knee wasn't killing him, he'd be tempted to believe it. But the pain was real, and this was real, and not for the first time he found himself thinking:

So, Jack, was retirement *really* that bad?

Leith stirred. Looking outwards again she said, "Moradh refuses to have any part in killing you. She doesn't like you but she says the choice must be yours to make."

"Moradh doesn't like me?" O'Neill echoed. "Well, color me surprised. And tell her the feeling's mutual." He bared his teeth in a smile. "Ooops. I forgot. I just told her myself."

Leith didn't reply. Her eyes rolled back so that only white slivers of cornea were visible. Her mouth dropped open, and he saw that all her mucous membranes had flushed a dark red. She began to tremble, then convulse. Frothy saliva dripped from her lips. Blood trickled from her nostrils; thinly at first, and then like a river in springmelt spate. She slid slowly sideways to the floor to thrash and jerk and flail on the flagstones like a suffocating fish.

"Leith!" he shouted. "Goddammit, don't do this! Stop! We'll get out of here, we'll be okay, don't do this! *Please!*"

But Leith was far beyond hearing him. There was nothing he could do but watch.

It took her—them— ten dreadful minutes to die. In the end the blood poured from every orifice, as though Leith's insides had turned to slush. As though she'd been cursed with Ebola. Her eyes flashed and faded, flashed and faded, like a Maglite with a dodgy battery.

It was a filthy, *filthy* way to go.

When it was over, and at last she lay still, he took off his shirt and covered her face.

It was a long cold night... and he slept through none of it.

Anatapas's Jaffa woke the slaves just after dawn, shouting and shooting their staff weapons into the air. Daniel sat up, startled out of the almost-sleep he'd fallen into barely two hours earlier. He had to shake Sallah awake; the poor little thing was drugged with exhaustion.

The cage was rank with the stench of unwashed flesh and the desperate relievings of human waste in one corner. They'd not even been provided with buckets. On the faces of his fellow captives Daniel saw, as though pressed into damp clay with vicious fingers, the marks of suffering and misery and despair.

Compared to this place, Yu's slave farm had been a paradise.

"What's happening, David?" Sallah whispered, her fingers like limpets around his hand. Why she'd latched onto him he didn't know. There were other adults locked in here that she'd grown up with but somehow, for reasons only she could understand, she felt safest with him. It was a toss-up whether he was touched by that, or driven to the edge of tears.

No, actually; it was both.

"I don't know, sweetheart," he whispered back. "Now hush. Don't give the Jaffa a reason to notice us."

Eyes wide and dull with fear she nodded, and fell silent.

A short time after waking them, the Jaffa opened the cage doors and herded all the stolen humans outside. Back up the long stone staircases and into the fortress courtyard where the al'kesh had disgorged them the day before. No al'kesh now, just hordes of Jaffa in a ring and bristling activated staff weapons. No hope of escape, even if he could bring himself to leave without Jack ... and Sam, if she was here. He looked and he looked but he couldn't see her.

He couldn't see Boaz or Mikah, either. He felt his guts tighten. Did it mean all three were dead? Or had they escaped, back on the farm?

Please, God. Let them have escaped.

The Goa'uld Anatapas was waiting for them. Dressed this morning in silks of indigo and emerald and dark blood red, he stood on a dais of inlaid mother-of-pearl. His right hand and fingers were encased in delicate gold, with crystals embedded where fingernails would be; a variation on the ribbon-device technology he hadn't seen before.

Daniel felt his skin tighten, crawling. Something very bad was coming...

The last of the stolen slaves were hustled and bullied and chivvied into place. He made sure he kept to the back of the crowd, with Sallah passed on to some other kind adult. Just in case things turned ugly and he was the target. As they waited he looked again for Sam. No luck. Still no Boaz and Mikah, either. He allowed himself to feel a flicker of hope.

The silence was unnatural. No dawn chorus of birds. Not even a whimper from the gathered humans. The morning air was cool and moist. Daniel breathed deeply, subduing fear, and waited to see what would happen.

The Jaffa Va'ton came up from beneath the fortress and into the courtyard. He wasn't alone. Jack shuffled with him, still favoring that knee, bare to the waist and chained at wrist and ankle.

He looked... old. As though he'd aged ten years overnight. Beneath dirt and stubble his face was haggard, carved with deep lines of grim endurance. It was a worse face even than he'd worn after days and nights of brutal toil in the spent naquadah mine on Shyla's planet. Worse than his face as he returned from Euronda and condemned Alar to death.

Daniel felt his breath catch in his throat.

Va'ton guided Jack to the dais and pressed on his shoulder till his knees buckled and he was on the ground.

"You're wasting your time, Anatapas," Jack said, breathing hard. "I'm here alone."

Anatapas gave him a single, gloating look then gazed at the crowded humans before him. "Daniel Jackson. Samantha Carter. One or both of you stands before me. Surrender now. Or I will make your friend here suffer in ways none of you *humans* can imagine."

Daniel felt a deluge of relief. No more murdered villagers? Oh, thank God! But the relief soured swiftly, curdling in his gut as he realized what that meant.

Jack was being used as bait.

No, no, no. He couldn't let this happen, he had to stop the torture before it started. They'd figure a way out of it later, together, they always did. But he couldn't just stand here and watch Anatapas do... whatever it was he planned to do. He *couldn't*.

But then he thought: *Wait. Think. What does Jack want you to do?*

Still as any statue he stared hard, trying to see if Jack was giving him a signal, any indication, the slightest hint of how he should handle this.

And there it was. Written plain in Jack's fiercely obdurate face, as though with pen and ink.

Keep your damned mouth shut, Daniel. Don't you say a word.

Well... crap.

"Anatapas, are you listening?" Jack demanded. "I'm on my own. Your Jaffa screwed up, they let the rest of my team escape back on Yu's farm."

Anatapas considered him. "You said you hadn't seen them for weeks."

"I lied. I'm sorry. It's a bad habit, I know."

"You lied then… you're lying now," Anatapas replied, disdainful.

"I'm not," Jack insisted. "The rest of SG-1 got away on a cloaked tel'tac. Cross my heart and hope to—Scout's honor. Your Jaffa missed them. I'm alone."

Anatapas smiled and raised his hand, fingers opening like the petals of a rose. The crystals in his gold fingertips flared into life, crimson as the silk edgings on his robe.

"We shall see."

He flexed his golden fingers, stepped down from the dais and pointed at Jack's right shoulder. His eyes narrowed. His expression… focused. And fire leapt from his hand-device to sear Jack's unprotected flesh.

Jack strangled a shout of pain. Now the moist air smelled of charring. Anatapas burned him again and again. Left shoulder. Right thigh. Right forearm. Right chest. Jack was swaying. Sweat poured down his face. Daniel looked away; his belly was empty and still it tried to heave.

Anatapas stopped. "I can burn him and burn him and he will not die," he said, sweeping the slaves with a molten gaze. "He will only suffer. You can stop it, humans of the Tauri. Come to me. Save your friend."

Keep your damned mouth shut, Daniel. Don't you say a word.

"Tauri, I lose my patience!" said Anatapas, and his eyes flashed hotter than the sun. "This is but a taste of what I will inflict!"

And he burned Jack directly over his heart. Jack screamed once then collapsed face-first on the ground.

To hell with orders. Daniel leapt forward. "*Stop!*" he shouted, waving his arms. "Anatapas, stop. It's me you want! Stop hurting him. *It's me!*"

CHAPTER EIGHTEEN

In between the fortress courtyard and their new, private prison cell, Jack remained passed out. On the whole, Daniel wasn't sorry. Not only because unconsciousness gave Jack some respite but because it postponed what surely promised to be a pyrotechnical encounter between them.

I don't care. I don't care. I - don't - care. All he can do is yell. I'm used to him yelling. And anyway I practically saved his life out there. He should be damned well grateful. Maybe for once I'll yell back…

There were no amenities in the stone room they were left in by Va'ton and his Jaffa subordinates. No benches. No blankets. No pillows. Typical Goa'uld hospitality. There was, however, a big messy dried bloodstain on the prison cell floor.

He wasn't going to think about that.

He took off his shirt, bundled it up, and put it beneath Jack's lolling head. It wasn't much but it was better than nothing. God, he was hungry. Light-headed. More than a little shaky. The cut on his hand had long since stopped dribbling but it still hurt. He was reasonably sure it was infected. Which was nothing compared to the trouble they were in. Standard O'Neill reply: *Don't worry, Daniel. We've been in worse.*

Okay. Maybe. Once. Sitting in a corridor covered in blood, having just been shot to bits by a Jaffa staff weapon, on a mother ship rigged to the rafters with C4, knowing his wound would probably kill him first, knowing Jack and Sam and Teal'c were going to die soon, too.

He'd survived that one. So had they. But even cats only got nine lives and he wasn't a cat. How many times could he tap-dance on the brink of death before that final, fatal plunge?

Please God. Let us be rescued soon.

Jack liked to say, There is always, *always* a Plan B.

"Not this time," he told his friend. "This time, Jack, it's a miracle… or nothing."

Jack didn't stir. His bitten lip was swollen and his burns looked wicked. It was good they were painful, though. That meant they were only second-degree. Not, thank God, third. Third-degree burns destroyed the nerve-endings. They didn't hurt, they just killed.

On the other hand... second-degree burns could be dangerous too, if enough of the skin surface was destroyed. More than ten percent total destruction meant Really Big Trouble. Massive fluid loss. Hypovolemic shock. Kidney failure. Heart failure. Death.

How much skin surface had Jack actually lost? Daniel couldn't be sure. Anatapas had burned Jack five—no, six—times. From what he could see, each burn was about two inches in diameter. Two times six was twelve inches. Was that less than ten percent total?

God. He'd always been hopeless at math.

Jack didn't look shocky. He wasn't leaking blood or tissue fluids all over the floor. Probably he was okay. Probably he'd stay okay until they got back to the SGC infirmary.

If they got back to the SGC infirmary.

Stop it. He'll rip you a new one if he catches you thinking like that.

He let his head fall back against the cold stone wall with a muffled thud. Look on the bright side, Dr. Jackson. At least you're still in one piece. Now that he's had his fun barbecuing Jack, Anatapas is leaving you alone.

Probably because Heru'ur wants the pleasure of dismembering us himself.

Heru'ur. One system lord who remained a mystery. They'd never had much to do with him. Although there was that time Jack put a commando knife through his hand...

I wonder if he holds a grudge?

Yeah. Right.

God, he was tired. Weary to the marrow of his bones. But he shouldn't sleep. Jack might come to at any moment. He shouldn't sleep. At least not deeply. Maybe a fast five minute snooze...

He jerked awake to the sound of Jack, muttering. About nothing pleasant, if his expression was any guide. "No—don't. I wouldn't follow us if I were you." Something else, an inaudible mumble. Jack's head rolled on the makeshift pillow. "Don't follow. Don't. Bastard Nazi wannabes..."

He was dreaming of Alar, his face an unguarded mirror reflecting every thought, every feeling, every knot of unresolved turmoil and guilt that he'd never, not once, shown the world while waking.

It was disturbing. Indecent.

"I wouldn't follow us if I were you."

Jack was getting more agitated. Daniel frowned. Should he try to wake him? That could be dangerous, couldn't it? Or was that sleep-walking? He couldn't remember, his brain had turned to cottage cheese. He was dangerously tired.

"Close the iris. *Close the iris*. Alar, you bastard, *why did you make me?*"

Jack's eyes flew open and he tried to sit up. For one single, horrible instant it was clear he didn't know where he was or what had happened.

Daniel reached towards him. "Jack, it's all right. You were dreaming. Lie still. You're hurt."

Slowly, slowly, the frozen expression on Jack's face thawed. He swallowed a groan. Lowered himself by inches back to the flagstone floor. "Daniel."

"Yeah." He pulled back his outstretched hand. "Are you okay?"

"I'll live," Jack grunted.

"Was Sam in the same cage as you?"

"No. Jacob got her out in the tel'tac."

"Thank God for that. Boaz? Mikah?"

"I don't know."

"Damn. They weren't in my cage. Jack—"

Jack closed his eyes. "Don't speak to me, Daniel. Don't even look at me. I could beat you to a bloody pulp."

Daniel let out a sigh. "Jack, I had no choice. If Anatapas had lost his temper he easily might've killed you."

"He wouldn't have *killed* me. You can't get information from a dead man. He was just using me to get to you and look! It worked!"

"Jack—"

Groaning aloud this time, Jack rolled over and made himself sit up. "Don't you *get* it, you *moron*? I was keeping my trap shut so you wouldn't end up in here with me!"

Daniel stared at him. "You expected me to let Anatapas keep on torturing you?"

"*Yes!*"

"For how long?"

"For as long as it took, Daniel! For whatever reason, the snake stopped killing people. If you'd just held your nerve he would've given up on me in the end, he would've bought my story that you escaped during the raid. You'd've been *safe*. But you blew a hole in that plan, didn't you? Same old Daniel, cherry-picking orders. *When* are you going to *learn*?"

"That's *bull*, Jack! You *never* ordered me not to—"

"You knew what I wanted," Jack retorted, vicious with anger. "*Don't* pretend you didn't know."

Daniel pressed his hands to his face, subduing the urge to lash out. *He's scared, he's hurt, he's having bad dreams. Cut him some slack… cut him some slack…* He lowered his hands. "Okay. Fine. So that means—and correct me if I'm wrong—that if, God forbid, Anatapas walks through that door and starts hurting you again to make me talk… you want me to let him."

Breathing harshly, Jack eased himself backwards and slumped against the nearest bit of wall. "Want it?" he said, his voice strait-jacketed with pain. "No. But does it have to be that way? Yeah, Daniel. It does."

He was serious. Was this insanity or the kind of courage that, in the end, defined him? Daniel didn't know. Wasn't even sure it mattered. It was just… Jack. All of it. The temper, the intolerance, the unpremeditated willingness to risk his life again and again, no matter the cost.

Jack nudged the bundled shirt with his foot. "This yours? Put it back on. No point both of us catching a cold."

"What happened to your shirt?"

"I lost it. What happened to your hand?"

"I cut it," said Daniel, retrieving his shirt. "It's nothing. Practically a scratch." A nasty thought pricked him as he pulled his shirt over his head. There was no such thing as a single-sided coin…

"Ah… Jack?"

"Daniel?"

"If the shoe ends up on the other foot. If Anatapas uses me to make *you* talk…"

Jack looked at him, unspeaking. His eyes were inexpressibly

tired. Shadowed with nightmares both waking and not. Echoes of a thousand cruel impossible decisions taken, and lived with, every minute of every day.

His heart thudded hard. "Oh," he said faintly. "I see." Then: "You'd really—"

"*Yes*, Daniel. If I had to. If there was no other way and it came down to one life, or millions? Yes. *Now* do you get why I wanted you to keep your big mouth shut?"

"I'm sorry," he said, after a moment. "I couldn't. I thought—"

"No, you didn't! Unless the question involves hieroglyphics, pyramids, ziggurats, cuneiform or alien kewpie dolls, you never do!"

Stung, he said, "Well, the point's moot now, isn't it? So let's focus on what we do next. I assume you've got a plan."

"The plan," Jack said, enunciating with care, "is to sit tight until Carter brings in the cavalry. Ordinarily I'd say escape, then sit tight, but I don't think we're getting out of here without outside assistance."

God, he wanted to believe that so badly. But… "Jack, we don't even know Sam's still alive."

Jack jabbed a pointed finger at him. "We don't know she isn't! Daniel, don't you start with me. We are getting out of this! *Without* giving up information to the Goa'uld."

"You don't know that either."

"You know my motto, Daniel. Never say die."

Daniel punched his knees. "Jack—look—I know you've survived some amazing disasters. We've both survived some amazing disasters. But sooner or later the luck runs out."

"Maybe," said Jack, scowling. "One day. But not today. Not this time. Are you listening, Daniel? *Not this time.*"

And maybe that was Jack's secret. Accepting that one day the rabbit wouldn't come out of the hat… but doggedly believing it wasn't today. Doing whatever it took to make sure that it wasn't today.

Daniel relaxed his fists and rubbed his burning eyes. Took a little time to breathe, just breathe, and rediscover his mental balance. Remembered his thoughts of regret on the al-kesh and decided it was now or never. "I'm sorry."

Jack snorted. "So you should be."

"I don't mean about this," he said sharply. "I don't care what you say, I'm not sorry I stopped Anatapas hurting you. I meant I'm sorry about Euronda. The way I handled things. You were right, back in Boaz's house. I shouldn't have contradicted you in public. I should've voiced my concerns privately. I just wanted to tell you that. You know. In case."

Jack looked away. "It's okay. It doesn't matter."

"If it didn't matter, Jack, you never would've mentioned it. Getting you to discuss anything personal is like pulling teeth with blunt tweezers."

"You say that like it's a *bad* thing," said Jack. Incredibly, he was almost smiling.

"I'm *serious!*"

Jack nodded. "I know." An awkward pause, then: "Thanks."

"I'll try harder in the future. I promise."

"In the future," said Jack, his tone wryly mocking, "you'll do exactly what you did before. What you always do. Follow your conscience and to hell with the consequences."

"You say *that* like it's a bad thing."

A long silence, then: "It's not," said Jack. "I suppose. But it can be damned inconvenient at times." His head rolled against the wall, his breathing harshening to a near-groan.

"Jack?"

"I'm fine."

Except he clearly wasn't. He was in pain and he stank of burnt flesh. "You need to rest."

"I would, if you'd shut up for five seconds," Jack retorted. But not unkindly. More resigned. Almost with affection.

Daniel raised his hands. "Right. Sorry."

"Fine."

"Just one more thing…"

"*What*?"

"When Sam and Teal'c come to the rescue can we take Yu's slaves home with us?"

"Oh dear God," Jack muttered. "*Daniel*…"

"I know what you said! I know what I agreed to!" he said quickly. "But—"

"*No*, Daniel. And don't ask me again."

It was the answer he'd expected. He even understood Jack's reasoning. But it still hurt. *Sallah* ...

Silence fell, and filled with unspoken regrets.

After a little while Daniel stirred, because the trouble with silence was it gave the brain time to think. To ponder. To imagine the unimaginable ...

"Jack ... "

Jack's head was in his hands. His shoulders were slumped, the closest he ever came to looking defeated. "Daniel?"

"Sorry. Um. Can I ask you something else?"

Jack sighed. "You know what they say. You can *ask*."

"No. Seriously."

Jack looked up. "What?"

Daniel moistened his suddenly dry lips. "Okay. So. You've been in prison before. In Iraq."

Jack's eyes narrowed, very slightly. "Yeah."

"And the Iraqis tortured you."

"Your *point*, Daniel?"

"My *point*, Jack, is I'm an archaeologist, not a Special Forces commando," he said, rattled. "We didn't study this stuff at university, you know."

"What stuff?"

"You know what stuff! How to deal with being tortured by ruthless enemies who'll use the most vicious brutal methods they can think of to get the information you have and they want!" He could hear his pitch escalating and didn't care. "So you have to teach me. Now. Before Anatapas comes in here with his hand-device and starts toasting my toes for the 'gate address to Earth!"

"Daniel, relax," said Jack. "Antipasto won't—"

"Anatapas."

"What?"

"His name. It's not Antipasto. It's Anatapas."

Jack rolled his eyes. "Like I *care*. This Goa'uld—"

"It could happen," Daniel insisted. "I want to be prepared!"

"Let me get this straight," said Jack, and rubbed a hand across his face. "You want me to teach you, right now, how not to break under torture."

"Yes. Please."

Jack snapped his fingers. "Damn."

"What?"

"I left my copy of 'Resisting Interrogation for Dummies' in the car."

"*Jack*..." Daniel leaned over and grabbed his friend's wrist. "I'm scared. We've fought the Goa'uld, we've killed the Goa'uld, and they've given us quite a few bumps and bruises along the way. I can deal with that." He took a deep breath and let it out. "I *can't* deal with this. I don't know how. And please, don't try to fob me off by telling me we're going to be rescued. Maybe we will. Maybe we won't. And maybe they'll get here five minutes too late."

Gradually, the impatience and mockery faded from Jack's face. When he discarded that particular mask he became... the warrior. The no crap, no fooling, nobody get in my freaking way guy who'd saved SG-1 more times than anyone could count.

"Okay."

Daniel let go of his wrist, and waited.

"The mistake people make about pain," Jack said eventually, his voice low, clinical, "is they make it personal. Subjective. It's not. Pain is just another sensation. Its origin is irrelevant. Whether it's stubbing your toe on a house brick or having some bastard shove an electrode where the sun don't shine... in the end it makes no difference. It's just a physical sensation. Attaching an emotion to it is counter-productive."

Daniel thought about that for a moment. "Yes, but... the house brick is an accident. The electrode—that *is* personal. That's someone *doing* it to you, deliberately. It has to make a difference. It can't be seen as anything *but* an emotional experience."

Jack shook his head. "Only if you let it. Don't. Getting emotional about it means they win. What you do is forget there's a person—or an alien—involved in the equation. You just stay focused on the physical sensation."

"Which in this instance happens to be blinding agony," he pointed out. "I don't see how that helps me much."

"It helps because it means you're not focussing on the *reason* for the pain," said Jack. "On why you're there and the questions they're asking. On your fears about whether or not you'll break and tell them what they want to know. And anyway, that's only step one. Step two is taking yourself out of the picture."

"I'm sorry, I don't follow you."

Jack's expression was intent now. Lethally, ruthlessly serious. "You step outside the moment. Outside your body. The pain. So that it's not happening to you, it's happening to some other guy who looks like you. You just…" He opened his hands. "Go away."

"Go away," he repeated uneasily. "There's a name for that, you know. Psychiatrists call it 'depersonalisation disorder'."

"I don't give a rat's ass what the shrinks call it, Daniel. You asked me how to handle being tortured, I'm telling you what I know. Take the advice, don't take the advice, it's entirely up to you."

Daniel held up his hands. "Sorry. Sorry. I didn't mean to—it's just—I thought it'd be more complicated. How can it be so easy?"

Jack smiled. "Did I say it was easy, Daniel?"

"No," he said, after a moment. "No, you didn't." He pinched the bridge of his nose. "What you *are* saying is it's not about the body, it's about the mind. Mental strength. Emotional endurance."

Jack shrugged, then pulled a pained face. "Pretty much."

Daniel sat in silence for a time, considering that. Jack's advice was like an iceberg; nine-tenths of its truth lay beneath the surface of the words. He turned those words over and over in his mind, examining them for their hidden meaning. Applying rigorous academic analysis to their structure. Their subtext. What had been said without being verbalized.

At length, he stirred. "Jack… I don't know if I'm strong enough. If I've got the emotional or physical endurance to do what you're saying."

Another shrug. Another wince. "Neither do I, Daniel," Jack said simply. "Nobody knows—'til they're dancing with the guy holding the electrodes."

"When you say 'electrodes'… " he said, feeling nervous. "You're being literal, aren't you?"

Jack just looked at him.

"Right." He cleared his throat. Now there was a mental snapshot he could live without… Distraction, distraction, he needed a distraction. "Did you know torture has been used as a political tool throughout human history? Elizabeth I's spymaster, Frances Walsingham, used it regularly to find out what the Catholics were up to. The Catholics were always—"

"Yeah," said Jack, gazing at the ceiling. "This would be what I'm needing right now. A lecture on the history of torture."

He subsided. "Sorry."

"No problem." Jack cocked his head. "Come here."

"What?"

"Come here. And give me your hand."

Baffled, he scooted closer. "Why?"

"For crying out loud, Daniel! Just give me your damned hand!"

Warily, Daniel extended his hand. Jack took it, cold fingers closing, thumb shifting as though it searched for something. It stopped. Stabbed. And a bolt of searing pain shot up and down his arm.

"*Ow*!" he shouted, outraged, and snatched himself free. "What the hell was *that*?" He rubbed at the slight discoloration on his wrist; he was going to have a bruise.

Jack's eyebrows lifted. "The theoretical part of the lecture is over, Doctor. Time for the practical demonstration."

"What practical demonstration? You didn't say anything about a practical demonstration. I don't *want* a practical demonstration!"

Jack looked at him. "Daniel, when you're hanging blindfolded from a meat hook and your feet are chained to the floor for good measure, or they've strapped you down on a table, you can't just pull yourself away. You're stuck there and you've got two choices. Tell them, or don't. And if it's don't, well … you're in for an exciting time. It helps if you're even a little bit prepared."

"You're crazy, you know that?"

Jack smiled. "It's been rumored."

Daniel sighed, and held out his hand again. "Okay. Okay. I take your point. This is what they do in the SAS, isn't it? And the Green Berets and the Rangers and all the other Special Forces outfits. They give you a taste of the real thing so you can handle the three course meal, if you have to. Okay." He tried to tame his ragged breathing. "Show me. Only don't break my wrist or anything. I'm going to need it for when we're rescued."

Another smile, gently derisive this time. "You ready?"

"No. Not really."

"Okay," said Jack, and once more made a cold hard bracelet of his fingers. "Here we go."

A callused thumb-tip, pressing on a nerve point. White hot pain flaring down his hand, up his arm. God, it *hurt*. The overwhelming urge to pull away, protect himself, make it *stop*.

"Don't fight it, Daniel," Jack's voice advised him. "Just let it be. Breathe it in, and breathe it out. Don't get involved with the pain. Don't have a conversation with it. Just observe it. And then… step away. Step outside. You're watching a movie. The sound's down low and you're a long way from the screen. Relax, Daniel. It doesn't matter. It's only pain."

He was sweating now, and his heart-rate was in the red zone. He tried to relax. Tried not to care. Tried to breathe through it. Step outside himself. Be the observer. *It doesn't matter — it's only pain. It's only pain. It's only pain.*

He couldn't do it.

"I'm sorry, I'm sorry," he panted, and pulled himself free. Cradled his bruised wrist in his unhurt hand and tried not to feel inadequate, and ashamed. "I can't do that."

Jack rested his head against the wall. "You might if you practised."

He pulled a face. "I'd rather not."

"It might be a good idea."

"I'll think about it." Maybe. Curious, still cradling his wrist, he added, "How come you never showed me that before?"

Jack's eyebrows lifted. "How come you never asked me to?"

Good question. And the answer was — was — because he was an archaeologist, not a Special Forces commando. He liked hieroglyphics and pyramids and ziggurats and cuneiform and yes… even alien kewpie dolls. He *didn't* like to think about dark deeds done in secret. In the kind of training exercises that got people killed, or maimed, or the attitude that said those deaths and injuries were acceptable collateral damage. It smacked too much of the Goa'uld's way of training for his comfort.

Jack said, "Daniel. Seriously. If you really want to know how to do that stuff I'll hook you up with the right people when we get home. They'll teach you better than I can."

"It's not the teacher that's the problem," he said wryly. "Jack—"

"Daniel?"

He tried for a devil-may-care smile and failed, miserably. "You realize if Heru'ur turns up with a Goa'uld symbiote or two, we're screwed?"

That made Jack scowl, ferociously. "*Daniel*—"

"I'm just saying…"

"Well, *don't*."

By tacit consent they each retreated into silence and private contemplation. After a while, finally defeated by dread and morbid curiosity, Daniel roused.

"Ah… Jack? Look. Not trying to be pessimistic or anything but—well—I can't help noticing there's a lot of dried blood on the floor of this cell. *Recently* dried blood."

Jack lifted his forehead from his bended knee. His face was drawn, his eyes dull. "It's Leith's. The Tok'ra operative you contacted. She killed herself."

Daniel felt a stab of sorrow. She was nothing more to him than a hurried whisper, a promise of help in the dark, but even so… "You were here? You saw it?"

"Yeah."

"Well, didn't you try to stop her, didn't you—"

"*Daniel*."

"Sorry," he muttered. "Of course you did. So where is she now?"

Jack shrugged. "Who knows? They must've taken her body while I was outside getting roasted."

Daniel considered the bloodstain, feeling queasy. "I don't understand. All this blood. I thought they used a poison capsule to kill themselves. The Tok'ra Aris Boch captured, he had a—"

"Antipasto found it. So she found another way."

This time Daniel didn't correct the deliberate mistake. "What, she slashed her wrists? How could they put her in here with a knife, didn't they search—"

"Not a knife," said Jack. "I don't know how she did it, exactly. But it looked like her snake self-destructed and took her with it."

Daniel stared at the bloodstain on the floor, his imagination painting obscene pictures. "God." He shivered. "And you really couldn't stop her?"

"Daniel, she killed herself from the inside out. How exactly do you suggest I could've stopped her?"

"Sorry. I didn't mean—of course you did everything you could. I just don't understand—"

"Daniel, she was a *snake*," said Jack. "That made her a head case, in every sense of the term."

"Not a snake, Jack," he said wearily. "A Tok'ra. There is a difference."

"Trust me, not that much," Jack retorted. "*This* Tok'ra was in half a mind—literally—to kill me first so I wouldn't talk."

Daniel frowned. "Oh."

"Yeah. *Oh.*"

"And that's different from you being prepared to let me suffer torture or die, even, to protect millions—how?"

Jack's face stilled. "I don't believe you'd want me to buy your life with the death of *one* person, let alone millions."

"I wouldn't."

"You'd sacrifice yourself in a heartbeat if it meant saving someone else."

"So would you."

Jack stared. "Then why are we having this conversation?"

"I guess because I think we have more in common with the Tok'ra than you like to admit."

"Daniel, you don't get it," said Jack, impatient. "If she'd killed herself because the situation was hopeless, *fine*. I'm on board with that. But she bailed before we got to that point. She wouldn't even consider the possibility of rescue or escape. That's just stupid. And short-sighted. And gutless. I'm telling you, I'll *never* understand the damned Tok'ra."

"I don't know. You understand Jacob, don't you?"

Jack grunted, and with some difficulty eased himself onto the floor. "Jacob's different. Now can we please be quiet?"

"Sure. But you know…"

"*What?*"

Daniel nodded at the bloodstain. "I was just thinking. Probably the details of how Leith died aren't something Sam needs to read in your report."

Jack's expression softened. "Yeah. Probably you're right."

Yes. He was right. The last thing Sam needed was another reason to worry about her father and his insane risk-taking on behalf of the

Tok'ra. The close call on Ne'tu had left her silent and pretending, as she so often pretended, that she was a big tough military commando who never got rattled by anything. The last thing she needed was her imagination running riot over images of a Tok'ra symbiote self-destructing and taking its helpless host with it.

Of course, for her to read Jack's mission report he'd have to write it first. And to write it he'd have to be somewhere that wasn't an escape-proof prison cell in a heavily guarded Goa'uld fortress...

Come on, Daniel. Think positive. We're going to get out of here. They won't leave us behind.

As far as he could tell, Jack was now sleeping. Daniel closed his eyes and tried to follow suit.

Jacob looked at High Councillor Per'sus's face on the Vorash comm room's viewscreen and thought, *God help me but I'm starting to agree with Jack. The Tok'ra need a great big kick in the butt.*

"Forgive me, High Councillor," he said, temper barely restrained, "but you're making a mistake."

"*Per'sus*," said Selmak sternly. "*You know we have to do this. Morally and politically, the Tok'ra have no choice.*"

"*The humans are probably compromised by now*," Per'sus objected. "*Our focus should be on evacuating Vorash.*"

Let me talk to him again, Jacob demanded. Selmak sighed, and relinquished control.

Jacob leaned close to the viewscreen and lowered his voice to his best 'pissed off General' growl. "Per'sus, if Jack or Daniel had given us up the base would be crawling with Heru'ur's Jaffa by now. It's not. In fact, Heru'ur hasn't even left for Anatapas's fortress. He's still going hammer and tongs with Cronos. Which means either Jack and Daniel's presence remains a secret or Heru'ur has put interrogating them on hold until he's finished his latest skirmish."

Per'sus didn't look too happy about being growled at. Tough. "*Or*," he said sharply, "*he has instructed Anatapas to conduct the interrogation for him. If that is so, compromise is merely a matter of time. Has there been further contact from Leith?*"

Jacob shook his head, trying to ignore a stab of anxiety. "No. But that doesn't necessarily mean anything. There's absolutely no reason to assume—"

"*That she is dead?*" Per'sus looked away for a moment; despite his anger, Jacob felt for him. The Tok'ra were too few, so precious. For Per'sus, the idea of losing another of their people was a special kind of agony. "*I know. But if she is discovered, Jacob, you know what will happen.*"

"Yes. Which is all the more reason for us to get off our fat asses and mount a rescue mission pronto," he retorted. "O'Neill's capable of holding out under torture—maybe Jackson is, too. I don't know. But if they're implanted with a Goa'uld symbiote then it's over, red rover. Per'sus, we have to act now. Before things go from bad to disastrous, for us and the SGC."

"*Jacob—*"

"No. You listen to me, Per'sus. George Hammond crawled a long way out on a very shaky limb for us. And now his people are in harm's way because of it and I'll be *damned* if we leave them there!"

Per'sus frowned. "*That is human thinking, Jacob. The Tok'ra are not human.*"

He felt like reaching through the view screen and shaking Per'sus till his teeth rattled. "High Councillor, do you want the Earth treaty or don't you? Because I'm telling you, as your resident Earth expert, refusing to participate in a rescue mission will be like blowing up the White House then wondering if we can still be friends. *It will never happen.*"

Per'sus looked away, his expression fretful. "*That is a risk I am prepared to take.*"

Jacob took a deep, sharp breath. "I'm not. If the Tok'ra won't help, I walk."

Shocked, Per'sus stared at him. "*Selmak would not permit that.*"

"*Selmak would open the door, my friend,*" said Selmak.

Now Per'sus looked furious. "*I am High Councillor of the Tok'ra! I will not be coerced in this fashion!*" He got up from his chair and walked away from the view screen. The sound of his angry footsteps, pacing his undisclosed location, echoed his displeasure.

Oh dear, said Selmak, unrepentant. *I think we've upset him.*

I'm sorry, said Jacob. But it can't be helped.

He's going to say you've been a bad influence on me.

Is he right?

Softly, Selmak chuckled. *Probably.*

Per'sus returned. "*You disappoint me, Selmak. You have allowed your host to affect your good judgement.*" Out of sight, his fingers drummed on a hard flat surface. "*I authorise the release of Tok'ra intelligence on the fortress of Anatapas and the loan of a tel'tac. But I will not endanger Tok'ra lives to rescue the Tauri.*"

"Not good enough," said Jacob flatly. "When Martouf asked Jack and Daniel to help him rescue me and Selmak from Ne'tu they didn't think *twice.* They are my friends, and our allies. I'm sorry, High Councillor, but I can't walk away from them."

"*Yet you can walk away from us?*"

"Not without bitter regret and genuine sorrow."

Per'sus fell silent for a moment, then nodded. "*Martouf can accompany you. Take no foolish chances. Selmak, I give you this clear directive: avoid getting killed.*"

Selmak nodded. "*That is our aim, High Councillor.*"

"*Bring the Tauri home unharmed,*" said Per'sus. "*I am not unmindful of the debt we owe them.*"

Jacob bowed his head. "Thank you, High Councillor. You won't regret this decision."

"*Let us hope not, Jacob. Contact me immediately upon your return.*"

Per'sus severed their connection. Wrung out, startled to find he was actually shaking, Jacob left the small Vorash base communications room to find Martouf waiting in the corridor outside.

"Per'sus has agreed to our involvement?"

"Yes," said Jacob, and clapped Martouf on the shoulder. "So let's get going, shall we? It's showtime."

CHAPTER NINETEEN

Sam stood at the base of the SGC 'gate ramp and looked at the assembled personnel looking back at her. Some of them she knew well, some not so well at all. Some she'd trained. A couple she'd recruited. Some she was fond of. Some she didn't like particularly ... and knew the feeling was mutual.

It didn't matter. They were the best of the best, gathered here to rescue the colonel and Daniel, and with that goal in mind squabbles and conflicts and personal differences were gladly set aside.

"So," she said, "thanks to Tok'ra intelligence, here's where we're up to. Lord Anatapas—" She flavoured the name with heavy irony. "— is an extremely minor Goa'uld in Heru'ur's hierarchy. Probably that's why he staged the raid on Yu's slave farm: he's bucking for promotion and he wanted to show Heru'ur what he could do. Anyway. His home base is the planet Elekba. It has a single small continent on which are sited a Stargate, his fortress and a gold mine. The mining operation won't impact on us. Elekba is the only inhabited planet in that sun's system and the nearest heavily occupied Goa'uld world is—" She glanced at her father, who was standing off to her left with General Hammond, Teal'c and Martouf.

"Forty-six light years away," he supplied, then smiled grimly at the gathered SG teams. "When the Major says 'minor', she isn't joking."

"Which of course works in our favor," Sam continued. "Anatapas has three al'kesh at his disposal and no access to a mother ship unless Heru'ur pays him a visit. So far we've seen no indication that a visit is on the cards; he's got his hands full with Cronos."

Sally Raismith from SG-4 raised her hand. "What are the chances of him anticipating our rescue mission?"

"It's possible, Captain," she admitted. "But remember, we don't know if he knows Colonel O'Neill and Dr. Jackson are among the stolen slave population. Or that Dr. Jackson's in possession of a Tok'ra communicator and has made contact."

Teal'c said, "Even if they have been identified as members of the

SGC and Heru'ur learns we have been alerted to their location, he will not believe any rescue mission could succeed. Of all the Goa'uld system lords he is one of the most arrogant. I have known him many years and can assure you, he thinks himself and his servants entirely safe from attack by petty humans."

"That's pretty freakin' dumb," said SG-5's Lt. Jim McRafferty, the SGC's class clown. "You'd think the Goa'uld would know us by now."

A ripple of laughter, of '*hell yeahs*' and '*you can say that again, Raffs*' ran through the gathered strike force. Sam allowed them a moment to blow off some steam, then gently reined them in.

"And it gives us a possible advantage, but let's not get complacent," she pointed out. "So. We know that Anatapas has a garrison of Jaffa stationed in his fortress. We need to eliminate them for this mission to succeed."

"Don't we get to kill Anatapas? And any other Goa'uld he's hanging around with?" said Mike Rodriguez, sounding plaintive.

"Killing Goa'uld will be a bonus, Major," she said, repressing a smile. "I know SG-11's got a rep to maintain but we can't lose sight of our primary objective: getting Colonel O'Neill, Dr. Jackson and the Tok'ra operative Leith out of the fortress and off Elekba alive."

Another ripple through the assembled personnel, this time of determination and agreement. In all their faces, keen focus and an iron-willed commitment. For SG-5, this was a replay of events from the other side of the looking glass. Last time they'd been the ones in trouble and SG-1 had saved their asses. Now they were returning the favor.

"Our attack will be two-pronged," she announced. "Teal'c, myself, my father and Martouf will be going in via a cloaked tel'tac, leaving from Vorash as soon we finish this briefing. All of you, led by Major Zammit and SG-2—" She nodded at Paul, who nodded unsmilingly back. "— will reach Elekba by Stargate from here. The good news is the Elekba 'gate has no iris or defensive armory of any kind. Once we're in synchronous orbit around the planet we'll subspace the 'go' back to you in a triple-coded burst and the mission will green-light. You'll have a head start on us in order to create a very loud, very messy diversion, disabling their al'kesh and anything else you can find that's a danger. This will draw the fortress's Jaffa towards your position and away from ours. When you give us the signal it's safe to proceed, we'll ring into the fortress complex itself and extract our guys. Thanks to one of Leith's previous reports we've got a detailed plan of the fortress's layout, including the al'kesh hangar location. You'll get copies at the end of the briefing."

Another raised hand. Megan Kostolitz, Jim's 2IC. "Yes, Lieutenant?"

"What's the transit time from Vorash to Elekba?" Megan asked. Her voice was taut, her eyes narrowed; she had all the leashed nervous energy of a greyhound in the starting gate.

"Ordinarily it's a 19 hour hyperspace journey," Sam replied. Then added, flicking a smile sideways, "But Martouf and I have taken some liberties with our tel'tac's hyperdrive. We estimate the transit time will be cut to six hours." As her audience muttered and nodded, impressed, she pulled a face. "Unfortunately, that pretty much guarantees the hyperdrive will be cooked by the time we reach Elekba, so we'll be 'gating out with the rest of you."

"Arrogant or not, Anatapas and his Jaffa aren't going to sit on their asses while we pay them a visit," said Rodriguez. "What's the distance from the Elekba 'gate to the fortress?"

"*Three hundred metres*," said Selmak.

"Basically, Mike," Sam added, "just start lobbing mortars as soon as you step through. You won't be lonely for long."

Muted chuckles. Knowing nods and elbow-digs. The adrenaline was starting to pump now. Heart-rates were accelerating. Pulses picking up speed. Anticipation was in the air.

"Anyone else have a query? No?" Sam breathed out, hard. "Good. Then I'll hand over to General Hammond for some last words. Sir?"

She stepped aside, allowing Hammond to take her place at the base of the 'gate ramp. Her father gave her a nod, the smallest of smiles curving his lips. *You done good, kid.* The unspoken compliment warmed her.

Hammond clasped his hands behind his back. "Thank you, Major," he said, his expression sombre. "People, there's not much more I can add to that. As soon as we're done here the ordnance crew will start bringing in the fireworks. When the time comes, go in hard and fast and teach these damned Goa'uld a lesson they won't soon forget. Dismissed."

Sam nodded. Trust the general to finish on the perfect note. As the strike team withdrew to wait out the next six hours or so in temporary quarters, she smiled at Hammond. "Thank you, sir."

Hammond snorted. "Don't thank me, thank your father and Selmak. I don't know what you two said to Per'sus, Jacob, but it did the trick nicely."

Her father exchanged an inscrutable look with Martouf, whose expression was equally unreadable. "Nothing we'd care to repeat, George, if it's all the same to you. I just hope you had the same sort of success dealing with your political masters."

The general pursed his lips. "Success might be too strong a word. Let's just say I've got them corralled, at least for the moment." He nodded to the technician currently on 'gate duty. "You'd best be on your way," he added, as behind them the Stargate began its ponderous, powerful dance. "It goes without saying that I wish you luck."

"Say it anyway," her father replied, holding out his hand. "There's no such thing as too much luck."

Hammond grasped her father's hand hard. "Find them, Jacob," he said. His voice was rough now. A trifle unsteady. "Bring them home. And your operative too. Bring them all home. We can't do without them."

"Yes sir," her father said softly. "That would be the plan."

With a roar and a whoosh the wormhole connected. Sam looked at the general. "See you soon, sir. All of us."

"I'm holding you to that, Major," said Hammond, self-control re-established. "Teal'c."

Teal'c nodded. "General."

There was nothing more to say after that. So they gave General Hammond a final nod and stepped through the wormhole to Vorash, leaving him behind ... and bereft.

"Right," said her father, as they exited the Vorash 'gate into scouring, wind-blown sand. "What say we get this show on the road?"

Damn, thought Daniel, and propped himself against a different bit of prison wall. Sleep was proving stubbornly elusive. His wrist ached all the way to his shoulder, vibrating with a remembered agony, and unresolved issues pricked him like needles.

Curled uncomfortably on the cold floor, Jack released an irritated sigh and let his forearm drop from over his eyes. "For God's sake, Daniel, I'm trying to sleep, here. Whatever the hell is bugging you just spit it out."

"What makes you think there's something bugging me?"

"How long have I known you?"

Oh. Right. "Okay," he said reluctantly. "I'll spit." He laced his fingers together and tried to pretend he wasn't just a little bit nervous. "Before. Earlier. You know."

"And people say *my* communication skills are lacking," Jack remarked.

"Before, in between them putting us in here and you coming to, you were dreaming. Okay? You were having a dream. Actually, I think it was more like a nightmare. About Alar."

And suddenly the cell was a whole lot colder. Jack's forearm returned to cover his eyes. "Yeah. Okay. You can stop now."

No, he couldn't. "*Did* you kill him for me, Jack? I have to know."

"*Daniel*—"

"No! You started this, Jack, you said you killed Alar so he wouldn't make deals *I* couldn't live with. I never asked you to do that. I *never*—"

"No, you never," said Jack. "It was a poor choice of words and I take them back."

"You can't un-ring a bell, Jack. Why did you say them at all? Because you were royally pissed at me and you wanted to score a point?"

"I guess."

"Well, gee. That's great."

"Sorry."

Daniel frowned and scrubbed at a mud stain on his trousers. "Because that's not something I want on my conscience, Jack."

"I know. And it shouldn't be. What I did had nothing to do with you. I killed Alar because—" Jack fell silent, his breathing strained. "It doesn't matter why. He's dead. It's done. Now drop it."

But it did matter. "I can't drop it. I meant what I said back on Panotek. This is eating you alive, Jack. God, if you'd seen your face while you were dreaming."

Jack didn't reply. Just breathed harshly with his forearm over his eyes.

Softly, Daniel said, "Jack. It wasn't murder."

For a passing ice age, Jack still didn't speak. Then: "Wasn't it?"

"You told him not to follow you. It was his choice to risk the wormhole. He knew we had an iris."

"And I knew he'd ignore me," Jack retorted. For whatever reason, deciding—for once—to share. "The bastard was desperate. The complex was coming down on top of him. It was stay and be crushed, or follow me. I knew he'd follow. And I closed the iris."

Daniel let that truth sit for a while, then said, feeling like a blind man in a minefield, "Is it because you hated him? Is that why it feels like murder?"

Another long silence. Then: "Yeah. I hated him."

"I can understand that. He had some pretty hateful ideas."

Jack snorted. "But you don't understand why I closed the iris instead of letting him through." He lowered his forearm. "Do you?"

"No," said Daniel, after a painful pause. "No, I don't. Alar could've been taken into custody as soon as he—"

"Custody? How?" demanded Jack, scathing. "We had no jurisdiction over him."

"Then we could've sent him away, sent him—"

"Where? To which unsuspecting planet?"

"I don't know, somewhere he—"

"Somewhere he could pick up where he'd left off on Euronda, fulfilling his father's dream of an Aryan nation?"

"No. Of course not," Daniel said reluctantly. "All right. We'd have been stuck with him. But I can't help thinking, maybe if we'd given him some time, talked to him, let him see how wrong he was, how misguided, maybe—"

"*Daniel*!" Jack rolled over and sat up, wincing. "Alar was a fanatic. You'd have had more chance convincing Apophis to renounce Goa'uldhood than of getting Alar to recant his belief in racial purity. And I closed the iris because I knew someone like Kinsey would ignore what he was and give Alar anything he wanted in return for his knowledge and what he could build us. I was afraid Alar would score an all-access pass to Earth . . . and we've already had one Hitler."

Daniel let out a deep, painful breath. Let it out. "Maybe you're right, Jack. Maybe there was no other way to resolve the problem. I regret not having the chance to try, but … probably if Alar had ended up in the SGC Kinsey would've auctioned off his first-born child and put his grandmother in hock if it meant getting his hands on the Eurondan technologies. His anger at our failure to procure them suggests we screwed up some big plan."

"Oh yeah," said Jack, very dry. "He was angry all right."

"So why is this haunting you? It's not like you haven't killed in the line of duty before. And don't tell me you're sorry you stopped Alar from getting his hands on that all-access pass. I know you better than that."

Jack lay down again, his forearm returning to his eyes. "For God's sake, Daniel, I'm not *haunted*."

"Then what word would you prefer? What do you want me to say?"

"Daniel, I don't *want* you to say anything," Jack retorted, scathing. "You're the one who started this conversation. *I* was trying to sleep."

"*Fine*," he said, unclenching his gritted teeth. "Forget I even brought it up. I was an idiot to think that my opinion would make any difference to how you feel about what happened."

More silence. Then Jack sighed again. "Try me."

Daniel cleared his throat. Waited for the moment when his voice could be trusted. "Okay. Alar was a war criminal, no question. To be fair, he was a victim of his father's psychosis but instead of acting like an adult and questioning the truths he'd been given he blindly accepted them, infecting a whole new generation with his sickness. And he had to be stopped from spreading that sickness even further. So you stopped him, the only way you thought you could. If that was all this was about, there'd be no problem. You wouldn't be … haunted. But it isn't."

Jack was staring at the ceiling. "Really?"

"Yes. Really. See, you didn't only hate Alar for his bigotry or attempted genocide. You hated him because he deceived you." Daniel shook his head, groping for the right words. For any words, to give his thoughts a voice. "No. More than that. Alar *seduced* you—with fancy toys and clever killing machines. He convinced you, only for a moment, but a moment's long enough, that the ends really can justify the means and that no smart person looks a gift horse in the mouth. And the only way he managed that was because you wanted to be convinced. Then, as if that wasn't bad enough ... he used you, manipulated you, tricked you into slaughtering innocent people for him. You found that unforgivable. Yes, you ordered the iris closed to stop him getting access to Earth, doing God knows what kind of damage to us. But it's not the whole reason. Alar injured your sense of honor—and you wanted to punish him for that."

Still, Jack said nothing.

"I guess the question is, does that make you a murderer? Being angry when you killed him. Being... hurt." Daniel shrugged. "I guess, in the end, only you know the answer. But for what it's worth... for the little that my opinion counts... no. You're not a murderer, Jack."

He sat back then, wishing he had a glass of water. Wishing he knew what was going on behind Jack's half-closed eyes, glittering in the smoky torchlight. The silence this time stretched on so long he actually started to drowse.

And then Jack spoke. Not looking at him, no. Still looking at the ceiling, his face an unreadable mask.

"I wish it hadn't happened. I wish there'd been another way."

"I know you do. I do too. But it is what it is. Like I said: you can't un-ring the bell."

Jack snorted. "Get some sleep, Sigmund. Dollars to donuts we're getting rescued in the morning... and we don't want to keep Teal'c waiting. You know how tetchy he gets when people keep him waiting."

Daniel cleared his throat. "Yeah. I had noticed."

And that, it seemed, was that.

Then, a little time later, just as the cell's single burning torch flickered and died, Jack said, quietly, "Thank you, Daniel."

In the sudden darkness, Daniel smiled. "You're welcome, Jack.

Twenty minutes after stepping through the SGC Stargate to Vorash, Sam and her team were rocketing through hyperspace like a cat with a lit firecracker tied to its tail. Beyond the tel'tac's main viewport window hyperspeed's familiar patterns, surreal like blue oil on shifting water, smeared and ran, unable to keep up.

"God," she said, and looked around the flight deck. "Is it my imagination or are the walls vibrating?"

"They're vibrating," said her father. "But don't worry. Everything's operating within tolerance levels."

"How neatly within?"

He pulled a face. "We may be coloring outside the lines here and there."

"Great."

"Relax, Samantha," said Martouf. "This ship can withstand the drive system modifications we made, at least for a journey of our intended duration. I would not have agreed to them if I thought we would explode into a million pieces halfway to Elekba."

She looked at him. "Oh. Well. That's very reassuring, Martouf. Thank you."

A sly smile touched his lips. "You are quite welcome."

Grinning, her father took her hand and pressed it to his lips. "Stop being a backseat driver, kiddo. I get enough of that from Selmak. Why don't you go take a nap in the cargo hold? You need to conserve your energy. We'll wake you when we're nearly there."

"Yeah. Okay. Are you sure?"

"Positive. We'll be fine," he said, and slapped her lightly on the butt. "Now scoot."

He'd dismissed her like that her whole life. Once upon a time it had angered her. Diminished her. Made her feel unwanted, unwelcome. Now, equally affectionate, she just smacked the back of his head and did as she was told.

But in the cargo hold's entrance she paused, uncertain. Teal'c sat cross-legged on the floor, eyes closed, head and spine in perfect alignment. His hands rested on his knees and his massive shoulders rose and fell, rose and fell, in time with his deep, silent breathing.

As she took a step backwards he said, "You may enter, Major Carter. I am awake."

"Oh," she said, feeling a little silly. "Sorry. It's just—I thought you were in *kel'noreem*."

His eyes opened. Warm, tranquil, welcoming. "No. I completed my required meditation while you and Martouf were adjusting the tel'tac's hyperdrive system."

She joined him on the cargo hold floor. "So this is—"

"Master Bra'tac calls it *jal'ka'rovan*. I believe on Earth it is known as Neuro-Linguistic programming. I was imagining our forthcoming attack on Elekba. Seeing it with my mind's eye as I wish it to unfold in reality."

"Rehearsing it, you mean?" she said, fascinated. "You know, I've heard of this. There was a POW in Vietnam, the Viet Cong hung him up for months in a bamboo cage barely big enough to stand or turn around in. He stopped himself going insane by playing rounds of golf in his head. He claimed that before he went to Vietnam his handicap was thirty-four. When he got home and played his first round of real golf in three years, it was twelve."

Sagely, Teal'c nodded. "Indeed. In skilled hands, *jal'ka'rovan* is a formidable weapon."

"And I'm guessing your hands are pretty skilled."

A small, self-deprecating shrug. "Master Bra'tac says I did not disappoint."

Sam punched his knee lightly with her fist. "You never do, Teal'c. You never do."

He inclined his head graciously, acknowledging the compliment. Looking, as he so often looked, like some exotic foreign plenipotentiary. Then he said, almost hesitantly, "I sense you are apprehensive about this mission, Major Carter. Did you wish to discuss your reservations?"

Looking like an exotic plenipotentiary, and talking like an Oxford don. He was the *most* extraordinary person. "I'm okay," she said. "A little nervous, I guess. But I'm always a little nervous before an important mission. And they don't come much more important than this one."

His hand, large and warm, came to rest on her shoulder. "You have devised an excellent plan, Major," he said quietly. "O'Neill will be impressed and proud."

Okay. If she wasn't careful this could get embarrassing. Breathing carefully, subduing treacherous emotion, she brought all her focus to bear on her interlaced fingers. "Thanks, Teal'c. That means something, coming from you."

"I am sorry," he said, and withdrew his hand. "It was not my intention to distress you."

"You didn't!" she insisted. "God, no. I'm grateful. I really needed to hear that. I'm an astrophysicist at heart, Teal'c, not a military tactical genius. When I was a kid I wanted to be Matt Mason, not—not Rambo Barbie. These last four years—they've been fantastic, don't get me wrong, I wouldn't trade them for anything, but I never realized there'd be so much fighting. So much bloodshed. I'm okay with it," she added, as Teal'c's expression deepened into concern. "Now. I'm okay with it now. It took me a while, though. And if I'm being honest I have to admit there are still days I wonder what the hell I'm doing in a frontline combat team. But I'm fine. I am."

Teal'c smiled one of his rare, sweet smiles. "You are more than fine, Major Carter. After O'Neill there is no warrior of the Tauri I would rather have by my side."

"Yeah, okay," she said tremulously. "Now you're *trying* to make me cry." She pressed her hands flat to her face. "Oh, God. I just want them to be okay, you know? I don't want them to be hurt. Or—or tortured. The colonel's had enough of that for one lifetime. For *ten*. And Daniel? God, what Daniel's been through. He's been hurt enough too. I just want them to be all right, Teal'c. I need them to be all right."

Slowly, she lowered her hands to her lap and looked at him, feeling small and helpless. Feeling desolate.

"I too am concerned for O'Neill and Daniel Jackson," Teal'c said gently. "But I find that performing *jal'ka'rovan* helps to allay my apprehensions. If you would like, I could teach you its rudiments as we travel to Elekba."

Sam nodded. "Yeah... yeah, I would like that, Teal'c. I'd like it very much. Thank you."

He nodded back, gravely pleased. "Very well. To achieve *jal'ka'rovan* you must sit like this..."

Hours later she woke to a hand gently shaking her shoulder. She sat up. "What?"

It was her father. "Okay, Sam. Time to lock and load. We're coming up on Elekba."

"Yeah. Right." She shook her head hard to clear the fog, then looked around. "Where's Teal'c?"

"Spelling me and Martouf on the flight deck."

"What's our status?"

Her father grinned. "Our status is the hyperdrive is on its last legs, but we're here in one piece. We've all had some sleep. We know what we're doing. In short, we're good to go. Get yourself together and come join us up front."

She nodded, and patted his hand. "Yeah. Okay. I'll be right with you."

He returned to the flight deck, and she made use of the head. Took a moment to breath and stretch the kinks out and replay, briefly, the mind games Teal'c had put her through before the need for sleep had claimed her.

Apparently they'd worked. She felt calm. Focused. Confident. Piranha fear, ripping and tearing and shredding her composure, was banished to the depths.

"Right," she said, under her breath. "Let's do it."

Up on the flight deck Teal'c had surrendered his seat to Martouf. As she took her place beside her father, Martouf dropped the tel'tac out of hyperspace. Directly ahead was the small planet Elekba, one vast green ocean with a single brown continent floating on its surface.

"We are assuming orbit," Martouf announced. "Prepare to send the scrambled signal to the SGC."

Jacob slid into co-pilot's seat and jabbed at the comm-console, coding the message and setting it to stand-by. He looked at Martouf. "Say the word."

Martouf eased the tel'tac into synchronous orbit directly above Elekba's lone landmass. Checked to make sure the ship's cloak was functioning, and nodded. "Send the message."

"Bombs away," said her father, and pressed the last button. With an electronic gurgle, the coded subspace message was sent.

"I estimate fifteen minutes tops before we hear from Zammit," said Sam. "Are the rings programmed, Dad?"

"Programming them ... now."

She left him to it and ducked back to the cargo hold to retrieve her P90, and zat-guns for her and Teal'c, as well as his staff weapon. Her sidearm and commando knife were already in place. These days she felt naked without them.

What was I saying about Rambo Barbie?

"Thank you," said Teal'c as she handed him his weapons.

She managed a tight little smile. "You're welcome. Martouf, if you're sure the cloak's still holding let's take the ship down closer to the fortress. Every second is going to count..."

Delicately, the tel'tac descended until through the view screen window she could see tiny buildings and tinier trees and what may have been, might have been, a sliver of dark grey Stargate.

"We should go no lower than this," Martouf advised. "If the cloak fails..."

Sam nodded. "Yeah. Good thinking. Are we okay for auto-pilot?"

"Auto-pilot is... engaged," said Martouf. "We should position ourselves on the ring platform."

"Took the words right out of my mouth," she told him, and flicked her vest radio onto 'receive'.

Her father was the last to join them, tossing Martouf a modified TER, holding his own weapon in confident, capable hands. On his left wrist, the remote ring control.

She glanced at Teal'c and his staff weapon, solid, silent and sentinel beside her. Took a deep breath, eased it out, and lifted her watch in front of her eyes.

Five minutes. Eight minutes. Eleven minutes. *God—*

"Major Carter! Major Carter! This is Zammit! You have a go!" Behind his bold voice the sounds of warfare. Guns. Mortars. Staff weapons. Grenades.

She hit the send switch. "Major Zammit, your message received. Keep 'em busy, we're on our way!"

No need for words now, no time for quips or questions. Her father remote-activated the rings. Blinding light, a heartbeat of nothingness, and they were standing in the fortress courtyard. It was still early, the sun wasn't high. Her brain took a snapshot: encircling red stone wall, flowering trees, blue gravel underfoot. No Jaffa. A flaming fireball rising into the sky. One of the al'kesh? Probably. Now she could hear things. Excited shouting. Running feet. Explosions coming from the direction of the 'gate. Rapid weapons fire.

"With me!" said Selmak, pointing. *"The prison cells are down there!"*

They sprinted behind him, towards large iron gates set into the fortress's ground floor. The gates were locked. Teal'c blasted them open with his staff weapon.

Torchlight inside, gusty and guttering. Wide stone stairs leading into the unknown. They ran in silence, taking treads four at a time. Heading for the human voices that were howling in fear.

Six armed Jaffa running to meet them. Six dead bodies, tumbling down the stairs. Leap. Land. Make sure to keep running. God, don't fall over. Broken bones will be fatal.

At last no more stairs. Safe footing to run on. Run faster. *Sprint*. The screaming louder now, filled with words. No time to listen. No time for compassion. Five large cages, three of them occupied. Reaching arms, waving hands. Desperate faces, pressed to the bars. Some looked familiar . . . but they weren't who Sam wanted.

"Colonel!" she shouted. "Colonel O'Neill! Daniel!"

"Major Carter, look out!"

She whirled as Teal'c shouted, weapon lifting, to see a Jaffa rushing at her. Her finger tightened on the trigger—

—and Teal'c crashed into him, knees driving hard into his solar plexus, smashing the Jaffa to the flagstone floor. One hand's fingers were wrapped around the enemy throat, throttling, the other full of knife and sliding inside unresisting Jaffa armor.

Behind her, Selmak and Martouf still searched for her team mates. "*Colonel! Daniel! Are you in here! Where are you!*"

Teal'c's ferocity was oddly calm. "Are there more prisoners?" he asked the captured Jaffa. "Human, or Tok'ra? Where will we find them? Speak, and you live."

The Jaffa's distant ancestors had been Caucasian, but now his white skin was shading to dusky crimson. His eyes bulged, bloodshot and furious. He was trying to buck Teal'c off him and having no luck.

"*Answer me!*" said Teal'c, in a voice like a dagger. "Or I will cut your symbiote to pieces in its pouch. Can you feel my knife there? Do you doubt I will do it?"

The Jaffa squealed through purpling lips.

Sam touched Teal'c's shoulder. "Let go of his throat, Teal'c, he's going to suffocate."

Teal'c loosened his grasp. "I will count to five," he promised the Jaffa. "One—two—three—"

"Up the stairs!" croaked the Jaffa. "In a cell up the stairs!"

Sam spun around. "Look for stairs! They're in a cell up the stairs!" She turned back—to see Teal'c draw his mucous-slimed knife across the Jaffa's throat. Blood sprayed in a pumping arc. She fell backwards to avoid it. Scrambled to her feet and pulled Teal'c to his.

"Here!" called her father. "There's a stone staircase here!" He and Martouf charged upwards and disappeared from sight.

Leaving the Jaffa and the still-screaming humans, Sam and Teal'c raced to the end of the prison block. As they reached the bottom of the narrow staircase they heard shouts of fury. Weapons discharging. The thudding of bodies hitting the floor.

The cell had been guarded. Of course, of course…

"Dad! *Dad*!"

Her father's grim face appeared at the top of the staircase. "Get Teal'c up here. We can't open the door."

Sam flattened herself against the wall so Teal'c could push past her, running easily, four treads at a time. She reached the top stair just as his staff weapon blew a hole in the cell door.

They all fell through it: Teal'c, her father, Martouf and herself.

And there was Daniel. And there was the colonel. Jack looked like a scarecrow. He was burned and bloody. Relief in his eyes, and a comical outrage.

"Well, Hallelujah! It's about damned time!"

CHAPTER TWENTY

"Sam!" shouted Daniel, and clambered to his feet. His infected hand hurt like hell, pushing against the wall, but he didn't care. It was like sunrise to see her, after a cold dark night. Sam, Teal'c, Jacob, and Martouf: his own private personal cavalry. His and Jack's.

Sam flashed him a taut smile, looking like an Amazon, and dropped to a crouch beside Jack. Her narrowed eyes swept over him, noting every singe, every blood smear, the way his gaze seemed blurred. Unfocused. "Sir, what's your status? Are you mobile?"

"Not so much," he said, with a twisted smile. "I've been moon-lighting as barbecue."

"Yes, sir, I can see that. Teal'c?"

As Teal'c crossed the small cell Jacob said, "Daniel. Our operative, do you—"

He pulled a face. "I'm sorry, Jacob. Leith's dead."

"Damn," said Jacob, his expression tight with pain. "*Damn*, she—"

"Hey, here's a plan," said Jack, teeth gritted as Teal'c helped him to his feet. "Escape now. Chit-chat later."

Jacob gave him a look, then nodded. "We'll make sure the coast's clear. Don't hang around once we give you the signal."

"But the room's paid up till the end of the week!"

"*Sir*—" Sam let out a harsh breath, and touched Jack lightly on the arm. "Teal'c, can you manage him on your own?"

"I can," said Teal'c. "If he does not cease talking I will club him unconscious and carry him to the Stargate."

Daniel took Sam by the arm and shuffled her a couple of paces sideways. Lowered his voice. "He's running a fever. I think he's delirious."

She rolled her eyes. "How can you tell?"

"Sam—"

"Save it, Daniel." She gave him her sidearm and a spare ammo clip. "Let's get out of here."

She led the way, he followed, and Teal'c brought up the rear supporting Jack, who muttered complaints and imprecations in an unsteady monotone. He really was running a fever. Hanging onto lucidity by his fingernails.

Whatever you do, Jack, don't let go.

Jacob and Martouf were guarding the bottom of the staircase. They moved into the prison proper as the rest of the team came down the stairs. Now Daniel could dimly hear the sounds of distant battle, gunfire and explosions and staff weapons, blasting. In the cages, the people were screaming. He heard a piping voice cry, "*David! David!*"

It was Sallah. She sounded terrified. Daniel stumbled as a fierce pain went through him, as though grief were a spear and had pierced his racing heart.

Jacob said, "We're clear. The rest of Anatapas's Jaffa must be taking on the strike team. Let's go — and keep your eyes peeled. We've got Goa'uld on the loose around here somewhere."

Daniel steadied himself against the nearest bit of wall. To hell with what he'd agreed to back on Vorash. Leaving Sallah and her people behind was wrong.

Sorry, Jack. You can kick my butt later.

"We can't go," he said. "Not without the—"

Jacob turned on him, his expression ferocious. "Daniel, remember the mission briefing!"

"But Dad—" said Sam. She was staring at all the desperate faces in the cages.

"Sam—"

"They're right, Jacob," said Jack, swaying drunkenly, still on his feet only because Teal'c was holding him upright. "We can't just leave them."

Daniel nearly swallowed his tongue. "*Jack?*"

"I know how you feel, Jack, I feel the same way," Jacob said urgently, "but you and Daniel are our top priority. We don't have time for anyone else. We have to get to the Stargate *now*. If we get caught this mission will have been for *nothing*."

Jack glowered at him. "We'll have plenty of time if you stop arguing."

"It's too big a risk! Jack, for God's *sake*—"

With a swallowed grunt of discomfort Jack pushed away from Teal'c and made himself stand unaided. Fixing Jacob with a baleful glare he said, almost snarling, "You want hosts? You want spies? Save these people and they'll owe the Tok'ra big time. We got into this mess to find you recruits, Jacob. And now you want to turn down *hundreds* of them?" His wildly swinging arm took in the packed cages. The weeping, anguished faces. The people with no futures ... unless a future was given to them.

Martouf stepped forward. "Colonel O'Neill, we—"

"Shut up, Martouf! I may be out of uniform but I'm still the ranking officer and this *is* an SGC operation. Right?"

A frozen moment, as Martouf, Jacob and Jack glared at each other. Then Sam toggled her vest radio. "Zammit? Carter. What's your status?"

A crackle of static, then Zammit's reply. "*The 'gate's secure but we're still taking fire. What's your ETA?*"

"Unknown. We've got a complication. Hold the fort and don't dial home till you see us coming."

"*Roger that. But get a move on, we ain't got all day.*"

Sam turned to her father. "You and Martouf go. Take Teal'c and the colonel. Cover them and help clear the way for us. Daniel and I'll be right behind you, bringing your recruits." When Jacob hesitated, she shook his arm. "Go on, Dad. *Go!*"

"*That way leads to the Stargate,*" said Selmak, pointing to a passageway off to the right. "*Samantha—*"

She was scooping up the staff weapon that must've belonged to the Jaffa with his throat cut, dead on the floor in a pool of blood. "Yes, Selmak?"

"*At the top of the stairs turn left. When you reach the fork turn right and keep going. The Stargate is at the end of the path.*"

"Got it."

"*And Samantha? Don't dawdle.*"

Then they were gone.

"You're right, Daniel," Sam said, making sure the staff weapon was operational. "The colonel's delirious."

"But in a good way," he said.

She just rolled her eyes, then turned to stare at the cages. "Daniel, what happened to the infants, do you know?"

All the littlest children, residents of the babyhouse. He hadn't seen one on the al'kesh that brought him here. He shook his head. "I've no idea."

"*Damn*." She bit her lip. "There's no time to look for them."

"I know."

She tossed him the dead Jaffa's activated staff weapon. "So we save who we can. Let's go."

He looked again at the crowded cages. "This'll be a lot simpler if I can find Boaz, they're used to listening to—"

"Daniel…" Sam touched his arm. "Boaz died. So did Mikah. During the raid."

Her eyes were too bright. He felt his own burn in sudden, sharp sympathy. "*Damn*."

"I know. Daniel—"

She was right. There wasn't time for sorrow, either. He spun the staff weapon and put a blast into the ceiling. The backdrop cacophony of wailing and tears ceased.

"Everyone listen!" he shouted. "We're taking you to safety but you have to do what we say or the Jaffa will kill you! Do you understand? No talking. No crying. No running unless we tell you. Adults, keep hold of the children. I know you've got a lot of questions—they'll be answered soon. Now everyone, stand back from the cage doors! Back! *Do it*!"

He blew the locks off the cage doors. Bullied the people to wait inside, wait, just *wait*, dammit, while Sam made sure the coast was clear.

"We're good," she said, coming out of the passageway. "It's now or never, Daniel. Move 'em out."

He turned back to the ex-slaves. "Okay, everyone, listen to me! We're leaving. Follow the group in front of you—and the first group, follow Sam. See?" He pointed. "That's Sam. Follow her. And I'll be right behind you."

They were used to being bullied, to being pushed and shoved and told what to do and brutally punished if they dared think for themselves.

Just at the moment, their docility was a godsend.

God. What a horrible thing to think.

Sam headed along the passageway, the first cageful of ex-slaves obediently following. Then the second. Finally the third.

"*David! David!*"

Daniel looked down as small thin fingers curled around his. "Sallah!"

"David, you take me!"

"Sallah, I—" He gave up. "Yes, all right, you stick with me. But you can't hold my hand. Just walk beside me, okay?"

Her smile was blinding. "Yes, David!"

Sam led them out of the prison complex, a blonde Pied Piper with a P90 for a piccolo. As soon as she reached the world beyond, she started to jog. Yu's ex-slaves began jogging with her.

After the prison complex's torchlit gloom the day's bright sunshine was dazzling. Everyone ran with their hands shading their eyes, stumbling a little along the uneven path that led to the Stargate. Daniel could just glimpse its shimmer over the top of the shifting sea of heads in front of him.

Over on the right, thick columns of oily black smoke billowed into the air. He caught the faint crackling of flames as structures burned. Strewn on both sides of the path were countless slain Jaffa and six dead Goa'uld, their rich robes bright in the sunshine. None of them was Anatapas, dammit. The sounds of battle had fallen silent. The atmosphere was eerie, the air laced with smoke. A little distance away he recognized Major Zammit, who was methodically checking bodies with two SGC team members.

They reached the Stargate miraculously unchallenged.

As the crowd of ex-slaves slowed and stopped, confused and alarmed and pointing at the open wormhole and the dead Jaffa tumbled in piles on the ground, Daniel skirted round them and kept on going until he reached Sam. Wide-eyed and pale, Sallah stayed with him. He didn't have the heart to foist her onto someone else.

Sam was standing in front of the activated Stargate with Jack, Teal'c, her father and Martouf. Strategically grouped around and in front of them, weapons still at the ready, were familiar faces from the SGC, all unscathed thank God. They looked pleased to see him. He was thrilled to see them.

"Hey Jack, what are you still doing here?" he demanded. "Get home to the infirmary!"

Stubborn to the last, Jack shook his head. His eyes were glazed, his stance unsteady. "Not till I'm convinced Anatapas is dead or on the run. I owe that snaky rat bastard…"

"Sir—" said Sam, in the tone that said she was repeating herself and getting tired of it. "You can hardly stand up. Please, go back to the SGC. We'll do a sweep and confirm he's a kill or a fugitive. And if we find him we'll make *sure* he's a kill."

"Who?" said Major Zammit, joining them.

Jack glared at him. "Are all the hostiles accounted for, Major?"

Zammit nodded. "Yes, sir. Sir, who are you talking about?"

"The head Goa'uld," said Jack. He was almost out on his feet. "Heru'ur's blue-eyed boy. Anatapas."

"I think you'll find he's a fugitive, Colonel," said Zammit, frowning. "We tagged one Goa'uld ship as it fled the vicinity. Didn't destroy it, but we hammered it pretty good. I'd say it's long gone."

"Wow," said Daniel. "That's it? We win? Just like that? It seems too easy, somehow."

"You're *complaining*?" said Jack, incredulous. "For once in our lives a mission goes smoothly and you're *complaining*?"

"No, no, but—"

"Unbelievable," said Jack, and ignored him.

"Sir, we'll do a final sweep of the fortress compound anyway," Sam said quickly, forestalling further protest. "Just to be on the safe side. Sir, *please*. General Hammond's waiting for you, he—"

Without warning, the air before them rippled into life.

Anatapas.

The milling ex-slaves screamed at the sight of a Goa'uld standing twenty feet high, and threw themselves face down on the ground.

"No!" shouted Daniel, as Sallah whimpered and clung to him. "It's all right, you're safe, he's not really here! It's a trick! It's a *picture*!"

The hologram shivered as though blown by a breeze. "*Tauri scum!*" Anatapas's voice boomed. "*You think you have defeated me? You think you are victorious? You fools. You and your traitor Tok'ra friends are marked for death. With my assistance Lord Heru'ur will find you and you will take one thousand years to die! Bid your loved ones farewell, you walking dead men! Your days are numbered and I am counting!*"

The hologram shivered harder, then disappeared.

Daniel flinched as Jack gave him a look and said, "You *had* to jinx it, didn't you."

"Sorry."

"God," Jack added, staring at the empty space where Anatapas had stood. "You gotta love such a piss poor loser."

Daniel looked at the empty sky. "Why isn't he dropping Goa'uld bombs on us?"

"Like I said," Zammit answered. "We hammered his ship pretty hard."

"And he's gone, and that's good, and now it's time for *us* to go," said Sam, with severe finality. "Before Heru'ur decides to show up. *Colonel—*"

"He is leaving," said Teal'c, and put an uncompromising arm around Jack's shoulders. "Do not wait long to follow us, Major Carter. When word of this defeat does reach Heru'ur you can be sure he will come at once. And he will not be in a good mood when he arrives." Then, before Jack had a chance to start arguing again, Teal'c hustled him through the Stargate.

Yu's ex-slaves, back on their feet, cried out in loud, fresh consternation as they vanished into the event horizon.

Jacob said, "You go through too, Martouf. Contact Per'sus and give him an update. I'll join you presently."

Martouf nodded and followed Teal'c and Jack through to the SGC.

Sam heaved a great sigh. "Okay then. Paul, are you and the strike team finished here?"

Zammit nodded. "Almost, Sam."

"Great." Her face relaxed into a smile. "And thanks."

His answering smile was characteristically wry. "You're welcome."

As he left to supervise the final mopping up, Sam turned. "So what was that plan again? 'Escape now, chit-chat later'?" She nodded at the crowd of dazed and muttering ex-slaves. "Give 'em another pep talk, Daniel, and let's get the hell off this rock."

He grinned at her, then jumped onto the Stargate's big stone platform. Sallah jumped with him. "Everyone, everyone, listen to me!" he called, and pointed to the 'gate. "This is a door, okay? A very big, very *special* door. And on the other side is safety, and freedom, and a chance for all of you to start over in a place where there are no Goa'uld and no Jaffa. No fire-brands. No beatings. No chains. No slavery."

He paused, then, and waited to see what effect his words would have. Heads turned. Voices whispered. Nobody stepped forward. Without Boaz it seemed they were lost.

"I know," he said, his heart breaking for them. For Boaz and for Mikah, denied their chance at freedom. "I know it's hard to believe. I know you don't understand right now, but you will. I promise. Sallah—" He dropped to a crouch before the little girl. "Will you do something for me? Something brave and important? Will you be the first of your people to walk through the door?"

Sallah considered him intently. "Will you walk through it with me?"

"I'll be right behind you."

Another moment's frowning thought. Then she said, "Yes, David. I'll do that for you."

Head high, dark eyes fearless in her thin, pinched face, Sallah walked towards the rippling event horizon. At its threshold she paused, turned, and looked at her people.

"Come along!" she said, waving her arm. "Follow me!"

The wormhole swallowed her: softly ... gently.

"If you don't recruit that kid, Jacob," said Daniel, his eyes pricking, "you're crazy."

Hesitantly at first, then with more confidence, Sallah's people walked through the 'gate, encouraged by members of the SGC strike team.

"I'd better get back," said Sam. "Do some explaining. General Hammond'll be having conniptions."

"I'll stay with Daniel and see the rest through safely," said Jacob. He smiled at her. "It was a perfect mission, kiddo. Objective achieved and no home-team casualties. Well done, Major Carter."

Under the sweat and grime, Sam's face flushed pink. "Thanks, Dad. I'll see you in a few minutes."

As she threaded her way to the front of the crowd and leapt lightly into the wormhole Jacob said, his voice not entirely steady, "*Damn*, I'm proud of that girl." Then he sighed, and looked up to the sky. "It's a shame I have to blow the tel'tac we came in. They don't exactly grow on trees."

Startled, Daniel stared. "Blow it? Why don't you just fly it home?"

Jacob sighed again. "Because we comprehensively burned out the hyperdrive getting here, which means I'd be a mummified corpse by the time I got back to Vorash. And while I could send it home on autopilot, if it fell into Goa'uld hands along the way they'd find out far too much about us. So ... it blows."

Daniel shrugged, and gestured at the dwindling crowd of humans fumbling their way to Earth. "I don't know, Jacob. Seems a fair trade to me. One machine for about six hundred lives. Don't you think that's fair?"

Jacob didn't answer. Just lifted his wrist and pressed a crystal on his armband. A moment later the air shivered with sound and the sky above them filled with fireworks as pieces of tel'tac flamed, flared and died.

Daniel nodded. "Very pretty. Now let's go home."

Swimming to the world's surface out of the depths of a dreamless sleep, O'Neill felt cool, impersonal fingers press against his pulse. Eyes closed he said, "Eeeerrrgggghhhh ... it's *alive*!"

"Yes, it certainly is," said Janet Fraiser, and put his wrist back on the bed. "How are you feeling?"

"That depends," he answered, and looked at her. "Will the truth set me free?"

She grinned. "Not for another twenty-four hours, at least."

"Damn."

"Seriously, Jack," she said, and shoved her hands in her lab coat pockets. "Tell me how you're feeling."

He was in one of the infirmary's small, private rooms. The door was shut and they were alone and yet again he'd come close to buying the farm, *no* pun intended, which was why she'd called him 'Jack', not 'Colonel'. Janet Fraiser was very proper, very correct, in all her dealings. It was one of the many things he liked about her.

He took a swift internal inventory. The first thing he noticed was a gratifying overall absence of pain. Based on numerous previous narrow escapes, it was a little unexpected.

"I'm good," he said, and let the surprise show in his voice. "I'm fine."

"Yeah," she said, tugged down his sheet and blankets and loosened his stupid hospital shift. "Notice the spectacular lack of burns?"

He inspected himself. "I notice. *And* I approve. Nice work, doctor."

"Don't look at me," she said, rearranging his various coverings. "Jacob healed them. And your face, and your knee."

He flexed the damned knee with habitual caution. Felt it move smoothly, sweetly, no barbed-wire tangling. "So he did. Go, Jacob. With that Goa'uld hand-operated healing thingumajig we've got lying around here?"

"The very same." She sighed, a connoisseur of medical thingumajigs. "I'd give my eye-teeth to have him on staff."

He sat up. "Well then, Janet, seeing as how I'm healed and hunky dory I'll—"

"Your injuries are healed, yes," she said, frowning, and pushed him back against the pillows. "And that fetching brand on your shoulder's gone, too. But you still need to rest."

He scowled. He knew that look, he'd seen it on her face too many times not to know that look. "What's Daniel been blabbing about this time?"

Her eyebrows lifted. "Not *blabbing*. Debriefing. Someone had to tell me what you'd been up to and you were too busy being unconscious to oblige." She sobered then, and considered him with her dark, all-seeing eyes. After a moment, he looked away.

Nobody in the SGC knew him like Fraiser. She'd tallied his scars both inside and out, every last damned one. He had no secrets from her: his past was her open book. She'd seen him in his weakest moments, at his most unprotected and humiliatingly vulnerable. She scolded him like the sister he didn't have. Was his strength when his own strength failed him. She'd saved his sanity. Saved his life. Theirs was a damned peculiar relationship; impersonal intimacy seasoned with genuine deep affection.

She patted his miraculously unscarred shoulder. "If you want to talk, you know where I am. Right?"

He did. And maybe he'd take up the offer. But most likely he wouldn't.

It felt good, though, knowing it was there.

"So how long was I out for this time, anyway?"

"Two days," she said. "A measly forty-eight hours. No time at all, for you."

"How's everyone else? Daniel cut his hand..."

"Oh, Jacob fixed that too. He's been a regular Hippocratic Santa Claus. I had to stop him from healing everyone, it really takes a lot out of a Tok'ra to do that."

"I like that Jacob," he said, smiling. "He's a good guy."

"Yes, he is," she agreed. "And he's hoping to see you... along with a few other people. You up for visitors?"

He hesitated, then nodded. "Sure."

"Sam wanted a minute in private first. Is that okay?"

A longer hesitation. "Yeah," he said at last. "Yeah, send her in."

"I'll page her," said Janet. "And the others. But the minute you've had enough visiting, you kick them out. Healed or not you're still convalescent. You've had a bad few days and we both know it."

He gave her a mock salute. "Yes, ma'am."

Carter must've been hovering in a nearby corridor; she turned up in less than three minutes. Spick and span, as usual. The faintest air of unease beneath her pleasure at seeing him.

He was pretty damned pleased to see her, too.

"Major. Good work, getting us out of that fortress."

She nodded. "Thank you, sir. Janet says you've made an excellent recovery."

."Thanks to your dad." He nodded at the visitor's chair. "Sit down. You're making me nervous, hovering like that."

She sat, spine as straight as a broomstick. "Sir..."

He knew that tone. "Spit it out, Carter," he said, feeling his guts knot and twist. "Bad news doesn't improve with age."

"No, sir." Her fingers clenched. "Boaz and Mikah didn't make it. They were killed during the Jaffa raid. I'm sorry. If it helps, I think it was quick. I don't think they suffered."

It didn't help. *Damn.* In a weird way, he'd already known. Some instinct, some sixth sense swimming in his subconscious. The pain was muted. He'd feel it more sharply later. Once he was alone.

"How many did we save?"

"In total, five hundred and thirty-seven adults, one hundred and sixty-two children. Three are infants."

He stared. "Only *three*? But—"

"Sir, we don't know what happened to all the children in the baby-house. When Dad, Martouf and I checked the farm after Heru'ur's raiders had left, it was empty. Aside from some bodies. We have no idea where those infants were taken."

She was distressed about that. Doing a good job of hiding it, but he could tell. "Carter—"

"I know," she said. "We saved nearly seven hundred people. It's glass half-full time. I know."

He nodded. "Good."

"Sir..."

Now what? Mixed in with her lingering sorrow for the babies, a distinct edge of nervousness. "Carter?"

She lifted her gaze and looked him square in the face. "There's something I need to ask you. Something about the Eurondan mission."

Oh, *crap*. He wanted to *forget* the frickin' Eurondan mission. "What?"

"When you ordered the iris closed..." She took a breath then let it out, incrementally. "Were you hoping I'd countermand you?"

"Countermand me?" He lifted his eyebrows. "You're a major, Major. I'm a colonel, you can't countermand me."

She frowned. "You know what I mean."

Yes. He knew what she meant. "Were you hoping I hoped that?"

"*Sir*—"

"I'm serious. Did you want me to want you to—"

"No," she said flatly. "I thought—*think*—you made the right call."

Until she said it, he'd had no idea how much that mattered. "Okay."

She leaned forward, just a little. "Do *you* think you made the right call? Sir, do you wish I'd stopped you? Now that some time's gone by, and we've had a chance to... think about it. Should I have argued to let Alar through?"

He shook his head. "Not in a million years."

She relaxed, as though relieved of some terrible burden. "Good. Sir—"

On the other side of the infirmary door, a brisk knocking. He looked at Carter. Shrugged. Raised his voice and said, "Come in."

"Sorry to interrupt," said Jacob, his hand on the doorknob, Martouf at his shoulder. "Only we have to get back to Vorash and we didn't want to leave without seeing you."

"Hey, no sweat," O'Neill said. "Come on in. The more the merrier. It's called visiting time at the zoo."

Behind the Tok'ra, Daniel and Teal'c. No conversation required there; they looked at him, he looked at them. A nod. A smile. The rest unspoken.

Jacob said, "You look a hell of a lot better than the last time I saw you."

"Thanks to you. Teal'c told me you had to kick some serious butt to join the rescue. Appreciate it. I owe you."

Jacob waggled a finger. "You owe us a tel'tac," he said, grinning. "As it happens."

O'Neill grinned back. "Bill me."

Martouf said, "We should not be speaking of debts, Jacob. Between friends, there is no such thing."

Friends? Him and Martouf? *Well, yeah. I guess we are.* "No debt? Damn. So that rules out me teaching you poker."

Jacob's grin widened. "I've already taught him, Jack. Trust me, he's doing you a favor."

It was a pity to spoil the mood, but... "Jacob. I'm sorry about your operative. Leith. I was with her when she died. All she cared about was protecting the Tok'ra. You'd have been proud."

"We are," said Martouf. "She will be remembered."

The sombre silence was broken by General Hammond's arrival. "Colonel! Good to see you awake."

He couldn't stand, so he sat up straighter. "Thank you, sir. It's good to be awake."

"This came for you this morning," said the general, showing him a flimsy envelope. "Thought you'd want it as soon as you were *compos mentis* again."

O'Neill blinked. "A telegram?"

"From Washington."

"Really? From the President?" he said hopefully.

Hammond's smile was very wry. "Not quite," he said, and handed the telegram over.

O'Neill read it. Nearly choked. Passed it to Carter, who made a strangled noise in her throat, eyes wide with outrage, and said, "Can I read it aloud?"

He nodded. "Sure. Why not. We're all fans of street theatre, aren't we?"

She held up the telegram. "*'To Colonel Jack O'Neill, USAF blah blah blah, from Senator Robert Kinsey, blah blah blah. Dear Colonel. Congratulations on your recent narrow escape. Do take care in the future. Next time you might not be so lucky. Sincerely, blah blah blah.'*"

A stunned silence, then derisive laughter.

O'Neill looked at Hammond. "I guess this means I owe the President. He's saved my unmentionables yet again."

Hammond nodded. "I understand there's to be a conversation, when you're fully recovered."

He could hardly wait. "Yes, sir."

"This must really be killing Kinsey," said Daniel. "Foiled once more by Jack O'Neill and SG-1."

Jacob shook his head. "Well, you know what they say, Jack. With friends like that…"

If O'Neill had been the sentimental type he'd have said something soppy, like: *With friends like you, who cares about Kinsey?*

But he'd never been soppy a day in his life, so he just shrugged and smiled his best feral smile. "Screw Robert Kinsey and the rat he rode in on. I won. He lost. What's next?"

"Next," said Jacob, with a look at Martouf, "we take our leave."

He felt sharply disappointed. "You really can't stay?"

"Sorry. There's a ton of work waiting for us back on Vorash," said Jacob, brisk and focused. "Almost three-quarters of the slaves you insisted on freeing have agreed to come and learn about the Tok'ra, with a view to joining our ranks. The others have been found homes on two non-Goa'uld occupied worlds. They have new lives now, thanks to you."

"So much for calling *me* Kunta Kinte…" Daniel murmured. "Have you met Mr. Kettle, Colonel Pot?"

"Shut up, Daniel," O'Neill said, with perfect amity.

"You were right to insist we save them, Colonel," added Martouf.

"High Councillor Per'sus is very impressed; he looks forward to thanking you himself when we finalise the treaty Dr. Jackson is drawing up between Earth and the Tok'ra."

O'Neill looked at Daniel, then. Daniel smiled, very pleased with himself, and O'Neill smiled back. No more tension, humming between them. Euronda was settled. They were settled. The world was returned to its proper axis, spinning gently...

"Treaty, eh?" he said to Jacob. "Gosh, that sounds like fun. All that talking—and writing—" He pretended to yawn.

"Yes, indeed," said Hammond, as pleased as Daniel. "Which is why we're lucky Dr. Jackson's been asked especially to draft the language. It's a singular compliment which the President has duly noted."

"A singular compliment and an awful lot of work," added Daniel. "So I'd better get back to it, as soon as I've said goodbye to Sallah."

"Sallah?" O'Neill prompted. The name rang a bell.

Daniel rolled his eyes. "It's a long story. I'll tell you later."

"I've got some goodbyes to say too," said Carter. "Berez, and Qualah. Sir, it's good to see you looking so much better. I'll stop by again this evening, if you'd like."

"Yeah," he said. "You do that."

"Okay!" said Fraiser, bustling in like the maitre-d at a swanky over-booked restaurant. "Show's over. I said ten minutes and I meant ten minutes. Everybody out! Vamoose! Scram! Scoot! Good-bye!"

Under cover of the resulting hubbub, Teal'c moved to the bedside. "Recover quickly, O'Neill," he said. His face was alight with grave amusement. "I wish once again to be entertained by your attempts to punch me on the nose."

He snorted. "Yeah, sure. I'll get right on that."

Teal'c's hand rested briefly on his shoulder. "Yet again, you have defied great odds and survived where most would perish." He wasn't amused now. "I am glad."

"Me too," he replied. "But the odds would've been a damned sight better if I hadn't let them talk me into sitting you out on this one. Do me a favor, okay? You punch *me* on the nose if I'm ever that stupid again."

Teal'c bowed. "With pleasure, O'Neill."

"Come on, come on, get out of here. *Go!*" said Fraiser, hands flapping. So they all shuffled out, his team, the Tok'ra. The room was suddenly empty. Too quiet.

"I need another minute," said Hammond, pleasant but unequivocal. Fraiser frowned, then nodded.

"Okay, General. But—"

"Yes, doctor. Thank you."

She let it slide. Took a moment to feel O'Neill's forehead, check his pulse. "I'll be back," she threatened. "You be sleeping."

She closed the door behind her, and then it was just him and the boss.

"Kinsey may be a wart on the face of humanity," said Hammond, entirely serious, "but for once he's right. You've been damned lucky, Jack."

Equally serious, O'Neill nodded. "Yes, sir. I know."

Hammond's eyes were hooded. Intent. "This is a dangerous life you've picked for yourself, Jack. If I were you I'd save whatever luck I have left for out there—" He made a vague gesture, indicating the universe. "Don't waste it by antagonizing pinheads like Kinsey. You're smarter than that. You're smarter than most people I know."

O'Neill let himself smile. "Yeah. Could we keep that our little secret, do you think, sir? I'd hate to make Carter feel threatened."

That made Hammond laugh. "Get some rest, Jack," he advised, and patted him on the shoulder. "You can consider that an order."

"Absolutely," he said, obediently. As Hammond reached the door he added: "Sir?"

The general turned. "Jack?"

"Thank you. For everything."

"You're welcome, Colonel," said Hammond, nodding. And then he was alone.

For three whole seconds.

"*Right*," said Fraiser, still bustling, but this time pushing a loaded cart. "Here is food. Here is fluid. Here is medicine. None of them is optional. I am your doctor, which means I'm God, and in case you'd forgotten there are ways undreamed of I can make you suffer if you don't do as you're told. *Capisce*?"

He eyed the cart with growing horror. "*Milk*? I don't drink no stinking *milk*. Is there scotch in it? I'll drink it if there's scotch in it. And what's that slop in the bowl? I don't do slop, either, with or without the scotch. And what the hell is—Needles? To hell with that, I don't need *needles*, even if the scotch is *intravenous*! Why do I need needles? Jacob healed me!"

Fraiser smiled at him. So would a barracuda smile, if it was wearing a stethoscope. "Consider them backup. Now, did I mention the word 'suffer'? I think I did. Shall I mention it again? No, I thought not. Roll over. Gown up. We'll start with the right hip, shall we?"

As she plunged the hypo into his flesh O'Neill yelped and thought:

God. It's good to be home.

ABOUT THE AUTHOR

Karen Miller has been a fan of Stargate SG-1 since the pilot episode back in 1996. She was born in Canada, but now lives in Australia where she's a full-time professional writer. Her Stargate fanfiction, the *Medical Considerations* series, introduced her to the enormous fun of writing in the Stargate SG-1 universe. Her first fantasy duology, *Kingmaker, Kingbreaker* was published by Voyager in 2005, and will be published in the UK by Orbit in 2007.

Karen's website is: www.karenmiller.net

SNEAK PREVIEW

STARGATE ATLANTIS: EXOGENESIS

by Sonny Whitelaw & Elizabeth Christensen

"It's possible that Rodney's still alive."

Elizabeth's eyes flared wide. "How can that be?"

"Apparently the villagers saw one of the local Wraith beam him onto a Dart." John leaned on the extended drive pod of Jumper Eight, currently down for maintenance, and willed his head to get its act together. "From what the Elders said, I didn't get the feeling that the hive was awake, just that a few Darts go out on occasional snack runs during the storms."

"If the Wraith have McKay, they may know about Atlantis by now." Caldwell looked none too thrilled with that possibility.

"Not necessarily. The villager said that Rodney was barely alive when he was taken."

"But the Wraith need healthy victims."

"Which means they might not feed off Rodney right away, or even at all. They might put him in one of those damned cocoons, dump him in a corner, and leave him to a slow and agonizing death." Elizabeth's horrified reaction told John he was hitting below the belt, but being delicate wouldn't serve anyone's purposes right now.

Caldwell was studying him a little too carefully. "Colonel, forgive me for sounding skeptical, but this seems like a risk we may not be able to take. For starters, you don't appear to be in any condition to lead a rescue mission."

"I just need a couple hours of sleep—"

"John, you're white as a sheet and barely upright," Elizabeth cut him off gently. "And your face and ear look… Well, you certainly need medical attention."

"Given the situation here," the *Daedalus* commander continued, "we're not in a position to go mounting an attack on a hive ship. An attempted extraction would most likely awaken the hive, and they'd be apt to finish the job the exogenesis machine started on Atlantis."

"This is not necessarily true," countered Radek. John hadn't noticed him break free from the science team, but the Czech now came over to join them. "We can still carry out the original plan to acquire the ZPMs and simultaneously flood the Wraith ship. But if I am to do this, I will need to return to the planet as soon as we have taken care of the worst of Atlantis's problems."

Elizabeth held up a hand to slow him down. "I understand the urgency here, but I need more information. What would be the impact to the Polrussons? You said they needed time to complete their move."

"They'll move fast enough now." That statement came from Ronon, and received a look of mild suspicion from Atlantis's leader.

Even talking was starting to hurt, but the anger John still felt toward Vené and his people spurred him on. "It took far more than it should have to get the Polrussons to be honest with us about the Wraith. Given the way we had to drag the information out of them, and the way we left, they have to assume that we've gone for good. When we go back, we can tell them that we'll only help if we're allowed to release the water now, because we're as worried about the Wraith threat as they feared. While Radek gets everything set up, we'll have the opportunity to take a team in to extract Rodney."

Caldwell didn't appear convinced. He turned to Radek. "How confident are you that we'll be able to acquire the ZPMs and flood the Wraith ship?"

The scientist's brief hesitation put the differences between Rodney and Radek into sharp relief. "I cannot guarantee," he replied truthfully. "We must remember that a hive is indeed a ship, and has the capability to seal itself against water as it does against the vacuum of space. Still, Atlantis was submerged for a reason. Perhaps the Wraith do not like water. But whatever the reason, we can only work to minimize the time the Wraith will have to recognize the threat and defend themselves or escape."

"What's your plan for shutting down the terraforming system and collecting the ZPMs?" Elizabeth asked.

In response, Radek withdrew his laptop from his pack and quickly called up a schematic. From what John could see through a fog of pain, it was a diagram of the ZPM locations on Polrusso. "The ZPMs form a type of power matrix across the surface of the planet. If we go by jumper to remove them sequentially from the matrix, the remaining units will attempt to compensate, and the system will weaken. We will remove the first ZPM from the area where we wish the force field to fail initially, but this does not assure that the water will rush out at once. It may do this, but equally it may take days or even weeks for the water pressure to break through the rock holding it back." Radek pushed his glasses up on his nose. "It may also still be possible for me to locate the second exogenesis machine. This I cannot promise, either, but if there is time—"

"Time we can only buy ourselves by doing everything in our power not to alert the Wraith," Caldwell interrupted.

Radek's head bobbed readily. "Hopefully by then we will have acquired sufficient ZPMs to power the city shield, against the Wraith as well as the nanites. That will give us time to repair the *Daedalus*."

Even before Caldwell spoke, John knew he wasn't going to like what he heard. "If you go barging into that hive ship now, the Wraith will be all over you before you can blink, and we'll kiss off any chance of acquiring even one of those ZPMs."

"Not necessarily," John insisted. "We've learned a lot about the layout of those ships. And if we do wake them up, we can go for some of the furthest ZPMs right away, before they can stop us."

"You don't know that you'll make it."

"You don't know that we won't!"

"Gentlemen." Elizabeth sounded utterly torn.

John felt for her, but there was nothing he could do to make this easier.

"Our best chance to save the most people is to initiate Radek's plan," she said at last. "With any luck, we'll also be able to find the second exogenesis machine and bring it back here, but that must be our secondary priority."

"Understood. Radek, is two hours enough—" John's world tilted again. By the time he managed to straighten up, four pairs of eyes were watching him with varying degrees of alarm and doubt.

"Major Lorne's team will go," Caldwell concluded. "You, Colonel, need to face facts and go see Dr. Beckett. You're injured, and you'd be a liability out there."

The sick feeling that settled in his gut had nothing to do with the sand or the pain, and everything to do with a disturbing sense of déjà vu. John looked to Elizabeth. "You're not going to let Lorne search for Rodney, are you?"

"John, we have to be realistic. The odds— "

"Since when has this expedition relied on the odds?" he demanded. "I recognize that Rodney's chances aren't good. But as long as there *is* a chance, don't we have an obligation to try?"

"Don't think that I like this any better than you." Elizabeth sighed. "God knows we can't afford to lose Rodney. But it's overwhelmingly likely that he is dead. It's my call, and with this level of risk I can't allow a rescue mission to proceed."

Starting to feel a flicker of desperation, John held her gaze. "You once asked me to tell you if I thought you were making a mistake," he said quietly, remembering the mission that had followed the long-past storm. "I'm telling you now."

Her eyes held endless empathy but also resolve. "The answer's no. I'm sorry."

And there it was. "You're sorry," he repeated, not bothering to mask the edge of contempt in his voice. "I feel better already."

Elizabeth flinched, but didn't falter. Caldwell moved in front of her, arms folded over his chest. "In case I wasn't clear before, *Lieutenant* Colonel, you're to stand down and report to the infirmary immediately."

Before John could figure out how to respond, Ronon stepped up beside him, staring the older man down. "You told me your people placed high importance on your loyalty to your comrades, Sheppard."

Bristling, Caldwell drew himself taller. "I don't like what you're implying."

John knew he should shut Ronon up before this got ugly, but he was too pissed off and too wrung out to try.

"I don't care what you like. *I* don't like leaving my teammates to suffer and die!"

"You are way out of line, Specialist!"

"Don't use my rank like it means something to you," the Satedan growled. "I didn't take your army's oath. You don't get to decide where my line is."

"Maybe not." Still as stoic as ever, Caldwell signaled to the Marines standing guard in the corridor. "Confine this man to his quarters until further notice," he ordered. "This much I *do* get to decide."

"Hold on a minute," John objected, only to feel Caldwell's iron gaze fall on him next.

"Infirmary, Sheppard. And under no circumstances are you to leave until cleared by Beckett."

Out of the corner of his eye, John saw another pair of Marines inching toward him. This day just kept getting better and better. "Is this a joke, sir?"

"Put yourself in my place, handling someone with a record that reads like yours," Caldwell said, unmoved.

So, because he'd bucked orders in a similar situation before, that justified preemptive confinement? What the hell kind of ship did this guy run? John stared at Elizabeth, willing her to stand up for him. "You're going along with this?" he accused.

"I hope Rodney can forgive me," she said softly. "But if it keeps you from blindly tilting at windmills, then yes, I am."

The feeling was familiar, and yet infinitely more of a betrayal. "Well, this has been...educational."

His body turned traitor next as a rush of dizziness sideswiped him, dropping him awkwardly to one knee. Elizabeth took a step toward him, but he pinned her with a fierce glare and staggered to his feet unassisted. With as much dignity as he could summon, he turned and started toward the infirmary, the two Marines moving to flank him as he went.

STARGATE
SG·1

STARGATE
ATLANTIS ™

**Original novels based on
the hit TV shows,
STARGATE SG-1 and
STARGATE ATLANTIS**

AVAILABLE NOW

**For more information, visit
www.stargatenovels.com**

STARGATE SG-1 © 1997-2008 MGM Television Entertainment Inc. and MGM
Global Holdings, Inc. STARGATE SG-1 is a trademark of Metro-Goldwyn-
Mayer Studios Inc. All Rights Reserved.
STARGATE: ATLANTIS © 2004-2008 MGM Global Holdings, Inc.
STARGATE: ATLANTIS is a trademark of Metro-Goldwyn-Mayer Studios Inc.
All Rights Reserved.
METRO-GOLDWYN-MAYER ™ & © 2008 Metro-Goldwyn-Mayer Studios Inc.
All Rights Reserved.

STARGATE SG-1: THE BARQUE OF HEAVEN

by Suzanne Wood
Price: $7.95 US | $9.95 Canada | £6.99 UK
ISBN-10: 1-905586-05-1
ISBN-13: 978-1-905586-05-9

Millennia ago, at the height of his power, the System Lord Ra decreed that any Goa'uld wishing to serve him must endure a great trial. Victory meant power and prestige, defeat brought banishment and death. On a routine expedition to an abandoned Goa'uld world, SG-1 inadvertently initiate Ra's ancient trial – and once begun, the trial cannot be halted. Relying on Dr. Daniel Jackson's vast wealth of knowledge, Colonel O'Neill must lead his team from planet to planet, completing each task in the allotted time. There is no rest, no respite. To stop means being trapped forever in the farthest reaches of the galaxy, and to fail means death. Victory is their only option in this terrible test of endurance – an ordeal that will try their will, their ingenuity, and above all their bonds of friendship…

STARGATE ATLANTIS: MIRROR MIRROR

by Sabine C. Bauer
Price: £6.99 UK | $7.95 US | $9.95 Canada
ISBN-10: 1-905586-12-4
ISBN-13: 978-1-905586-12-7

When an Ancient prodigy gives the Atlantis expedition Charybdis — a device capable of eliminating the Wraith — it's an offer they can't refuse. But the experiment fails disastrously, threatening to unravel the fabric of the Pegasus Galaxy — and the entire universe beyond. Doctor Weir's team find themselves trapped and alone in very different versions of Atlantis, each fighting for their lives and their sanity in a galaxy falling apart at the seams. And as the terrible truth begins to sink in, they realize that they must undo the damage Charybdis has wrought while they still can. Embarking on a desperate attempt to escape the maddening tangle of realities, each tries to return to their own Atlantis before it's too late. But the one thing standing in their way is themselves…

STARGATE SG-1: ROSWELL

by Sonny Whitelaw &
Jennifer Fallon
Price: $7.95 US | $9.95 Canada | £6.99 UK
ISBN-10: 1-905586-04-3
ISBN-13: 978-1-905586-04-2

Series number: SG1-9:

When a Stargate malfunction throws Colonel Cameron Mitchell, Dr. Daniel Jackson, and Colonel Sam Carter back in time, they only have minutes to live. But their rescue, by an unlikely duo — General Jack O'Neill and Vala Mal Doran — is only the beginning of their problems. Ordered to rescue an Asgard also marooned in 1947, SG-1 find themselves at the mercy of history. While Jack, Daniel, Sam and Teal'c become embroiled in the Roswell aliens conspiracy, Cam and Vala are stranded in another timeline, desperately searching for a way home. As the effects of their interference ripple through time, the consequences for the future are catastrophic. Trapped in the past, SG-1 can only watch as their world is overrun by a terrible invader...

STARGATE SG-1: RELATIVITY

by James Swallow
Price: $7.95 US | $9.95 Canada | £6.99 UK
ISBN-10: 1-905586-07-8
ISBN-13: 978-1-905586-07-3

Series number: SG1-10

When SG-1 encounter the Pack—a nomadic spacefaring people who have fled Goa'uld domination for generations—it seems as though a trade of technologies will benefit both sides. But someone is determined to derail the deal. With the SGC under attack, and Vice President Kinsey breathing down their necks, it's up to Colonel Jack O'Neill and his team to uncover the saboteur and save the fledgling alliance. But unbeknownst to SG-1 there are far greater forces at work—a calculating revenge that spans decades, and a desperate gambit to prevent a cataclysm of epic proportions. When the identity of the saboteur is revealed, O'Neill is faced with a horrifying truth and is forced into an unlikely alliance in order to fight for Earth's future.

STARGATE SG-1: SURVIVAL OF THE FITTEST

by Sabine C. Bauer
Price: $7.95 US | $9.95 Canada | £6.99 UK
ISBN-10: 0-9547343-9-4
ISBN-13: 978-0-9547343-9-8

Colonel Frank Simmons has never been a friend to SG-1. Working for the shadowy government organisation, the NID, he has hatched a horrifying plan to create an army as devastatingly effective as that of any Goa'uld. And he will stop at nothing to fulfil his ruthless ambition, even if that means forfeiting the life of the SGC's Chief Medical Officer, Dr. Janet Fraiser. But Simmons underestimates the bond between Stargate Command's officers. When Fraiser, Major Samantha Carter and Teal'c disappear, Colonel Jack O'Neill and Dr. Daniel Jackson are forced to put aside personal differences to follow their trail into a world of savagery and death. In this complex story of revenge, sacrifice and betrayal, SG-1 must endure their greatest ordeal…

STARGATE SG-1: ALLIANCES

by Karen Miller
Price: $7.95 US | $9.95 Canada |
£6.99 UK
ISBN-10: 1-905586-00-0
ISBN-13: 978-1-905586-00-4

All SG-1 wanted was technology to save Earth from the Goa'uld … but the mission to Euronda was a terrible failure. Now the dogs of Washington are baying for Jack O'Neill's blood—and Senator Robert Kinsey is leading the pack. When Jacob Carter asks General Hammond for SG-1's participation in mission for the Tok'ra, it seems like the answer to O'Neill's dilemma. The secretive Tok'ra are running out of hosts. Jacob believes he's found the answer—but it means O'Neill and his team must risk their lives infiltrating a Goa'uld slave breeding farm to recruit humans willing to join the Tok'ra. It's a risky proposition … especially since the fallout from Euronda has strained the team's bond almost to breaking. If they can't find a way to put their differences behind them, they might not make it home alive …

STARGATE SG-1: CITY OF THE GODS

by Sonny Whitelaw
Price: $7.95 US | $9.95 Canada | £6.99 UK
ISBN-10: 0-9547343-3-5
ISBN-13: 978-0-9547343-3-6

When a Crystal Skull is discovered beneath the Pyramid of the Sun in Mexico, it ignites a cataclysmic chain of events that maroons SG-1 on a dying world. Xalótcan is a brutal society, steeped in death and sacrifice, where the bloody gods of the Aztecs demand tribute from a fearful and superstitious population. But that's the least of Colonel Jack O'Neill's problems. With Xalótcan on the brink of catastrophe, Dr. Daniel Jackson insists that O'Neill must fulfil an ancient prophesy and lead its people to salvation. But with the world tearing itself apart, can anyone survive? As fear and despair plunge Xalótcan into chaos, SG-1 find themselves with ringside seats at the end of the world...

• *Special section: Excerpts from Dr. Daniel Jackson's mission journal.*

STARGATE SG-1: SIREN SONG

Holly Scott and Jaimie Duncan
Price: $7.95 US | $9.95 Canada | £6.99 UK
ISBN-10: 0-9547343-6-X
ISBN-13: 978-0-9547343-6-7

Bounty-hunter, Aris Boch, once more has his sights on SG-1. But this time Boch isn't interested in trading them for cash. He needs the unique talents of Dr. Daniel Jackson—and he'll do anything to get them. Taken to Boch's ravaged home-world, Atropos, Colonel Jack O'Neill and his team are handed over to insane Goa'uld, Sebek. Obsessed with opening a mysterious subterranean vault, Sebek demands that Jackson translate the arcane writing on the doors. When Jackson refuses, the Goa'uld resorts to devastating measures to ensure his cooperation. With the vault exerting a malign influence on all who draw near, Sebek compels Jackson and O'Neill toward a horror that threatens both their sanity and their lives. Meanwhile, Carter and Teal'c struggle to persuade the starving people of Atropos to risk everything they have to save SG-1—and free their desolate world of the Goa'uld, forever.

STARGATE SG-1: A MATTER OF HONOR

Part one of two parts
by Sally Malcolm
Price: $7.95 US | $9.95 Canada |£6.99 UK
ISBN-10: 0-9547343-2-7
ISBN-13: 978-0-9547343-2-9

Five years after Major Henry Boyd and his team, SG-10, were trapped on the edge of a black hole, Colonel Jack O'Neill discovers a device that could bring them home. But it's owned by the Kinahhi, an advanced and paranoid people, besieged by a ruthless foe. Unwilling to share the technology, the Kinahhi are pursuing their own agenda in the negotiations with Earth's diplomatic delegation. Maneuvering through a maze of tyranny, terrorism and deceit, Dr. Daniel Jackson, Major Samantha Carter and Teal'c unravel a startling truth—a revelation that throws the team into chaos and forces O'Neill to face a nightmare he is determined to forget. Resolved to rescue Boyd, O'Neill marches back into the hell he swore never to revisit. Only this time, he's taking SG-1 with him...

STARGATE SG-1: THE COST OF HONOR

Part two of two parts
by Sally Malcolm
Price: $7.95 US | $9.95 Canada | £6.99 UK
ISBN-10: 0-9547343-4-3
ISBN-13: 978-0-9547343-4-3

Returning to Stargate Command, Colonel Jack O'Neill and his team find more has changed in their absence than they had expected. Nonetheless, O'Neill is determined to face the consequences of their unauthorized activities, only to discover the penalty is far worse than anything he could have imagined.

With the fate of Colonel O'Neill and Major Samantha Carter unknown, and the very survival of the SGC threatened, Dr. Daniel Jackson and Teal'c mount a rescue mission to free their team-mates and reclaim the SGC. Yet returning to the Kinahhi homeworld, they learn a startling truth about its ancient foe. And uncover a horrifying secret...

STARGATE SG-1: TRIAL BY FIRE

By Sabine C. Bauer
Price: $7.95 US | $9.95 Canada | £6.99 UK
ISBN-10: 0-9547343-0-0
ISBN-13: 978-0-9547343-0-5

Trial by Fire follows the team as they embark on a mission to Tyros, an ancient society teetering on the brink of war. A pious people, the Tyreans are devoted to the Canaanite deity, Meleq. When their spiritual leader is savagely murdered during a mission of peace, they beg SG-1 for help against their sworn enemies, the Phrygians. Initially reluctant to get involved, the team has no choice when Colonel Jack O'Neill is abducted. O'Neill soon discovers his only hope of escape is to join the ruthless Phrygians — if he can survive their barbaric initiation rite. As Major Samantha Carter, Dr. Daniel Jackson and Teal'c race to his rescue, they find themselves embroiled in a war of shifting allegiances, where truth has many shades and nothing is as it seems. And, unbeknownst to them all, an old enemy is hiding in the shadows...

STARGATE SG-1: SACRIFICE MOON

By Julie Fortune
Price: $7.95 US | $9.95 Canada | £6.99 UK
ISBN-10: 0-9547343-1-9
ISBN-13: 978-0-9547343-1-2

Sacrifice Moon follows the newly commissioned SG-1 on their first mission through the Stargate.

Their destination is Chalcis, a peaceful society at the heart of the Helos Confederacy of planets. But Chalcis harbors a dark secret, one that pitches SG-1 into a world of bloody chaos, betrayal and madness. Battling to escape the living nightmare, Dr. Daniel Jackson and Captain Samantha Carter soon begin to realize that more than their lives are at stake. They are fighting for their very souls.

But while Col Jack O'Neill and Teal'c struggle to keep the team together, Daniel is hatching a desperate plan that will test SG-1's fledgling bonds of trust and friendship to the limit...

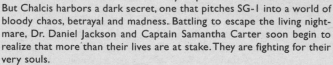

Series number: SGA-7

STARGATE ATLANTIS: CASUALTIES OF WAR

by Elizabeth Christensen
Price: £6.99 UK | $7.95 US | $9.95 Canada
ISBN-10: 1-905586-06-X
ISBN-13: 978-1-905586-06-6

It is a dark time for Atlantis. In the wake of the Asuran takeover, Colonel Sheppard is buckling under the strain of command. When his team discover Ancient technology which can defeat the Asuran menace, he is determined that Atlantis must possess it — at all costs. But the involvement of Atlantis heightens local suspicions and brings two peoples to the point of war. Elizabeth Weir believes only her negotiating skills can hope to prevent the carnage, but when her diplomatic mission is attacked — and two of Sheppard's team are lost — both Weir and Sheppard must question their decisions. And their abilities to command. As the first shots are fired, the Atlantis team must find a way to end the conflict — or live with the blood of innocents on their hands...

STARGATE ATLANTIS: BLOOD TIES

Series number: SGA-8

by Sonny Whitelaw & Elizabeth Christensen
Price: £6.99 UK | $7.95 US | $9.95 Canada
ISBN-10: 1-905586-08-6
ISBN-13: 978-1-905586-08-0

When a series of gruesome murders are uncovered around the world, the trail leads back to the SGC — and far beyond. Recalled to Stargate Command, Dr. Elizabeth Weir, Colonel John Sheppard, and Dr. Rodney McKay are shown shocking video footage — a Wraith attack, taking place on Earth. While McKay, Teyla, and Ronon investigate the disturbing possibility that humans may harbor Wraith DNA, Colonel Sheppard is teamed with SG-1's Dr. Daniel Jackson. Together, they follow the murderers' trail from Colorado Springs to the war-torn streets of Iraq, and there, uncover a terrifying truth... As an ancient cult prepares to unleash its deadly plot against humankind, Sheppard's survival depends on his questioning of everything believed about the Wraith...

STARGATE ATLANTIS: EXOGENESIS

by Sonny Whitelaw & Elizabeth Christensen
Price: £6.99 UK | $7.95 US | $9.95 Canada
ISBN-10: 1-905586-02-7
ISBN-13: 978-1-905586-02-8

When Dr. Carson Beckett disturbs the rest of two long-dead Ancients, he unleashes devastating consequences of global proportions. With the very existence of Lantea at risk, Colonel John Sheppard leads his team on a desperate search for the long lost Ancient device that could save Atlantis. While Teyla Emmagan and Dr. Elizabeth Weir battle the ecological meltdown consuming their world, Colonel Sheppard, Dr. Rodney McKay and Dr. Zelenka travel to a world created by the Ancients themselves. There they discover a human experiment that could mean their salvation. But the truth is never as simple as it seems, and the team's prejudices lead them to make a fatal error—an error that could slaughter thousands, including their own Dr. McKay.

STARGATE ATLANTIS: ENTANGLEMENT

by Martha Wells
Price: £6.99 UK | $7.95 US | $9.95 Canada
ISBN-10: 1-905586-03-5
ISBN-13: 978-1-905586-03-5

When Dr. Rodney McKay unlocks an Ancient mystery on a distant moon, he discovers a terrifying threat to the Pegasus galaxy. Determined to disable the device before it's discovered by the Wraith, Colonel John Sheppard and his team navigate the treacherous ruins of an Ancient outpost. But attempts to destroy the technology are complicated by the arrival of a stranger — a stranger who can't be trusted, a stranger who needs the Ancient device to return home. Cut off from backup, under attack from the Wraith, and with the future of the universe hanging in the balance, Sheppard's team must put aside their doubts and step into the unknown. However, when your mortal enemy is your only ally, betrayal is just a heartbeat away...

STARGATE ATLANTIS: THE CHOSEN

by Sonny Whitelaw & Elizabeth Christensen
Price: £6.99 UK | $7.95 US | $9.95 Canada
ISBN-10: 0-9547343-8-6
ISBN-13: 978-0-9547343-8-1

With Ancient technology scattered across the Pegasus galaxy, the Atlantis team is not surprised to find it in use on a world once defended by Dalera, an Ancient who was cast out of her society for falling in love with a human. But in the millennia since Dalera's departure much has changed. Her strict rules have been broken, leaving her people open to Wraith attack. Only a few of the Chosen remain to operate Ancient technology vital to their defense and tensions are running high. Revolution simmers close to the surface. When Major Sheppard and Rodney McKay are revealed as members of the Chosen, Daleran society convulses into chaos. Wanting to help resolve the crisis and yet refusing to prop up an autocratic regime, Sheppard is forced to act when Teyla and Lieutenant Ford are taken hostage by the rebels…

STARGATE ATLANTIS: HALCYON

by James Swallow
Price: £6.99 UK | $7.95 US | $9.95 Canada
ISBN-10: 1-905586-01-9
ISBN-13: 978-1-905586-01-1

In their ongoing quest for new allies, Atlantis's flagship team travel to Halcyon, a grim industrial world where the Wraith are no longer feared—they are hunted. Horrified by the brutality of Halcyon's warlike people, Lieutenant Colonel John Sheppard soon becomes caught in the political machinations of Halcyon's aristocracy. In a feudal society where strength means power, he realizes the nobles will stop at nothing to ensure victory over their rivals. Meanwhile, Dr. Rodney McKay enlists the aid of the ruler's daughter to investigate a powerful Ancient structure, but McKay's scientific brilliance has aroused the interest of the planet's most powerful man—a man with a problem he desperately needs McKay to solve. As Halcyon plunges into a catastrophe of its own making the team must join forces with the warlords—or die at the hands of their bitterest enemy…

STARGATE ATLANTIS: RISING

by Sally Malcolm
Price: £6.99 UK | $7.95 US | $9.95 Canada
ISBN-10: 0-9547343-5-1
ISBN-13: 978-0-9547343-5-0

Following the discovery of an Ancient outpost buried deep in the Antarctic ice sheet, Stargate Command sends a new team of explorers through the Stargate to the distant Pegasus galaxy. Emerging in an abandoned Ancient city, the team quickly confirms that they have found the Lost City of Atlantis. But, submerged beneath the sea on an alien planet, the city is in danger of catastrophic flooding unless it is raised to the surface. Things go from bad to worse when the team must confront a new enemy known as the Wraith who are bent on destroying Atlantis. Stargate Atlantis is the exciting new spin-off of the hit TV show, Stargate SG-1. Based on the script of the pilot episode, Rising is a must-read for all fans and includes deleted scenes and dialog not seen on TV.

STARGATE ATLANTIS: RELIQUARY

by Martha Wells
Price: £6.99 UK | $7.95 US | $9.95 Canada
ISBN-10: 0-9547343-7-8
ISBN-13: 978-0-9547343-7-4

While exploring the unused sections of the Ancient city of Atlantis, Major John Sheppard and Dr. Rodney McKay stumble on a recording device that reveals a mysterious new Stargate address. Believing that the address may lead them to a vast repository of Ancient knowledge, the team embarks on a mission to this uncharted world. There they discover a ruined city, full of whispered secrets and dark shadows. As tempers fray and trust breaks down, the team uncovers the truth at the heart of the city. A truth that spells their destruction. With half their people compromised, it falls to Major John Sheppard and Dr. Rodney McKay to risk everything in a deadly game of bluff with the enemy. To fail would mean the fall of Atlantis itself—and, for Sheppard, the annihilation of his very humanity…

THE OFFICIAL MAGAZINE

STARGATE
SG·1 ◆ ATLANTIS

- ● Interviews with cast & crew
- ● Latest *Stargate SG-1* & *Stargate: Atlantis* news!
- ● Behind-the-scenes secrets revealed

Subscribe now and save 10%

UK call 0870 428 8217 or visit www.titanmagazines.co.uk
US call 1877 363 130 or visit www.titanmagazines.com